Jodi Taylor is the internationally bestselling author of the Chronicles of St Mary's series, the story of a bunch of disaster-prone individuals who investigate major historical events in contemporary time. Do NOT call it time travel! She is also the author of the Time Police series – a St Mary's spinoff and gateway into the world of an all-powerful, international organisation who are NOTHING like St Mary's. Except, when they are.

Alongside these, Jodi is known for her gripping supernatural thrillers featuring Elizabeth Cage, together with the enchanting Frogmorton Farm series – a fairy story for adults.

Born in Bristol and now living in Gloucester (facts both cities vigorously deny), she spent many years with her head somewhere else, much to the dismay of family, teachers and employers, before finally deciding to put all that daydreaming to good use and write a novel. Over twenty books later, she still has no idea what she wants to do when she grows up.

JODI TAYLOR

A CATALOGUE OF CATASTROPHE

HEADLINE

First published in Great Britain in 2022 by
HEADLINE PUBLISHING GROUP

5

Cataloguing in Publication Data is available from the British Library

ISBN 978 1 4722 8689 5

Typeset in Times New Roman by CC Book Production

Printed and bound in Great Britain by Clays Ltd, Elcograf S.p.A.

Headline's policy is to use papers that are natural, renewable and recyclable
products and made from wood grown in well-managed forests and other
controlled sources. The logging and manufacturing processes are expected
to conform to the environmental regulations of the country of origin.

HEADLINE PUBLISHING GROUP
An Hachette UK Company
Carmelite House
50 Victoria Embankment
London EC4Y 0DZ

www.headline.co.uk
www.hachette.co.uk

This book is dedicated to the memory of
Leslie Robert Steian – honorary member
of the St Mary's Institute of Historical Research.

DRAMATIS THINGUMMY

Max	Going quietly mad.
Markham	Founding – and only – member of Pros and Cons. Marches to the beat of his own drum. Frequently followed by a crash, bang and clatter because the little drummer boy didn't look where he was going.
Lady Amelia Smallhope	Upmarket bounty hunter.
Pennyroyal	Her butler.
Bridget Lafferty	Max's boss. The nicest one she's ever had.
Eddie Middleditch	Non-talking non-toupee wearer.
King John	Not a happy bunny.
Peterson Sykes Sands Roberts Keller	Co-opted historians and one enthusiastic security guard.

Dr Bairstow	In the process of being rehomed.
Mrs Brown	With mixed results.
Evans	
Mrs Proudie	Definitely no longer on Team
Kathleen	Winterman and Feeney.
Sarah	
Maggie	
Sally	
Mary	
Rat Face	Miscreants – as Lady Amelia would
Smuggy	call them.
Lady Nicola de la Haye	Hereditary chatelaine of Lincoln Castle.
Her steward	
Her maid	
Her guards	
Her runners	
Her garrison	
Falk de Breauté	
His archers	
William Marshal senior	A bit of a legend.
His army	You surely don't want me to name them all.
A smith and his mates	Pissed as newts, the lot of them.
Guy Fawkes	Well, we all know about him. Failed mass murderer.

Thomas Ward	One of the most important people in History. Remember his name.
Guards Soldiers Boatmen	
Dr Dowson	Master forger.
Major Guthrie	Seeing even more of St Mary's than when he worked there.
Leon	Good thing someone knows where the plunger is kept.
Matthew	Nervous about his exams but 'Algernon, take me, take me, my body is on fire for you,' should see him through.
Professor Penrose	Matthew's teacher.
Adrian and Mikey	Making trainspotting cool.
Commander Treadwell	Bringing new meaning to the phrase 'Getting shot of . . .'
Captain Hyssop Gallacio Cox	Head of Security.
Keller	Mentioned twice!
Harper Jessop Glass Lucca	

The one whose name no
one can remember
including the author

Dr Stone	Bearer of some unwelcome news.
Nurse Fortunata	Hair stealer.
Martin Gaunt	I think we all knew we hadn't seen the last of him.
His minions	Leaving their master to sink or swim. SPOILER ALERT – he doesn't swim.
Two paramedics	Who wander in and then wander back out again.
Janet Thompson from the kitchen	Markham's personal Spotted Dick provider. Possibly the best job description ever.

Various other members
of that accursed
organisation who zip in
and out of the story as
the fancy takes them.

They came in the night. No warning. No nothing. The first I knew about anything was when I opened my eyes to find the dark shape of Pennyroyal leaning over me, which, trust me, is enough to propel anyone into full consciousness in record time.

He had his hand over my mouth. Not threatening – just a light pressure which nevertheless conveyed the necessity for utter silence.

I nodded understanding. There was the faintest clunk as he left something on my bedside table before ghosting silently back into the dark.

I swung my legs out of bed, pulled jeans and a sweatshirt over my pyjamas, jammed my feet into trainers, and had a quick look at what he'd left me. Night visor, blaster, handgun, stun gun. It would seem something fairly dangerous threatened. Jehovah's Witnesses, perhaps.

I had no idea what time it was. There was complete silence and it was cold. Very cold. Shivering, I pulled on my night visor, took two deep breaths to calm myself and then eased my head around my bedroom door. I could see a bright green blob further down the landing, which I hoped very much wasn't just some carelessly discarded nuclear waste. Since I wasn't at

St Mary's any longer, it seemed safe to assume the blob was only Markham.

Keeping to the long runner that ran down the middle of the landing, I made my way to the top of the stairs, found my own patch of deep shadow, checked my weapons, tried to slow my heart rate . . . and waited.

We'd practised for this. The sudden appearance of unwelcome visitors. All of us knew where to go and what to do when we got there. Dr Bairstow and Mrs Brown would take themselves down to the special cellar – 'bunker' would be a better description – with instructions only to open the door when they heard the safe word, no matter who or what was happening at the time.

Pennyroyal and Smallhope would cover downstairs – Pennyroyal stationed at the back door that led from the barn where we kept our pods, and Smallhope at the front door. I had the stairs and Markham the long landing. Between the four of us, we had every inch of Home Farm covered.

We'd always known this day would come. With our lifestyle, it was almost inevitable. We had two likely scenarios here: one – we'd finally managed to well and truly piss off the Time Police and they'd decided to wipe us off the face of the earth, or two – what Lady Amelia always persisted in referring to as the criminal classes had come to the conclusion we were too good at what we did and turned up to murder us in our beds. Since our main occupation was to descend on said criminal classes, arrest them and then sell their arses to the Time Police for extremely handsome bounties, this was the more likely option.

Alone in the silent darkness, I adjusted my night visor, eased my position and waited. Whoever they were, wherever they'd come from and whatever they wanted, we were ready for them. The house was surrounded by a complicated network of sensors, which was obviously what had aroused Pennyroyal, who takes security very, very seriously indeed. We were well armed, well prepared and knew exactly what to do. Unless these intruders had brought a battalion or two, the odds were with us.

'Anything?' said Pennyroyal in my ear.

'Negative,' said Markham.

'No,' said Smallhope.

I opened my mouth and in the crackling silence of the house, I heard a faint sound. Directly over my head. A very slight chink.

I whispered, 'Heads up. They're coming over the roof.'

The loft hatch was to my left, further down the landing. I inched my way past two empty bedrooms and crouched in an open doorway. The hatch was about ten feet away. I sensed rather than heard Markham move up to take my place at the head of the stairs.

'I'm coming up,' said Pennyroyal softly – presumably so we wouldn't shoot him – and the next moment he'd joined me in my doorway.

That slight sound came again. Difficult to identify. And then I had it. Someone was very slowly and very carefully taking the tiles off the roof. I could picture the scene. A sharp knife to cut through the waterproof membrane and insulation and then they'd have access to the attic. This was a Pennyroyal attic. There would be no generations of ancient furniture and useless bric-a-brac. The space would be clean and clear. Easy for them to move around in.

I looked up. I doubted they'd use the hatch – it would be a pinch point. We'd easily be able to pick them off as they dropped through. No, they'd come straight through the ceiling. I endeavoured to convey this to Pennyroyal through the medium of mime.

He shook his head either in exasperation or admiration – it really wasn't clear. He obviously didn't have my skills.

I wasn't too worried. There were three of us up here – and two of those were Pennyroyal and Markham. Unless our uninvited guests had armed a small thermo-nuclear device, all the advantage lay with the home team.

It would seem Pennyroyal didn't share my optimism. 'Back,' he breathed. 'All of us.'

We retreated back along the landing and not a moment too soon. With a massive crash and a ton of dust and plaster, the whole ceiling at the end of the landing disintegrated. I jumped, swallowed and brought up my gun. Pennyroyal had provided me with a neat, medium-range blaster. Light, accurate and very effective. Trust me, if I'd been Horatius Cocles, I could have held that bridge forever.

Three figures emerged from the billowing dust, raking the corridor with fire, all of which went straight over our heads because we were safely on the floor. I heard the roar of their blasters and felt the heat. At the same time, I heard Smallhope open fire downstairs. We were being attacked on at least two fronts.

I aimed low. Smallhope always likes us to try to take people alive because we get more for undamaged – or nearly undamaged – illegals. And a bit extra for the amount and value of any intel they might provide, as well. So far, in the course of our new careers as bounty hunters – sorry, recovery agents – Markham and I hadn't felt the need to kill anyone. Tonight might be different. I could feel the milk of human kindness curdling within me.

4

They raced down the landing, firing as they came, hoping to drive us back. Perhaps the blasters had just been to soften us up because now bullets thudded into the wall above me, showering me with yet more plaster, and trust me, it's a bugger to get out of your hair.

Pennyroyal moved up to return fire. Someone went down with a thud. I'd lost sight of the three intruders. Night visors are all very well but even they're pretty useless when everything's enveloped in clouds of dust, plaster and shattered wood. I didn't want to hit Pennyroyal by mistake – I had an idea that wouldn't go down at all well – so all I could do was wait for the situation to resolve itself.

There was a shout from behind. Markham yelled at me to get clear.

I rolled into the shelter of the bedroom to my left and as I did so, twin streams of blaster fire roared past the door. I swear I felt my hair curl in the heat.

I heard Markham shout, 'Clear. Fire at will,' so I rolled back out again, firing as I came.

My role was simple. To keep them pinned down while Markham and Pennyroyal used my covering fire to move forwards. I kept playing the flame from right to left and back again. The long carpet was on fire, as were the curtains at all the windows. Unless the buggers had taken cover in one of the bedrooms, they were toast.

Pennyroyal called to cease fire so I rolled back into the bedroom again to check my weapons. The blaster was nearly empty. No matter – it had done its work. I suspected it would be handguns from now on.

I saw the blur that was Pennyroyal whip past the door.

I tossed aside my blaster and pulled out the handgun and waited.

The next few minutes were confused. I had no idea who was where. Somewhere I heard Pennyroyal shout, 'Max, hostiles at your two o'clock.'

I rolled back out of the bedroom, fired two shots and heard something hit the floor. I stayed where I was. We all had our own part to play – our own position to hold. Markham at the rear providing long-range cover and watching our backs. Me holding the middle ground, ready to move forward or back as circumstances demanded. Pennyroyal up front, all ready to go in and do as much damage as he pleased.

Bullets and blaster fire criss-crossed the narrow passage. The heat and noise were intense. I could hear the same happening downstairs. I had no idea how many intruders there were altogether. Nor did I have any idea how Smallhope was coping on her own, although I was prepared to bet she was carving her way through wave after wave of miscreants with the winning combination of bad language, brutally accurate gunfire and margarita fumes. If she wasn't, then they could be coming up the stairs behind us at this very moment.

I couldn't spare the time to worry about that. Concentrate on the now, Maxwell. My job was in front of me: to do my best and trust others to do theirs.

A plaster-bedecked figure loomed through the dust. I think we were both equally surprised to see each other. He raised his weapon. I had nowhere to go. I made a split-second decision and rolled under his gun, knocking his legs out from under him. He fell across me and my first thought – because I'm not famed for my focus in a crisis – was that he was wet. Very wet.

6

The second was that he didn't weigh anything like as much as I thought he would.

He was crushing my gun into my body. I couldn't get it free. We rolled around. At some point I was back on top again. I had a vague impression of armour, a helmet and Chanel No. 5. That didn't seem right. Had I banged my head?

A voice hissed in my ear. 'You bitch – I could have loved you.'

I wonder if that's come as much of a surprise to you as it did to me.

It was enough for me to lose concentration. The next minute she was back on top of me. I needed to separate her from her weapon, but the only way I could do that was to relinquish my own and she already had an advantage over me with her armour and helmet and so on while I was still, technically, in my pyjamas.

I let go of my own gun and concentrated on just keeping the business end of hers pointing away from me. The battle raged around us. This close combat wasn't to my advantage. She was dealing short, sharp, vicious punches to my ribcage, each one extremely painful. And then I got an elbow in my face. I tasted blood from a split lip. Was this personal? It felt personal. It was very fortunate that most of her blows were either deflected or went astray in the dark, otherwise I'd have been finished there and then.

She headbutted me which really, really hurt because only one of us was wearing a helmet. I blinked to try to clear my vision and she drew her head back to do it again.

I didn't think I could handle another one and so, in desperation, I twisted and bucked like an old mule. Anything to get her off me. There was a confused and tangled moment in the dark during which I became quite disoriented and then, suddenly, the floor disappeared beneath me and we were both falling down the stairs.

They were wooden but carpeted. I've fallen down worse. And they were fairly wide and shallow. Trust me – I'm an expert on stairs. You should have seen the murderous death trap that ended Amy Robsart.

The next few seconds were jumbled. As they tend to when you're tumbling down stairs. The good news was that she let go of her gun as she fell. We both grabbed at it – she to retrieve it and me to get it out of the way. We both missed. I heard it falling down the stairs ahead of us.

The bad news was that she didn't let go of me. Her momentum propelled her downwards – as did mine – and there was rather more of me. We tumbled over each other. I know my knee must have caught her somehow because of the sudden flash of hot pain in my right leg. Like a big red sunburst. And then I was upside down. I was on the bottom, bearing the weight of both of us and I was bruised all over. And, for the record – carpeted stairs are no better than bare wood. I would be looking at savage carpet burns.

Something bashed my arm and I instinctively grabbed at what turned out to be one of the carved wooden spindles that made up the banisters. It jarred my shoulder and the old pain started up again but it did arrest my fall. Not so my dancing partner, who rolled right over the top of me and continued the trip solo. I heard a rather nasty sound as she hit the stone flags at the bottom.

I followed her down, all ready to give her a seeing-to if she looked like getting up – because for some reason, she'd had a real desire to do me harm – but she wasn't moving. She sprawled at the foot of the stairs, face down and quite still. Out cold by the look of it.

'Hold your fire – it's me,' I said breathlessly before Small-hope could make an unfortunate mistake in the dark.

I jammed my gun between my assailant's shoulder blades and shouted, quite redundantly as it turned out, 'Don't move.'

She didn't, so taking advantage of this unexpected cooperation, I pulled her arms behind her back and zipped her tight.

'Prisoner secured,' I said to Smallhope, found a spot on the bottom stair and waited.

There was more gunfire upstairs. They were going at it hammer and tongs up there.

Smallhope called for me to watch the back door just as it burst open and two gas canisters rolled across the floor. Instinctively – well, I call it instinct, everyone else calls it blind stupidity – I stood up, took two steps and kicked them straight back out again.

'What?' shouted Smallhope. 'Gas canisters? That's just rude. If you want us, come and get us, boys.'

The shooting upstairs had stopped. For what I could only hope were good reasons.

Smallhope and I were pouring fire through the open back door, keeping whoever was out there completely pinned down. I heard someone on the stairs and Markham said, 'I'm behind you,' which wasn't anything like as reassuring as he thought it was.

'Where's Pennyroyal?'

'Gone out the window,' he said tersely. 'Not in a good mood. Wouldn't want to be them.'

9

Home Farm is a long, low building. The bedroom windows aren't that high. Pennyroyal would be heading towards the barn to come up behind them.

I flexed my fingers. My gun was hot in my hands and my forearm ached with the strain. My shoulder was throbbing from when I'd fallen down the stairs.

A couple of flashes and an enormous bang told me Pennyroyal was busy doing some damage outside. The three of us waited, weapons raised, all ready for whatever came through the door next.

I heard Pennyroyal shouting not to shoot. Which meant he was in the barn with our unwelcome visitors. Coming up behind them probably. Which also meant they would very soon be regretting their decision to get out of bed this morning. I was crouching to one side of the stairs, my legs on fire and I was covered in dust, but otherwise unscathed. Was it all over? I could hear Markham reloading behind me.

We waited. We waited some more.

Suddenly, there was a shout, a burst of gunfire, and then, finally, after one almighty bang – silence. Dust and black smoke poured in through the shattered back door. I brought up my gun, all ready for whatever came through the door next.

Which was Pennyroyal. 'All clear,' he called, emerging through the smoke. 'Two of them out here. One dead. One not very well.'

'Two up on the landing,' reported Markham. 'Dead.'

'One down here,' I said. 'Unconscious.'

'Well, sodding arseholes,' said Lady Amelia. 'Struggling not to feel left out.'

Markham told her she could have one of his.

I went to see if mine had come round yet. I lifted her visor and got rather a shock. I'd gathered she was female because you can't roll around with someone and be completely unaware of their gender, but I'd envisaged some battle-hardened veteran with the scars to prove it. Given the viciousness of her attack, I think that had been a natural assumption. But she wasn't. She was younger than me. And pretty. She was also dead. I swallowed. Her blue eyes stared straight at me.

'Dead,' I called.

Her head lay on her shoulder. Like a broken doll. Had that been the sound I heard? Her neck breaking?

I think the first thing that flashed through my mind was the randomness of fate. Or luck. We'd both rolled down the stairs. At some point either impact or an awkward position had ended her life, but it could just as easily have been mine. I shivered. When I think of the number of times I've fallen down a flight of stairs. I just pick myself up, dust myself down, swear a bit and carry on. And not just me. Many of us believe Bashford is constitutionally incapable of descending a staircase without tumbling from top to bottom. And these weren't even particularly steep stairs.

Around me, silence had fallen.

Markham appeared beside me. 'Is there something you want to tell us?' I realised he must have heard what she'd said.

You bitch – I could have loved you.

'No.'

'Sure?' He bent down to take off her helmet.

I made myself look at her face again. A little younger than me. Chin-length, glossy black hair, flattened now by her helmet. Very blue eyes. 'I've never seen her before – I swear it.'

11

'You sure? You do know you can be a bit forgetful at times, don't you? You sure you haven't had some sort of relationship that's just slipped your mind?'

'I don't think so.' I took a deep breath. 'Unless you're saying I bewitched her from a distance with my beauty.'

'No. No one's saying that.'

I looked again. 'Do *you* know her?'

'Don't know any of them.'

'Who are they? What's this all about?'

'Absolutely no idea. And why are they all so wet? They've definitely been in water in the last hour . . .'

I looked again. The woman had a couple of long black scorch marks along her breastplate that I didn't think had been my doing.

Markham sniffed gently. 'She smells of burning.'

'Perhaps that's why she's wet – trying to put out a fire some-where.'

'Mm.' He looked around. 'I suspect they'd had a rough day even before they turned up here, don't you think?'

We dragged them all into the hall and zipped them hard. Even the dead ones.

'The ties are coded to us,' Pennyroyal had said during our induction. 'The Time Police tot them up and reward us accordingly. Eventually.'

This is a long-standing grievance for Pennyroyal. The Time Police always cough up in the end, but they often make us wait and as he says, the invoice clearly states payment within twenty-eight days of delivery.

Markham and Pennyroyal went off to search upstairs – just to make sure we hadn't missed anyone – while Smallhope and

12

I did a room-to-room downstairs. Then we all went outside and searched the farm buildings and garden.

Nothing and no one. Just the five inside. We traipsed back in again to inspect the damage. At least, Pennyroyal and Markham inspected the damage; Smallhope searched the prisoners and I put the kettle on. We all have our own areas of expertise.

'Well,' said Smallhope, 'wasn't that exciting while it lasted? What's the bad news? Is the house about to fall on our heads, Pennyroyal?'

'There's a big hole in the roof, my lady,' said Pennyroyal. 'That's not going to be cheap. Bastards.'

He scowled at our unwelcome guests. The five of them lay in a neat row along the narrow passage because Pennyroyal does like things to be tidy. Four men and one woman, and definitely not included in the kitchen festivities because, as Lady Amelia had kindly informed the survivor – they weren't really our sort of people.

'Part of the landing ceiling's come down and I can see the sky,' continued Pennyroyal. 'Your rooms are OK.' He nodded at me and Markham. 'And your end of the building is untouched, my lady. The worst is the damage to the back door leading from the barn. We are no longer secure.'

'The pods?'

'Unharmed. We can check them over later but there's no visible damage.'

I nodded. It's almost impossible to gain entry to a pod if you don't have the right biometrics or password or door code or whatever. You can kick the door all you like – you can whine, beg and plead – but you ain't getting in.

'Well,' Smallhope said, getting the mugs out, 'I wonder what

13

that was all about. There wasn't anything in their pockets. Not that I thought there would be.'

'Let's ask the survivor,' said Pennyroyal, getting to his feet.

The others congregated around the zipped survivor while I stared down at the woman again. Medium height, medium build. Those bright blue eyes still stared sightlessly over my shoulder. Once again, it crossed my mind that that could easily have been me. If I'd been the one to fall awkwardly . . . If I hadn't grabbed the banister . . . If I'd . . . Stop that, Maxwell.

Now the light was better, I could see the others had scorch marks on their armour and clothing as well. I sniffed. It was hard to tell with the dust and smoke mingling with their damp clothes, but they all smelled . . . burned . . . to me. Perhaps they had been in a fire after all.

Smallhope was examining their weapons. 'There's some good stuff here. I think we'll hang on to some of this.'

'Not some second-rate organisation,' said Markham, turning a blaster over in his hands. He looked down at their black clothing, boots, body armour, helmets. 'A professional outfit.'

'Good to know,' said Lady Amelia. 'I refuse to be terminated by people at the unfortunate end of the social scale.'

'Indeed, my lady,' said Pennyroyal, nodding his agreement.

He addressed the sole – but possibly not for much longer – survivor. 'Name?'

The man shook his head. He was, I think, the youngest, but none of them looked older than their mid-thirties. I didn't think he'd talk. Markham was right – they were professionals. And if they'd been hired, they might not even know for whom they'd been working.

I made the tea and then went off to let Dr Bairstow out of

the cellar because – and don't tell him this – we'd forgotten he and Mrs Brown were still down there.

I made very sure to tap on the door and give the safe word, because no one wants the phrase 'friendly fire' on their death certificate. My caution was more than justified. He and Mrs Brown had built themselves a completely unnecessary barricade out of all the sort of stuff you usually find in cellars and were manning it with considerable enthusiasm. I could see a couple of heavy-duty blasters pointing in my direction. Really, I don't know why Markham and I had bothered getting out of bed.

'We won,' I said, standing in the doorway.

'I never doubted it for one moment,' said Dr Bairstow, shutting down his blaster. 'Report.'

'Five of them. Four men, one woman. One survivor who isn't talking. Or wasn't when I left. Pennyroyal may be able to change his mind.'

Mrs Brown shouldered her blaster. 'Are we secure?'

'No,' I said. 'Big hole in the roof. Ceiling down on the landing. Back door blown off its hinges. Otherwise, all OK.'

They trotted up the stairs. Dr Bairstow especially can get around considerably more quickly than you might think. Ask Markham, who, several times in his career, has come across Dr Bairstow at the most inconvenient moments. He can be quite eloquent on the subject.

Dr Bairstow bent over the prisoners. 'Anything?' he enquired of Pennyroyal, who shook his head.

'Do *you* recognise them at all, sir?'

Dr Bairstow shook his head. He and Mrs Brown had recently spent some time as unwilling guests of the government. It had not ended well. For the government, that is. Was it possible the targets of tonight's little adventure were Dr Bairstow and Mrs Brown, rather than Pennyroyal and Smallhope as I'd assumed? There was also an outside chance they'd been after Markham – who isn't who he seems, and that's all I'm going to say. It seemed safe to assume no one was after me. I tried not to feel too aggrieved because no one likes being left out, do they?

'I think,' said Lady Amelia, 'that we should get these fellows off the premises as soon as possible. I don't like having dead people about the place. Pennyroyal can drop them off with the Time Police and claim any bounty. With luck it'll be enough to cover the damage.'

She bent down. 'You hear that, you bastard? We're selling you to the Time Police. Pennyroyal, be sure to tell them how uncooperative the prisoner has been. Invite them to try out all their latest interrogation techniques. Say goodbye to the world, my friend. You'll never see it again. Get them out of here.'

We carted them into Pennyroyal's pod, huffing and puffing away because some of us are not as fit as we should be. His pod disappeared and we retreated back into the kitchen.

'If you've no objection, Lady Amelia,' said Markham, 'I'll take Max and we'll have a look around outside. I know we've covered the farm buildings but I'd like to extend the search. They must have come from somewhere.'

'You're expecting to find a pod?'

'Given the quality of their weapons, I wouldn't be surprised.'

'In that case, have at it. We'll have breakfast on your return.'

I threw on my old riding mac, slung a new blaster over my shoulder, and set off to look for any clues as to the origin of our night visitors. Which I quite enjoyed, actually, because it gave me the opportunity to ride one of those quad bike thingies and they're great fun. Although surprisingly wilful. There had been that incident when the sheep had herded me instead of vice versa. Which wasn't half as funny as Markham would have you believe.

We worked in increasing circles from the farmhouse. Markham clockwise and me the other way. I'd say widdershins but that would only set him off on his Fun Facts again as he attempted to explain the origins of the word, and one can only take so much cataclysm in one night.

I bumped across fields, swerving around sleepy sheep who made absolutely no attempt to get out of my way. I couldn't help wondering how Markham was faring because he's a priority target for the animal world. I had a proximity meter, and apart from a few hazy green blobs that could have been either sheep or Markham – very similar readings, for some reason – I was alone.

And then, north of Home Farm and about three fields away, in a small copse, a brief flicker. A pod signature.

I opened my com. 'Hey.'

'Good morning,' he said reproachfully, because he does like standards to be maintained.

'Possible signature. Hundred yards to my right. That small copse we can see from the kitchen window. Find me. I'll wait for you.'

I parked the bike, adjusted my night visor, followed the hedge, and approached the copse with caution, because I had no idea whether anyone would've been left on board. Finding a handy bush to crouch behind, I settled down to wait for the young master.

He's really very good. I never heard the slightest whisper of either him or the quad bike. I was blithely looking in the wrong direction for him when his voice said, 'Two trees to your right.'

I squinted through my visor at what was either a very strangely shaped tree or a normal tree with a wayward ex-Head of Security crouching behind it.

Following his hand signals, we moved silently towards the pod, ghosting from tree to tree. The ground was damp so I didn't have to worry about rustling leaves. The morning was still dark but if they had proximity alerts and night vision, they'd know we were here anyway. I couldn't see any signs of life from the pod which led me to believe it was unmanned. Surely the driver would have legged it by now, having lost all contact with his comrades well over an hour ago. Even so, we weren't going to take any chances.

I can't believe I just said that. Do you think that's what they call personal growth? Moving on . . .

We both fetched up at the pod together – Markham on the right and me on the left. The door was midway between us.

I remembered an old trick. I held up my hand to signal 'wait'. He lowered his gun. I pointed to the roof and cupped my hands.

He nodded, took two steps forwards and I boosted him up. Well, actually, I performed the basic functions of a ladder and he scrambled up me like a monkey up a stick. Good job he's small and light because I have the upper body strength of damp cotton wool. There was a brief, perilous moment when we both nearly toppled into the mud but then I leaned against the wall and braced myself and generally saved the day.

He jumped down. I massaged some life back into my hands and he shook his head. No one up there.

If there was anyone inside, they were taking their time coming out and shooting us. We both looked at the door. There had been five of them. This was a small pod. They'd have been cramped. It would appear no one had called the pod for reinforcements. Or to tell them to get out while the going was good. On the balance of probabilities, this pod was empty.

I looked at Markham, whose thoughts, I suspected, were running along the same lines. I backed off behind a tree and brought up my blaster to give him cover.

He said, 'Door,' and at the same time threw himself to one side.

Nothing happened. He picked himself up and I advanced cautiously.

Both St Mary's and Time Police pods are fitted with the latest in biometrics, meaning most people can't gain access unless they're programmed in. However, it's expensive enough to build a pod, without struggling with the cost of optional extras. Even programmed passwords. When I was at St Mary's, I could barely remember my head of department login and frequently had to ask my assistant, Rosie Lee. Rather in the same way I have to get Matthew to open things with childproof locks. We – they – St Mary's – don't password our pods because trying to remember a complicated set of numbers and letters that must include at least one punctuation symbol, one number, and one uppercase letter in the middle of the Great Fire of London or with a hungry T-rex bearing down on you is quite difficult. So mostly, we – they – just call for the door and as long as we're programmed in – it opens. Occasionally, if things are expected to become really hairy, we have a code woven into the fabric of our costumes. Just in case you've had your tongue cut out, they told me during training.

'Door,' however, wasn't the word.

I frowned. 'Open.'

Nothing.

Markham leaned over my shoulder. 'Open, please.'

The door opened.

'I keep telling you,' he said, radiating smugness, 'standards should always be maintained.'

I informed him I could maintain my own standards by shooting him now, and we entered the pod.

It was empty. No people inside and nowhere to hide. There was a very basic console, six metal seats bolted around the walls, and some sort of weapons locker. That was it. No decon lamp. Not even a kettle. Certainly no bathroom. Bloody amateurs.

The next thing that grabbed my attention was the smell of burning. There was a big impact burn on the wall opposite the door. It looked as if something fiery had come through the door, ricocheted off that wall, hit the wall over the console – damaging the screen and leaving another long scorch mark – and then dropped to the floor, where it had obviously burned for some time because there was a small melted crater, at the centre of which were the remains of a burned-out fizzer.

Fizzers are a form of emergency flare made to fire into the air. I've used them myself. They hover for ages, painting everything a lurid red and convincing your enemies/dinosaurs/religious fanatics/whoever that the end of days is at hand and to push off while they still can.

What you don't do – what you don't *ever* do – is fire one inside. They're only for exterior use. They go off with considerable force and once they're lit, you can't put them out. Even if they land on water, they'll still fizz for a while. Like phosphorous. Do I mean phosphorous? Or magnesium, perhaps? Anyway, you never fire a fizzer inside because they'll just keep going – bouncing off the ceiling, walls, people, whatever – until they expire. Which takes a while. I remembered our assailants had all been wet. Had they had an accident with a fizzer and tried to put it out?

I looked around. No fire extinguisher. No fittings on the wall where a fire extinguisher could be mounted. Sloppy. Very sloppy.

Markham rummaged through the contents of the locker, shoving it all into a small cardboard box, while I sat at the console and checked the coordinates. Surprisingly, there were quite a lot. Far too many to remember.

'We need to download these,' I said, 'and I don't have a gizmo.' Neither of us had thought to bring one.

'You go back,' I said. 'I'll be fine here. I'll have a poke about and see what else I can find. Anything interesting in the locker?'

'Yes. Take a look at this while I'm gone. I'll be ten minutes – no more.'

Markham handed me a scrap of A4 paper torn in half, with *LC 0900 20/5* scribbled on it. There seemed to be some kind of logo in the top left-hand corner. Part of a hand, perhaps, holding an ice-cream cone.

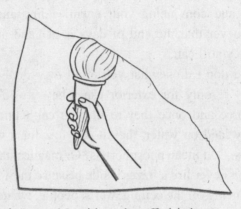

'An appointment,' I said, and stuffed it into my pocket.

'Don't open the door to strangers.' He disappeared and I heard his bike start up in the distance.

Now that all the excitement was over, the night had turned even colder. I was glad of my scruffy, smelly, but very warm riding mac. Shivering, I stood in the doorway and shone my torch around the little wood outside. The light picked out gaunt and skeletal trees. And eyes. Lots and lots of eyes. Which was really creepy. And did I mention how cold it was?

I shut the door against anyone or anything attempting to gain access – either human or a passing badger, wanting to get into the warmth. It seemed the sensible thing to do at the time. As I explained to everyone afterwards. You'd think I'd know better by now. When does being sensible ever keep you safe?

I settled myself down at the console for a bit of a think.

Everyone does it occasionally. You sit down and reflect on how you got to this point in your life. Ponder your life choices. What would you have done differently? What *should* you have done differently?

Quite a lot in my case.

My world was upside down. The reported death of Dr Bairstow had brought John Treadwell to St Mary's. It really hadn't taken me long to fall foul of him. And the knowledge he was really a Time Police officer had not endeared him to me even a little bit. And then there'd been Hyssop – Markham's replacement as Head of Security. I'd really managed to fall out with her. And the people she brought with her. I suppose the only surprise was that it had taken me so long to be sacked. Perhaps I was losing my touch. Or mellowing with age. Although, remembering the head-bursting rage with which I'd confronted both Treadwell and Hyssop – probably not.

And now, here I was with Markham – who, for reasons of his own, had also left St Mary's and was here with me. *Here* is Home Farm, owned by Lady Amelia Smallhope and her alleged butler, Pennyroyal. They'd recruited us and now Markham and I were both pursuing successful careers as . . . recovery agents. Hey, how about that? I remembered.

Very successful careers, actually. Trust me, being on the slightly wrong side of the law is considerably more lucrative than being on the right side of it. Markham and I were doing very nicely, thank you. Due, in no small part, I suspected, to our naturally unlaw-abiding natures. The phrase *ducks to water* had been used. And by Dr Bairstow, no less. It's a long story but both Dr Bairstow and Mrs Brown are wanted by government security.

Especially since Markham and I had snatched Dr Bairstow from the clutches of Martin Gaunt, superintendent of the Red House and one of the few people who genuinely frightened me. I was definitely in no hurry to see him again. But – should all this ever resolve itself into a happy ending for everyone – Markham and I would be very nicely placed to make a fresh start with our respective families.

So the situation wasn't desperate. Not for us, anyway. And Peterson would look after St Mary's in the meantime. He was far more adept at dealing with idiots than me. As someone had pointed out, St Mary's would probably do much better now I wasn't there. But even so . . . none of this was ideal. And there was Leon out there somewhere, conducting the world's longest field trial on a pod. Sooner or later . . .

No – nothing I could do about that. Have some faith in other people, Maxwell, and concentrate on the job in hand.

Good advice. I should take it.

I was leaning over the console to make an in-depth analysis of the data available – or as in-depth as I could get until Markham turned up with the right equipment – when the chronometer went clunk.

Something lit up on the console. A metallic voice said, 'Auto-pilot engaged. Enter code to disengage.'

I leaped out of the chair.

Shit. Shit, shit, shit. It wasn't anything I'd done. I swear it wasn't anything I'd done. I hadn't touched a thing. Honest.

And I hadn't got a clue what the code might be. I didn't even intend to try. I had only a second or two and then I was going to be in very deep trouble indeed.

I shouted, 'Door,' out of sheer habit, completely forgetting

24

that wouldn't work, and then lunged across the pod, meaning to pull the trip switch and cut off the power, but it was too late.

'Code not entered. Jumping in three, two, one . . .'

Shiiiiiiiiit . . .

OK – in a life that's had more than its fair share of bad moments – here was another one.

The pod landed well. Peterson – the world's worst lander – would have been proud of that one. I was on my feet at the time, still halfway across the pod and reaching for the switch, and I barely staggered.

There was a moment's stillness while I wondered what the hell to do next.

My first instinct was to get out of the pod as quickly as possible and find somewhere to hide, before its owners came to claim it and discovered they'd acquired a stowaway.

Second thoughts convinced me that might not be a good idea. If the pod jumped again – as it seemed distressingly prone to do – then I'd be stranded in an unknown time and place with no way of getting back.

Third thoughts said to hang on for a moment and see what happened next. Which, I worried, would consist of a hail of gunfire and me dying on the floor. Seriously, if I ever got out of this, it was definitely time to review my life choices. Get that nice office job I was always banging on about.

Fourth thoughts said to hang on another minute. Where was

everyone? I was still in here on my own. Why hadn't anyone turned up to find out what was going on? No one was trying to access this pod. Was that a Good or a Bad Thing?

I stopped having a mental twitter and pulled myself together. I should go. A prudent and sensible historian – not that I'd ever met one of those – would bang in the appropriate coordinates and get the hell out of here.

On the other hand – and I think everyone will agree – this was a god of historians-given opportunity. This could be the place from which the pod had originated. I should take the opportunity to investigate. Do a little detective work.

Most importantly – make a note of the current coordinates while I still could. I flicked through the controls. Here they were. The last set. I tried to calm down. To remember them. Why the hell didn't I have anything to write on?

Actually, I did. I had that piece of paper in my pocket. Problem solved.

No, it wasn't. I didn't have anything to write with.

This was not turning out to be the best day ever.

I yanked open the locker door, rummaging away in Markham's cardboard box. Stuff went everywhere but nothing to write with.

All right, Maxwell – improvise.

There was a small med kit. Nothing to write with in there either, but there was a scalpel in a protective sleeve.

I took a deep breath. Imaginative improvisation is all very well when someone else is doing it, and surely I'd shed enough blood over the years, but needs must, etc., etc. I bared my forearm – the one with the rather nasty scar from when Leon had tried to remove my tag. That hadn't turned out so well – mostly because he was operating on the wrong bloody arm. A fact I return to whenever I'm losing an argument.

I took another deep breath – the first one had run out while I was dithering – and made the cut. Rather unenthusiastically, tiny beads of blood welled up and then stopped so I had to do it again. Equally painful. And my blood flow was equally unspectacular.

I couldn't understand it. In films you're always seeing people take a blood oath. The hero, his profile sharp and clear against the full moon, drags his giant knife across the palm of his hand and suddenly there's blood everywhere.

Well, let me tell you – *no, there bloody isn't*. There's a reluctant trickle – like politicians lining up to act in the public interest – and then it starts to go sticky almost immediately. Good news, obviously, should I ever be bleeding to death, but not today. Not right now.

Returning to the console, I flattened the piece of paper, dipped the blunt end of the scalpel into my reluctant blood and painstakingly began to write. It wasn't easy – neither blood nor upended scalpels are a professional scribe's instruments of choice – but I kept at it.

I used coordinate shorthand and symbols wherever I could, conscious of time ticking away. There could be people bursting through the door at any moment.

After a painful few minutes, I had something I thought I'd be able to read. Or, should things go horribly wrong, something Pennyroyal would be able to retrieve from my lifeless corpse and make some sense of.

That done, I left it to dry and turned my attention to what I thought might be the camera controls. After a lot of fiddling and cursing – because they were configured differently to those at St Mary's and I kept going in the wrong direction – I got the hang of things. There was only the one camera but I could pan about a little bit.

I'd been worried that wherever I was would be in complete darkness and I'd be none the wiser, but fortunately that wasn't the case. I was in a largish indoor space. I couldn't see to the corners but that was because it was lit only with what appeared to be emergency lighting. Far from hordes of angry hostiles heading towards the pod, there was only silence and stillness. I peered at the screen. I seemed to be in a warehouse of some kind.

The bit that I could see was beautifully organised. And clean. No clutter, no overflowing bins, no scruffy notices stuck skew-whiff on the walls. Even the floors were swept clean.

I shouldn't leave the pod. I really shouldn't leave the pod. Really, really shouldn't leave the pod. There would be security cameras everywhere. At the moment all they could see was this pod, sitting still, minding its own business. If there was anyone monitoring this, they might give it a few minutes before turning up to investigate the lack of activity, but if they saw me – a complete stranger – emerge from the pod and start poking around their facilities, they'd be here faster than the History Department on the last biscuit.

I panned around again. At the other end of the space were pallets of what appeared to be books and pamphlets, all shrink-wrapped. Office furniture was neatly stacked against one wall, with flatbeds and sack barrows against another. So far, so innocuous. There was a wire cage in one corner. That was probably where they kept the valuable and accessible stuff. I tried for a close-up but everything seemed to be carefully packed up in anonymous boxes that could contain just about anything. All the evidence said this was just what it looked like: a small warehouse and loading bay.

Except ... further along the wall was a familiar sight. Markham would have identified them instantly. Gun safes. Four of them. And a row of lockable metal boxes, contents unknown. Ammo, I suspected. Or grenades. Whatever. They were all keypad-operated – as was the wire cage.

I twisted and turned the camera. No other pods as far as I could see, although there did appear to be a row of Parissa fittings along one wall. I didn't dare hang around much longer. Surely someone must be on their way to investigate this strangely inactive pod. I should go while I still could.

And I genuinely would have departed except as I was turning away, I saw it. I couldn't believe I hadn't spotted it before. A small piece of paper, light against the dark floor, as conspicuous and out of place as an honest politician at a party-political conference.

I flicked the camera back to the pallets. Yes, one of the bundles on the end was ripped. The pamphlet must have spilled out and somehow been kicked half under the shelving.

To be clear, I wasn't expecting it to be a full confession or a five-point explanation of our assailants' activities, but something – anything – would be useful. I couldn't – just couldn't – miss this opportunity.

I tried for a close-up but the camera wouldn't zoom any further.

I mentally measured the distance. I could do it. I could definitely do it.

Door open. One, two, three, four steps. Grab the bit of paper. Turn. One, two, three, four steps and back inside. Door closed. Five seconds. Seven at the most. I could do it. I slipped off my riding mac for ease of movement.

Time was of the essence but I still took a valuable moment to run through it all again in my mind. No athlete ever prepared more thoroughly for her world-record ten-foot sprint and leaflet pickup than I did.

Wait – stop and think, Maxwell. Enough people know who you are and want a quiet word. Don't go adding to the list.

I pulled my sweatshirt over my head to cover my hair. The way I did when I was a kid and a superhero. And yes, I was still wearing my PJs underneath. I could only hope any observers were too distracted by my bizarre dress sense to see what I looked like, but I tied the sleeves around the lower part of my face, just in case.

Ready . . . steady . . .

No. Hang on a minute. A word to the wise. Always set up your return coordinates in advance. Just in case a quick getaway is needed. I took a second to flick back and found the ones for Home Farm. I moved the last three digits forwards a couple of hours because you can't be in the same place twice unless you want to die a horribly unpleasant death.

Right – this was it – go. I hit the door control and was moving across the pod before it even began to open.

Everything worked like a dream.

I vaguely remember the air was cold. They obviously didn't bother heating this space. And there was a strange combination of smells. Old paper, perhaps, and musty somethings. And something sharper, more chemical. No time to think about it now.

One, two, three, four. I grabbed the paper.

The bloody thing was stuck to the floor. I felt a part of it come away in my hand.

And then the bloody lights came on.

Bloody, sodding, bollocking motion sensors.

I jumped a mile. Understandably, I think. A thousand thoughts crashed through my mind, ranging from *Shit, busted*, to a mad moment, possibly induced by blood loss, when I half expected people to leap out shouting, 'Surprise!'

I was already spinning around.

I heard voices. They were coming.

My previous record for the ten-foot dash went straight out of the window. I don't even remember covering the ground. I was back to the pod in a flash, crashing into the console at full speed. The god of historians, obviously not realising I was no longer a fully paid-up member, thoughtfully arranged the universe in such a way that I sprawled only inches from the jump controls. Whether people were already in the warehouse or not – I don't know. I was past caring. My little heart was going like one of Lingoss's steam engines. I slapped the door control and less than a second later, I was gone.

Considering the circumstances of my departure, my return journey was very smooth. I hardly noticed the touchdown at all. It was a real shame Peterson wasn't there to see how it should be done.

I pushed myself off the console, weak with relief. I'd done it. I was home. And possibly with something useful. I opened the door – because I wasn't taking any more chances with this pod – donned my mac because now I was cold, sank into the seat, regretted the lack of kettle and smoothed out my bit of pamphlet.

Typical. Abso-sodding-lutely typical. The bloody thing was blank. On both sides. Just a scrap of white paper. I'd done all that – I'd risked all that – for absolutely bugger all.

I raised it to my nose and sniffed. Well, at least I'd traced the source of the smell. The paper had been treated with some sort of chemical. And that was all the info I had.

I threw myself back in the seat and closed my eyes.

And then, because my night from hell still wasn't over, a voice said, 'Safety codes not entered. Presumed hostile incursion. Life support to shut down in . . .' and the bloody door began to close.

I didn't wait. I was sick of this bloody pod doing its best to kill me. It was still intoning something dire as I squeezed through the rapidly narrowing gap – an incentive to lose weight if ever there was one – and fell face down on the ground.

What saved me – what saved everyone – was my left foot. I didn't get it out of the way in time and the door closed on it. And stopped. Safety protocols are a wonderful thing. I don't ever want to hear anyone say differently. Safety protocols are the only reason the world isn't full of one-legged historians. The door stopped. The countdown stopped. Everything stopped. Except for my heart which was, by now, in overdrive.

And my foot hurt, too, because I wasn't wearing my trusty boots.

Not daring to move too much in case I inadvertently triggered pod destruction, radiation, smoking craters, dead sheep, and the wrath of Pennyroyal, I carefully rolled over and found a decent-sized rock.

Fortunately the door was too stupid to tell the difference between me and a rock. No comments, please – Markham has more than made them all. I rammed the rock into the gap, very cautiously withdrew my throbbing foot and lay on my back, staring up at the sky. Just for a minute.

A pale sun shone weakly through the trees; it was now daytime. My adventures in the warehouse had barely taken the time needed to describe them, but I seemed to have been away for a couple of hours at least.

There was so much still to investigate but if I left the pod here, door wedged open, with my luck a casual passer-by would discover it and press the wrong button and *boom*. Or a family of rabid badgers would move in. Or the local council would bung it in band B and send us a council-tax demand. Or prosecute us for failing to get planning permission. Or a couple of ley-line-walking ancient astronaut-seeking nutters would stumble across it to worldwide publicity and all the conspiracy theorists would go into meltdown. It really shouldn't be left to its own devices. Not least because we hadn't had time to plunder its secrets.

I sat up and opened my com. 'Hello.'

There was a long silence and then Markham said very cautiously, 'Hello?'

'Hey,' I said. 'Where are you?'

There was a bit of a silence and then he said, 'Never mind that, where are *you*?'

'Here,' I said, not very helpfully, looking around at the trees. 'Where we were before. The pod jumped. I think it had some sort of automatic return system programmed in. Which makes sense.' I had a sudden thought. 'Have I been gone long?'

There was just the veriest suggestion of gritted teeth. 'Three days.'

Oh. Shit.

'Sorry,' I said meekly. 'I was in a slight hurry and didn't have time to check the coordinates very carefully.'

'Pod OK?'

'Absolutely fine,' I said. I looked at my bloody arm and throbbing foot. 'Probably better than me.'

'On our way.'

I climbed to my feet and cautiously approached the pod. I could just about wriggle through the partly closed door. I stepped carefully over the rock, intending to retrieve the contents of the cardboard box, and it was a good job I did because just as I slipped the bloodstained piece of paper into my pocket, deliberately or otherwise, the whole console went bang. All the lights went out and sparks flew everywhere and there was a really nasty smell of dying pod. I grabbed the box, squeezed myself out through the door, and rolled across the clearing just as Markham and Pennyroyal appeared on quad bikes.

I picked myself up, brushed myself off, and Pennyroyal regarded me without noticeable enthusiasm. 'So what did you do, then?'

'Nothing,' I said indignantly. 'It did it all by itself.'

'Interesting,' said Markham, dismounting and going inside, flapping his arms in the smoke. 'If no one returns from their assignment, then the pod quietly takes itself home, leaving no trace. Neat.'

'I don't know about that,' I said. 'How would you feel knowing that if you're delayed for any reason, then your transportation will go home without you and you're stranded. Forever.'

'Hell of an incentive to get the mission successfully completed on time.'

'Well, it's just gone bang so I think it's programmed to self-destruct if some sort of safety routine isn't performed.'

'Where did it take you?'

'Don't know.' I told them about the warehouse and my adventures therein.

Pennyroyal stared at me. 'It's like *The Perils of Pauline* wherever you go, isn't it?'

I didn't dignify that with a reply.

'What about the sack barrows and flatbeds?'

I stared. 'What about them?'

'Get a chance to check them out?'

'No. Why?'

'Chances are they'd have had "Property of Whoever" on them somewhere – if only to prevent external delivery drivers making off with them.'

Bugger. I hadn't thought of that. 'No,' I said, 'sorry.'

He shook his head. 'Disappointing.'

'I know,' I said, casually. 'If only they'd dragged me out of the pod and brought me before their leader who would, with luck, have had a very helpful desk diary, showing not only the date, time and place, but that day's plans for world domination, as well. Some people just don't deserve to be supervillains.'

'No doubt,' Pennyroyal said, coldly. 'But some idea of the coordinates would have been useful.'

'The thing exploded,' I said indignantly.

I was the recipient of his dead-eyed stare. 'Even so, Dr Maxwell.'

I grinned at him – because I know that winds him up – fished for the blood-inscribed coordinates and held them in front of him.

Typically, his first words were not, 'Magnificent, Dr Maxwell. Your quick thinking has saved the day and there's a massive bonus in this for you.' Although, to be fair, I don't think those have ever been anyone's first words. Not to me, anyway.

He regarded the paper distastefully. 'Is that blood?'

'Yes. Some of mine. Finest vintage. Any chance of the traditional cup of tea and a biscuit?'

He nodded at Markham. 'He'll give you a lift back. I'll take a look around here and follow on with whatever I can salvage.'

Since by now I was desperate for a tea and pee break, I didn't argue. Pointing to the box lying on its side, I said, 'I was able to save most of the locker contents, but I was in a hurry.'

He nodded.

'And before you do anything, trip the switch. To be on the safe side. This thing is just full of surprises. Wouldn't it be dreadful if it exploded while you were still inside it?'

He just stared at me and then disappeared into the pod. I heard a thunk as he tripped the switch.

'See you soon,' I called, climbing up behind Markham, and we roared off.

They'd cleared a lot of the damage to Home Farm while I'd been away. The back door was heavily boarded so we had to come in through the front. Dr Bairstow and Mrs Brown emerged as we pulled up. Both were festooned with weapons. I have to say considering they were supposed to be from the respectable end of the behaviour spectrum, they'd embraced the shady side of the law with even more enthusiasm than me. When you think one was the ex-Director of St Mary's and the other a senior member of the Civil Service . . . well, what can I say?

I was instructed to go and tidy myself up, which actually I was quite glad to do. Not only was my bladder twanging but I still had plaster in my hair from our recent unpleasantness. I shot off for tea and a pee, and not in that order, either. And a shower and change of clothes. Not least because underneath everything, I was still wearing my PJs.

Some time later, much refreshed and with proper clothes on, I was brushing my hair when Markham knocked at the door.

'I'm glad you're here,' I said, letting him in. 'I've been having a think.'

He settled himself in the window seat. 'About the attack?'

'A little. But I had concerns before that.'

He nodded. 'Yeah. Me too. About Dr Bairstow's safety?'

'And about Martin Gaunt, as well.'

Martin Gaunt supervised the department of the Red House responsible for housing Dr Bairstow during his recent incarceration. He was an unpleasant man – Gaunt, I mean, although Dr Bairstow can have his moments as well. I'd committed an unforgivable sin, however – I'd made Gaunt look small. In front of his own people, too. He wouldn't forgive and he certainly wouldn't forget.

'I don't think Gaunt's the type to let things go. It's possible that Dr Bairstow may never be able to return to his proper time and place.'

He sighed. 'None of us can at the moment, can we? You and I are guilty of breaking him out, remember. The authorities aren't going to forget that in a hurry.'

'And,' I said, 'don't forget the very unlikeable Commander Treadwell currently presiding over St Mary's.'

'Isn't he supposed to be a mate of Dr Bairstow's?'

'He's also Time Police,' I said grimly.

'Friendly Time Police, though.'

'Right up until he receives orders to the contrary. Suppose the Time Police decide this is the perfect moment to move in and dismantle St Mary's?'

'Blimey, Max. When you do paranoia, you really don't mess about, do you?'

'I haven't even started.' I lowered my voice. God knows why – no one downstairs could possibly have heard us. Not unless they'd riddled the room with sophisticated listening devices. Always a possibility, I suppose.

'Then there's those two – Pennyroyal and Smallhope,' I continued. 'Yes, I know they took us in and made Dr Bairstow's rescue possible, but only because they were paid to do so. Suppose someone offers them more money to hand him over? To hand us all over? I'm pretty certain they would, aren't you?'

'I'm not so sure. Yes, they work for money – lots of it – but I don't think there's enough money in the world to make them do something they don't want to.'

'I don't disagree, but suppose handing us over for a giant reward is something they suddenly *do* want to do?'

Markham folded his arms. 'I'm assuming, from your expression, you've had some sort of Brilliant Idea.'

'I have. I don't think there's anywhere beyond the reach of Smallhope and Pennyroyal, but we do need to get Dr Bairstow out of the sight of lesser mortals. And out of mind.'

He looked at me. 'And out of time?'

I nodded. 'I've been considering those two lowlives, Feeney and Winterman and . . .'

'Low*lifes*,' he said.

I frowned. 'You sure?'

'Pretty sure, yes.'

'Well, Dr Bairstow and Mrs Brown would be safe in that house. It's all set up and provided with servants – all of whom owe us big time. They could look after Dr Bairstow and he could look after them.'

He sat in silence. I waited.

'It's a good scheme,' he said at last. 'But what about Penny-royal and Smallhope? They know the location of the house as well.'

'They do but we can't do anything about that. And frankly, if Pennyroyal and Smallhope are looking for you, then I don't think any time or place is safe, do you?'

'What does Dr Bairstow say?'

'I haven't mentioned it to him yet – or anyone – but I think it's worth considering. I don't think he's quite recovered from his treatment at the hands of Martin Gaunt, either.'

He glanced at my hair. 'Neither have you.'

I shrugged because I didn't want to talk about that. That bastard Gaunt had hacked off my hair and I hadn't been able to do a thing about it. Yes, I know – it wasn't important in the scheme of things but even so . . . 'It'll grow.'

'How are your arms and shoulders?'

I didn't shrug again because I'd had more than a twinge the first time I'd done it. I'd recently had my arms forced nearly out of their sockets and I wasn't healing as quickly as I would have liked. And falling down the stairs hadn't helped much, either.

'Again – I'll heal.'

He sat for a moment, considering.

'It's a good plan,' I said. 'All my plans are good plans.'

'Like all your ideas are Brilliant Ideas.'

I beamed. 'You've noticed that too?'

Markham stirred. 'We should go downstairs. There's your unscheduled jump to discuss.'

'Agreed.'

There were bacon butties. I can't tell you how pleased I was to see them. I was slightly less pleased to discover they weren't all for me, but never mind.

Pennyroyal had returned while I'd been wallowing in hot water. The remaining contents of the pod's locker and the cardboard box were on the kitchen table. Mostly odd bits of clothing – no helpful name tags, sadly; the remains of the med kit; four or five half-empty sports drinks, brands unknown; and a sock. Why would anyone take their socks off? And why only one? We examined everything carefully but there were no clues anywhere so we moved on.

'The console's blown,' said Lady Amelia. 'Probably a deliberate strategy to prevent honest, God-fearing people like us from downloading useful information and using it to track down the miscreants and bring them to justice.'

Yes, she really does talk like that. Especially after her third margarita.

'And to prevent us collecting our rightful reward,' said Markham.

She scowled. Lady Amelia is very big on rightful rewards. 'And that as well.'

'In this case,' said Pennyroyal, 'and thanks to the always resourceful Dr Maxwell, I believe their strategy has been unsuccessful.'

He laid my torn scrap of paper gently on the kitchen table. Smallhope poked at it with a knife. 'Is that . . . ?'

'Written in my own life blood,' I said dramatically. 'You're welcome.'

No one would touch it.

'Coordinates,' I said. 'Where and when the pod originated.'

They all looked at me. I looked back. They looked at me some more.

I sighed. 'Fine – I'll do it, shall I?' and took myself off next door to the office. Firing up the data table, I took a long swig of the tea I'd remembered to bring with me and got stuck in.

The *where* was London.

The *when* was sometime in the future. Which I wasn't tremendously enthusiastic about. For very good reasons.

I'm an historian. My passion is the past. Ancient civilisations, actually. I really can't understand how people can be bothered to get out of bed for anything after 1485. I'm not much interested in the present and I certainly couldn't give a rat's arse about the future. I've been there – I was in it now – but like a polar bear in the Namibian desert, it wasn't my natural environment. The thing about jumping into the past is that you know it's actually there. It exists. The same thing can't be said about the future. Suppose a nuclear strike wipes out all life? Although I have to admit I do sometimes look around and think pressing 'reset' might not be a Bad Thing. Or, suppose there's some sort of future planetary collision and the earth is destroyed. What then? Where do you land? How do you get back? My point is that the future is uncertain and there's enough grief and catastrophe in my life without taking on comets and nuclear apocalypses. Besides, the Time Police are all over the future and they don't like me much. I can't think why – I'm delightful – but there you go. They're not bright.

I flattened my data stack and returned to the kitchen to find the others had been joined by Dr Bairstow and Mrs Brown so this was to be a full conference.

All six of us gathered together in our official discussion spot – i.e., around the kitchen table, where it was warm and a jug of margaritas was never that far away. It was the first time we'd really had a chance to discuss recent events.

'Right,' said Smallhope, setting down her margarita. 'What do we know?'

'We know we were attacked the other night,' said Pennyroyal.

'We don't know why,' I said.

'We don't know their intended target,' said Markham.

'We don't know who they were,' I said.

'We don't know where they came from,' said Markham.

'We don't know . . .' I began.

'Yes, all right,' said Smallhope, obviously regretting asking what, with hindsight, I suspected might have been a rhetorical question.

Pennyroyal topped up her glass. I sipped my tea.

They all looked at me.

'London,' I said. 'The pod originated from and jumped back to somewhere in the region of Great Russell Street.'

I was quite unprepared for the response.

'Not the British Museum again,' groaned Mrs Brown.

'I wouldn't be at all surprised,' said Dr Bairstow gloomily.

'Nor I,' said Lady Amelia.

44

Markham and I exchanged glances. Was there another British Museum somewhere? One that had drifted to the dark side?

'But . . .' I said. 'I mean . . . the British Museum . . . ?'

Mrs Brown turned to Dr Bairstow. 'Do you remember that incident – oh, eight or nine years ago . . . ?'

'When they had to evacuate the entire area? Vividly.'

'They blamed it on a gas leak, of course.'

Dr Bairstow nodded. 'They always do. You'd think, wouldn't you, that if the British Museum is going to keep opening doors best kept shut, then they could at least come up with a better cover story.'

'Or just stop opening doors to underground vaults when no one knows exactly what's on the other side.'

'Or be more careful in the placement of some of their exhibits. Do you remember when they laid out those artefacts in the wrong configuration and inadvertently raised . . . ?'

She grimaced. 'Exactly. There was hell on over that one. Quite literally, at one point.'

They seemed to become aware they weren't alone.

'Sorry,' said Mrs Brown. 'A bit off-topic there.'

'No, no,' said Markham. 'Do please tell us more about this sinister organisation masquerading as a national treasure. And its secrets.'

'Can't, I'm afraid,' she said regretfully. 'Suffice to say they make St Mary's look like a Sunday-school outing. Why do you think the Leaning Tower leans?'

'Well, that was just carelessness,' said Dr Bairstow.

'Wait,' I said. 'Are we talking about *the* British Museum? Big place. Pillars outside. Nice cafés. Aching feet. Borrowed one of our Botticellis for their Renaissance thing.'

'Yes, that's them.'

Markham shook his head mournfully. 'Academia is not what we think.'

'Don't knock them,' said Lady Amelia, refilling her margarita. 'They pay well.'

'Eventually,' said Pennyroyal, darkly.

'Well, true, we've had to call on them occasionally when they've been a bit slow settling an invoice. I always say you can't beat the personal touch.'

All eyes slid to Pennyroyal – the epitome of the personal touch.

Dr Bairstow cleared his throat. 'To return to the main topic of discussion – our little excitement the other night – all we know is that our security was breached. We now have a possible suspect – which is probably *not* the British Museum. Would the situation be clearer if we could identify which of us was their target? We are somewhat spoiled for choice.'

Smallhope shrugged. 'Well, we just don't know, do we? Nor likely to, unless the Time Police manage to get something out of our former prisoner.'

From the tone of her voice, she wasn't optimistic.

There was a pause. Now, Maxwell.

'Actually,' I said. 'Arising out of Dr Bairstow's comment, I've had some thoughts.'

I paused, half hoping someone would say, 'Not now, Maxwell,' which, to be fair, is the usual response to an awful lot of my Brilliant Ideas, but no one did, so, encouraged, I ploughed on. 'As things stand at the moment, we have no idea as to their target the other night. It could have been any of us – although probably not me – but until things are clearer, I think we need to spread the risk a little, so I have a plan.'

'Which is?'

'Winterman and Feeney.'

I suspect I need to bung in a bit of backstory at this point.

Part of what we do – and one of the most lucrative areas of our business – is to track down and bring back people whose criminal deeds have made their own time too hot to hold them. The authorities are poised to pounce with extreme prejudice, so, being rich and powerful people, they – the criminals, not the authorities – nip back in time, taking a considerable portion of their loot with them and begin a new life. Safe, as they think, from retribution.

Enter Smallhope and Pennyroyal – from whom no one is safe – and lately Markham and Maxwell as well – also from whom no one is safe, but for completely different reasons – to retrieve them from their little hideaway and – and this is the important bit – to sell them on to the Time Police for a truly colossal sum of money which we then gloatingly divide between us.

Winterman and Feeney were two such naughty people. Markham and I had popped back to 1893 to apprehend them. Not without a bit of a struggle on my part, I should say. They'd been a thoroughly unpleasant pair – ask their female staff who hadn't fared at all well under their masters. However, we'd got there in the end. Exit Winterman and Feeney. Mrs Proudie and her girls had been living quietly at Number Six Swan Court ever since. A house and servants just looking for a master and mistress and here were a mistress and master just looking for a home. Sometimes, even I can't believe how brilliant I am.

I turned to Dr Bairstow. 'Sir, I propose you and Mrs Brown go to live in their house. As a perfectly normal, respectable

Victorian couple. You will have a ready-made house and household. In turn, I think you'll be able to provide some security for the servants there which they badly need.'

I turned to Smallhope and Pennyroyal, sitting together opposite me. 'What worries me is that if anyone tracks us here, whoever they've come for, they find all of us. So – as I say – we should spread the risk a little. What do you think?'

Smallhope stirred. 'I think the most important opinions are those of Dr Bairstow and Mrs Brown. I myself think it's a stonking idea but I'm willing to go along with whatever they decide. Dr Bairstow? Your thoughts?'

He clasped his hands on the table in front of him. 'I think it seems an excellent plan. I don't want to seem ungrateful – especially if we were the unwitting cause of the other night's excitement – but the idea has merit. If anything should happen here . . .' He tailed away, looking at Mrs Brown.

'Then not all our eggs are in one basket,' she finished. 'By splitting our forces, we double our chances of success. If anything happens to one group – there's another to follow up this line of investigation. I think it's an excellent idea.'

'Practicalities,' said Lady Amelia, briskly. 'Some clothing can be provided from our wardrobe here and we can have the rest made there.'

'There's plenty of money already on site,' I said, 'which Winterman and Feeney had to leave behind in the drama of their exit. You wouldn't be short a bob or two.'

'I don't think either of us will have much trouble with social protocols,' said Mrs Brown, looking at Dr Bairstow.

I nodded. Mrs Brown – aka the Dowager Lady Blackbourne – would be more than equal to running a Victorian household.

And, not to put too fine a point on it, Dr Bairstow had Victorian patriarch nailed. Since birth, probably. All we had to do was create an identity for them. A married couple, obviously – they all had separate bedrooms in those days so that wouldn't be an issue – or rather it would be an issue they could work out for themselves. Their relationship wasn't something any of us were happy speculating over. As someone had once said – it was like your parents, wasn't it? Or the king and queen. Just not something you wanted to think about.

Not military, I thought. Yes, he had the bearing, but it would be too easy to search the Army or Navy lists and discover there had never been a Colonel Bairstow. Or even an Admiral Bairstow. Obviously they couldn't go by the name of Bairstow, either, but . . . how about North? North was Mrs Brown's family name. Brown was her professional name. Blackbourne was her title. Seriously – how many names could one person have? We'd stick with North, I think. The last thing we needed to do was chuck yet another surname into the mix.

Everyone was nodding. Everyone was impressed with my Brilliant Idea. A bit of a first for me.

While Dr Bairstow and Mrs Brown sorted themselves out with Smallhope's assistance, Markham and I were lumbered with finishing the clearing up and repairs.

The priority was getting the back door fixed, which meant not only a new door but sorting out the keypad lock, the electronics, the alarms, and the sensors, which meant we had to shift the pods while the experts were in.

Additionally, the farm – yes, it was an actual working farm – stopped for no one, so the Faradays – who ran it on behalf of

Lady Amelia – were continually shunting livestock about the place, to the consternation of Markham who never knew when he was going to find himself confronting some random member of the animal kingdom. Giant pieces of farm machinery were always being reversed in and out of the archway, the dogs ran everywhere and Markham managed to get himself bitten. There was extensive debate as to which of them was most likely to get rabies. Markham failed to see the funny side.

Possibly in self-defence, he went up on the roof to fix the tiles. Pennyroyal worked inside the attic to effect repairs from below. I was allowed to sweep up and cart it all away. It all took several days and many trips. And I had plaster in my hair again.

At the end of our efforts, we still had a gaping hole in the ceiling that Markham and I taped over with plastic which rustled in the wind and got on everyone's nerves.

Pennyroyal wanted the builders in as quickly as possible. Security was a subject very dear to his heart. Me lifeless on the ground might evoke a mild concern but socking great holes in the fabric of the building were making him very grumpy.

'Won't they be suspicious,' I said to him, pausing for a brief rest in my rubble-shifting labours. 'The builders, I mean. What will you say to them?'

'I shall say, "Here, accept this enormous sum of money and keep your mouths shut," and they will say, "Cor, ta very much, guv'nor, we certainly will."'

I stared up at him. 'You're just taking the piss, aren't you?'

He stared down at me. 'Why have you stopped working?'

Three days later, his builders turned up. Well, I say builders – first time I've ever seen tradesmen arrive before dawn in an unmarked van with no registration plates. One wore a knife strapped to his boot. Pennyroyal scowled and he whipped it out of sight in a nanosecond. There was a mutual, if unspoken, feeling that we'd all be better off elsewhere while they got on with things. Lady Amelia, Mrs Brown and Dr Bairstow went shopping; Pennyroyal took Markham to visit his family and then returned to supervise 'the builders'.

And me? I went off to meet with Leon.

5

I parked my pod – Leon's pod – in the woods at the top of the village, and crossed the road to peer into the churchyard. Believe it or not, there were still faded crimson petals caught among the headstones – the last remnants of Peterson's red-and-black-themed wedding. To Lingoss – just in case anyone had any doubts. No zombies – even though they're very fashionable at the moment – although there had been a carnivorous horse and two temptingly tasty bridesmaids.

Never mind the bride and groom – the real stars of the show, of course, were me and Markham, heavily disguised as the most normal wedding guests in the world. Our behaviour had been impeccable – obviously – except that close study of the wedding shots would reveal that Commander John Treadwell had unexpectedly sprouted bunny ears. I'd found myself standing behind him in the photo line-up and unable to resist the temptation. Don't judge me. No one could have.

I strolled down the hill to the Falconburg Arms and in through the front door. Technically, I still had a room upstairs, although I was slightly vague about how long I'd been away. And how long I'd remain away. I don't know if anyone's noticed but my life is a little unpredictable at the moment.

Ian looked up as I came through the door and groaned. The traditional Caledonian welcome whenever the English heave themselves over the horizon.

'What ho,' I said.

He looked over my shoulder. 'Markham's not here as well, is he?'

'Nope – shot off to visit Hunter and Flora. Whereabouts unknown, so don't ask.'

'Wasn't going to. One of you is bad enough.'

'I am a paying guest,' I said with dignity.

He snorted one of those all-purpose Caledonian snorts that can be interpreted in so many different ways. The most common being *give us back our cattle and our women, ye thieving English bastard*. Or the equally popular *you will never take our freedom*. Although that last one is a comparatively modern invention.

Ian looked very well. He'd kept the beard and the eyepatch and both suited him. I told him he looked like the lead in one of those historically inaccurate epics that were so popular these days. The ones where Troy is saved by a sword-wielding Helen who goes on to lead an attack on Rome and sleeps with Julius Caesar just before he invades Britain to seduce Boudica – who's an alien. And everyone is aged between twelve and fifteen. And clean. And all the costumes and hairstyles are wrong and the prudent historian steers clear of any scheduled fittings with Mrs Enderby in Wardrobe because there is inadvertent but still quite painful pin-stabbing.

Obviously having never attended Hospitality 101, Guthrie folded his arms and demanded to know why I was here.

'I'm hoping to see Leon. We tried to arrange something when I saw him last Christmas.'

'It's August,' he said.

'Not where and when I've come from. Is he here?'

He shook his head. 'Not yet. Shall I take you up to your room?'

'That's very impressive customer service, Ian. Almost like a real pub landlord.'

'I just want you out of sight as quickly as possible. We work quite hard to project a respectable image, you know.'

'Yeah – the beard and the eyepatch must be a huge help. They don't make you look like Fourth Villain in *Pirates of the Caribbean* at all.'

'May I remind you no one knows you're here. I am ex-military. I could kill you where you stand and no one would ever know.'

'You're from North Britain,' I said with confidence. 'You won't kill me until I've paid the bill.'

'Get up those stairs while you still can.'

Pleasantries observed, we went upstairs.

My room was exactly as I'd left it, which was a little concerning.

'Ian, have you been keeping this room for me?'

'No need,' he said, checking the supplies of tea and biscuits were adequate. 'Once I tell people you've been in here, no one ever seems to want it. When all this is over . . .' he looked at me, 'and it will be over one day, Max, then I'm going to bill you for a major refit.'

I grinned. 'Your words have no power over me. Not to toot our trumpets but the young master and I are doing rather well. We'll just buy you out.' I paused. 'The . . . um . . . the things we left with you . . . ?'

54

'Fine,' he said. 'Not accessible and quite safe.'

I nodded, satisfied. If Ian Guthrie said a thing was safe then it was. In our capacity as recovery agents living on the wild side, Markham and I had attended a Flying Auction selling off historical artefacts and we'd ... acquired ... a few goodies which, out of the goodness of his heart, Ian was keeping safe in his concealed cellar. Which now you know about, too.

He looked me up and down. 'You have time to tidy yourself up before Leon arrives.'

I was indignant. 'I tidied myself up before I jumped.'

'Really? Rough landing, was it?'

'Why are you still here?'

He laughed and closed the door behind him.

Barely had I dropped my bag on the bed when someone knocked at the door.

I stiffened. Leon wouldn't knock. This was trouble.

There was one of those ornamental fire sets in the fireplace. I seized the poker, raised it on high and whipped open the door to find Commander John Treadwell standing on the threshold.

Which was a bit of a shock. On the other hand, Guthrie must have had a reason for letting him come up so maybe I should let him live. For a minute or two.

I stared at him. He stared at me.

'Can I come in?'

'No.'

I really don't know why I bothered. He did something – something ninja and faster than the eye could see – well, my eye, anyway – and suddenly he was inside the room and calmly locking the door behind him. I planted my feet, gripped my poker and prepared to sell my life dearly.

'Should he turn up, I have asked Major Guthrie to detain Chief Farrell for twenty minutes. Therefore, my time is short. Oblige me by not passing any facetious comments until I have finished and am halfway back to St Mary's.'

Very slowly and ostentatiously I laid down the poker and folded my arms.

'Three things,' he said. 'Firstly, Mr Black is dead. Yes, that Mr Black. Friend and ally of Dr Bairstow. He died last week. This changes things considerably. There is now no one in government circles who has ever known Dr Bairstow personally. Mrs Brown's replacement is still under discussion and Green has always been unknown to me. I was deliberately inserted into St Mary's with the knowledge and cooperation of Brown and Black but I now think it very likely I shall be replaced. And quite soon.'

I wasn't given any chance to react.

'Secondly, I am unaware of the current location of Dr Bairstow and Mrs Brown and intend to remain so. However, it occurs to me that some attempt might be made to rescue . . .'

'Possibly already happened,' I said.

'Indeed?'

'They're both safe and well.'

'From where – and when – did this attempt originate?'

I wasn't going to tell him that. 'Unknown.'

'Move them,' he said abruptly.

I nodded. 'In hand.'

He paused and then said, 'For your own sake and that of St Mary's, you should make this your last visit here. There is someone out there who would give a very great deal to get his hands on you for a second time.'

56

For a moment I couldn't think who he was talking about. And then I could. My throat closed.

'Gaunt,' I said.

He nodded. 'This is only a suggestion – please do not reject it because it comes from me – but you should consider sending Matthew back to the Time Police. For his own protection. And yours. He is your weak link.'

I nodded again. He wasn't wrong. 'A question.'

He looked at his watch. 'Make it a quick one.'

'This shadowy organisation Dr Bairstow and I have talked about. The one pulling people's strings behind the scenes – the one who planted Laurence Hoyle – the one possibly linked with Clive Ronan – is it possible it's based in the future?'

'I think it very likely,' he said. 'May I ask what led you to that conclusion?'

'We were attacked. We're not sure if it was just a normal working-day hazard for Pennyroyal and Smallhope, an attempt to get at Markham, or whether it was Dr Bairstow and Mrs Brown they were after.' I tried not to sound too mournful. 'They didn't seem to want me at all.'

'My own opinion is that they must be completely unaware of your existence.'

'What makes you say that?'

'No normal person who has even the slightest acquaintance with you would be able to resist the temptation to kill you on the spot, Dr Maxwell.'

I informed him coldly that his twenty minutes was up.

Treadwell ignored me. 'What was the outcome of this attack?'

'Four dead, one handed to the Time Police. Their pod

attempted to self-destruct but Pennyroyal might find something that we can work with. What was your third thing?'

'Thirdly, you will not be surprised to hear that after the Security Section's disgraceful performance in front of the Parish Council, I have had no option other than to dismiss Mr Evans.'

We stared at each other for a very long time until the penny dropped for me. 'Understood,' I said.

'His last working day will be Friday but if it gets him off the premises more quickly, I would have no objections to him leaving early.'

I looked at Treadwell. With Evans, Dr Bairstow and Mrs Brown would acquire one of the best bodyguards money couldn't buy. They could end up being the safest people on the planet. This was an unexpected bonus arising out of St Mary's embracing World Naked Gardening Day. And then my brain moved up a gear. Exactly whose idea had that been? Not the worldwide *get your kit off and watch the roses bloom* thing – yes, WNGD is a real thing – but the idea that our Security Section should participate. Surely Evans at least must have realised the consequences . . .

I gave up. I had my world view of Treadwell, and like most people, I was unwilling to give it up even when faced with evidence to the contrary.

'Understood,' I said again. 'I shall be here until tomorrow evening. Tell him to bring a suit if he's got one.'

'Understood,' he said. 'And I say again – this must be your last visit. You do not want to fall into the hands of Martin Gaunt. Nor do you want Matthew falling into the hands of Martin Gaunt.'

A cold hand gripped my heart. No – I didn't.

He continued. 'Chief Farrell can, I am certain, look after

himself and has not, as yet, brought himself to the attention of the authorities, but you and Markham are wanted criminals. As are Dr Bairstow and Mrs Brown. Be aware Pennyroyal and Smallhope are not the only bounty hunters on the block.'

I nodded. Shit – this was just going from bad to worse.

'Will you return to the Time Police – once you're finished at St Mary's?'

'My course of action is not clear at the moment.'

I took a chance. 'Who does Captain Hyssop work for?'

'An excellent question to which I do not have the answer. She appears to be a genuine Army officer with eleven years' service. Distinguished service. If St Mary's could only realise how lucky they are to have her as their new Head of Security, everyone's life – especially mine – would be a lot easier. On an unrelated subject, I suspect either Chief Farrell has been conducting the longest field trial in history, or he hasn't yet succeeded in finding a home for your Archive. He needs to wrap that up and return to St Mary's. As for you – try to stay out of my sight.'

He unlocked the door and left.

I sat on the bed and had a think.

Five minutes later I went down to see Guthrie in his office.

'Have you got a minute?'

He closed his tablet. 'My spreadsheet doesn't balance so of course I do.'

'Did you know about all this?'

He knew exactly what I meant by *all this*. 'Some, yes.'

'Did Leon?'

'Everyone was briefed on their own particular role.'

Except me. I hadn't been briefed on anything.

'So only trusted people were briefed on their "particular role"?'

He didn't answer. Which was answer enough.

'Never mind,' I said. 'I can ask Leon.'

Who turned up about five minutes later.

Another one with a beard. He looked well and healthy. I walked into his arms and we stayed together for a long time. He felt good. He smelled good. Eventually, I lifted my head and smiled at him. 'Where's Matthew?'

'With Professor Penrose. They're both fine.'

'And Mikey and Adrian?'

'The same. They're all fine. They'll be along later. Me coming ahead was their idea of being tactful.'

There was something in his voice. 'How are you, Leon?'

He sighed from the depths of his soul. 'There are no words to describe my suffering.'

'Oh dear,' I said, patting him, because that always helps.

'The four of them . . .'

'Four?' I said, startled.

'Oh, come on, Max. As if you don't know Professor Penrose is as bad as the other three put together. You have no idea how many times I personally have saved the world.'

'Well, the world is very grateful. As am I. Perhaps there's some way I can show my gratitude.' I tickled his neck.

He closed his eyes. 'I spent all last week dissuading Mikey from inventing a portable time-travelling device that could end the world. None of the other three supported my well-presented arguments. In fact, none of them were any help at all. Sometimes I think I'm just a lone voice in the wilderness, struggling against a tsunami of irresponsible enthusiasm – or possibly enthusiastic irresponsibility – and now all I want to do is sit quietly and stare at a wall.'

I patted him again because it seemed to be helping. 'You poor thing.'

'You've no idea.'

'What can I do to end your torment?'

'Alcohol,' he said, which wasn't what I'd had in mind at all but I forgave him because he was obviously suffering.

And yes, I did go downstairs and bring him back a nice bottle of wine. And a ginormous ham sandwich, because sometimes even a hero can't handle full-on head-banging sex and needs a ham sandwich instead.

While he was building up his strength with that and two glasses of wine – so that his wife could dangerously deplete his energy levels again, he said – I had a grumble about Treadwell.

'And after what she did to Clerk and Prentiss at Babylon, why is Hyssop even still walking the earth?'

Leon sighed. 'Are we going to waste our short time together talking about those two?'

'Sorry. Can't help it.'

'I think you're selling him short, Max. If he really is Time Police, he's doing a cracking job of protecting St Mary's. No,' he continued, as I prepared to annihilate him on the spot. 'I know you resent Treadwell giving Hyssop's team all the top jobs over Evans' team, but think about it. It's Hyssop's people who are never at St Mary's. If something unfortunate were to threaten the unit, then it's Evans' team who'll deal with it. I suspect that, like you, Treadwell's not sure who Hyssop is working for. By getting her and her team out of St Mary's at every opportunity, he's leaving the people we do trust on site and in charge. And don't worry about the History Department. Sands is more than capable of keeping them safe. Hyssop's people might kid themselves they're providing Security but they're not. Sands takes an extra historian along on every jump just to keep an eye on the Security Section, instead of vice versa, and it's working well so far. If Evans had refrained from participating in World Naked Gardening Day, he'd be there still. I can't believe he did that. He left Treadwell no choice other than to sack him.'

'He did it on purpose,' I said, thoughtfully.

'Who? Evans or Treadwell?'

'Evans,' I said. 'And possibly Treadwell. It's wheels within wheels.'

And it was. For all my enthusiasm over his relocation, I'd been worried Dr Bairstow might be a little exposed in 1893 and now, suddenly, here was Evans. Another one manipulated out of St Mary's at the perfect time. Were we all just pawns? Given just the right amount of information to do the job and no more? And in my case – almost no information at all.

'I'm just a pawn,' I said to Leon.

He smiled and kissed my hand. 'Pawns turn into queens.'

'Unless they're sacrificed for the greater good.'

He suddenly looked worried. 'Max . . .'

I wasn't going to let my gripes about being outside the loop ruin our time together. 'I know. Don't worry about it. It's good to see you again.'

'And you.' He looked around. 'Nice room. What's the bed like?'

'I don't know. Don't laugh – I haven't actually been in it yet.'

'In that case . . .'

Someone thumped erratically at the door.

Leon uttered a heartfelt groan. 'Your son is here.'

I grinned, warned him I'd give him something to really groan about later – if he was lucky – and went to open the door to Matthew.

We spent a lovely evening together. Professor Penrose looked no different. Bright-eyed and bushy-tailed, he was plainly enjoying life on the run.

'Max, my dear, how are you? No need to ask – as radiant as ever. Perhaps because you've been away from Leon for so long. My dear, are you sure you've made the right choice there? If you should change your mind, you have but to utter and I will happily lay the world at your feet.'

Leon turned his head. 'Professor, are you still trying to steal my wife?'

'And succeeding, I think. She's looking very impressed. What do you say, Max?'

'I'm tempted, professor. Very tempted. It's not as if Leon's ever offered to lay the world at my feet.' I linked my arm through his. 'Tell me more.'

Wisely, Ian had parked us all at a table in the corner. Where we couldn't upset his proper customers, he said, and for heaven's sake, keep an eye on those two.

Those two – Mikey and Adrian – astonishingly tidy for the occasion, grinned in what they mistakenly considered to be an endearing manner. Professor Penrose very kindly talked to them for most of the evening, leaving Matthew to tell me what he'd been up to.

There was a lot of laughing and joking which didn't completely disguise the strain we were all under. By unspoken consent we talked of nothing important. I drank rather a lot of wine. I told Leon he had some difficult decisions to make

63

regarding the world and the laying at my feet thereof. Although my grammar became rather entangled.

Leon and I spent the night together at the Arms. The others returned to the pod under the dubious supervision of Professor Penrose. And for those still interested – Leon laid more than the world at my feet. Several times, actually.

Matthew joined us for breakfast. Somewhere along the way he'd encountered Mr Evans who had allowed him to carry his bag. Matthew staggered in, red-faced with effort and completely unwilling to admit it was too heavy for him. A grinning Evans was on his heels. I tried hard to unsee Evans as I'd last seen him.

I put my hands on my hips. 'Seriously? World Naked Gardening Day?'

Evans smirked. 'An important event in every gardener's calendar. Like propagating your corms or pinching out your trusses.'

How does the Security Section manage to make even gardening sound slightly improper? I blame Markham. 'I don't see why any of that needed to be done in the nude.'

'Letting the air in,' he said, innocently. 'Opening my pores. Beneficial effects of sunlight. Reducing the risk of mildew. Or black spot. I asked Mrs Mack if she'd ever considered hosting World Naked Cooking Day.'

Yes, I know I shouldn't have asked but I just couldn't help myself. No one could. 'And what did she say?'

'Actually, Max, she was unexpectedly enthusiastic. Although she was manipulating an electric carving knife in a way that was making my eyes water so I decided to give any further discussion a miss.' He grinned at me. 'So how are you?'

'Virtually speechless,' I said, my mind running on electric carving knives and trusses.

He grinned complacently. 'Then my work here is done.'

I'd forgotten Big Ears flapping away at my side.

Matthew plucked at my sleeve. 'Did Uncle Evans really take all his clothes off?'

'No,' I said, lying to my child without a second thought.

'What's a pore?'

'It's how your skin breathes.'

'Why does he need to open his pores?'

'He doesn't.'

'But he said . . .'

To continue the gardening theme – I decided to nip this in the bud.

'Uncle Evans' pores are open enough. In fact, they positively gape. His pores are actually the size of Tycho Crater.'

'Does he really have mildew?'

'I don't know but it would account for a lot.'

'Is Aunty Mack really having World Naked Cooking Day? Will we all have to take our clothes off?'

Leon had had this for months. Together with Mikey and Adrian as well. He really is a hero.

I have to say Evans didn't seem too upset at being chucked out of St Mary's. He told me he was following a proud tradition. Leon rolled his eyes again.

I had a lovely hour with Matthew after breakfast. Just the two of us in the pub garden. He chatted happily, describing some of his adventures, and I began to perceive I'd underestimated Leon's suffering. *And* I suspect I was getting the 'edited for

Mum' version. But I was thrilled to see how much his vocabulary had improved. And his social skills. And his manners. And he'd grown again. He was now nearly tall enough to look me in the eye which seemed very strange.

'You've grown,' I said, trying to smile.

He grinned. 'Yeah – Dad says he's giving me too much meat.'

I had a sudden picture of Matthew as he'd been when Leon had rescued him from his brutal life as a climbing boy. A grey-faced skeleton. Covered in scrapes and half-healed burns. Terrified of everyone. My heart broke all over again. As it always did.

For me, his whole life was a series of snapshots. Matthew as a baby grinning at me from his cot. Matthew as a baby, screaming with fear as the gun went off and Helen died. Matthew cowering in the pod when Leon finally got him back. Matthew going off to the Time Police. Matthew talking to Mikey. Matthew and Professor Penrose wrestling with Markham's PA. Sadly, there never seemed to be enough snapshots to make a moving picture.

Evans had been one of Guthrie's team when Guthrie was Head of Security at St Mary's. The two of them had a quiet word together and while they were occupied, I took Leon to one side.

'Listen, a message from Treadwell. You need to come back to St Mary's. He advises we send Matthew to the Time Police again. For safety.'

Leon frowned. 'I don't think sending Mikey and Adrian . . .'

'No,' I said. 'Definitely not. For everyone's sake they need to be kept well away from the Time Police but I've had an idea about that.'

I passed him a slip of paper with a series of coordinates. 'There's a house in London in 1893 where Dr Bairstow and Mrs Brown are about to take up residence. Evans is to join them there. I think you could drop Adrian and Mikey there too.'

He stared at his feet. 'And the professor?'

'Can make up his own mind what he wants to do.'

'And the Archive?'

'Could also be stored there, even if it's only a temporary measure. It's a big house and they have extensive attics and cellars. What do you think?'

'I think it's a good idea.'

'We all need to stay apart. You at St Mary's. Markham and me at Home Farm. Dr Bairstow et al. in London. We're spreading the risk.'

Leon nodded and then it was time to go our separate ways. I told myself it was good that Matthew seemed perfectly happy with his current nomadic lifestyle. I didn't dare ask him if he missed me in case he said no. I told myself that self-reliance in a child is good. I told myself he was getting too old to need his mum. I told myself I was fine with all of this.

I didn't think he'd want to hug – not in public, and he was getting a bit old for that sort of thing, anyway – but when the time came, he put his arms around me, told me I was shrinking and he was making me a present for when he saw me next.

I swallowed a lump and said that sounded lovely. He didn't ask where I was going or what I was doing. I told myself that Leon had probably warned him not to ask and that it wasn't because he didn't care.

He trotted off into TB2 with the others. I turned to Leon. 'I wish we could have had longer.'

He took my hand. 'One day, Max. One day we'll have all the time we need. I promise you.'

I smiled. 'Just not right now.'

'No. But all things pass, remember?'

'Stay safe,' I said, suddenly. 'Promise me.'

'If you want me,' he said, not answering me at all, 'you can leave a message here.'

There was a crash from inside the pod and the sound of young people arguing.

I grinned. 'Off you go.'

Leon stared at the pod. 'You don't want to swap, do you? I go to Home Farm and you attempt to assume control of this lot?'

'Poor old man.'

'Are we bad parents?'

'The world's worst, I should imagine.'

'I'll see you soon, Max.'

The sounds of argument grew more urgent.

'I have to go before someone kills someone.'

'You, probably.'

He kissed me, squared his shoulders and marched up the ramp.

A minute later the pod disappeared and I went back into the Arms.

I asked Guthrie for the bill and he said Leon had already taken care of it. I scowled. I hate being paid for. However, he said, if I wanted to assert my independence and pay him twice, he, Guthrie, would have no problem with that.

Ten minutes later Evans and I bade him farewell and made our discreet way to my pod.

'Where am I going?' he said, dropping his bag on the floor.

'It's a secret,' I said, mysteriously.

'OK,' he said, completely incurious.

And the world went white.

6

The appearance of Mr Evans was greeted with great enthusiasm by Lady Amelia. A while ago, she and Pennyroyal had been guests of St Mary's – quite voluntarily, I assure you – and Evans had been detailed to provide them with close protection. As it turned out, so fervently had he embraced his duties where Lady Amelia was concerned that neither of them had been seen in public for nearly forty-eight hours.

Evans and Markham were hugely delighted to see each other, too.

'All right?' said Markham, barely looking up from a file he was studying at the kitchen table.

'Fine,' said Evans casually, dropping his bag. 'You?'

'Not too bad. Got yourself sacked, I see.'

Evans blinked. 'I'm not the one who stole Mrs Huntley-Palmer's Bentley. Sir.'

'And I'm not the one who pranced naked in front of the Parish Council.'

'I had no choice. It was World Naked Gardening Day.'

Markham closed the file. 'Well, we have an assignment for you. Sit down, pour yourself a brew and I'll catch you up.'

*

Three days later we set off for London, 1893. Present were Dr Bairstow and Mrs Brown, who already looked as if they'd spent their entire lives in the 19th century, the massive Mr Evans, and me.

We assembled outside my pod. In an effort to look as if I had more hair than I actually did, I'd bundled the stumps into a pretty snood and plonked my hat with the irritating feather over the top. I was wearing the same outfit as the last time I'd visited Number Six Swan Court. The time I beat up Jack Feeney on his own hearthrug, and what an enjoyable experience that had been. I had some idea the servants would remember me more easily if I was wearing the same clothes.

'You all but wrecked their living room, Max,' said Markham, as we arrived at the pod. 'They won't have forgotten you in a hurry.'

He was staying behind for this one – not least because Evans took up over half the available space inside the pod and I still had two other people to cram in. Evans was embracing his new role as personal manservant and bodyguard, wearing his own not particularly accurate dark suit because we had nothing to fit him. He could sort something out when they'd got themselves settled. A too-small bowler hat perched on top of his head. Like a pimple on the Matterhorn. No one said a word.

Mrs Brown was elegantly attired in brown silk that rustled imposingly with every movement. Dr Bairstow, frankly, didn't look any different. He was Dr Bairstow in every time and place.

I'd like to say everyone made themselves comfortable but there was only one chair and I made sure I had it.

'If we're all ready,' I said. 'Computer, initiate jump.'

'Jump initiated.'

The world went white.

We exited the pod to a dank and foggy day in late-Victorian London which suited me down to the ground. I'd aimed for just after eight in the morning. Early, but not suspiciously early to pay a call.

I'd noticed on my previous visit that there was a small patch of derelict land behind Swan Court. A few optimistic souls had attempted to grow something since I'd been there last, and several skinny horses nosed a pile of mouldy hay, but mostly it was just mud, puddles and drifting tendrils of yellow, throat-catching fog.

Mrs Brown and I were very careful to keep our skirts out of the mud until we achieved solid ground.

'It's just down here,' I said, striding along the pavement to warm myself up.

Even this early in the morning the roads were as crowded as the last time I'd been here. The weather then had been autumny and boisterous – today it was cold, damp and still. This time, however, there were far more pedestrians than carriages. I suspected the carriage trade were still in bed. Muffled men, their scarves across their mouths to keep the fog out, pushed their way in both directions. Off to work, I suppose. There were very few women around and certainly no well-dressed women. Dr Bairstow eased Mrs Brown on to the inside of the pavement and Evans did the same for me. Social etiquette decreed ladies were not to be exposed to the hazards of oncoming traffic. I couldn't see the point, actually. Two hefty-looking horses drawing a coal dray were trotting towards us and if they should take fright, then, on the inside or not, I'd just be a stain on the already very stained pavement.

For a respectable area, the streets were filthy. Wet straw and hay lay thick in the gutters and if there were any drains, they were completely overwhelmed. Steaming horse shit lay in dollops everywhere, despite the best efforts of urchins with buckets and shovels. I assume they sold it to the market gardens.

Street traders were setting up their stalls. A knife grinder had a prime spot on one corner. I could hear his wheel turning and smell the hot metal. A grimy sweep pushed his way past us, his brushes over his shoulder. He had no cart and no boy.

Many people were pushing handbarrows full of vegetable produce. They would have been to the early-morning markets. Meat and fish would be delivered later, I guessed. The barrows took up a lot of room, both on the pavement and in the streets. There didn't seem to be any rhyme or reason to the flow of traffic. No one kept to one side of the road. Carts and cabs just weaved about, looking for the next gap to open up.

A grey, exhausted-looking man sat cross-legged in a doorway, an empty metal cup set carefully in front of him. As I looked, the door opened behind him and a voice shouted at him to move on. Without a word, he picked up his cup, heaved himself to his feet and shambled off. If I'd had any money, I would have given him some.

'Around the next corner,' I said to Mr Evans, and suddenly, we were there.

The square looked just the same as it had before. There were fewer people out and about, though – servants on early-morning errands, I guessed. I could hear someone sweeping their front steps somewhere. A window rattled open as we passed and I caught sight of a maid fluttering her duster. Some of the pavement was wet where the steps had already been scrubbed. Not a pleasant job on a chilly day.

The giant plane tree was still in the centre of the square, safe behind its ornate railings. I must remember to tell Markham, who had developed a fondness for it on our last visit.

'Here we are,' I said, bringing our little convoy to a halt. 'This is it.'

The steps were wet outside Number Six, so the inhabitants were clearly up and about.

I left my party standing on the pavement outside, so we didn't look too much like a posse, while I climbed the shallow steps to the front door. Reaching the top, I paused for a moment, thinking that nothing seemed to have changed very much since my last visit, and that's when it happened.

Everything blurred. My head swam as I struggled with the familiar feeling that I was here and the world was here – but one of us was wrong. This wasn't the first time I'd experienced this. Nor the first time I'd been in one world but seen another. Usually, though, it only happened at St Mary's, where I'd once spent a year in the 14th century, which seemed to have imprinted on me. Sometimes I saw things as they'd been then. I would try to go through doors that didn't exist any longer. Or walked into walls that hadn't been there in 1399. I'd had this problem for a while now, and ignored it on the grounds that it would go away eventually, but I'd never had it this badly before. And not away from St Mary's.

I was unable to move. Time lost its meaning and the world stretched away from me as if it were elastic. I couldn't focus properly. The crisp outline of the door with its well-polished knocker, framed by the two pillars of Portland stone, was super-imposed over another image of a door with its well-polished knocker and two pillars of Portland stone. The two images were identical but didn't quite line up.

My arm wavered, as I reached for first one knocker, changed my mind and went for the other one, and then changed back again. It was the weirdest sensation. Like coming downstairs while looking at someone else's feet. Your legs can't make sense of what your eyes are seeing. So it was with me and the knocker.

I broke out into a cold sweat. I could feel it prickle on my forehead and top lip. For one nasty moment I thought I was going to embarrass myself by throwing up all over the spotless porch.

And then, thank God, Evans grasped my arm. He did it hard enough for me to find a bruise later but it was what I needed.

He said, 'Max?' and I came flying back again as the world reassembled itself around me like a mended kaleidoscope. I heaved in a breath – I didn't seem to have breathed for a hundred years – and then another. Gradually everything fell back into place and I was myself again, standing on the wide porch in front of Number Six Swan Court.

'All right?' said Evans, softly.

I swallowed. 'Yes. Thanks.'

He reached up and rapped the knocker for me. 'Mr Markham said to watch out for this.'

I let that pass without comment, merely noting that I'd been the subject of a Security Section briefing and wondering what else they'd said about me, and then the door opened a cautious couple of inches and a face appeared. I suspected we were the first people to knock at this door since the exciting afternoon that took Jack Feeney and Mr Winterman out of their lives forever.

I peered. 'Is that you, Kathleen? Do you remember me? It's Mrs Farrell. I've come to see how you all are.'

She opened the door wide. 'Mrs Farrell?'

'Yes,' I said. I gestured at the infinitely more respectable people standing behind me. 'And I've brought some friends to meet you. Is Mrs Proudie in?'

'Yes, madam.' She stepped back and we entered the hall. I'd like to say it was considerably less dreary than last time but this was Victorian England so there was no chance. Gloomy and cold, pictures of dead animals and past battlefields hung all around the walls, hideous ceramics stood on over-ornate tables, and vertigo-inducing black and white tiles covered the floor . . . I closed my eyes and looked away.

The door beside the stairs opened and Mrs Proudie appeared, cap tied firmly under her chins, starched apron rustling and her keys swinging from her waist. All the maids clustered behind her. They were still doing safety in numbers, then. We all ignored the brass candlestick Mrs Proudie was holding behind her back.

I'm still not sure of the difference between housemaids and parlourmaids – you need Markham for the finer definitions – but I recognised Kathleen and Maggie. The other one must be Sarah whom I hadn't seen on my previous visit. She'd been too knocked about to work.

Not any longer. They all looked well; their bruises had healed. Kathleen's wrist was no longer bandaged. They were wary, but not terrified. I wondered what had happened to the next-door neighbour, Mrs Leyton, who had come to the attention of that bastard Winterman. And not in a good way. I must remember to ask later.

Time to do the gracious-lady bit. 'Mrs Proudie.' I held out my hand. 'How are you?'

There was a moment's confusion with the candlestick which Kathleen discreetly took off her and then Mrs Proudie touched my hand and bobbed a small curtsey. 'Very well, thank you, ma'am. We all are.'

'And you must be Sarah?' I said. 'Back to work?'

Mrs Proudie answered for her. 'She is, ma'am. Light duties but better every day.'

Right – I must remember that. Mrs Proudie was in charge of the servants – I spoke to Mrs Proudie – Mrs Proudie spoke for them. Got it.

'I'm very glad to hear that. I'd like to introduce some friends of mine who are looking for somewhere to live during their stay in London. It occurred to me that this house would be ideal.'

I waited. Mrs Proudie was not a stupid woman. She'd kept the staff together through some difficult times. Those days were gone but sooner or later someone was going to remark on the lack of Winterman and Feeney. Yes, they might have gone away, but in that case the house would have been shut up and the servants paid off. If my scheme worked, however, the house would have very nearly legitimate tenants again, thus giving the servants some much-needed protection. And Mrs Proudie's household would protect Dr Bairstow and Mrs Brown. A mutually beneficial arrangement. I hoped she would see things that way.

I need not have worried. She turned to Dr Bairstow and dropped him a much more respectful curtsey than the one I'd merited.

I performed the introductions. 'Mr and Mrs North, this is Mrs Proudie, who is in charge of the house at this moment.'

Mrs Brown, of course, had the situation well in hand. As the

Dowager Lady Blackbourne, she was accustomed to running a large household. She was a member of the government and a political hostess. It was in her blood, so to speak. And managing the house was woman's work, anyway.

Somehow, the maids had managed to line themselves up. Mrs Proudie took her along the row. 'Sarah, ma'am, and Kathleen and Maggie.'

Mrs Brown – sorry, Mrs North – nodded at each one and they bobbed back again. 'And this is Sally, the kitchen maid, and Mary from the scullery.'

This was going very well.

And having Evans made a huge difference. He stood respectfully behind Dr Bairstow – sorry, Mr North – his bowler under his arm, every inch the enormous, reliable, trustworthy manservant. They couldn't take their eyes off him. It was a good job I hadn't brought Markham as well. What is it with our Security Section? Housemaids just melt all over them.

Mrs Proudie was suggesting tea. Kathleen had already scuttled off to light the fire in the drawing room. Maggie relieved Mr and Mrs North of their hats and coats and ushered them in. Evans grinned at me and disappeared downstairs into the probably much warmer and more comfortable kitchen. Everything had gone much more smoothly than I could ever have anticipated. I actually felt quite optimistic for a change. This was one of the best Brilliant Ideas I'd ever had; it was actually going to work.

And then – believe it or not – someone knocked at the front door.

We all stopped dead. Dr Bairstow and Mrs Brown were just entering the drawing room. Kathleen was holding the door open for them. Mrs Proudie was chivvying the remaining servants back through the door into the nether regions. And me, standing around like a spare part, as usual. We all stared at the front door. Tension twanged in the air. I could see the servants' first thought was that Feeney and Winterman were back. I knew that was utterly impossible – the Time Police were entertaining them for as long as it took to extract everything they needed to know, after which their usefulness would be at an end. And, probably, their lives, too.

I looked at Mrs Proudie. It was still quite early. Not yet nine o'clock. Far too early for a social call. Not that anyone had ever made any social calls here anyway. I had a very bad feeling about this.

I said, 'I'll handle this,' and was proud of my confident tone. True, I had no idea how I would handle it, but I was positive I'd think of something in the next six or seven seconds.

Dr Bairstow drew Mrs Brown into the drawing room, leaving the door slightly ajar behind them. He had his swordstick and if both he and Mrs Brown didn't have a small arsenal distributed between them then they weren't the people I thought they were.

Kathleen came out into hall, staring at the door.

I said, 'One moment, Kathleen. Mrs Proudie, may I have your keys, please.' I gestured at her chatelaine.

She stared for a moment and then handed them over. I took them off her, saying, 'I am the housekeeper, Mrs Farrell. Make sure everyone knows that.'

She nodded and melted back through the door. I could only hope Evans would be on the other side of it and not warming himself by the kitchen fire with a cup of tea and his boots off.

I took off my coat, rolled it up, whipped off my hat, and

shoved it all behind an overstuffed red armchair in the corner. Its fellow, a smaller red armchair, stood in the opposite corner.

I fastened the keys at my waist and there I was – Mrs Farrell, housekeeper – a person to be reckoned with.

The knock came again.

Kathleen looked at me, her eyes wide with panic.

I took a deep breath and lifted my chin. 'Answer the door, please, Kathleen.'

She trod across the black and white tiles and opened the door.

I clasped my hands in front of me and waited at the foot of the stairs. The house was suddenly very quiet.

I heard Kathleen say, 'Good morning, sirs. Can I help you?'

'Yes,' said a man's voice, quite clearly. 'Is Winterman at home? Or Feeney?'

I called, 'Who is it, Kathleen?'

Bless her, she answered without a tremor. 'Two gentlemen for the master, ma'am.'

'Ask them to come in, please.'

She held wide the door and two men entered.

I knew immediately. Their clothes weren't quite right. I mean their clothes were right, but the way they wore them was wrong. Their attitude was wrong. And most damning of all, they didn't remove their hats as they entered. I watched an historical drama holo last week. Not one of Calvin Cutter's, before you ask. This one was actually very good – they got nearly everything right. Except Elizabeth I walked past and not one single courtier removed his hat. If I'd been her, I would have removed their heads instead.

Where was I? Yes. These weren't contemporaries. These were, like me, people from another time. Except I was making a bloody sight better job of blending in than they were. Amateurs. Bloody amateurs.

I've said this before and I'm going to keep on saying it, so just shunt on a couple of paragraphs if you're easily bored. Living outside your own time is not as simple as you think. You can't just rock up anywhere you like and expect to be accepted into society. Presumably anyone leaving their own time to live in another would demand a comparable standard of living – which usually meant at least middle class – which was fine but only to a certain extent. Contemporaries would want to know who you were, who your people were, where you hailed from, mutual acquaintances and so forth. Letters of introduction would be required. Enquiries would be minute and persistent.

The aristocracy were even worse. There was absolutely no point in me calling myself Lady Maxwell because as soon as I did so, the stock books would be consulted, family lines explored, marriages and alliances recalled, and the sad truth that Lady M was a fraud would soon emerge. There would be scandal and notoriety – none of which those fleeing from justice would welcome.

And then there were the ordinary everyday problems. How to manage your clothing – don't laugh, I've frequently been overwhelmed by my own underwear. How to wear a hat. When not to wear a hat. Gents take theirs off – ladies keep theirs on. There was glove etiquette, what clothes to wear on what occasions, manners, how to address people above and below your station, the names of common household objects. For women especially, the social customs would be very different from those they'd been accustomed to. And on top of all that – as amply demonstrated by the two troglodytes currently standing in the hall – modern people just don't look quite right. There's always that indefinable air of not quite fitting in. Yeah – living outside your own time is not easy.

I sailed forwards with all the confidence that being encased in three petticoats and twenty-five yards of fabric can bestow.

The man on the left was skinny and rat-faced. His top lip didn't quite cover his front teeth. His dark eyes slid about all over the place. Especially all over me.

The other was chunky with an air of well-fed smugness about him. He wore his bowler on the back of his head because he probably thought it made him look rakish and Jack the lad, and actually just made him look a complete pillock. Although I rather thought that, of the two, he would be the one to watch.

Kathleen, bless her, was standing in the shadows on the other side of the hall. Just outside the dining room. Ready if needed.

Time to earn my pay. 'I am Mrs Farrell, the housekeeper. Can I help you?'

Rat-face was obviously happy to leave the talking to Smuggy. 'We're here for Winterman.'

Well, that was just plain rude. 'I'm sorry to inform you, gentlemen, that neither Mr Winterman nor Mr Feeney are at home at the moment.'

'Where are they?'

I paused for a moment to allow him to reflect on his bad manners. He failed to avail himself of the opportunity so I said, 'Their whereabouts are, at this moment, unknown.'

They eyed each other and then the other one said, 'When did they leave?'

'Approximately three weeks ago.' Always tell the truth if you can. If you can't – make it up.

'You haven't seen them for three weeks?'

I drew myself up. 'We are accustomed to Mr Winterman and Mr Feeney absenting themselves occasionally.'

'What for? Where do they go?'

I looked down my nose. 'Neither Mr Feeney nor Mr Winterman are in the habit of informing us of their movements.' I was proud of myself for remembering to use the present tense. 'Business trips, I believe, is how they describe them. If you care to leave your cards, I will apprise them of your visit on their return.'

Will you listen to me? It's all that underwear. You just can't help yourself.

They had no visiting cards, of course. What they did have, however, was something heavy dragging down and distorting their right-hand pockets. I was certain these men were armed. Not that I was bothered. With Evans behind the servant's door, Dr Bairstow across the hall in the drawing room, and Kathleen standing next to a particularly hideous vase whose demise no one would mourn, I reckoned we possessed more than enough firepower.

That wasn't what was worrying me. There was something slightly ... odd ... about this. It seemed safe to assume these two men were from the same time as Feeney and Winterman, that they knew all about them and why they were here, but what could these two want with them? Monitoring? Checking everything was OK, that they had everything they needed? Or was it a genuine social call, to chat over old times? Perhaps they themselves had been transplanted into this century and that formed the basis of a social group? No, none of that seemed very likely. These two weren't in the same league as Feeney and Winterman. If I didn't know better, I'd say they weren't much more than armed thugs. And they certainly weren't happy to find the occupants of the house absent. Perhaps, at some point, an appointment had been made. And not kept.

Something tickled the back of my brain. In between wrestling with Jack Feeney, chucking tea all over him, spraying him with pepper, zapping him with my stun gun, wrecking his front room and kicking the living shit out of him – yes, it had been a crowded afternoon even by my standards – but even while all that had been going on, I'd found a moment to speculate on the possibility of the existence of an organisation that provided an escape into the past for people who had made their own time too hot to hold them. An organisation that, for a not inconsiderable sum of money, would provide a new life in the century of your choice. They'd prep you, clothe you, install you in appropriate living accommodation, thank you for your business, and move on to the next client. But suppose they didn't. Suppose a few months after you'd settled in, these two turned up. To do . . . what?

I dragged my attention back to the here and now.

That they were concerned was very apparent. They'd definitely expected to find Winterman and Feeney here. I could imagine the conversation.

Just checking up on you, old chap. How's it going? Everything all right?

I stared at them as they stared at each other, and wondered what would happen next. They still hadn't taken their bloody hats off. And then one of them, making yet another rookie error by assuming people in the past were thick and couldn't hear properly, said quietly, 'What shall we do? We can't bring in the new people until . . .'

Not so much the penny dropping as the entire Royal Mint plummeting from thirty thousand feet. They were hitmen. Assassins. Paid killers. Hired guns. Murderers. And they'd come for Feeney and Winterman because . . . because . . . oh my God, because that's how it worked. They pretended to set people up in a new life. They resettled them in a new home – charging them a fortune for the privilege, obviously. Then, having given them a few months to relax, drop their guard and start enjoying their new life, they sent the boys round to take them out. A short while later they would install a whole new set of people – who would also have paid handsomely – give them a few months, dispose of them, re-let the house to yet another set of fugitives and do it all over again. No one would ever survive long enough to grass them up. There would never be any inconvenient witnesses. Do that three or four times a year and you were on to a real winner. More than ever, I was convinced that somewhere out there was an organisation that needed the close attention of Markham and Maxwell – bounty hunters. Sorry, sorry, sorry – recovery agents.

I resurfaced to find Rat-face and Smuggy both looking at me. Shit – because the next logical thought was that if you take out the owners then you should probably take out the staff as well. Definitely no witnesses then. And guess who'd just firmly identified herself as staff? Planning ahead – not always my forte.

I smiled at them and said, 'I have an address for emergencies if you think that might be helpful.'

Their faces brightened. Problem solved.

I began to rummage in the vast folds of my skirt. I knew there was a concealed pocket in here somewhere, it was just a case of finding the bloody thing . . . ah – here we go.

I pulled out my stun gun and got one of them, no trouble at all. Rat man crashed to the tiles with rather a nasty crack that possibly did him more harm than the actual zapping. I left him where he was because Smuggy was already going for whatever he had in *his* pocket. It was all a bit like one of those party games. *What has it got in its pocketses, my precious?*

I was whole seconds too slow. These guys might not be the brightest hangmen on the gallows but they knew their stuff. He was already bringing out his gun. And a nasty-looking thing it was. A Webley, Evans said afterwards. British Bulldog. Hugely popular – a lot of them about. Fits easily in a coat pocket. He was right. It had.

I flung myself sideways, although that was going to put me on the floor – not the best place from which to mount a counter-attack, but I didn't have a lot of choice.

And then he too jerked and shuddered as Evans zapped him neatly from behind. This is why every historian should always be accompanied by her own member of the Security Section. Although don't tell Markham that because he's convinced he and his team are indispensable, and sadly, all the evidence bears out his conviction.

Evans' efforts weren't completely flawless. Unfortunately, one of Smuggy's spasms tightened his trigger finger and something sang past my ear – I swear I felt the slipstream although Evans says no, I didn't, and stop being such a drama queen – and shattered the hideous porcelain vase. I heard the pieces tinkle to the tiled floor. So not all bad, then.

I hit the ground, rolled over and sat up. Evans was standing over Smuggy, stun gun crackling in his hand. Dr Bairstow – who, as previously stated, can move like lightning when he has to – was standing over Rat-face, drawn sword only microinches from his right eye.

I felt a quiet pride. I know I sometimes liken St Mary's to performing chimps – to the advantage of the performing chimps – but on the days we get it right, we are magnificent.

An opinion obviously shared by Mrs Proudie and *L'Équipe Domestique*, who were all gazing at both Evans and Dr Bairstow, mouths open in shock, awe and admiration. Never mind whose quick thinking had brought about this happy turn of events – I'll just sprawl here on the cold floor, shall I?

I kicked myself free of my encumbering skirt and clambered to my feet. Dr Bairstow enquired politely whether I was hurt.

I shook my head. 'Absolutely fine, thank you, sir.'

'Oh dear,' said Mrs Brown, wandering over to inspect the sad remains of the vase. She too was armed with a small pistol, not quite concealed in the folds of her skirt. I could see her prestige rocketing as well. I might as well go home now. I said as much to Evans, who agreed.

We all stared at the former hitmen who were probably catching their death lying on this cold floor.

'Now what do we do?' I said. 'We can't carry them back to the pod in broad daylight.'

'They can walk,' said Evans, unsympathetically.

One of the men slurred something along the lines of no, they bloody wouldn't.

'Yes, you bloody will,' said Evans. He picked up Smuggy and threw him hard into the panelled wall. The impact reverberated around the hall and something else fell over. I never found out what it was.

86

Smuggy slithered bonelessly down the wall to lie in a pathetic heap on the tiles. Evans leaned down, picked him up again, virtually one-handed, and threw him into the wall again.

I winced. That had to have hurt.

'I can do this all day,' said Evans, bending over him for the third time.

Smuggy groaned.

Rat-face shrieked.

Startled, I jumped a mile and looked around.

'My dear fellow,' said Dr Bairstow. 'I'm so sorry. Did I inadvertently catch you with my sword? Huge apologies – that looks quite painful.'

'We could swap, sir,' said Evans. 'I'll throw yours and you can stab mine.'

'An excellent idea,' said Dr Bairstow. 'It is the duty of every conscientious employer to bring variety and interest to their employee's working day.'

'Your efforts are greatly appreciated, sir,' said Evans, bending over Rat-face in a not particularly reassuring manner. 'Do you think he knows he's bleeding?'

'Won't matter once Pennyroyal gets hold of him,' I said, because sometimes just mentioning Pennyroyal's name was all it took and people couldn't talk fast enough. Seriously. Was the guy some sort of legend? I suspected yes was the answer to that – and for all the wrong reasons.

Not this time, however. The two of them closed their eyes and refused to cooperate. It was too much trouble to shunt them out of the hall so we left them where they were. Evans zipped them tightly and then searched them, but apart from their weapons, their pockets were empty. These were professionals.

Evans crouched off to one side – out of range of anything they might try – and I made myself comfortable in the smaller red armchair.

Evans smiled his big friendly smile because he's a big friendly bloke. 'Let's start with the easy stuff, shall we? Names?'

They shook their heads and refused to speak.

'Who sent you?'

Nothing.

'Why are you here?'

Still nothing. Well – there was the occasional whimper or curse, but you know what I mean.

I leaned forwards. 'What did you mean by new people coming?'

Their eyes flickered.

'When do they arrive?'

Still nothing.

Evans tried again. 'Do you live here? Do you have a pod? Where is it?'

Nothing. Just a couple of blank stares.

Evans stood up and took me to one side. 'We're not going to get anything from them, Max.'

'No,' I said, watching the two men. 'Best leave it to Pennyroyal, I think. He's not as squeamish as us.'

Evans crouched again. 'I expect you'd like us to let you go, wouldn't you?'

They couldn't help it. They were professionals but hope flickered in their eyes.

'Give us something to work with and we'll tell Pennyroyal you cooperated and that was all you knew. Put in a good word for you, so to speak.'

Rat-face made a slight sound and immediately Smuggy twisted to glare at him. He subsided.

'OK,' said Evans, standing up again. 'You had your chance. A nice cup of tea, Max, after all our exertions, and then back to base.'

'Good idea. We'll leave them here where we can keep an eye on them, shall we?'

Time for tea.

Tea was served in the drawing room. Silver teapot, Royal Worcester crockery, silver cutlery, sugar tongs, little cakes still warm from the oven – everything anyone could possibly want. Which rather summed up Victorian England – elegance and sophistication in the drawing room, blood and violence on the other side of the door.

'Well,' said Dr Bairstow, sitting back and stirring his tea. 'I suspect you got nothing from them.'

I shook my head and bit into a cake. 'Nor do I think we will, sir. Unless we're prepared to torture them in the hall, of course.'

'An option,' he said, calmly, 'but only a last resort, I feel. What do you intend to do with them now?'

'Take them back to Pennyroyal for onward transmission to the Time Police. Either of whom will certainly persuade them to tell us what they know. Which I suspect will be the bare minimum they needed to function. Setting that aside for one moment, sir, did you hear what they said about new people coming in?'

'I did indeed and I can see you have a theory you are bursting to share with us . . .' he became aware of Kathleen bringing in more hot water, 'Mrs Farrell.'

We waited while Kathleen rearranged everything on the tray to her liking, bobbed a curtsey in the general direction of Mr and Mrs North – who had lost no time in literally getting their feet under the table, let me tell you – and closed the door behind her.

'Well, sir, if this is standard procedure – and I very much suspect it is – my first point must be – are we leaving you in an even more precarious position than before? It seems safe to assume this has happened before and will again.'

He stretched out his legs to the now very pleasant fire. 'Fore-warned is forearmed, Dr Maxwell.'

Mrs Brown poured herself another cup. 'What do you think will happen when those two . . .' she indicated the hall with her head, 'don't return?'

I had no answer to that but fortunately I didn't need one. Dr Bairstow set down his cup. 'I really don't know but it will be interesting to find out, don't you think? These little cakes are excellent, Mrs North. Be sure to present my compliments to Mrs Proudie.' He settled back with another one.

I must confess, I was slightly shocked at his attitude. I'm supposed to be the reckless one here. On the other hand, a long time ago in the future, he had been an historian. In fact, jumping back to found St Mary's was probably the most reckless thing any historian could ever have done.

He turned to Mrs Brown. 'I do think we should stay, don't you?'

'Oh yes, if only for the sake of those poor girls out there. And this does appear to be a very comfortable house.'

I was pretty certain I should be warning them of the dangers of their proposed course of action, making strong and cogent arguments, but before I could get going, Mrs Proudie entered with the dinner menu.

'There isn't a lot in the pantry, madam, not for the likes of you and the master, but with your permission, lunch will be an omelette. I've sent the girls out to the shops and dinner this evening will be a clear broth, salmon in hollandaise sauce, a roast chicken with dauphinoise potatoes and green peas, lemon tart and a nice cheese for the master.'

She bobbed the master another curtsey.

The master was looking more cheerful with every passing moment.

'Mr Evans is inspecting the rooms upstairs.' She turned to me. 'If I might have the keys, madam . . .'

I handed them over and she ceremoniously handed them to Mrs Brown who equally ceremoniously handed them back again. Seriously, they couldn't have done it any better at the Tower.

'Halt – who comes there?'

'The keys.'

'Whose keys?'

'Mrs Proudie's keys.'

'Pass then – all's well.'

Mrs Proudie took herself off, beaming. Kathleen bustled in with a plate of tartlets. Just to tide them over until the lunchtime omelette, I suppose. Outside, it began to rain. Inside, the fire blazed. Mrs Brown topped up the teapot again. Dr Bairstow took another little cake and made himself comfortable.

And I had to go out in the rain with our prisoners.

In the end, they did walk back to the pod, courtesy of Evans and his stun gun. The consequences of disobedience had been made very clear to them when we'd freed their legs. We took them out via the kitchen door. At Evans' suggestion, the staff were absent, busy making up the beds upstairs.

Dr Bairstow shook my hand. A lesser man would have told me to take care but he's never been one to waste his breath. We took our prisoners through the back area and from there it was only a hop, skip and a jump across the mud to our pod.

A horse, wisps of hay trailing from his mouth, watched us pass with complete disinterest and then turned back to his mid-morning snack.

'I wonder what happened to their pod,' I said to Evans, poking Smuggy with the end of my stun gun, just to let him know who had complete control of the situation.

'If they came in one,' said Evans. 'I know they're not contemporaries – you can see that a mile off – but suppose they live here semi-permanently. They're the ones who acquire the house, set things up, and make the initial disbursements. The newcomers settle in – these two turn up to make a friendly call – just keeping an eye on things – and bang. Clear the house and ready for the next lot. If you think about it – that would make sense.'

I nodded. It did make sense. I could just picture the scene.

Hello, Winterman, old chap – and Feeney too. Just come to see how you're doing. Everything running smoothly? Any chance of something to keep the cold out?

And then, when Winterman and Feeney's backs were turned – and with that precious pair, it would have to be while their backs were turned because they were a very wide-awake pair of criminals – out come the guns and bang-bang, you're dead. Not forgetting to nip below stairs and do the staff, as well. I remembered Mrs Proudie telling me she and the maids had come from an agency I'd thought might be in league with Winterman and Feeney because trafficking seemed right up their street. I'd warned Mrs Proudie not to let any of the girls go back there and shuddered to think how close they'd come. If they had returned to the agency, that would definitely have been the end of them.

And then, having killed them all, presumably our two prisoners would have had some sort of local arrangement. A cart would turn up around the back after dark, they'd load the bodies, and away they'd go.

How would they dispose of them?

Easy – the same way as everyone else. There was a socking great river over there. Where everyone else disposed of their bodies. They might even have to queue for the privilege.

I was recalled by Evans demanding to know if I was all right because my eyes had gone funny again.

'Absolutely fine,' I said, marching up to the pod door.

I could see the exact moment they decided to make a break for it. Which, sadly for them, coincided with the exact moment Evans decided to give them another ten million volts or whatever. They even fell neatly inside the pod. It makes all the difference having a professional along, as I told Evans, who nodded modestly. 'It always pays to use the best, Max.'

He kicked their legs inside so I could get the door shut and looked at me. 'You going to be all right?'

'I am,' I said. I gestured back to the house. 'And I think you've fallen on your feet here.'

'Yes,' he said. 'Nice girls.'

'Mrs Proudie is a tyrant. Just a friendly warning.'

'Unnecessary,' he said reproachfully. 'I am, at present, spoken for.'

94

'Would you like me to give your fond regards to Lady Amelia?'

'Already done that,' he said, grinning. 'Several times, actually.'

'You are disgusting.'

'Yes,' he said, looking extremely cheerful about it. 'There is no hope for me.'

'Well, good luck.'

'You too.'

'One of us will check in at least every fortnight,' I said, 'but I don't think you'll need us.'

'Only to take the bodies away,' he said, and he wasn't joking.

I turned towards the console.

'Just a minute,' said Evans, stepping into the pod and zapping Rat-face and Smuggy all over again. There wasn't any real necessity – they were still very wobbly – but as he said – just a top-up and wasn't it fun when you didn't have to play by the rules any longer? And I wondered again whether Dr Bairstow deliberately selected staff who were only one step away from criminal behaviour. In some cases, a very short step.

I shut the door behind Evans, stepped over the twitching bodies and initiated the jump.

The world went white.

I called up Pennyroyal the moment we landed at Home Farm.

'Hi – I have another two for you.'

'Another two what?'

'Another two sad sacks for you to translate into ready cash.'

There was a pause. 'How long were you actually gone?'

'Couple of hours. Do you want them or not?'

'On my way,' he said curtly and closed the link.

He turned up thirty seconds later bearing such a vast number of zip-ties that I wondered if some of them were for me. And two hoods.

He leaned over the prisoners. 'This one has a broken arm.'

'Mr Evans accidentally threw him against a wall.'

'And a nasty gash to his head.'

'Mr Evans accidentally did it again.'

'And this one's bleeding.'

'Dr Bairstow accidentally stabbed him.'

'A real catalogue of catastrophe,' he said grimly.

I rather thought that should be catastrophes – with an s – and for one suicidal moment toyed with the idea of pointing this out. However, my overworked survival instincts hoisted themselves wearily to their feet and I refrained. Pennyroyal wasn't fond of the Time Police – I suspected he'd have no time at all for the Grammar Police.

Nor had he finished complaining. 'You do know I get more for them if they're undamaged?'

'Would you like me to take them back to Victorian London?'

He sighed. Every inch the sorely put-upon psychopath, struggling endlessly against a sea of troubles. 'Other than that, how did it go?'

'Perfectly,' I said, not even bothering to cross my fingers behind my back.

I was reluctant to leave the pair of them in the pod so we shoved them into our special accommodation – or one of the cellars, if you want to be strictly accurate. Neither of them gave us any trouble. Pennyroyal has that effect on people. We let them lie down because of their injuries but, for safety's sake, zipped them together – Rat-face's ankles to Smuggy's wrists and vice versa. I dropped a blanket over them and Pennyroyal didn't argue.

In the kitchen, I poured myself a cup of tea and joined everyone else at the kitchen table.

'Shall I open the batting?' said Lady Amelia. 'Extrapolating from the sudden appearance of two more unexpected guests, I am assuming things in London did not go completely according to plan.'

'Yes and no,' I said. 'Yes, Dr Bairstow and Mrs Brown are nicely settled in. Mrs Proudie and her team are completely on board with everything. When I left, they were discussing household arrangements, menus and such. I think we can assume everything is fine in that area.'

Pennyroyal frowned. 'And in which area are things slightly

less fine?' I tried to tell myself that was his normal expression and not directed specifically at me.

'We had unexpected visitors. Those two downstairs,' I gestured downstairs, 'turned up at the front door. They asked for Winterman and Feeney by name. They obviously weren't contemporaries and they were armed. I had a choice between letting them return whence they came – with all the problems that might entail for Dr Bairstow and Mrs Brown – or stopping them in their tracks. I went for the latter.'

'How long before they're missed, do you think?' enquired Lady Amelia, topping up her glass.

'I don't know,' I said, honestly. 'Best-case scenario – they don't have a pod and live there semi-permanently.'

'For what reason?'

I shifted in my seat. The moment had come.

'I've long been convinced there's an organisation behind all this resettling people in another time and place. It's almost certainly not something your average felon could arrange on his own. I think there are people out there who, in return for a large sum of money, create new identities for criminals, or disgraced heads of state, or anyone with oodles of cash who needs to discreetly disappear. This outfit provides them with somewhere to live, arranges assimilation sessions and so forth. We all know it's not easy living outside your own time but an operation like that would go a long way towards solving the problems of integration.'

'Yes,' said Smallhope, thoughtfully. 'That had occurred to us, too.'

'But,' I said, 'after today, I think there's more to it than that.'

'Go on.'

'The two who turned up this morning – Rat-face and Smuggy – were looking for Winterman and Feeney. They asked for them by name.'

'So you said, but for what purpose?'

I shrugged. 'Could be anything. To check they haven't been rumbled by the Time Police. To provide customer care services – although I think we can all agree that's unlikely. Or – and this is my first choice . . .'

I paused. This was the moment to lay out my theory.

'I think they'd come to kill them.'

'Are you saying Winterman and Feeney had turned on their . . . benefactors?'

'*Au contraire*. I think their benefactors turned on them. I think they wanted to clear out the house and install another set of high-paying customers. I think that's what this organisation does. They set up people in their new life and then, after a couple of months, after their clients have let down their guard and relaxed, they kill them and install another set. It's not as if anyone's ever going to miss them. Or even come looking for them. And imagine if you could do that two or three times a year. And that's not counting all the personal effects – money, jewellery and so forth – that could be harvested. I wouldn't mind betting that anything the killers find is theirs to keep as their fee.'

'In that case,' said Markham, 'have we made a wise decision in leaving Dr Bairstow and Mrs Brown there?'

'Well, they have Evans, who's the equivalent of an entire battalion and only slightly smaller,' I said, 'so I don't think there's too much to worry about there – not for the time being, anyway – but you're not thinking it through.'

'Indeed?' said Pennyroyal and I didn't much care for his expression so I hurried on.

'Think about it – if people do keep turning up, then they'll be walking straight into the arms of Dr Bairstow, who's just looking for something to slaughter these days. If we can neutralise these future clients and hand them over to the Time Police, then *you* . . .' I indicated Smallhope and Pennyroyal, 'could have a very nice little earner. Don't tell me anyone attempting to reside in Swan Court won't be worth an absolute fortune to the Time Police. If the miscreants have gone to all the trouble and expense of arranging a new life in another time, then I'm betting they'll be at the very top of the Time Police's *People We'd Like to Have a Quick Chat With* list. What do you think?'

'I think,' said Pennyroyal, 'that after a very short period of time, whoever is in control of all this will tumble to the fact that all is not well at Number Six Swan Court, and despatch a considerable force to investigate.' He paused and then continued. 'However, concerning though that thought is . . .'

'. . . It's not our top priority at the moment,' said Smallhope. 'We should be focusing on the people behind the recent attack on Home Farm. I appreciate your point concerning Swan Court, and we will certainly need to turn our attention there before very long but . . .'

'. . . We can't afford another incident like the one the other night,' I finished for her.

'No.'

'OK,' I said, because she and Pennyroyal were right. 'Well, we already have the coordinates from the pod of the people who came to kill us.'

I stopped and reviewed that last sentence because it sounded a bit like a French lesson. *Where is the letter written by the pen of my aunt* style.

'I mean, we know from when and where they originated. Easy enough for me to track them down.' I looked at their unenthusiastic faces. 'Although I'm not saying it has to be me that does it. We can make that decision when we know what and who we're dealing with. If I – and I'm only saying that for convenience – if I can get in somehow, then I'd be in a position to feed you all sorts of useful intel. And then, when we're ready, we take down the whole organisation.'

Smallhope blinked. 'The four of us.'

'But what a four,' said Markham, topping up her glass.

'To be clear,' said Smallhope, 'are you implying that the people behind Swan Court and those behind the attack the other night might be one and the same?'

I stopped. Was I?

'I don't know,' I said, honestly. 'Possibly not – but ...' I tailed away.

'A rather large coincidence ...' said Pennyroyal.

'True,' I said. 'But we've all been in this game long enough to know massive coincidences frequently occur. Strange strokes of luck. Effect before cause. And so on.'

'I'm not saying you're wrong,' said Smallhope. 'Recent events may very well be linked in a way we cannot yet see, but it's a case of priorities.'

'And resources,' said Pennyroyal.

'Yes,' said Markham. 'While we *think* something bad is happening around Swan Court, we *know* someone's trying to kill us here. It makes sense to deal with that first. We can deal with Swan Court when our backs are safe.'

There was more silence and then Pennyroyal said, 'That is a very valid point. We have two areas where further action may prove necessary, but we start in Great Russell Street.'

'It *is* the British Museum, isn't it,' cried Lady Amelia. 'I knew it. The villains. They still haven't paid those invoices from last year, either. Pennyroyal, make sure the buggers settle before we wipe them from the face of the earth.'

'Regrettably, my lady, I think we can discount the British Museum. For the time being,' he added, as she seemed inclined to argue.

'Thank God,' said Markham. 'I really didn't fancy bringing down a national treasure. I've been there, you know. They actually let me in.'

'They let anyone in,' I said witheringly before he developed delusions about being an acceptable member of society. Turning back to Pennyroyal, I said, 'The British Museum might very well be innocent . . .'

'They *are* innocent,' he said firmly.

'In that case, we should be the ones to establish their innocence. The point I want to make is that only my on-site investigation will clear them.'

Pennyroyal closed his eyes. 'They don't *need* clearing. Could we please stop assuming the British Museum are a bunch of murdering, criminal masterminds.'

'Easily done,' I said. 'I'll go there and check it all out.'

'You will not,' he said, and you don't argue with that tone of voice. Everyone stared at the table, deep in thought. Well, actually I was worrying about lunch because I was starving. Lady Amelia was possibly considering how to take down the entire British Museum and subdue the thousand-plus people who worked there.

Pennyroyal got up to attend to something in the oven that smelled great and God knows what Markham was thinking.

I knew what I wanted to do but I wasn't Head of the History Department any longer. Doing the right thing was of secondary importance now. Smallhope and Pennyroyal would weigh the various courses of action open to them and select the most profitable. That was a foregone conclusion.

'I think we all need to consider our next actions very carefully,' Smallhope said, eventually. 'Pennyroyal will drop off our prisoners with the Time Police and we'll reconvene after lunch.'

We enjoyed a pleasant lunch – chicken in white wine sauce. I suddenly realised I'd been woken in the middle of the night, fought a bit of a battle, located a hostile pod, been kidnapped by said pod, whirled off to pastures unknown, whirled back again, jumped to London, subdued a couple of potential assassins, successfully relocated my boss and his . . . friend . . . and returned to base, bringing the aforementioned potential assassins with me for Pennyroyal to transmute into gold, and still been able to construct and present a compelling argument for doing something amazingly stupid. And I hadn't eaten since 1893. You have to admit – as an employee I'm excellent value.

I explained all this over lunch. The lack of response from my colleagues was disheartening so I took myself upstairs to review my actions to date – which is historian speak for having a nap. And to give them all the opportunity to discuss things in my absence, of course.

Markham woke me with a cup of tea – which was a nice gesture. I thanked him politely so standards would be maintained.

'Downstairs when you've finished,' he said. 'They've made a decision.'

'Without me?'

'You were there in spirit,' he said soothingly. 'Plus, we could hear you snoring.'

They had indeed reached a decision. They'd even come up with a tentative plan, which was that Markham jump to Great Russell Street to investigate.

I got all set to protest.

'No,' said Pennyroyal, and I closed my mouth again. 'He goes in first, susses things out, reports back here and we put together a proper plan based on actual facts rather than an unexplained and unexplainable attempt to pin everything on to a much-loved institution. That will be when you step in, Dr Maxwell. Teamwork.'

'Another job for Pros and Cons,' said Markham happily.

Oh God, he was back to that again.

9

The thing about Smallhope and Pennyroyal is that they don't mess around with formal procedures. There's none of this 'setting up working groups to study proposals and consult with everyone under the sun'. A decision was reached, where and why sorted, and the personnel delegated, given the freedom to act as they saw fit and told to get on with it.

Markham was there and back less than twelve hours later and he had a lot to report.

Firstly, to relieve any unnecessary stress among anxious readers – we must all do what we can in these difficult times – let me assure everyone that the British Museum was completely innocent. Well, innocent as far as we were concerned, anyway. As Markham said, God only knew what went on behind that portentous pillared portico, but as far as we were concerned – not the BM.

'If not them, then who?' I said, quite unwilling to let it go. I'd been in a warehouse of sorts. A secret, sinister underground basement – exactly the sort of thing with which, for all we knew, the British Museum could be riddled. I was envisaging long cobweb-bedecked corridors with ancient, warped wooden doors, opening into cavernous chambers that had remained unexamined since the Dawn of Time, containing dark and dangerous knowledge forbidden to man and . . .

'It's not them,' said Markham, impatiently. 'Will you please get over this fixation with the British Museum?'

I subsided.

'Given the coordinates,' he said, returning us to the business in hand, 'I've narrowed it down to one of three establishments. There's a dark, old-fashioned second-hand bookshop – and we all know they're always a lot more sinister than they appear; a very posh gent's outfitters making bespoke suits; and . . .' He paused dramatically. 'A highly visible outfit called Insight.'

I blinked. 'Incite? As in provoke, inflame or motivate?'

'No, Insight. As in perception, vision or understanding.'

'So what exactly is Insight as in perception, vision and . . . thingummy?'

Markham grinned at me. 'Believe it or not – an historical research organisation.'

I gaped at him. 'You're kidding.'

'Nope.' He brought up an image. 'This is their HQ. Incorporating SPOHB – remember them? And SPERM, of course. The Society for the Preservation of English Regalia and Monuments. And they house the people from the Historical Ships Records. And they also hold part of the National Archive.'

I was actually quite disappointed. 'That all sounds very respectable. It can't be them, surely. My money's on the second-hand bookshop. It's always the second-hand bookshop. They're portals to another universe and inhabited by sinister beings disguised as little old men with spectacles and carpet slippers.'

'Well, not wanting to rain on your parade, but no, it's not. Take a look at this.'

Markham took his recorder back off Pennyroyal and brought up an image of a promotional pamphlet. The name Insight was emblazoned across the top and the capital I was a stylised hand holding a flaming torch.

I blinked. I'd seen that before. I wasn't the only one. Silently, Pennyroyal produced the bloodstained scrap of paper.

'Not an ice-cream cone,' I said, enlightened. 'A torch.'

Which, on mature consideration, would make more sense. As did their logo – 'Keeping Alight the Torch of Knowledge'.

Markham grinned. 'You have to watch out for these historical research societies, you know. Not one of them is what they seem. Do you think they're all a mask for sinister activities?'

'Yes,' said Pennyroyal. He narrowed his eyes and looked at me. 'And one day we'll take them *all* down.'

Pennyroyal has a very specialised sense of humour. At least, I was hoping he had. Because that wasn't worrying at all, was it?

'So, our next move is for me to infiltrate . . .' I felt quite proud of that word, 'this organisation, gain an *insight* into their activities – see what I did there? – and somehow bring them to their knees. Then we hand them over to the Time Police who will charge them with illegal time travel, possession of illegal pods, and anything else we can pin on them, and give us oodles of cash in return. Job well done.'

'An oversimplification,' said Pennyroyal, 'but yes.'

I think that was the moment I stopped listening. I picked up Markham's recorder and began to flip through the images. Promotional literature, services offered to the public, price lists. Their credentials were impeccable. They supported the teaching and learning of History at all levels – something of which I could only approve. They promoted historical research and their proud mission statement was to make history accessible to all. I couldn't argue with any of that. Markham had got it wrong, surely. I began to inch back towards suspecting the BM.

And that wasn't all. Insight influenced government policy regarding History and the national school curriculum. Although considering the amount of History taught in schools these days, that wasn't much to be proud of. And it provided practical support as well, distributing grants, awards, bursaries and scholarships to needy students. They funded research grants; there was a hardship fund . . . they were a real force for good.

I read it all through as the discussion ebbed and flowed around me then I picked up my mug, sat back and sipped, and had a bit of a think.

It wouldn't be the first time I'd jumped into the future to work for a sinister organisation. I'd done it with the Time Police and I could do it again. I did at least have a nodding acquaintance with the future – how things worked and so forth. I wouldn't be going in completely blind. And I had the historical know-how to blag my way through any sort of situation where specialist knowledge was required. *And* – forgive me, Dr Bairstow – I had a time-travelling background. Seriously – I was tailor-made for the job.

I mentioned this.

'Sadly,' said Markham, 'she is.'

'You can't go alone,' said Smallhope, decisively.

'She won't be,' said Markham.

The discussion went on for hours. Everyone had a great deal to say. We stopped for a mid-afternoon break. It began to get dark outside. My mouth was dry – even tea wasn't helping. Everyone was talking over everyone else and I could see Pennyroyal growing annoyed.

'Stop,' I said. 'Please, can we stop for a moment. This isn't how we usually work – any of us. If I were back at St Mary's, I'd be sitting down and devising something realistic and achievable – which I would then present to Dr Bairstow. Allow me to do the same here. At the very least it will provide a starting point and focus for our discussions and we can take it from there. Can you give me a couple of hours?'

'We can do more than that,' said Lady Amelia, getting up. 'Tomorrow, Dr Maxwell. We'll reconvene after lunch tomorrow.'

I nodded, climbed stiffly to my feet and wandered next door to what they normally referred to as their office. Markham followed me in. I fired up the data table and we got stuck in.

'Accommodation could be a problem,' he said after a while. 'I don't fancy living in a tiny pod with you. Not for any length of time anyway. You snore.'

Yes, I do, but it was hardly polite of him to mention it – as I pointed out.

'And not just snoring,' he said. 'You make these funny whiffly noises.'

'Shut up, will you.'

'That's what I say to you and you just ignore me and carry on. Sometimes the windows rattle.'

He was exaggerating. There are no windows in a pod. 'Just shut up about my snoring. We'll delegate.'

'What will we delegate? And to whom?'

'Those two . . .' I jerked my head in the direction of the kitchen, 'can be in charge of securing accommodation. I'm sure they'll be more than up to the challenge and I could find myself in something rather plush.'

'We.'

'What?'

'We.'

'We what?'

He sighed. '*We* could find ourselves in something rather plush.'

'What about my snoring?'

'I'll find a way to cope. The thing is you shouldn't go alone.'

He was right, of course, and I was pleased to hear he intended to accompany me, but there is such a thing as professional pride.

'I can manage.'

'No, you can't, but that's not the main reason I'm not letting you go alone.'

'Which is?'

'I'm not looking Leon in the eye and saying, "Well, yeah, mate, sorry, but your wife had one of her daft ideas and we all just stood back and let her get on with it. Sorry about the way it turned out. Fancy a drink in her memory?"'

'Whereas the news that we've been shacked up together – possibly for months – will bring a happy smile to his face.'

'Probably happier than mine since I'll have been the one bearing the brunt of the shacking. He'll probably have to buy *me* a drink. Many drinks.'

I glared at him – for all the good that did – and we carried on.

Considerably less than twenty-four hours later, we had our proposal ready.

I told myself it was just another briefing. I don't know why I felt so nervous about this one. We didn't actually need Smallhope and Pennyroyal's approval. Yes, we worked for them, but we were free to leave any time we weren't actually in the middle of an assignment. If they didn't like our plan, then we – Markham and I – could do it by ourselves. Probably. Although if you have access to assets like Pennyroyal and Smallhope then it makes sense to utilise them. They could make everything very much easier for us. If they chose to. So yes, I was nervous.

'The proposal is this. Markham and I jump to sometime before the date Insight tried to kill the six of us. We need to be in and out before that happens.'

'Agreed,' said Smallhope. 'Shall we say six months before? I think if you haven't discovered what they're up to in six months, it will be time to withdraw and readjust our strategy.'

'Agreed,' I said. 'Markham and I establish ourselves somewhere. I apply for a job with Insight . . .'

'Won't they know who you are?' enquired Smallhope.

I shook my head. 'It's six months before the attack. Hard to believe if they knew who I was they'd wait six months before attacking me.'

'Suppose they shoot you as soon as you walk through the door?' said Pennyroyal, working very hard to suppress the note of optimism in his voice.

'Problem solved,' I said. 'All our suspicions confirmed. Take them down.'

No one replied to that so I pressed on.

'From reading through their bumf, it seems they're always recruiting. Perhaps they're utter shits to work for and have a high turnover. Or the fact that we put five of them out of circulation the other night might have something to do with their high attrition rate. For whatever reason, they say here . . .' I brought up the relevant blurb, 'that they're always on the lookout for enthusiastic and experienced people with historical and archaeological backgrounds. I think they would jump at the chance of having me on board.'

Silence. Now for the difficult bit.

'Except . . .'

I stopped.

'Except what?' said Smallhope.

'Except that won't be the sort of job I'll be applying for.' I took a breath and braced myself. 'I want an admin job.'

'Why?' enquired Pennyroyal.

I marshalled my arguments.

'Because admin staff can go pretty well anywhere. All you need to do is look serious and clutch a few files. If you catch a researcher poking around the financial department, eyebrows could be raised. An admin assistant, on the other hand, has a perfect right to be anywhere from the stationery cupboard to the switchboard, from the basement to the boardroom.'

I began to gather speed. 'Plus, admin staff are invisible most of the time. Until something goes wrong, of course, when they tend to find themselves alone and unprotected on the front line, but most of the time no one ever notices them. They're just there. And besides, I applied for a research job at St Mary's and look what that led to.'

'You might find another husband,' Markham said, nodding.

Pennyroyal rolled his eyes. 'I can't think of anyone else who'd be prepared to take you on, but by all means give it a shot.'

I don't think he was referring to my attempt to infiltrate Insight but I decided to misunderstand him.

'Great,' I said. 'Thanks for your support.'

He opened his mouth and I rushed on.

'So – tasks. I'm afraid there's going to be a lot of delegation on this one but I can't see any other way. Markham's offered to accompany me and although we could live in the pod . . .' Markham made a faint noise like a stricken antelope discovering the waterhole to be infested with predators, 'we would prefer proper accommodation. It's more comfortable in the long run and will give me an address.' I looked at Lady Amelia. 'I was hoping you could . . .' and tailed away.

She made a note. 'Very well. Leave that with me.'

'And a wardrobe. Nothing flashy. A cheap interview suit and some very basic office clothes. I'm not well off. That's why I need a job.'

She made another note. 'Anything else?'

And so we worked through it all. Who I was. What I was. How I would proceed. What I would do if this happened, or that. They were very thorough. I noticed Smallhope would ask a question, move on and then ten minutes later Pennyroyal would ask the same question but in a slightly different format. Whether they were testing me or my plan was never really clear. In their own way they were worse than Dr Bairstow and when I eventually left the table, I was exhausted. I wouldn't mind betting I was more knackered than if I'd actually done the job itself.

Markham and I made ourselves some sandwiches and took them to his room to watch TV. We could hear them talking downstairs. About us, I assumed.

10

A week later and after a lot of background work . . .

'Right,' said Lady Amelia, placing a large envelope in front of me. 'I think it's all there. References – which will check out. Employment history – ditto. Details of your accommodation. Your wardrobe will be on site when you arrive. A line of credit has been opened for you . . .'

'Don't go mad,' interrupted Pennyroyal.

'As if,' I said.

'Citizen's ID card. You're Maxine Forrest. We kept the Max just in case you somehow slip up or – very unlikely, but you never know – someone recognises you. Someone shouting "Max" in the street can easily be explained away if you're Maxine Forrest.'

As always, I was gobsmacked by their groundwork. Everything was creased with just the right amount of wear and tear. New docs are always suspect. These genuinely looked as if they'd been in and out of files, folders and bags. There was even a passport full of stamps because Maxine Forrest had obviously knocked around a bit. I sighed. Lots of homework to do there.

I wondered – not for the first time and certainly not the last – exactly which time these two were from. They seemed at home everywhere they went. I knew if I asked them they'd just fob me off. Smallhope was Lady Amelia Smallhope, so consulting Debrett's should sort out who and when she was. If that was her real name, of course. But that didn't solve the riddle of Pennyroyal, who probably hadn't actually been born of a mortal woman but forged instead. Was he from a different time to Lady Amelia? Had they met on a job? Speculation was tempting but fruitless. I should just happily accept all my first-class forgeries, enjoy my no doubt comfortable accommodation, utilise the credit facilities set up for me, and get on with it.

'You'll have to get the job yourself,' Smallhope said, jolting me back. 'But they publish their vacancies every month and there always seems to be a reasonable selection, even if it's only in the cleaning and caretaking departments.'

I nodded.

'Here's your new address. The accommodation has a garden, I believe. For the pod. Or you might find yourself close to an area of public allotments where no one's going to notice an extra shed, scruffy though it might be.'

This was true. Since the greening of London with roof gardens, living walls and a massive plant-a-tree scheme, thousands of small allotments had been made available. We'd find somewhere for the pod. And if things were truly desperate there was always the camouflage device which would render the pod almost invisible. It gobbled up the power though, so we'd have to be careful.

'What are you doing about your hair?'

'Eh?'

'Your hair.'

And now I need to explain about my hair.

I think I've mentioned breaking Dr Bairstow out of the Red House. Unfortunately, while the operation itself had been successful, things hadn't gone so well for me. I'd been caught. I came round in some sort of medical ward, handcuffed to a bed. Not the first time but definitely the most unpleasant. And then that bastard Gaunt strode in, hacked off my hair, tossed it into the waste bin and strode back out again. For which he would one day pay.

Contrary to everything you see in the holos, it's impossible to just lop off someone's hair and have it result in a perfect hairstyle afterwards. Or any sort of hairstyle at all. My hair was up around my ear on one side and down to my chin on the other. With a sort of nearly bald spot at the back. Like me, my hair was still in a state of shock and had barely even begun to think about regrowth.

'I could tell people I was growing it.'

'The unkempt look is never fashionable. Get it trimmed.'

'Nearest hairdressers?'

'About seventeen miles away.'

Shit.

I looked at Markham, Markham looked at me.

'I'll give it a go if you like,' he said. 'Then we can just bung some product on it. The important thing is to pretend it's supposed to look like that. That's what I always do.'

I looked at his hair. 'You look like a small coconut.'

'A small but fashionable coconut,' he corrected. 'I'll go and get the kitchen scissors.'

Oh God . . .

Afterwards, everyone said how much better it looked. Apparently long bits and short bits and then long bits again were very fashionable this year. I looked like a badly mown hayfield. I don't really want to talk about it.

The brief was clear. Get the job. By hook or by crook – get the job. Wander vaguely around seeing what information I could pick up. Don't get into trouble. Don't set fire to anything. Return to base with enough useful info to formulate Stage Two. Markham would remain in the background just in case.

'Simple and straightforward,' I said. 'What's the worst that could happen?'

I won't bore you with the response. I stopped listening and used the time to grow my hair instead.

We landed just before dawn. I activated the cameras. As far as I could see we were where we should be – when, however, was wrong. We were a day early.

'This pod is beginning to drift,' I said, checking over the controls.

'Not a problem at the moment,' said Markham. 'We're not going to be using it very much. If at all. And we can still access the flat. It's all good. Stop worrying.'

We left the pod as the sun was struggling over the horizon. Markham had a hand-drawn map and I followed blindly. There were some lovely houses in this area. From different periods, but all making a harmonious whole and sensitively divided into neat little flats. I felt my spirits rise.

Ours wasn't any of that. Our destination was a four-storey brick box, designed and built during the architectural desert that was the latter part of the 20th century. Tiny. Dark. Ugly. Flat-roofed and water-stained, it enjoyed a stunning view over its correspondingly depressed-looking sibling on the other side of the street. But it had a garden. Well, it had a small patch of uneven, broken-glass-strewn, thistle-ridden ground at the back, which was where we had landed. There was no direct access from the garden to the block, but if we scrambled over a wall and trotted down a damp, narrow passage and turned right, we would find ourselves only fifty yards or so from the block's front door. As Markham said, let's hope we never had to make a quick getaway and, apparently under the impression this would solve the problem, announced his intention of buying a rope ladder.

As far as I could see, the ground floor was completely unoccupied.

'Probably a crack den,' he said as we passed the boarded-up doors. Our flat was on the second floor. There were two flats to each floor and we were on the right. Markham unlocked the door and in we went.

I dropped my bag and looked around. The entire flat was nearly as small as my first room at St Mary's and had probably cost twenty times as much. Per day. I made a mental note to wrap up this assignment asap – before Pennyroyal began to get shooting pains in his wallet. Not that we'd end up paying for any of this. All our costs would be shunted on in one way or another. I have to admit, I was rather enjoying my time as a recovery agent.

Markham settled us in while I opened the windows. It smelled as if the previous tenants had kept goats in there.

The scant furniture was exactly what you'd expect from rented accommodation in the most expensive city in the world. Despite being billed as a two-bedroomed flat, there was one bedroom and what looked like a large cupboard.

'You're the working girl,' said Markham. 'You can have the bedroom and I'll take this one.' Which was good of him.

I activated our private dongle and fired up the ancient data table. Despite my misgivings, it worked. A little bit trembly but so was I.

I brought up the Insight situations vacant site and read through the list. There were two possibilities. One was in admin proper and one was a filing clerk. I registered an interest in both and went off to explore my wardrobe. Which took approximately seven seconds. The application forms came back by automatic return and I enjoyed a creative hour or so.

Two days later – much more quickly than I had anticipated – I was invited to interview for the filing clerk's job. Markham and I celebrated quietly.

I dressed carefully that morning. An anonymous high street trouser suit with a plain white shirt. All the fabrics were light and comfortable – and self-cleaning. How about that?

I'd applied just a little make-up. I don't normally wear it but I wanted to look as if I'd made the effort. My hair looked . . . let's go with unique. 'You have your own look,' said Markham. 'That's what you need to tell yourself.'

He wasn't coming with me. 'I don't want to risk myself,' he said. 'I'll stay safely at home in case you don't come back.'

To increase his chances of survival even further, he hadn't bothered to get out of bed.

'There are cameras everywhere,' he said, thumping his pillows, 'so I don't want to be seen in public with you. Understandable, I think.'

'And I don't want you queering my pitch with any future

employers so don't go showing your scruffy self anywhere near my – with luck – future place of employment.'

'I meant,' he said with dignity, 'that I will be available to get you out in case anything goes horribly wrong.'

'Such as?'

'I don't know,' he said, pulling up the covers and preparing for another selfless half hour or so in bed. 'It's you. Could be anything. Use your imagination.'

I looked at him in his squalid nest on the floor. 'I'm trying not to.'

It was just over a forty-minute walk to the Insight building. I trudged the pavements, following the street map I'd downloaded the night before.

To begin with, all the streets were residential and reasonably quiet. As I drew closer, small hotels and posh B&Bs began to emerge. Pubs appeared on the corners. I love London – a pub on every corner and all of them festooned with flowers. Perhaps smothering your pub in flowers was a condition of the licence. And I rather liked the way I had to thread my way through all the small tables and chairs strewn across the pavements. Getting home after work without stopping anywhere to avail myself of the facilities was going to be enjoyably challenging.

As I drew closer to Great Russell Street, the pavements stopped being manual – or footual, I should say. There were automated walkways for those already worn out – for a small fee, of course – and energy-generating walkways for the fitter and poorer. I only had to swipe my ID card and our home address would be credited with the value of the electricity I was out generating while the young master still sprawled in his foetid bed.

I wasn't a complete stranger to the future. I'd been here before when I'd had myself seconded to the Time Police as part of a brilliant strategy to take down Clive Ronan. Which had worked – believe it or not – and then the bastard Time Police let him go.

Before anyone asks – I'm not a fan of the future. Yes, there's canals crammed with boats, and airships chugging everywhere and everything's very green, but the weather's a bit shitty. Overly hot and dry in summer – which is when you need the rain – and cold and wet in winter, when you don't. That's the problem with solar power: when you need the hot water – when you fancy a lovely hot bath after a cold walk home – there isn't any. Because the bloody sun hasn't been shining. And on the days when you fancy a lovely cool shower after a hot walk home, there isn't any because it's so bloody hot even the cold water is warm. Although, to be fair, on four or five days of the year the system works really well.

And, sadly, still no flying cars. In fact, very few cars at all. Emergency vehicles, official transportation for important people, and that was it. Most people cycled or walked or used the extensive waterways system.

But there were lovely roof gardens, and living walls bloomed everywhere. There were trees at street level for shade and to soak up the CO_2. Markham would be delighted by the number of plane trees lining the streets. And there were smaller trees above street level as well. To see a small wood of silver birches fifty feet in the air is quite a sight.

Arriving at my destination, I stood on the other side of the road – it was the only way I could get a proper impression of the building as a whole.

Wow. Impressive. Seriously impressive. It made St Mary's look like a lean-to.

In front of me reared a massive building some six storeys high, and that wasn't counting the labyrinth of cellars and basements that almost certainly existed below street level. Five very impressive steps, flanked by stone lions, led up to wooden double doors. The brass plaque beside them gleamed like a second sun.

The edifice was built of red brick – real red brick – not the cheap cladding used in the *only designed to last as long as the life of the mortgage* buildings you get these days.

A wrought-iron balcony ran around the first-floor windows. I don't know why – in the days when the house was built, no one would ever have gone out there. Too noisy and smelly by day, and the night air would've been considered most injurious to the health. Especially if you were female and barely surviving the rigours of life anyway.

The architect – whoever he was – must have been smoking some seriously good stuff. The complicated frontage was festooned with turrets, arched windows supported by mini pillars, crests, gables, barley-sugar chimneys, stained glass and parapets. A second balcony ran around the fourth floor and was no doubt as unused as the first.

The ornate roofline rose up to a kind of dome with a clock face embedded. Five to ten. Time for my second job interview with an historical research organisation. Because the first one had turned out so well, hadn't it?

With luck, this would turn out to be a nice indoor desk job offering no opportunities to be eaten by dinosaurs or trampled at the Battle of Bosworth Field, or drowned in the tsunami that brought down Bronze-Age Crete.

Being a recovery agent wasn't any less hazardous, but probable causes of death were disappointingly dull. *Shot dead* seemed most likely. And the shooter would probably be Pennyroyal when I pushed him too far – as I was bound to do one day. Although if it *was* Pennyroyal, they'd certainly never find my body.

For God's sake, Maxwell – focus.

Dodging e-bikes and pedestrians alike, I crossed the road to peer through the glossy black-painted railings. There was at least one floor below street level, possibly two. That would be where one's servants had led their subterranean existence.

Sighing, I smoothed the sad results of Markham's first attempt at free-form haircutting, climbed the steps and went inside. Two terrifyingly chirpy receptionists regarded me with delight. My appearance had obviously made their day.

'Good morning. I have an interview with Bridget Lafferty at ten. My name is Forrest.'

'You do,' said the one on the right, consulting her screen. They issued me with a visitor's badge and asked me to wait. The badge had one of those clip things that I can never work out how to operate. They watched me struggle for a while and then, in pitying silence, popped it on a lanyard for me. Not the best start.

'This way,' said the other one and led me to the lift.

She pressed the basement button. I sighed. People always keep their filing in the basement. It's a conspiracy by the entire world to deprive filing clerks of fresh air and sunshine. I could feel early-onset rickets kicking in already.

The lift pinged and the doors opened. Not entirely sure what to expect, I stepped out cautiously. The smell hit me immediately. Old paper, must and chemicals. Much stronger here than it had been in the loading bay. I took a deep breath.

'Good luck,' she said, and left me standing there. I heard the doors close behind me. I took a quick look around. I was in a large office area. There was a notice board with everything pinned in neat rows, two enormous photocopiers, a stationery cupboard with a skull and crossbones and the words *Keep out – yes, this does mean you* stencilled across the front, three metal filing cabinets against one wall and two desks. The one on the right was empty. A man was seated at the other, peering at his screen with such intense concentration that I would have put good money on him playing a game of some kind. Behind the desks a big metal grille stretched from floor to ceiling behind which was a massive – and I do mean massive – filing system. The only access was through a key-padded door. It was hard to tell whether the door was keeping people out or the files in because, trust me, if this lot ever became sentient and escaped then they could take over the world. The cavernous space just went on and on, row upon row of metal shelves stretching off into the distance. The Cheddar Gorge of filing. And it wasn't all enclosed in those nice modern rolling stacks, either. The shelves were all open. There would be dust. And miles and miles of walking.

I stared. I don't know if it's just me, but does anyone else have difficulty equating filing with sinister organisations doing sinister things?

'Excuse me, Ms Lafferty? Does World Domination go under W or D?'

I was still staring in disbelief when a cheerful voice said, 'Hello there.'

I turned and got the shock of my life.

Smiling warmly at me, her arm extended all ready to shake hands, was the woman who'd attacked us at Home Farm a couple of weeks ago.

And died in the attempt.

11

I could only hope she put it down to interview terror.

For long moments I was paralysed. Was I in the right time? Had she recognised me? Was this a trap of some kind? The last time I'd seen her she'd been dead. What the hell was going on here?

And then I pulled myself together – mostly – smiled, and shook her hand. 'How do you do?'

'Bridget Lafferty,' she said. 'Nice to meet you,' and it sounded genuine.

I was utterly dumbfounded. My mind was filled with alternate universes, hypnotism, hallucinations, or that it was all a terrible dream. My instincts were screaming at me to get out of here now while I still could. Sadly, all that took a few seconds and by the time I pulled myself together again, Bridget and the world had moved on.

'Shall we go into my office?'

She had one of those glassed-in affairs. Something that gave her a good view over the general office and the filing cave behind it. There would be no hiding anything from her. There was a desk – suspiciously tidy from my point of view – with the usual desk furniture: in- and out-trays, pen holder, desk calendar, a screen – nothing I wouldn't expect to see. The only solid wall was behind her, with a door in it, flanked by three filing cabinets. There was just the faintest whiff of Chanel No. 5 about the place, triggering memories I really didn't need just at this moment.

Bridget took a file from under her arm. 'Let's just check I've got the right person, shall we? I once got all the way through an interview and it was only at the end, when she produced her documents for me to pass on to our personnel department, that I realised I'd been interviewing the wrong candidate.'

She smiled, inviting me to laugh with her, so, because I hadn't a clue what to do next, I did. 'Whatever did you do?'

'I discreetly put down the file, distracted her, picked up the correct file, smiled and carried on as if nothing had happened.'

'Impressive,' I said. 'Would you like me to look away while you check?'

'No need.' She looked down at a list of names pinned to the front of her file. 'I'm only guessing, of course, but I don't think you're Thomas Coulter.'

'No, I don't think I am, either. Maxine Forrest.'

She ostentatiously ticked off my name on her list of four. I was one from the end – the last being Thomas Coulter, presumably.

'I'm head of Admin Services. Which, sadly, means that everything that goes wrong is my fault. My department covers everything admin-related. I apologise for my office but it is actually my choice. Senior staff all hang out on the top floor and this is as far from them as I could get.'

Well, I could relate to that.

She smiled. 'Can I ask how you like to be called?'

'Maxine is fine.'

'Take a seat, Maxine.'

She closed the door behind us, cutting off all the building sounds. This office was clearly soundproof. I made myself comfortable, and bearing in mind I'd come for a clerical job where organisational skills would be a key qualification, I ostentatiously placed my notebook and pen on the desk between us.

She busied herself setting out her papers thus giving me a chance to study her properly. Yes – the same dark hair, cut in a glossy bob. The same vivid blue eyes. I put her age as younger than me – although I've jumped around the timeline so often I've really no idea what my true age is any longer. She was slightly taller and slightly thinner but most people are. You'd really have to work at it to be any shorter and fatter than me.

She looked very smart. I was conscious of my cheap suit and shoes. Her crisp white blouse was uncreased – and clean. No idea how she'd managed that. Anything I wear that's white usually has a shelf life of about twelve minutes. On a good day. I wasn't going to look down at my own shirt. I didn't want to know.

She wore a tight black skirt and comfortable walking shoes. Her jacket hung off a peg behind her and smart court shoes were lined neatly against the wall underneath. Everything was tidy and in its place.

She smiled again. 'So – Maxine, can you tell me a little bit about yourself.'

It was all on my application form. She was checking I was literate and could string two words together. I gave her a potted version of what she'd read. And I didn't make the mistake of going on too long. Five or six sentences covered my historical and archaeological experience, all drawn from my early life before I joined St Mary's. I talked up some of it but only a little. Most of it was genuine.

After I'd finished, she was silent for quite a long time, frowning. Bugger. Surely I hadn't blown it already.

'Maxine, forgive me, I have to ask. You do know you're massively overqualified for this job, don't you? Why haven't you applied for a research job upstairs? They're always looking for people like you. You wouldn't even have to go in at entry level. Not with your experience. And this is not a permanent position, you know. Six months – possibly ten – but certainly no more.'

I smiled. 'I know, but research isn't the sort of job I'm looking for. I'm looking for something quiet and simple that I can switch off from at the end of the day.'

'Well, we can give you quiet and simple but again – why?'

'I travel,' I said. 'That's what I really like to do. I go all over the place. When my money's run out, I come back to this country, find a nice job with no stress and no responsibilities. Then I work like stink to get some more money under my belt – that usually takes around six months – and then I shoot off on my travels again.'

'Anywhere in particular?'

'Not really. Wherever the fancy takes me. I usually avoid large centres of population.' I patted my hair. 'Sometimes I've been a long way from basic facilities.'

She smiled. 'Well, I did wonder, but didn't like to say anything just in case . . .'

'In case I was suffering from a bad case of mange.'

'Something like that, yes. Did you do it yourself?'

129

'No, I'm blessed with a short-sighted flatmate with blunt scissors and delusions of adequacy.'

'Well – it'll grow.'

'I certainly hope so,' I said, gloomily.

'Just in time for your friend to hack it all off again with a ceremonial khopesh.'

'Please don't give him ideas.'

She laughed. This seemed to be going well.

And then the phone bleeped.

I jumped a mile.

She frowned. 'I'm sorry – I said to hold all calls. Will you excuse me, please?'

I nodded, hoping for a moment to get myself back together again.

She listened for a while and then said, 'When? And where? . . . OK, got it.'

She yanked a piece of paper out of her top drawer, scribbled *LC 0900 20/05* and tore the sheet in half. Right there and then. Right in front of me. I can't tell you how weird it felt to see that message actually created. To know that somehow it would find its way into the pod for Markham to find and for me to write all over in my own blood.

I actually felt a little queasy.

'Sorry about that,' she said, putting down the phone.

I smiled weakly and we picked up where we'd left off. As if I hadn't just had my second massive shock of the last ten minutes.

I cleared my throat. 'Perhaps I shouldn't seem overeager but I have to tell you this job is perfect for me. A temporary contract suits me very well. That way I don't inconvenience my

130

kind employers when I decide to push off and explore Nepal. Or Iceland. Or Japan.'

'But how will you manage for accommodation? How can you afford to live here in London on what we pay?'

'I'm flat-sitting. A friend of mine is married. An unwise seven-year contract that I suspect isn't working. Well, I know isn't working. She wants to be able to return to her flat – you know, when the contract is up. She doesn't want strangers in the place so I flat-sit for her when I'm in the country. It works really well for both of us. I get a reasonable place to live, she knows her property is safe and maintained, and there won't be a problem getting the tenants out when she calls time on her marriage.'

She closed my file. 'Oh my God – can I have your life?'

We both laughed. I took a chance. 'That depends on whether I get this job or not.'

'Well, let me tell you a little bit about Insight while you're still keen. We're quite small – nowhere near as big as bully boy across the street – the BM – but we're very prestigious.

'There are three main departments: Admin – which is us; Policy – which comprises the professional staff and the mystique with which they surround themselves; and Finance. They're in a separate building in Chelsea and we never see them which suits everyone.

'Obviously, we in Admin do most of the work. We're responsible for reception, including the switchboard. We manage appointments, people's diaries, arrange meetings and conferences. We sort out travel arrangements, itineraries, tickets, visas – everything. This is a filing post but you will occasionally be asked to cover elsewhere.'

I nodded.

'The main Admin offices are on the second floor, along with Procurement, who like to regard themselves as belonging to Finance. I've had to tell them several times that they're part of Admin and to get over it. And then there's the jewel in the crown – filing.'

She waved her hand in the direction of the giant cave. 'Our filing system. It's massive. It probably distorts time and space. We call it the Cave. We haven't actually lost anyone in there yet but it's only a matter of time. In fact, hacking your way through rainforests or navigating featureless deserts will have been ideal experience for this job.'

'Well, there you are,' I said. 'Unknowingly, I've been training for this my whole life.'

We both laughed again.

'It's a simple system,' she said. 'Files are numbered and arranged in order of century, geographical location, event and date. For instance,' she unlocked her top drawer and pulled out a pink file, 'Magna Carta would be 13th century, area 044 – which is England – followed by the date. Which gives us 13/044/15/06/1215 and then the actual number of the file – one, two, three, twenty-seven or whatever. The file is then cross-referenced with anything a researcher thinks is relevant – say, King John, Runnymede, the Great Charter, William Marshal.' She held up the file again. 'As you can see, this is file twenty-four.'

'Goodness,' I said. 'I should perhaps say that my speciality is Ancient Civilisations, with secondary and tertiary areas being British and European Middle Ages, and the Tudors. I'm amazingly ignorant about anything after the 17th century. I'm not sure how accurate I could be when it comes to file numbering.'

'You can relax. All that sort of thing is done upstairs. The researchers take responsibility for the setting up, assembling and numbering of files. All we do is retrieve and deliver the files themselves, keep the shelves in order, make sure everything's accessible and keep track of everything taken out. We're very protective of our material.'

She replaced the file and locked the drawer. 'Another important thing. We operate a tidy-desk policy here. You clear your desk at the end of every day, lock all your material away and hand the key to me.' She gestured at a locked key box on the wall behind her.

I blinked at the Cave again. 'What have you got in there? The Bank of England gold reserves?'

'Much more valuable than that. Original documents, signatures, seals, some artefacts and so on. Not world-shattering stuff by any means, but it would be valuable to someone.'

I nodded. 'Not to cast any aspersions but the British Museum is within spitting distance.'

'And we do occasionally,' she said. 'Spit, I mean. When they pip us to the post on something we particularly wanted or use their massive clout to try and bully us. On the other hand, Insight is small, agile, innovative and fast. We don't do too badly.'

I've always known the academic world is cold-blooded and cut-throat but this was a revelation. 'And how do they respond to that?'

'A frigid memo in a dead language usually.'

'They don't send the boys round to break your legs?'

She drew herself up. 'We at Insight do not respond to threats.'

'And I bet you have your own team of leg-breakers.'

'Of course we do – what respectable academic establishment doesn't?'

'I am entranced by this fresh insight – see what I did there? – into the working methods of respectable national institutions.'

She said darkly, 'You don't know the half of it.'

'In that case, sign me up. I'm a dab hand with medieval weapons. I could knock you up a trebuchet out of two desks and a fax machine. And I'm not a bad shot, either.'

We both laughed again. For her it was just another interview. I was pretty certain cold sweat was gluing me to my seat and I'd never be able to get up when the time came. Because I was talking to a dead woman. And I really liked her.

My impression of Bridget Lafferty – right up until the moment she tried to kill me – was that she was a lovely person. Warm, open, friendly, smiling, intelligent, sympathetic . . . the lot. You knew instinctively she'd be a great boss, going in to bat for her people, fighting her corner for funding . . . and she liked me. There was a connection. You can always tell.

'One more thing,' Bridget continued. 'No electronics are allowed in the working areas. Or handbags, either. Lockers are provided in the staff area behind reception. You won't even need your purse. You'll be issued with an ID card. Simply swipe at the vending machines or when the sandwich man comes round and it'll be deducted automatically from your pay at the end of the month.'

'So, to be clear – nothing comes into the building?'

'Nothing past reception, no. And nothing goes out, either. No one is allowed to take work home. Occasional spot checks are carried out at the door by security staff. Any of this likely to be a problem?'

'Not at all.'

She began to stack her papers together.

'Any questions?'

I flicked open my notebook, to the first of my prepared questions.

'Is there a dress code?'

'Oh, yes, thank you for reminding me. We walk miles in this job. Miles and miles. It's a big building and the lifts don't work half the time. Wear comfortable shoes. In fact – Top Tip for the day . . .'

I hope I didn't jump. For a moment it could have been Markham talking.

'Top Tip?'

'Bring in a second pair and change after lunch. Something with a different heel height eases the strain on your feet and ankles.'

'Good to know.'

'Otherwise, apart from no jeans or leggings, you can wear whatever you like. Make sure it's self-cleaning. We have extensive filter systems in the Cave, but it's still dusty. You'll be covered in it by the end of the day. Am I putting you off?'

'No, it's fine. Nothing I wasn't expecting.'

'You'll be paid at entry level, I'm afraid,' she said. 'Your wages will go into your bank account on the last day of every month. HR will need the usual two pieces of photo ID in line with government regulations. Your citizen's ID card is acceptable, together with passport, driving licence, NI card, anything like that. And we'll require verification of your address from the council. All the usual stuff. Still interested?'

'Yes,' I said. 'Very much so. It sounds the ideal job for me. I hope I'm the ideal person for the job.'

'Well, my main concern was your overqualification or that

you'd misinterpreted the job description, but both of those misgivings have been addressed. If I offered you the job, would you accept?'

'Like a shot.'

'I have one more person to see but we can let you know yes or no by the end of the day.' She stood up. 'We'll be in touch.'

'All right.' I stood up. Or rather, I peeled myself from my seat. I was certain my face was glistening with sweat. I could only hope she'd put it down to interview nerves.

'Nice to have met you,' she said, smiling.

Dammit – I liked her. A lot.

'And you,' I said.

'Just let me check I have your contact details . . . yes, it's all here.' She extended her hand. 'Thank you for coming today.'

'Thank you for seeing me.'

'I'll introduce you to Eddie who will show you out.' She lowered her voice. 'It's not a toupee.'

I wasn't sure how to respond to that. Who should I congratulate on Eddie's non-toupee-wearing status?

Eddie was the guy sitting opposite the empty desk – potentially mine, I hoped. He didn't stand up.

Bridget had lied to me. He was wearing a toupee. He had to be. No one could have hair like that. Two-tone. A grey fringe at the back and hanging around his ears with a strange, nut-brown thatch of a completely different texture on top of his head. It had to be a toupee.

'This is Eddie Middleditch. Eddie, could you show Maxine out, please.'

Smoothly, he blanked his screen, stood up and, without waiting for me, headed for the door.

I glanced uncertainly at Bridget.

'He's not very chatty,' she said. 'Bye.'

I scooted after him.

As I reached the stairs, I looked back.

Bridget had returned to her office and was talking animatedly on the phone. As I watched her, she picked up the piece of paper and stared down at it. Given where I'd found it, I couldn't help a twist of unease. I was just turning away when she looked up and saw me watching. For one moment we looked at each other. Then she smiled, gave me a small wave and turned away.

'I think I've got the job,' I said to Markham when I met him on the steps of the British Museum – which, I might add, I was seeing through new eyes these days.

'So I should hope,' he said. 'You'd really have had to work at it to screw that one up.'

'Actually, I very nearly did,' I said. I looked around and then sat beside him on the step. 'We're in the right place, anyway. It's definitely them.'

'You were only inside half an hour. You can't possibly know that.'

I lowered my voice. 'Bridget Lafferty – who interviewed me – is the woman who tried to kill us at Home Farm. The one who fell down the stairs with me.'

He stared. To the uninitiated it simply appeared as if he'd gone into a light trance, but I knew better.

'Interesting,' was all he said at the end of it. 'You're sure they didn't recognise you?'

'No,' I said, 'because I think they got the timeline wrong. I was thinking about it during the interview.'

'Glad to see you giving the mission your full attention.'

'I'm an historian. I can multitask.'

'Not with any visible success.'

'Do you want to hear or not?'

'Sorry.'

'Anyway, I'm certain I'll get the job. Obviously – I don't know how – perhaps I'll never know – I do something that gives the game away. Somehow, they realise who I am. Or who I work for. They do some digging – they're an historical research organisation, for heaven's sake – and come after us. But they get the dates wrong. You know what Dr Bairstow always says – sometimes you get effect before cause. This is one of those instances. They try to kill us before we manage to do the thing for which they want to kill us. And the thing is – I can't do anything to prevent discovery, because if I do, then they won't jump back to kill us, so I won't be investigating them, and we'll have paradoxes jumping all over us.'

He put his head in his hands. 'Oh God, why do historians have to make everything so bloody complicated?'

'I don't know. It's a gift.'

'It's a bloody curse.'

'Well,' I said, 'at least it solves the problem of who they came to kill. You all sneered at me because I wasn't important enough and now it turns out I am.'

'Max – stop. Listen a moment. This changes things some-what. At some point – we don't know when or how – but at some point, it's all going to go pear-shaped. Are you sure you still want to continue with this?'

'Well, yes,' I said. 'So something goes wrong – it would be more unusual if it didn't. And whatever it is, I obviously survive, otherwise they wouldn't be coming after me at Home Farm, would they?'

'I can see so many things wrong with that fallacious piece of reasoning.'

'Come on,' I said, getting up. 'You can buy me lunch. I've earned it.'

The message flashed up on my scratchpad at around half past six that evening. Not Bridget – someone from Personnel. I'd got the job. They'd need to get me security cleared first – and there was a ton of other bureaucratic stuff – but my provisional start date was the first of next month.

As easy as that. How good am I?

12

My first day nearly killed me. I don't mean assassins leaped out of the stationery cupboard or a rack of shelving mysteriously fell on me or they poisoned my food or anything like that – I mean I probably walked the equivalent of Land's End to John o' Groats. Twice. Uphill both ways. Bridget had been right about the comfortable shoes – which I had – and the lifts not working – which they didn't – and it being a big building – which it certainly was. As I had suspected, there was far more of it than was visible from the street and it went back a long way as well.

I arrived bright and early. The new girl making a good impression. I left Markham in bed. Self-defence, he said. Apparently, I'm not all bright and sparkly first thing in the morning. I crashed around the tiny kitchen making as much noise as I could, and then opened the chiller and found he'd made sandwiches and a drink to take with me so I didn't slam the front door on my way out.

The walk to work was pleasant. The day was crisp and clear and I strode along, swiping my card for the energy-generating walkway along Great Russell Street because it was still a novelty for me. I walked briskly, building up a nice credit – or so I hoped – to offset our power bill back at the flat, and eventually swung in through Insight's doors, all ready to begin my new job.

They were very efficient. My ID card was ready and waiting for me – and on a lanyard, too, because I think we'd all learned from our previous experience. I used it to swipe open my allocated locker, deposited my backpack and spare shoes, and went downstairs.

Bridget was waiting for me. I'd been right about mine being the desk opposite Eddie Middleditch.

'Right,' she said, sitting me down and activating my data table. 'This password is temporary. Just for today. You'll need to set up your own. You'll be prompted to change it every twenty-eight days. File requests – we call them File Forms – are routed to you almost continually. The standard procedure is to print out a bunch of forms, curse all researchers and leap to your feet with well-simulated enthusiasm that will be gone by this time next week.

'Now – the first thing to remember is *No Form – No File*. Verbal requests are not accepted. From anyone. You must have a paper trail. If only to cover your arse when some idiot researcher loses his file and tries to blame you. Clear?'

'Yes,' I said.

'Secondly – and this is important . . .' She nodded towards the Cave. 'No one goes in there but us. No matter how prettily they plead – and they will. No one but us. They all know that so don't be taken in by *I just need a quick look – I won't be a moment*. Tell them to fill out the requisition and get it authorised. It's the usual conflict between professional and admin staff, I'm afraid. Apparently, we're too stupid to file properly but that's all right because they're too stupid to put the files back in the right place. The different file colours do make it easy to spot a misplaced file, but on the other hand it is practically another country back there. Trust me, trawling through that lot looking for a lost file is not something you want to spend your weekend doing.'

'No indeed,' I said. 'So, no one in or out but us.'

'You've got it,' she said. 'A couple of times a day you print out your lists – you'll soon identify peak and trough periods – grab your trusty trolley, assemble said files, deliver them and pick up the ones that are being returned. Take no nonsense from anyone. You are File Queen and don't let anyone forget it.'

'File Queen,' I said. 'Gotcha.'

She looked at me. 'I may be wrong but I don't think you'll have any trouble handling troublesome historians.'

'None whatsoever. Professional historians – pains in the arses, all of them.'

'Oh God – I'm going to love having you here. Come on – let me introduce you to . . .' She paused dramatically. 'The Cave.'

I leaped to my feet in well-simulated enthusiasm that was gone by the end of the day, let alone by the end of the week.

She showed me how to access the Cave using my Insight card and in we went.

The smell was much stronger here. Too strong to be ignored.

I stopped. 'Um . . . I don't want to be rude but what is that smell?'

'The chemical smell?'

I nodded.

'Every piece of paper in the place is treated with fire retardant. We're terrified of fire here.'

'Oh, yes. I can understand that.'

The Cave was vast. And it had grown organically so there were no nice neat rows of files all logically arranged. 'You'll just have to learn the layout as you go,' she said. 'Sorry – but if it was easy then researchers could do it.'

I was given a smart red file trolley – which was a great deal better behaved than a supermarket trolley, believe me, with four working wheels and no squeaks. It was divided into two – incoming and outgoing files.

'Don't get the two mixed up,' said Bridget. 'Triumphantly presenting a file to someone who's just returned it makes you look such an arse. We've all done it.'

I nodded.

'Each file has an out card,' she continued, pulling one off a shelf to show me. 'You take it out, enter your initials here, the date, and the initials of the person for whom it's intended and leave it in place of the file so we know who's got it. Then, when you get the file back, you do the whole thing in reverse. As you can see, this one . . .' she showed me the card, 'is something to do with Tesla and was taken out last week by Eddie – who must have actually done some work that day – and is still upstairs with KAd – Kofi Adomako, one of our senior researchers.'

I nodded.

'OK,' she said. 'You see that central desk over there?'

I nodded again.

'That's the work table. Use it to collate files, get your breath back, whatever. It's also a useful landmark because everything behind that is BC. Everything this side is AD. It's not strictly chronological, I'm afraid – there are a few endearing quirks where we ran out of space or started a new category or something. Each row of shelves is clearly marked. Don't lay down a trail of breadcrumbs because it attracts mice. If you're not out in an hour, Eddie and I will rope ourselves together and come and get you. Here's your first list. Only five files. Take your time. Files in your trolley and lock the door behind you when you leave. Then I'll show you what to do next. Off you go.'

And off I went. I found the first two files easily enough, was inclined to think she'd overstated the difficulties, found the third by accident, and the fourth and fifth not at all.

What I did find was a small, caged room she hadn't mentioned. I knew my file wasn't in there because the covers of these files were all black but I tried the door anyway. Locked.

'Those are the black files,' said Bridget, appearing from nowhere and frightening me half to death. 'You'll never be asked for one of those.'

'OK,' I said, turning away, careful to show no interest at all. 'I'm still looking for Prague 1432.'

'Over there,' she said. 'Second row along – the section runs chronologically upwards instead of downwards like all the others. Don't ask why – no one knows. And the Garibaldi files are over there.'

I assembled my five files and we left the Cave. Back at my desk she pulled up a building plan for me.

'You'll usually have fifteen or twenty files to deliver and the same number to pick up so save your feet,' she said. 'Arrange your files in order of floors otherwise you'll be criss-crossing the building all day long and wear your legs down to stumps.'

'God forbid,' I said, shuffling files. 'I'm short enough. I have to say, it's nice to see old-fashioned paper files like this. Digitisation is all very well but . . .' I tailed away, invitingly.

'No, we don't digitise,' she said. 'Researchers like to lay

144

everything out on a long table and have an overview. They think that makes them look important. And this way we control access to the files. There's only ever one copy of anything and we always know who's looking at it.'

By lunchtime, I'd have paid for the whole bloody lot to be digitised myself. I was nearly on my knees. Requests came through thick and fast. I was scampering about all over the place. And I had a suspicion the lovely Eddie was routing a lot of his stuff my way as well. He didn't seem to be a big fan of mobility, our Eddie. He came in, sat down, fired up his data table, and apart from the occasional comfort break, that was it for him. I was the one racing around like a lunatic.

On the other hand, this job was brilliant for getting around the building. And as a newbie I could legitimately go anywhere and then pretend I'd lost my bearings. I was politely turned away from the top floor which was no surprise because only senior managers and the Board had access.

And it wasn't a straightforward building, either. There were narrow corridors that didn't seem to go anywhere, changing levels, strange staircases that ended in locked doors, tiny rooms with just one desk, and vast open rooms full of desks with everyone beavering away doing God knows what.

I trotted around with my trolley, giving and receiving files, in and out of the Cave, ate my lunch in the small canteen next to the locker room, remembered to change my shoes, drank copious amounts of water, discovered the whereabouts of all the loos pretty damn quick, and cursed the almost perpetually non-working lifts.

Eddie was out of the door like a whippet on the stroke of five. Fastest I'd seen him move all day. He didn't say goodnight. I lay back in my chair and wondered if I'd ever move again. Bridget came out of her office and laughed at me but not in a nasty way.

I remembered to clear my desk, locked everything away, handed the key to Bridget and took myself off home. Although not without a quick spot check by security on the way out. Because I was the newbie, I suppose. They wanded away and checked my backpack and then, finally, I was free.

Except I had another forty-minute walk home. I never before realised how lucky I'd been to live and work at the same location. Still, at least it was walkable. I didn't have to battle the ancient Underground system or queue for the clippers or water taxis. And I was offsetting our power bill so it could have been worse. And it wasn't an unpleasant walk – past squares with parks and gardens and attractive houses. Not our block of flats, obviously. Our brick monstrosity and its partner stood out like massive carbuncles. I was almost ashamed to let myself in through the front door.

Markham was waiting for me. I kicked off my shoes, dropped everything and sprawled in a chair. He handed me a cup of tea on which, I was prepared to bet, no duty had been paid. Yes, the tea tax was criminal but only if you actually paid it. We preferred to be criminal by not paying it. Trust me, illegal tea tastes even better.

'Well? How did it go?'

'I think I died about three this afternoon. After I'd had to traipse up to the fourth floor for the fourth time. I hate bloody stairs. If they had any bloody sense, they'd kick their listed building status into touch and install half a dozen escalators. Can I have a refill?'

'Did you find anything interesting?'

'There's a locked area containing what they call the black files that I can't access.'

'Why not?'

'I don't know. There aren't many of them. Only just over thirty.'

'You counted them?'

'Didn't have to. Ten files to a shelf. Three and a bit shelves. Basic maths.'

'If an historian's doing maths, then it would have to be basic.'

'I'm too tired to get up and slap you.'

'That's what I was banking on. Plus, dinner's nearly ready and you have to keep me alive to open the oven door because you won't know how.'

'I hate you. You know that, don't you?'

'You have, once or twice, subtly conveyed that message. Go and have a shower because you're getting dust and God knows what all over everything and I tidied today.'

Meekly, I did as I was told while Mrs Markham crashed around in the kitchen.

I managed to stay awake through his lasagne. Which wasn't bad although there's no need to tell him that.

I left him watching the football – some kind of punishment, I could only assume – and went to bed.

The next few weeks were all repeats of Day One. With the exception of the lasagne. Actually, Markham wasn't a bad cook. No need to tell him that, either. In fact, he was turning out to be quite a domestic goddess. You can tell him that.

I did once enquire how he was spending his days while I was slowly killing myself in the cause of taking down an evil empire and earning us a great deal of dosh at the same time.

He sipped his tea and reached for another chocolate biscuit – disappointingly still not available on the English National Health.

'Well, after the echoes of your departure have died away – that usually takes about an hour – I rise gently, tidy the environment, do a little mild shopping and check the pod. Then I enjoy an historian-free lunch, take a spot of quiet exercise in the nearby park, returning in time to prepare yet another delicious meal, watch as much TV as I can absorb with an historian yammering in my ear the whole time and then retire, exhausted, to my sleeping cupboard.'

By which he meant he was keeping an eye on the pod and familiarising himself with the area in the not unlikely event of us needing to make a run for it.

He was scoping out Insight, as well. He'd presented himself to their librarian, seeking to avail himself of Insight facilities. He was a freelance researcher, he said, investigating the Princes in the Tower. He'd been welcomed with great enthusiasm, the appropriate expert had been summoned, and he'd received a full tour of the public parts of the building, together with a list of the services offered. And their price list.

'You can walk around quite freely,' he'd reported. 'I didn't even have to use the "looking for the Gents" excuse. The clerical areas are out of bounds, of course, together with the top floor and the basement. Although I can easily see why they'd want to keep you away from the paying public.'

He'd even walked around the block to suss out the back of the building, where he reported the usual bog-standard loading bay and storage areas. Absolutely nothing that shouldn't be there. Well, there wouldn't be, would there?

According to his account, he'd actually taken a few steps into the yard and been politely but firmly turned back on the grounds of Health and Safety. Bloody Health and Safety – sucking the joy out of life since the day they'd been invented.

I was pursuing a theory of my own. The basement, vast though it was, was smaller than the floors above. Considerably smaller. It wasn't immediately apparent – the layout of the Cave might have been designed deliberately to mask its dimensions. As I said to Markham, there might be any number of good reasons for this, of course – although I couldn't think of any and neither could he – but I still remembered the place that pod had whipped me off to. I'd been in no state to carry out a methodical survey, but I couldn't help wondering if it was the other half of the Insight basement. Discrete, separate, inaccessible to all but the favoured few. It might only be on the other side of the wall, and if it was, how could I get in there?

Under the pretence of searching for obscure files, I'd wandered all around the Cave and had completely failed to discover any hidden doors or secret passages, which I think everyone will agree was pretty disappointing. It was only when I was handing Bridget my key one evening that it came to me – her door. The door in the wall behind her desk. Perhaps it didn't, as I'd assumed, lead to a little bathroom, or a cupboard, or a safe – perhaps it was access to the hidden basement and Bridget was the gatekeeper and that was the real reason her office wasn't on the top floor with the others.

I couldn't think of any way to access the door, either. She didn't lock her office whenever she left – which was quite often – but bloody Eddie was always at his desk so I couldn't get in to have a poke around.

It was only as I was walking home one evening that it suddenly dawned on me. Eddie did sweet FA as far as work was concerned – but perhaps that was the true reason for him being there. He wasn't a paper-pusher like me – he was security.

The more I thought about it, the more it made sense. It also made sense for me to be much more careful around Eddie than I had been. I used the time walking to and from work to try to come up with an imaginative scheme which would discreetly remove Eddie from the office without him noticing. So far, I hadn't come up with a single idea.

I have to say, potential murderers or not, Insight were excellent employers. Even though I was on a fixed-term contract, I was called into Bridget's office for the mandatory two-week formal assessment.

I seated myself and regarded her somewhat nervously.

'Well, Maxine, how do you think you're getting on?'

I sighed. 'I'm shorter, thinner, older, and even more knack-ered than I was a fortnight ago. Good thing it's only a temporary contract or there'd be nothing left of me.'

She laughed. 'I think you worry unnecessarily. I've seen the amount of chocolate you put away. Daily.'

'Keeping up my strength,' I said, straight-faced. 'A valiant effort to prevent the job from killing me.'

I thought she'd laugh but she didn't. Instead, she fidgeted with her pen. I shifted uneasily. I'd thought we had a good working relationship. Had I read things wrong? I was still on probation. Was she about to sack me?

'I am aware,' she said, slowly, 'that there are two of you and that one does much more than the other.'

'Well, yes,' I said, 'but it's not a major issue.'

'I inherited him, I'm afraid. And he's been here long enough to be entitled to his own bodyweight in compensation should we try to chuck him out.'

I nodded. As an explanation for Eddie's immobility, it was a good one. Every office has someone who doesn't really pull their weight but isn't bad enough to be sacked.

'It really is OK,' I said, because it was. The upside was that with Eddie's bum firmly planted on Eddie's seat, I had the opportunity to zip around the building and poke my nose into all sorts of places. And at least I always knew where he was. The downside, of course, was that I couldn't get to that door in Bridget's office.

She smiled at me. 'Well, that's good of you, Maxine. Don't think I'm not grateful.'

'Please feel free to express your gratitude in chocolate form.'

She picked up my personnel sheet. 'How about I simply mark you down as "exemplary in all areas"?'

'A poor second,' I said, 'but I'll take it. Thank you very much.'

'I'm enjoying having you here, Maxine.'

'Thank you,' I said. And meant it.

'And our file delivery statistics have soared,' she went on, 'so you're making me look really good.'

'Astonishingly, you're the first boss ever to say that to me.'

'Well, to celebrate the occasion, how about we nip up the road and have a quick lunch at the BM?'

'That sounds lovely,' I said, surprised. Dr Bairstow had never taken me out to lunch. Definitely worth mentioning it next time I saw him. Should either of us ever return to St Mary's, of course.

Lunch was lovely. And longer than we intended. Not that I cared. I was out with the boss so timekeeping wasn't a problem. And although neither of us said anything, I think we were both happy at the thought of Eddie actually having to do a spot of work for a change while the womenfolk of the office enjoyed a leisurely meal.

We talked History, art, travel, food – all my favourite topics. I really enjoyed it and I think she did too. I really, really had to work at reminding myself that – for some reason not yet clear – she would try to kill us all.

Two hours later we returned to Eddie. Who, I was prepared to swear, hadn't moved since we left. I sat at my desk and sighed.

I had no idea what to do about Eddie's bum being perpetually on Eddie's chair.

And then . . . one day . . . the god of historians remembered my existence and deigned to lift a finger . . .

It was just a normal day. Bridget was at a meeting on the top floor. I was preparing my files for delivery around the building, sorting them into order and stowing them in my trolley, when my phone rang. Which was a surprise in itself. Bridget spent a lot of time on the phone, Eddie didn't answer his, and mine rarely rang because I suspected most people were still unaware of my existence.

I picked it up. 'Maxine Forrest.'

It was Bridget. 'Oh Maxine, thank God. I was worried you'd be in the Cave and I'd get Eddie instead. I'm up on the top floor. There's a big meeting and I've stupidly forgotten a file. Can you bring it up? Asap?'

'Of course,' I said. 'Which one and where is it?'

'In my pending tray. Right-hand side of the desk. It's the only one in there.'

'Understood,' I said. 'On my way.'

'You're an angel.' She hung up.

I found the file and set off for the top floor. The lift wasn't working – obviously – so I toiled up the stairs, telling myself I was strengthening my heart. And weakening my legs as well, so, you know, swings and roundabouts.

There was a receptionist at the top of the stairs. One of those immaculately turned-out specimens who probably moonlights as a fashion model. I was suddenly very conscious of my dust-streaked clothes and slightly dirty hands.

Automatically I held out the file. She didn't actually recoil at the sight of me – not recoiling from scruffy lowlifes was probably Reception 101 – but there was no way she was touching me or my file. She simply nodded me through.

There were four sets of doors along the corridor.

'Boardroom Three,' she called, hardly bothering to look up. 'Just go straight in.'

Well, this was unheard of. From snippets picked up around the building, I knew there were people who'd worked here for years and never even been near the top floor. Was it possible I'd been rumbled? I braced myself because this bunch had tried to kill me a few weeks ago and I had no idea what was waiting for me on the other side of the door.

I stopped outside Boardroom Three, tapped, took a breath and entered a large corner room. Light streamed through tall windows on two sides. The walls were panelled in oak. In fact, everything was oak. Walls, furnishings, floor, the lot. The whole effect was rather old-fashioned. There was no tubular steel or glass here. Portraits in heavy frames hung around the walls. Mostly old, bearded blokes but there were two silk-clad women among them. One was dressed in 1920s gear and flourished a dramatic cigarette holder. The other wore a 1980s power suit. The only thing bigger than her shoulders was her hair.

A podium stood at one end of the room and a large oval table at the other, big enough to seat sixteen people. I filed that away for future reference. Was that how many board members there were?

Everything in the room gleamed. Solid and prosperous. Old-fashioned. Family values. And we all know how unpleasant they can be.

There were five people in the room – Bridget and four others.

Two men and two women. Bridget was the youngest there. They stopped speaking as soon as I entered. A number of files were spread across the table, including, I was interested to see, a black one.

I hesitated, unsure whether to take the file to them or wait for someone to collect it from me.

Bridget stood up and held out her hand. I held out the card. After all, she'd been very specific. No Form – No File.

She shot me a look and then grinned and scribbled her initials on the card.

Taking the file, she turned to the room. 'Have you met our latest recruit? This is Maxine Forrest; she joined us a month ago.'

I thought I might get a frigid nod or two but they all smiled quite pleasantly. Someone said, 'Welcome, Maxine, how are you settling in?'

'Very well, thank you,' I said. 'Nice place to work.'

Everyone beamed. 'We think so, too,' said someone else.

I picked up the card and left. Seriously, if I hadn't actually seen members of Insight blow a hole in our roof then I would never have believed it. And it wasn't only the people I'd just met. Everyone in the building was pleasant and friendly and helpful. They had to be the nicest, politest, most inclusive sinister organisation up to no good in the whole history of sinister organisations up to no good.

Even with Bridget providing living proof, I still had difficulty believing I was in the right place, that my boss had tried to kill me. Even if she didn't know it yet.

I wondered how she'd felt about being instructed to kill me. Had she protested? Or had she simply nodded, assembled her team and jumped back to carry out her instructions without even the slightest pang of regret? She liked me – I was sure of it. I liked her – which was a bugger. How would I feel if Dr Bairstow put a gun in my hand and instructed me to kill her? Would I do it? That was an interesting thought, wasn't it?

And I still didn't know what I'd done – or would do – to betray myself. That moment standing outside the boardroom door had really set my heart racing.

I dropped off my regular files then sat back down at my desk and busied myself with my file list. Eddie was still doing his impersonation of a human being – although not very well. I pulled open my top drawer. I had stats to compile ready for the end of the week and needed the list of files I'd handled so far.

Someone had been in my drawer. I deliberately kept my stats list right on the top, at the front, so all I had to do was whip open the drawer, add a figure in the appropriate column and shut it again. The list was still on the top but pushed towards the back. Definitely not how I'd left it.

I stared.

'Oh,' said Eddie's voice and I started – for a moment I couldn't think who was talking. 'I needed a pair of scissors and went into your drawer. Hope you don't mind.'

'No,' I said. 'Of course not.'

Well, what else could I say? I didn't know what the office etiquette was for rummaging in people's drawers. Was it acceptable or not?

He held out my scissors. 'Thanks.'

I nodded and took them back, hoping I didn't look as unsettled as I felt.

I remembered, when I worked at St Mary's, I'd rather had the feeling that the new Head of Security, Captain Hyssop, had been poking around my desk drawers at night, after Rosie Lee and I had left the office. I'd never said anything but one night I'd scribbled, *Fuck off, Hyssop*, on a piece of paper and left it in my top drawer.

Obviously there had never been any reaction from her and I'd never had anything incriminating in my drawers in the first place but it wasn't a pleasant thing for her to do. I'd mentioned it to Rosie Lee because she was quite capable of having all sorts in her desk, from banned literature to anthrax spores. Not that I had any objections to Hyssop infecting herself with anthrax spores but some of them could have blown my way.

Anyway, whatever his motives, Eddie wouldn't have found anything there that shouldn't be. I should remember I was just a normal, innocent person and proceed accordingly.

Sadly, I wasn't given a lot of time. Another call from Bridget. The meeting was finished. Could I come up and collect the files, please.

I sighed, heaved myself to my feet and set off again for the top floor.

Again, I was waved through. I tapped and went straight in.

They were all gathered at the far end of the room by the windows, talking quietly, cups of coffee in hand. The files were still scattered across the table. Four pink, one red, one blue, two green, and . . . and, half hidden under the pile, the black one.

This was far too good an opportunity to miss. I moved around the table, collecting the files, stacking one on top of the other. Take it slowly, Maxwell. Don't scrabble at them. Don't draw attention. One pink, one red, one black, three pink, one green, another green, and the big blue one on the top. A nice file sand-wich with the black one in the middle.

I didn't catch anyone's eye. Clutching them to my chest, I quietly opened the door and let myself out. I nodded to the receptionist and, without hurrying, made my way down the stairs.

There was an empty loo on the next floor. It was as if this was meant to be. No file should ever be left unattended, so naturally I took them all in with me. It was a little crowded but I could cope. I lowered the lid, sat down, and pulled out the black file. I didn't waste time trying to decode the file number – I opened it up and waded straight in.

The contents were very sparse. I was looking at a map of some kind. There was no heading. An arrow pointed north. I twisted it the right way around. It was fairly large scale. A thick blue line with the word 'Windsor' and an arrow pointing off the map. I frowned. If Windsor was nearby, then this could be the Thames. I turned over the sheet. Blank.

OK – what was next? A timetable. I scowled at it. From what I could see, it detailed the movements of two groups of people. Purpose unknown.

And at the bottom of the page – a long line of . . . surely not. Coordinates. They were coordinates. Yes! Eureka! Bingo! Maxwell the Magnificent strikes again. I must remember to tell Markham. Several times.

Time to act.

Calling down multiple blessings on an organisation that had never moved on from paper, I whipped out a pen and then found myself without anything to write on. Again. No matter – I was Maxwell the Magnificent. I could do this.

The coordinates were too complex to memorise so I dropped

my trousers – as you do – and copied them on to my thigh. Much safer than writing them on paper should I be spot-searched on the way out. And there was no way I was dropping my trousers for anyone at Insight.

Time was ticking on. They'd have missed the black file by now. What else could I see? There wasn't much else. A list of initials which I assumed were the people whose movements had been timetabled. I went back to the map. It seemed very basic so I moved to the other leg and drew it as best I could. The possible river, the arrow pointing to Windsor, some stylised trees. And . . . I peered more closely. That looked like an X. And another one. And was that a J? And that was just about it. No scale. No details. Only Windsor.

It would have been sensible to look at the other files – the chances were that the black file wouldn't have been studied in isolation – but I wasn't given the chance. The outer door banged open.

'Maxine, are you in here?'

'Yes,' I shouted. 'Out in a minute.'

Noiselessly, I replaced the map and list and inserted the black file back into the middle of the heap. Then I yanked on the toilet roll, zipped up my trousers, and pulled the chain. Picking up the files, I unlocked the door.

Bridget was standing there, a slight look of strain around her eyes.

'Did you want me?' I said, rather stupidly since she probably didn't normally stand in the fourth-floor toilets shouting random women's names.

'Goodness,' she said, staring at the files. 'Did you take them in with you?'

'Well, yes,' I said, slightly embarrassed. 'We're not supposed to leave files lying around, you said.'

'Well, I don't think I quite meant . . .'

'It's OK,' I said. 'I didn't wee on them or anything.'

I don't think she was listening. 'Can I just . . . ?' She took them off me and rummaged through them, pulling out the black file. 'You walked off with this.'

I stared in horror. 'Oh my God, I'm so sorry. I didn't notice. I just grabbed all the files. It never even registered.'

'No, it's OK.' And with that she thrust the other files back at me and whirled out of the door, leaving me still unsure how much trouble I might be in.

The thing now, obviously, was to get my legs home where I could have a better look at them, and then back to the pod to check out the coordinates.

Despite being God's gift to the filing world, I wasn't wearing a watch. I didn't really need one and in my former job I'd usually been in a time when watches didn't exist, and when I was at St Mary's, Rosie Lee always made damned sure I knew the time – especially when it was time for me to make the tea. Although actually, I haven't expressed that very well. For some reason, it was always time for me to make the tea.

Back at my desk, my data table said quarter past four. How soon could I get out of here? Not before five o'clock. I didn't want to arouse any suspicions. To have accidentally walked off with a dodgy file was something anyone could have done but to walk off with said file and then dash home early was just asking for trouble.

I opened my drawer, pulled out my stat returns and tried to concentrate. Not that easy.

I packed up as early as I could. No sign of Bridget, which I tried to regard as a good sign. Unless she was off organising my assassination, of course. My stomach jolted. Was this the incident that had precipitated the attack?

No, of course it wasn't. Pull yourself together, Maxwell. I slowly tidied my desk, put everything away, locked all my drawers and was just crossing the room to leave my key in her office when she turned up. Minus the black file.

'I'm just off,' I said, casually handing her the key. 'Unless you want me for something.'

She smiled. 'I'll walk up with you.'

Shit. She'd never done that before. She locked my key away and we set off together.

'While I think of it,' I said, seeking to distract her from my possibly imminent extinction. 'What's the policy on going into someone's desk?'

She looked at me shrewdly. 'Eddie been rifling through your drawers?'

'You could have put that another way,' I said. 'If I have nightmares, I shall know who to blame.'

'He does it, I'm afraid. I've never actually caught him so I can't do a great deal. Do you want to make a formal complaint?'

By now we were halfway up the stairs. I could hear the bustle of people leaving the building through the front doors. My blouse was sticking to my back. I had a sudden thought that between sweat and the friction from my trousers, I might accidentally rub off the vital info currently inscribed on my thighs.

Now there's a sentence I've never used before.

'No,' I said. 'He told me what he'd done. Looking for scissors, apparently.'

161

'I could have a word if you like but it's a difficult situation. Officially it's not forbidden because it would be too stupid to need something urgently and not be able to go into someone's desk to get it. It's one of the reasons we ask everyone to leave their personal stuff in their lockers – nothing gets nicked that way.'

By now we were in the locker room. I swiped my locker open, retrieved my backpack and changed my shoes. 'Well, goodnight. See you tomorrow.'

Not giving her time to reply, I headed for the line to get out of the building, slightly concerned that Markham might have chosen today to meet me from work. He did sometimes, in case, he said, he had to rescue me again. There had followed a vigorous discussion on who had rescued who most often. Now, with Bridget close behind me, I very much hoped he wasn't here today.

Guess who was waiting at the top of the steps, loitering with intent, looking clean and very nearly normal.

He waved.

Pillock.

I waved back because what else could I do?

'Who's that?' enquired Bridget.

I didn't reply immediately because I was next up in front of the guard. Between him, Bridget and Markham, I didn't know where to look or what to do.

The guard waved me through. I strode out, still seeking to shed Bridget, but he waved her through as well. Bloody bollocking hell. It was too late for him to get out of the way so he went for it.

'Hi,' he said, addressing both of us.

'Hello,' said Bridget.

'Hello,' he said. 'I'm Maxine's flatmate.'

'Nice to meet you. I'm Bridget.'

I waited with interest to hear how he'd introduce himself.

'Ham,' he said. 'Mark Ham.'

She blinked. I didn't blame her. If I hadn't been wearing my backpack then I'd have slugged him with it. As it was, thanks to my magnificent self-control, he remained unslugged. Although not once I got him home.

Bridget looked from Markham to me and back again. I knew that look. She was trying to work out our relationship. Or at least I hoped that was what she was doing and not entertaining suspicions about me, the files and the toilet. She smiled suddenly. 'Got to go. See you tomorrow, Maxine. Nice to meet you, Mark.'

'You too,' he said and then, thank God, she was gone.

I clutched his arm. 'For God's sake, buy me a drink.'

'What happened to today's modern girl?' he said, reproachfully. 'Buy your own drink. And one for me while you're at the bar.'

'Buy me a drink or die,' I said, which pretty much clinched the matter.

Once back at the flat I made Markham close his eyes.

Not unnaturally, he demanded to know why.

'I'm going to drop my trousers.'

'I'm off,' he said, scurrying away. 'Food on the table in ten minutes.'

Some of my careful writing was a little blurry but it was all still there. I copied everything out on more conventional writing material – paper – and we pored over the sheets during dinner.

'The coordinates will be easy,' I said. 'I'll nip out to the pod as soon as it's dark. The map's a puzzle, though.'

'One will solve the other,' he said. 'Eat up and we'll go and look.'

As soon as darkness fell, we trotted down the dingy alleyway and tackled the obstacle course in the back garden. Glass crunched under my feet and something scuttled away in the dark.

The coordinates were easy.

'You're right,' I said. 'One solved the other. The coordinates are for a point midway between Windsor and London. 1215 AD. Runnymede.'

I remembered the day of my interview. The Magna Carta file

had been in Bridget's drawer. She'd used it to demonstrate the file numbering system.

He took the map off me and looked at it. 'I'm assuming then that the J is John. What do the Xs show?'

I remembered the list of people's initials. 'Positions,' I said. 'Two groups of two people. Four altogether. Two to the east and two to the west.'

We laid the map on the console and stared at it.

He pointed to a symbol. 'Is that broccoli or a tree?'

I scowled. 'Trees.'

He saw it at once. 'So,' laying a pen along the paper, 'clear lines of sight between both the Xs and the J.'

We looked at each other.

'Are you thinking what I'm thinking?'

'Well, I wasn't, but now I am.'

'Snipers,' he said. 'Betcha. They're going to shoot King John. To stop him signing Magna Carta.'

'John didn't sign,' I said automatically. 'He couldn't write. His signature wasn't necessary. All that was needed was the Great Seal.'

'Seal, signature – doesn't matter if he's dead, does it?'

'I suppose not,' I said, thinking it through. 'But what's the point? He's dead eighteen months later, anyway. We know that. He reneges on Magna Carta, the barons rebel, he flees, loses the Crown Jewels in the Wash and dies of a nasty combination of dysentery, peaches and brandy. Why go to all the bother of assassinating him?'

'Don't know.'

'We'll have to check it out, won't we?'

Markham frowned. 'Haven't you already been? Years ago? I'm sure I saw something . . .'

He tailed away.

I took a moment to answer. 'Well, I remember the History of Democracy assignment – Peterloo, Runnymede and so forth – but then we lost Grant at Peterloo, didn't we? My recollection is that the assignment was never revived. Didn't Kal have appendicitis? And Peterson was in shock. And I wasn't properly qualified . . . or Sussman, so . . .'

'Yes,' he said, 'that's my recollection too.' He paused. 'We'll have to check this out, won't we?'

'Oh, I think so. It's why we're here, after all. It's Friday tomorrow – we'll jump after work.'

He blinked. 'You're going into work tomorrow?'

'I think I have to, don't you? We don't want to arouse any suspicions. And you'll need time to prepare.'

I fired up the console and began to check over the power levels. 'The pod's fine. Greens across the board.'

'OK. What are your measurements?'

'What?'

'Height? Circumference? That sort of thing.'

'I'm not telling you that.'

'You want me to guess?'

I sighed. 'Either this is for some sort of costume or you've developed yet another weird perversion and should, ideally, be removed from society. I'm going with the latter.'

'Theatrical costumier,' he said. 'I'll hire us something tomorrow morning, make some sandwiches and then we'll be off tomorrow night.'

'Get something generic,' I said. 'And accurate. I don't want to find myself in Sexy Medieval Wench costume with my bosom hanging out.'

He shuddered. 'I don't think any of us would want that.'

Markham walked me to work the next morning. He was clutching his list of measurements. I'd written mine down for him. He'd blinked, said, 'Good heavens,' and then disappeared out of the door before I could get to him.

I'd spent the previous evening reading up on King John, Runnymede and Magna Carta.

Well, we all know about King John, don't we? Subject to violent rages, shifty, unreliable, lusty and greedy. So bad that no king has ever been called John since. Last of the many children of the first Plantagenet king, Henry II, and the formidable Eleanor of Aquitaine. The Devil's Brood, as they were all known.

John more than lived up to the name. He attempted to rebel against his brother, Richard the Lionheart – who, to be fair, made it easy for him by being out of the country on those never-ending Crusades. The repercussions of which still rumble on today.

John murdered the other claimant to the throne, Arthur of Brittany. There were rumours he personally had gouged his eyes out, or that he had had him castrated and the young prince had died of his wounds.

More tellingly, his personal vindictiveness extended even to the family members of those who had offended him. On capturing the wife of one of his many enemies, Maud de Braose, together with her son, John imprisoned them in Corfe Castle and left them to starve to death in a dungeon. Eleven days later they were both discovered dead. In her desperation, Maud had eaten her son's cheeks.

Outrage over this act was immediate and widespread. Condemnation came from all sides – if John could do that to the powerful de Braose family, what could he do to others? – and this led to the famous Clause 39 of Magna Carta:

'No free man shall be seized or imprisoned, or stripped of his rights or possessions, or outlawed or exiled, or deprived of his standing in any other way, except by the lawful judgement of his equals or by the law of the land.'

Echoes of Clause 39 can be found all over the world, even in the American Bill of Rights – when they still had a Bill of Rights, of course.

In the meantime, John had lost the Duchy of Normandy and most of his French lands. His Angevin Empire, which had stretched from Hadrian's Wall to the Pyrenees, collapsed.

England was, at the time, regarded as a very second-class country and John's priority was to use his kingdom to regain his French empire. To raise the dosh, he taxed everyone and everything until the country broke. Armed with this massive fortune, he bought himself an army, but since he was such a crap king, strategist, husband, son, brother, human being, everything, he was spectacularly defeated at the Battle of Bouvines. It was a rout. He lost everything – the battle, his army, his money, the lot.

Nothing daunted, his proposals to tax the country all over again to pay for the rematch led to the Barons' Revolt which led to Magna Carta – the Great Charter.

He also managed to get himself excommunicated by the pope – which was no small matter in those days – and was basically so useless he would easily have been overthrown had there actually been anyone to replace him – but there wasn't, and there's no point overthrowing a king unless you have a spare standing by. The king's son, Henry, was very young – too young – and so the barons did the unthinkable – they looked to France and offered the crown to the son of the French king, Prince Louis, who said, 'Thank you very much,' or possibly, '*Merci bien*,' and hopped over the Channel with seven thousand troops.

The two sides jostled for a while and then, in 1216, John lost the Crown Jewels in a devastating storm surge in the Wash – Markham and I were there and he really did – and died shortly afterwards.

This left the barons in the embarrassing position of having a French prince who was suddenly surplus to requirements. John's son – Henry III – was now old enough to ascend the throne under the protection of a strong regent, William Marshal. The mighty William Marshal, soldier and statesman, served five English kings: Henry II, young King Henry, Richard I, John, and Henry III. According to Stephen Langton, Archbishop of Canterbury, William was 'the best knight who ever lived'.

A disgruntled Louis returned home, England heaved a sigh of relief that all that was over, thank heavens, and got on with things under their shiny new king.

The only good thing to come out of all this turbulence was Magna Carta. Lacking a human focus for their rebellion, the barons had turned instead to constitutional reform. These reforms were to benefit only themselves, of course. There was no mention of the common people, and women wouldn't catch up for centuries, but the foundations were laid – and strong ones they were too. It was enshrined in law that no man could have his property taken from him, that he was entitled to a trial and so on. It certainly curtailed the powers of the king who, up until that point, had been able to do pretty much as he pleased.

I should mention that John turned up at Runnymede to 'sign' the Great Charter but had no intention of abiding by its conditions. Although, to be fair, there's no evidence the barons considered it particularly binding, either. John successfully appealed to the pope – another head of state who believed in unlimited power at the expense of others. Presumably forgetting he'd previously excommunicated John for four years, the pope condemned the Charter and all those who supported it.

Magna Carta survived, however, was revised, copied, and issued throughout the land. And went on being revised and reissued, forming the base of our laws today. Its effect down the centuries has been massive. It has been described as the most important document in History. Countries all over the world – with some notable exceptions and we all know who they are – have adopted the principles of Magna Carta.

But suppose John didn't die in 1216, but at Runnymede instead? Assassinated. There would be shock, turmoil and rebellion, and in the ensuing chaos, Magna Carta would be forgotten. Everyone would argue that with John gone, there would be no need for the Great Charter. The king is dead, they would say. And I never liked the look of that Charter thing anyway – silly liberal nonsense. Burn it and let's press on. And the world would be poorer for it.

I sighed. Markham and I were going to have to get out there and save worthless John's worthless arse, weren't we?

And it wouldn't be easy. This wasn't going to be a case of just recording and documenting and dealing with whatever

History threw at us. We were jumping back to foil what no doubt Markham would, any moment now, be referring to as a dastardly plot. A plot, moreover, hatched by people who might possibly know my face. And I'd stand out because there weren't likely to be many women there. We were going to have to box very carefully with this one.

For the record, when I awoke the next morning, I wasn't that enthusiastic about going back to Insight. I think if Markham had said, 'I'll phone in sick for you,' I'd have jumped at it. He didn't, however, so I did. Go to work, I mean.

We strode along the walkways with me thinking cheerful things like *this could be the last time I ever do this*, although I think *this time tomorrow, I could be dead* was my favourite.

We parted on the pavement outside Insight.

'I'll be fine,' I said, even though he hadn't said anything.

Markham shook his head. 'She walked you out of the building yesterday. You said she'd never done that before.'

I thought for a moment and then said, 'I don't think you should turn up here again. Keep your distance from now on. If anything happens to me . . .'

'Oh.' He looked disappointed. 'Actually, I was considering trying my luck with your boss. You know – invite her out for a drink and a fun-filled evening and use my charm to winkle out her secrets.'

'Wasting your time,' I said. 'Delightful though you are, I'm pretty certain she bats for the other team.'

'Ah,' he said. 'I'll leave that to you, then. Are you sure you don't want me to come in with you?'

I shook my head. 'You're keeping your distance, remember?'

'OK. Good luck.' He disappeared into the crowds of people streaming along the pavement.

I stared up at the building wondering what horrors were in store. I pictured the Insight staff waiting for me. Silent and implacable. Or gunning me down as I changed my shoes. Poisoning the coffee. My imaginings became wilder and wilder until even I had to laugh, and it was with a very nearly merry smile on my lips that I climbed the steps.

All ridiculous when you think about it. I knew this lot didn't mess about. If they'd had any doubts about us, then Markham and I would have enjoyed the traditional dawn raid so beloved by governments and other illegal organisations everywhere.

I took my place at my desk. Eddie ignored me as usual. Bridget was in her office, head down and typing away. She gave me a vague wave as I entered and passed me my key.

Somewhat reassured, I unlocked my desk and got stuck in.

There's nothing like a guilty conscience to make you work harder. I think I thought if I kept moving, they couldn't catch me. I raced around the building like a maniac. Files flew in all directions. At one point Bridget came out of her office and asked if I was on medication.

'No,' I said, seizing the excuse, 'but I was hoping perhaps to finish a few minutes early tonight.'

'Plans for the weekend.'

'A few, yes.'

'Sure,' she said. 'If you've nothing major outstanding then how about finishing at four?'

'Thank you,' I said, beaming. 'Much appreciated.'

After that I took care to calm down a little.

*

I worked until five to four and then started clearing my desk. I called goodnight to Eddie – just to annoy him because he really hated participating in social intercourse – and was out of the doors by five past.

I called up Markham as soon as I gained the safety of Great Russell Street and he stepped out from behind Duke of Bedford's statue as I walked past Russell Square. He was bearing two covered hangers and a bag and banging on about the heat, the length of the journey, the cost, and having to have his inside leg measured twice because they hadn't believed it the first time. I've no idea what that was all about and I wasn't going to ask. His inside leg had always looked moderately normal to me – especially compared with the rest of him.

Back at the flat I left him murmuring discontentedly on the sofa and made him some illegal tea. He sipped and subsided while I investigated the results of his day's work.

There was a long brown dress – not wool, but it looked like wool, which was even better. Runnymede is full of water meadows which was why it was chosen. The king would be surrounded by his own loyal followers. The barons would arrive with theirs. Should things turn nasty – which they might well have done as neither had any love for the other – it's quite difficult to have a full-scale bloodbath when you're up to your ankles in muddy water and the place is full of cows. Wool's a bugger when it gets wet. It's heavy. It stretches. It smells. And sometimes the colour runs. So fake wool was good.

The downside was no concealed pocket. I've no idea why the universe has decreed women aren't entitled to pockets but there we are. My stun gun would have to go up my sleeve.

A linen slip went underneath the dress to show at the neck

and wrists and I had a belt to rest on my hips – waistlines were low in that period. And some sort of mobcap – not quite the right period – nowhere near the right period, actually – but I could jiggle it about. Or even turn it inside out so the frilly bits didn't show. I had my own stout shoes, so yes, it would all do very well.

Markham himself was also in brown, a long robe falling past his knees with a pair of boots underneath. He also wore a chaperon – a hood that came down to cover his shoulders. Very like a gugel but without the point. They were popular at the time. Not so much on a hot June day, I suspected, but it all added to his look.

'We'll change in the pod,' I said.

He told me he'd brought sandwiches. 'And fruit, cheese and biscuits. I know we have compo rations but we can't replenish those so I'd rather not use them unless we absolutely have to.'

I nodded. 'Right. Soon as it gets dark, we'll dump this lot in the pod and be off.'

I changed while Markham stowed our kit in the lockers. He changed while I laid in the coordinates.

'All set?' I said as he emerged from banging his elbows in the tiny bathroom.

'Ready when you are.'

'Right, let's jump into a situation where we don't know what's happening and the chances are that we'll be recognised and shot as soon as we set foot out of the door, shall we?'

He grinned. 'I can hardly wait.'

'Computer, initiate jump.'

'Jump initiated.'

The world went white.

And I fell apart.

15

I was lost. Untethered. Drifting in time. The centuries closed in, towering over me like cliffs. Joan of Arc burned even as Randall tried to save her. The ground gaped beneath my feet at Troy. Clive Ronan and I clung together as a sandstorm enveloped us, flaying the skin from our bones. A blood-covered Thomas Becket sprawled in a pool of bright candlelight as his cathedral rang with screams of grief and fear that found an echo inside my own head. An acoustic snake lay on my chest. A small neat bullet hole appeared . . .

Something grabbed my arm and pinched it hard. Right on the fleshy bit. Incredibly painful. My world collapsed into reality again.

'Ow,' I said indignantly, rubbing my arm.

'Sorry,' said Markham. 'What happened there?'

I blinked. 'Not sure. I'm getting the occasional dizzy spell. I think I might have a slight inner ear infection.'

I stuck my finger in my ear and waggled it about so he could see I had an inner ear infection.

'Only Evans mentioned something odd happened to you in London.'

'Yes,' I said. 'It's getting to be a bit of a nuisance but dealable withable.' I rubbed my arm. 'Even at the cost of great pain.'

'You're welcome.'

'Right,' I said, changing the subject. 'I'm shutting down everything I can to save power. We don't have any means of charging so let's not be profligate. I'll leave the cameras on but the camouflage device is off so be aware people can see us.'

'OK,' he said, amiably. 'Where and when are we?'

'Just where we want to be. Coming up to midnight on the 11th June 1215.'

Not wanting to appear in front of everyone and start a panic-stricken riot, we'd decided to arrive the night before. And since we weren't far off midsummer, we'd had to wait a while for darkness to fall.

'Dawn is around 0400,' I said. 'We can't do anything in the dark except be eaten by a cow, perhaps.'

Markham shuddered. 'We should get our heads down while we can.'

So we did.

He woke me at ten to four with a cup of tea and reported the sun had made its traditional appearance. He was sitting at the console panning the camera around.

'Lots of people here already. They must have been arriving through the night. No idea what time everything kicks off but I shouldn't think they'd want to be here in the noonday sun so it's quite possible it could all be over with by ten thirty.'

He squinted at the screen. 'They seem to be erecting some sort of wooden stage. Keeping the king out of the mud, I suppose.'

I yawned. 'Give me a few minutes to finish my tea and then we'll go and have a look around. There should be enough people by now to give us some cover but not so crowded we won't be able to get an idea of what's where.'

'No,' he said and folded his arms.

'What?'

'Sorry, Max – but you're known. You work for Insight. You might not know the team they despatch today, but we can't take the chance someone will recognise you. You'll stay here and be my eyes on this one. Let me know if you see anything untoward. I'm off for a look around.'

'But . . .'

'Stay here and finish your tea. You know it makes sense.'

I scowled horribly and he completely ignored me so I pulled out the copy of the map and handed it to him. He tucked it into the purse hanging from his belt.

'Ready?'

He nodded. I opened the door for him. We stood in the doorway for a few minutes, taking it all in. The sun was rising on a beautiful, sparkling morning. The dew sparkled on the grass. The sunlight sparkled on the river. The early morning was still a little chilly but not for long. Clear blue skies promised a long hot summer's day. I sighed.

'Com check,' Markham said.

I sighed again. 'Loud and clear.'

'And give me regular time checks as well.'

'I will. Good luck.'

He set off. I closed the door behind him and seated myself at the console.

The area was crowded already and more people were arriving

every moment. They streamed across the meadows. On foot, on horseback, on carts. Large numbers were arriving by boat. The river was packed with craft waiting to moor up.

I was pleased to see there were a few women among them – setting up pie stalls, fetching water – not enough to camouflage me, though.

Bollocks. But nothing I could do about it. I should get on with the job. I started moving the cameras around, methodically quartering the area. I split the screen, allocating one camera to follow Markham, one to the nearly completed stage, and panned around the crowd with the rest.

People milled around everywhere. Horses were led under the trees. Dogs trotted between people's legs. There was even a pig. No, I've no idea why, either. I spent a lot of time focused on each of the areas I thought had been marked X in the Insight file but I couldn't see anything that looked even remotely out of place.

Time ticked on – as it does if you don't keep an eye on it. I glanced at the chronometer and opened my com.

'. . . ing for Site Alpha. Wait one.'

That wasn't Markham.

Another voice said, 'Confirmed. Be aware of Team Two one hundred yards to your right.'

'Confirmed.'

There was a brief burst of static and then silence.

Very carefully and very quietly I shut down my com.

What the hell was that? I'd never known anything like that happen before but the answer seemed fairly obvious. There was someone else here and they were using the same frequency as us. Or channel. Or whatever the stupid technical term was.

Now what did I do?

Half of me was thrilled to bits. Working from a scrap of paper and with assumptions piled upon guesswork heaped upon speculation, we were, nevertheless, in the right place at the right time. A cracking piece of work by Markham and Maxwell.

The other half of me was shitting bricks because this meant I couldn't contact Markham. As soon as I spoke, they'd hear me as I'd heard them. They'd know someone else was here. It wouldn't take them long to find a rickety old hut among the cluster of stalls, tents and lean-tos rapidly being erected around us. Especially if they had kit that could read a pod signature. They'd find us in minutes.

And what if Markham tried to contact me? He wasn't stupid – as soon as he heard strange voices in his ears he'd realise what had happened – but if he spoke first they'd hear him and we'd be blown.

I could see him circling a booth purporting to be selling beer although it could as easily have been ditch water. There's no difference in the taste. I could get to him in a few minutes. I stared at the screens and plotted my route because I couldn't afford to get lost once I was out there. I had the sound down low and could just hear faint music and shouting and laughter from the crowd. No one was passing up this splendid excuse for a knees-up. My sort of people.

How much time did I have? I suspected the barons would arrive last. In reverse order of importance, because precedence was key and lots of people were making a statement today. The barons chipping away at the absolute power of the king and the king resisting every inch of the way. I was certain John would make sure he was fashionably late. Late enough for them to begin to worry he wasn't coming. He was setting out from Windsor Castle, the barons from London. Runnymede was approximately midway between the two. A nice compromise.

Come on, Maxwell. The longer I sat here, the more Markham was at risk. Insight had every reason to believe that, apart from contemporaries, they were alone. They might not spot me if I was clever, but at some point, Markham was definitely going to open his com. He might even refer to me by name. At which point, I didn't mind betting, we might have only seconds to live.

I stood up, smoothed my skirts, made sure my stupid cap covered all my hair and quietly exited the pod.

The cameras in Leon's pod are excellent. Manoeuvrable and responsive, they had given me sharp images of the scene outside – but the one thing they can never convey is the smell of a place. The day had warmed considerably as the sun rose higher in the sky and a vast and complicated smell hit me at nose height. Roasting meat. Someone had a pig on a spit somewhere. Hot horses. Hot men. Hot horse shit. The muddy smell from the river. Crushed grass. And a familiar, strange, sweet smell – crushed bullrushes.

And the place was packed. Teeming. As one chronicler put it, 'Nearly all the nobility of England were there.' And not just the nobility – there were plenty of commoners here, too. All jostling for the best positions. To see and be seen. Personally, given John's track record, I'd have been a bit wary of the king's gaze falling on me – especially on what was never going to be one of his favourite days. The Great Seal would be fixed to Magna Carta, but John wasn't going to be happy. Matthew Paris states that the king was well aware he had just surrendered a vast amount of royal power and that afterwards he gnashed his teeth, rolled his eyes, caught up sticks and straws and gnawed them like a madman, or tore them to shreds with his fingers. I'd rather like to see that but first things first.

The Thames was wide here. The far bank was tree-lined and green but my side was packed with boats. Small rowing boats, coracles, punts, rickety rafts I wouldn't have stepped on if you'd paid me to – they were everywhere.

I looked around. This was a wide, open meadow, filled with flowers and dotted with oak trees. Further down, willow trees overhung the banks and people were taking advantage of the shade.

I could see Markham over by the stage. He had his back to it and was surveying the terrain. Looking for sniper points, I guessed. I looked around. Always carry something if you can. It helps you to blend in. That said, I didn't want some goodwife chasing me because I'd nicked her bucket. I couldn't see anything small and portable lying around so I'd just have to risk it.

I set off for Markham, waving to attract his attention. I was careful not to hurry. I walked at the same pace as everyone else, weaving and smiling my way between groups of excited, chattering people who'd turned up to see the king today.

What with watching where I put my feet, avoiding bumping into people and keeping my eyes fixed on Markham in case I lost him, I really wasn't looking where I was going at all. I skirted a group of well-dressed merchants who were going to regret all that fur when the day really warmed up and walked smack bang into Peterson.

16

We stared at each other. Probably his surprise was more justified than mine. Being here today was part of his job, after all. I had no idea how to account for my presence. However – first things first.

I grabbed his arm. 'Don't use your com.'

Peterson blinked. 'Why not?'

'There's someone else here and they're up to no good and they're on our wavelength. Frequency. Whatever.'

He rolled his eyes. 'Channel, you ignoramus.'

'Smart arse.'

Pleasantries over, we grinned at each other.

'Good to see you, Max.'

'And you. Who's here?'

'Sykes.' Good – another woman. 'Roberts and Sands.'

'Who's on security?'

'Keller. No Hyssop or anything Hyssop-related.'

Well, that was a stroke of much-needed luck.

'Where are they?'

'They're behind you,' said Sykes, very nearly causing me to jump ahead in my bowel-evacuating schedule.

'Look who I found,' said Peterson, unjustifiably taking the

182

credit because *I'd* found *him*. There was a chorus of hellos. I was surprised how pleased I was to see them. Just when I thought I'd got St Mary's out of my system I realised I hadn't. I suspect St Mary's is like some sort of dreadful malaise from which you never really recover.

'Don't use your coms,' I said. 'Whatever you do. And can someone fetch Markham? He's over there. They know me and I need to stay as hidden as possible.'

'Who knows you?'

'The people who've come to kill King John.'

Keller grinned at me. 'We've missed you.' He slipped away.

'Oh God,' said Peterson. 'What have you got yourself into now?'

I watched Keller thread his way through the crowd. 'Let's wait for Markham. How's things at St Mary's?'

'Not too bad,' said Peterson. 'Treadwell's doing OK. He and Kal are the dream team when it comes to securing funding. We're really busy these days. Hence my presence here.'

'Yes, but you're only making up the numbers, surely. It's everyone else actually doing the work.'

'Do you know, I haven't missed you one little bit.'

Markham arrived, grinning like a lunatic.

'Or him.'

Markham grinned some more. 'Or him what?'

'You mustn't use your com,' I said to him. 'The opposition are on the same . . . channel. If we can hear them, then they can hear us. I came to warn you. And before you say anything, I'm carefully standing behind Mr Roberts – who's being really useful for once – and no one can see me.'

'Well,' said Peterson, rubbing his hands together. 'We do

183

seem to have become embroiled in something exciting. Tell us all about it. Who's about to kill John?'

'My employers.'

He stared at me. 'Good God . . .'

'I know.'

'No, I was expressing astonishment you'd actually found someone prepared to employ you. Who are these desperate souls?'

'Believe it or not, an historical research society who may not be what they seem. Well – I think most of them are but some of them aren't.'

'Your usual concise and accurate delivery of vital information, I see.'

I grinned. 'Are you available for some extracurricular activity?'

'Need you ask?' said Sykes with enthusiasm. 'What's the plan?'

Peterson groaned.

'We think they've got two teams of snipers,' I said. 'They were just setting up when I accidentally overheard their conversation.'

Markham pulled out his map and shunted about, trying to orient himself.

'There,' said Keller, peering over his shoulder. He pointed at a small stand of trees over to our right. 'There's the river . . . there's the stage . . . so those must be the trees.'

'Or over there,' said Markham, pointing to a similar clump a hundred yards to our left.

'Or even over there,' said Sykes, nodding in the direction of even more trees to our right. 'This is not the most accurate map in the world.'

'Doesn't have to be,' I said, making sure I stayed in the centre of the group. 'I've had a Brilliant Idea.'

Peterson sighed in exasperation. 'Until you accidentally fell over us, there were just the two of you, and from what you say, fifty per cent of you should have stayed in the pod in case you were recognised. What is this Brilliant Idea? Just how did the pair of you imagine this going down?'

'Flawlessly,' said Markham, loyally. 'We're Pros and Cons.'

Peterson turned to me. 'Just when you think he can't get any worse . . .'

'You think you've got problems. He recently threw me out of an upstairs window wearing tights.'

Peterson gave the matter some thought. 'Just to be clear, was it you, him, or the window that was wearing the tights?'

Markham grinned evilly. 'Guess.'

'Anyway,' I said, dragging them all back to arguably more important matters. 'I'd like you guys . . .' I indicated the men, 'to find somewhere with a reasonable point of view, open your coms and have a nice chat.'

'About . . . ?'

I grinned. 'You're the Time Police. You've tracked them here and you're closing in. Flush them out. Sykes and I will stand here and watch for any groups showing signs of agitation. Or even just plain running away. We can't participate because there aren't that many women in the Time Police and I certainly don't want to do anything that would cause our friends out there to associate me with them.'

'No one in their right minds would associate you with the Time Police,' said Peterson scathingly. 'And they don't take kindly to being impersonated.'

'They'll never know anything about it,' I said, reassuringly.

'They're still looking for a good reason to shoot you on sight, you know.'

I waved all this aside. 'We don't have the manpower to do this any other way,' I said. 'Are you armed?'

'The usual,' said Sands. 'Stun guns and pepper.'

'I think it's a great plan,' said Sykes enthusiastically, although to be fair she's enthusiastic about everything. As far as she's concerned, the dodgier the better.

'Two teams,' I said. 'Markham takes one – Keller the other. You should be able to work up a nice bit of dialogue between you. Flush them out and we'll record as much of them as we can. The important thing, though, is to save the king.'

Markham looked at me. 'You stay quiet and out of sight.'

'Roger Dodger,' I said, and he frowned because standards weren't being maintained.

They began to move out.

'And lay it on thick,' I called after them. 'We need to smoke the buggers out.'

They disappeared into the by now much larger crowd, most of whom were gathering around the stage.

Sykes grinned at me. 'Hang on, Max, I don't know what you've got on your head – it looks like a pair of drawers.' She pulled off her veil and passed it to me. 'Pull it forwards and it'll hide your face.'

I gave her my cap. She pulled a face and put it on over her wimple. I stepped back in horror. Dear God, had I really been walking around looking like that?

'Your sacrifice is recognised and appreciated,' I said.

'An honour and a privilege, Max. I'd better do some work or

Treadwell will have my guts for garters. You know what he's like. You keep watch.'

She hauled out her recorder and began to pan around. The usual stuff. Establishing shots first. The crowd. Minor barons standing in small, grim-faced groups, their grooms and servants around them. No one was armoured and they were all bare-headed but everyone carried a sword. As far as I could see, there were about ten to fifteen of the actual rebels, although more were still arriving. There should be twenty-five of them altogether.

We kept our distance from the stage but that wasn't neces-sarily a disadvantage. Besides, the crowd was thicker there and feet were trampling the water meadow into mud. People were slipping all over the place. Whoever had chosen this site was a genius.

Sykes was still panning around the ranks when there was a disturbance. A trumpet sounded from somewhere behind us. I could hear cheering and shouts of welcome.

'William Marshal junior,' she said in excitement, moving sideways for a better view.

And there he was. I could see his badge. Party per pale or and vert, a lion rampant gules. William Marshal junior. His father, William Marshal senior, would be appointed future regent when the young Henry III came to the throne next year.

I wondered if his father were here. It was very possible. William senior supported the king, while his son sided with the barons. Usually, they took very good care to avoid any sort of confrontation with each other but not today. I couldn't help wondering if having one Marshal on each side was just simple pragmatism on their part, ensuring that, whatever the outcome, at least one member of the family would be on the winning team.

That would all crash to the ground when William junior would fall out with Prince Louis big time and join his father. He would go on to fight for the king at Lincoln but that was all in the future.

The barons drew together to welcome him as their attendants melted away. Colourful standards flapped in the breeze, bright against the blue sky. I could make out the red chevrons of the de Clares, the three seashells of William Malet and, exactly as recorded by Matthew Paris, the flag of Henry de Bohun – azure, a bend argent cotised two lions rampant or. The rest I'd have to check when I got back to St Mary's.

I shook my head. No, I wouldn't. I didn't do that sort of thing any longer. I'd taken the girl out of St Mary's. Taking St Mary's out of the girl was proving more difficult. Focus, Maxwell, for heaven's sake. Remember why you're here. Speaking of which . . .

Cautiously, I opened my com, indicating to Sykes the channel was now open. She nodded, mimed zipping her mouth, and continued recording.

All the common people – e.g. me – were standing at the back of the crowd, but we could see the raised stage well enough. There was a great air of anticipation. Men chattered in small groups, constantly looking around for the arrival of the king. For most, this would be the one and only time in their lives that they ever saw him. And one of the last opportunities as well – he'd be dead next year.

Vendors and purveyors of ale and bread – meat and wine for the upper classes – bawled their wares in competition with each other. Their voices rang above the general hubbub as they did a roaring trade.

188

Dogs, picking up on the excitement, ran around barking and nosing for scraps. All in all, a great day out for everyone although I think it was more excitement at the prospect of actually seeing the king rather than the significance of the moment. I wondered how many people here actually knew what was happening today.

John, of course, had no intention of honouring the Charter. I didn't have a great deal of faith in the barons, either, but the thing about John was that he made everyone else look good. For the barons, I suspected the Charter was simply the focus of their rebellion. The symbol of their dominance over him.

Images of the event always show a scowling king reluctantly signing an important-looking document, but it wasn't like that at all. I shouldn't say this, but big Historical events are often nothing like we imagine them to be. John would simply affix the Great Seal of England, without which no document could be passed into law. There were two sides to the Great Seal. One depicted the king dispensing justice. The other showed the king as war leader. John, obviously, was crap at both.

Faintly, in the distance, I could hear the sound of horns and men shouting. Heralds were clearing the way. A great stir of excitement ran through the crowd. Surprisingly, given that pretty well everyone in England hated the king, there was even some ragged cheering. The cynic in me wondered if they'd been paid to do so.

John obviously wasn't going to get his feet wet. Unlike the rest of us, he approached on horseback, riding a fine white horse with a deep saddle and richly decorated bridle. Heralds preceded him, roughly shoving people aside.

Most people knelt as he passed. Including me and Sykes,

so there went Markham's deposit as I stood up with big, wet, muddy knee patches on my dress. Those barons at the front bowed their heads in token respect but kept one hand on their swords. The king cast them an evil glance as he dismounted at the foot of the steps. The air was thick with suspicion and distrust. Seriously, you could have cut the atmosphere with a knife.

King or not, I wouldn't have let John through my front door. It's rare that people look what they actually are. Many shiftless, devious, untrustworthy bastards have the face of a smiling angel. John, however, looked exactly what he was. And you could add cruel and merciless to the mix as well. I remembered Maud de Braose and her son, and shuddered.

Unlike most of the Plantagenets, he was short and stocky. His brother had been six feet four inches tall. John was a foot shorter, which wasn't particularly short for this age, but I wondered how he'd felt as big, golden, charismatic Richard towered over him. Still, John had the Plantagenet nose. The one you could probably slice cheese with. He wore a long robe, appropriately of royal blue, with a crimson cloak tossed back over his shoulders. The sun glinted off a large silver brooch holding it in place. His hair was dark and chin-length, but he'd lost a lot at the front. He sported a small, neat beard. His dark eyes glittered with suspicion and his complexion was heavy and red. High blood pressure was my guess. I wondered if having a nasty look about you was part of the job spec for being king. Edward I, his grandson, once famously frightened a man to death and they always reckoned Elizabeth I could make men wet themselves just by looking at them.

Grooms led the king's horse away. John turned slowly and surveyed the twenty-five rebels, all their retainers standing behind them, and the massed commons standing behind them. Everyone stared back. The sun was beginning to climb high in the sky and I'll swear the air sizzled between John and his barons. There was no love lost here.

John was not alone, however. As well as William Marshal senior – who had arrived very quietly and was taking care to stand well back among his own small retinue – there were several clergymen, one of whom might be the Archbishop of Canterbury, Stephen Langton. He'd been the pope's choice, imposed upon John against his will. Langton was accompanied by a small gaggle of what I assumed were clerks and secretaries. Intentionally or otherwise, however, John was almost completely surrounded by other people. I glanced around. It wasn't going to be easy for Insight to get a clear shot at him.

Someone was bearing John's standard. Gules three lions passant gardant or, which was proudly displayed as, with great pomp, the king slowly mounted the wooden steps. The never very enthusiastic cheering had completely died away by now and the king's steps sounded hollow on the wood. I used to be an historian and we're not supposed to use our imagination, but to me, it was as if he were mounting a scaffold.

A table and high-backed chair had been set for him but he stood for a while, examining the crowd around him. Memorising faces, perhaps. There were a lot of people here, and a crowd can never be completely silent, but this one was as quiet as it could manage, staring back at him.

The moment dragged on. I suspected that John, having embarked on this staring contest, had no idea how to disengage without losing face. And – whether the stage had been deliberately set that way or not – he had the brilliant sun shining directly into his eyes.

It was the A of C who saved him. I hoped John tossed him a decent bonus at Christmas. Touching his arm, the archbishop murmured briefly to the king and gestured to the table and chair.

John pretended to start – striving to give the impression he'd forgotten why he was here – and then, with an attempt at the appearance of good grace he couldn't quite bring off, seated himself at the table, leaning back in his chair and gazing around.

The small band of monks and clergymen were showing signs of agitation. It would seem the most important document in the world had been mislaid. I was just idly speculating on what would happen if someone had accidentally left it at home when I got the shock of my life.

'. . . and wimple. I say again – hostile believed to be wearing brown dress and white wimple.'

I looked down. Brown dress. White wimple. What?

Sykes swung around to stare at me in consternation, laying her finger across her lips.

A man's voice said, 'Confirm description.'

'Description confirmed. Brown dress, white wimple. Awaiting instructions.'

There was a pause. 'No action at this moment. Continue with original target.'

'Confirmed.'

What? What the . . . ?

And then, as if that wasn't enough – I got the second shock of my life.

Glancing casually around to see if anyone was heading in my direction, I saw a horribly familiar figure in a cream-coloured dress and crimson girdle. Bloody hell, it was Bridget Lafferty. Here. Now. And not ten feet away from me. Shit. Shit, shit, shit. Now what?

At exactly the same moment, Markham spoke in my ear. Crisp. Clear. Completely in control.

'Attention all units. This is Red Leader. Red Leader to all officers. I have eyes on the primary targets. Moving in.'

Keller replied immediately. 'This is Blue Leader. Secondary targets identified. Awaiting the word.'

'The word is go, Blue Leader. Terminate with extreme prejudice. No survivors. Leave the bodies here.'

'Copy that, sir. Blue Team – go go go.'

For a moment, Bridget stood rigid. I half expected her to stare wildly around. Even put her hand to her ear – always the sign of an amateur.

She did none of that. Actually, she remained motionless for a good ten seconds, apparently thinking.

I was impressed. In a crisis, most people's instinct is to move – and quickly. It takes balls to do nothing and take a moment to make the correct decision rather than a swift one. I made very certain I stood behind a pie seller who had obviously sampled too many of his own wares.

Bridget came to a decision. Her voice sounded in my ear. 'The Time Police are here. Abort, abort, abort. Board authorisation. Regroup at the evac point. Three minutes.'

Neat. A quick summary of the problem, instructions given, timescale advised. I guessed three minutes was the amount of time until the pod jumped. And judging by my own experience the pod *would* jump whether everyone had returned or not. I know I'd likened this outfit to St Mary's but this was the one major difference. Insight might be lovely employers (as opposed to Dr Bairstow glaring down at us from the gallery), with great working conditions (as opposed to being blown up by R&D every ten minutes) and decent pay (with no Deductions from Wages forms zipping across your desk), but, when push came to shove, Insight *were* prepared to leave their people behind. I wondered if anyone on the sniper teams found that as chilling as I did.

And, of course, it meant they wouldn't let anyone or anything stand in the way of their escape. They would mow people down if they had to. Especially if they thought they were about to fall into the hands of the less than humanitarian Time Police.

Instinct said to warn Markham and the others. Common sense told me to shut up and stay out of it. They all knew what they were doing. Bridget, meanwhile, had spun on her heel – or squelched on her heel in the mud – and begun to work her way back through the crowd.

I should have stayed quietly where I was. I was surrounded by people and relatively safe. Staying put would have been the sensible thing to do.

I mouthed, 'Good luck,' to Sykes and set off after Bridget.

She was easy to follow. She was cleaving the crowd like an icebreaker on its way home after a hard winter. Shouts and grumbles followed in her wake. I simply rode her slipstream, modestly holding Sykes' veil across the lower part of my face.

I could hear confusion in my ear. Men were shouting contradictory instructions. One was shouting, 'Abort,' while another was requesting what sounded like clarification. I couldn't make out any specific words but the tone was urgent and panicked. The Time Police were here. Everything had gone tits up. They had only three minutes to get out. It rather sounded like every man for himself.

Not that I cared. John was safe – that was the main thing. I didn't dare lose sight of Bridget. I did look back at the stage – just once – but all I could see were people's backs.

I tried to move slowly but not slowly enough to lose her. The important thing was not to draw attention to myself. I was just a woman looking for a bush to squat behind with some broad-leaved plants nearby. Markham and Keller would have everything in hand. It was Bridget I was after.

17

Everyone's attention might be on the king but the more exciting stuff was going on offstage, so to speak.

Markham and Keller were still doing sterling work, playing their little drama to the hilt.

'Red Leader, this is Blue Leader. Targets acquired. Neutralising now.'

'Copy that.'

From the corner of my eye, I thought I saw movement under the trees but I dared not take my eyes off Bridget.

Her light dress was easy to make out in this sea of earth tones. She walked quickly, holding up her hem, which was dark with muddy water. Her veil streamed out behind her.

I had a nasty moment as she drew level with our own pod, partly concealed under the overhanging branches of an ash tree, but she passed it without a second glance.

I heard a faint cheer in the distance and slowed my pace a little. Was that it? Had I missed the famous moment? I dropped back a little, wishing again I had something in my hands. A bucket, a basket, anything. The crowd was thinning out as I moved further from the stage. If she looked back now . . .

But she didn't. Not once.

Her pod was about fifty yards beyond ours. I hoped to God she hadn't been here when Markham exited, but surely, if she had, she would have raised the alarm. Interference from the Time Police must be constantly in Insight's thoughts. I know it was constantly in mine.

This pod was identical to the one which had carried me away the night of the attack. Obviously, it wasn't camouflaged. That told me a lot. Probably they couldn't. Too sophisticated for them. And they didn't have a pod tracker. Or a gizmo that could read recent pod activity by locating signatures, otherwise they'd have picked up our pod. Again, possibly too sophisticated.

Having reached her pod, Bridget paused outside. There was no cover anywhere so I crouched on the ground as if adjusting my shoe. My veil fell over my face and every second woman here was wearing a brownish dress.

And, to be fair, she didn't just abandon her people. She stood by the door, turning her head from left to right, searching the crowds for them. I kept my head down – literally – and watched her through the folds of my veil.

Bridget spoke quietly but I could hear her in my ear. 'Withdrawing to tertiary site. Final transmission.'

She paused another moment then went inside, and the pod vanished almost immediately.

I breathed out and used Sykes' veil to wipe the sweat off my face. OK – what did that tell me?

One – that the pod hadn't been left unmanned because Bridget hadn't had time to fire up the console.

Two – she'd said 'withdrawing' rather than 'withdraw'. Information rather than an instruction.

Three – that she was prepared to leave her people behind.

And four, that they weren't finished. That they had contingency plans in the event of everything going tits up here. Another site.

I made my way back to Sykes, still recording like the trooper she was. The king appeared to have buggered off but everyone else seemed to be settling down to make a day of it. Someone was enthusiastically carving the roast pig and a crowd had formed.

I stood alongside her. 'Is it done?'

She nodded happily. 'Yep. Done and dusted. You missed it all.'

Bugger.

I looked around. 'Has the king gone?'

'He has. Didn't hang around. Left without a backward glance.'

Bugger.

'We could go back to your pod and I'll download a copy for you.'

I nodded. A good idea. Not just for watching John do the deed but for any clues the recording could offer about why the hell Insight were intent on messing with History.

We set off.

'So,' she said, chattily. 'How's things, Max?'

'Not too bad,' I said, skirting a lively bunch of apprentices who certainly shouldn't have been here today but were and seemed determined to take every advantage of their freedom. 'I see you didn't bring Hyssop with you.'

'No. Treadwell sent her off with Van Owen and Bashford. They're poking around Pasargadae in the vain hope Cyrus has carelessly left a ton of valuable stuff lying around that they can help themselves to.'

'Hmm,' I said, neutrally.

'Actually, he's not a bad bloke.'

Presumably she meant Treadwell, not Cyrus the Great, founder of the Achaemenid Empire.

'Hmm,' I said. 'He seems to know what he's doing. It's Hyssop that worries me.'

'Yeah. Me too.'

'Has anyone mentioned me and Markham? Officially, I mean.'

'Not that I know of. You two in trouble again?'

'I'm not sure,' I said, unsure how much to say. Markham and I had broken Dr Bairstow out of a secure establishment but it would seem the authorities hadn't made that public. Well, they couldn't, could they? Not without mentioning that Dr Bairstow hadn't died in a car crash, as St Mary's had been told, but had actually been kidnapped by a semi-official government department and held illegally. According to Magna Carta, anyway.

'Oh, I expect you are,' she said, with what struck me as very inappropriate cheerfulness. 'In trouble, I mean. You just don't know it yet.'

We were approaching a stand of trees. Some welcome shade at last.

Or would have been had we actually been allowed to enjoy it. A figure – wearing modern woodland camouflage – came racing out from between two large trees. He was looking over his shoulder and neither Sykes nor I managed to get out of the way in time so he collided with the pair of us. We all went down like a trio of skittles, hitting the muddy ground with a squelch.

Sykes recovered first. Not bothering to extricate herself from her skirt, she wrapped herself around his legs and hung on like a bulldog. The back of her head and neck were horribly exposed.

Our assailant – although given what happened to him, I suppose I should call him our victim – had dropped his rifle as he fell. I got a foot free and tried to kick it away across the tussocky grass. It didn't go very far. I gave that up and threw myself on top of him. At the very least it would knock the wind out of him and if I was really lucky, I might manage to stave in a couple of ribs.

Sadly, that completely failed to work. In fact, I took a couple of punches to the ribs myself.

Neither Sykes nor I were large – not lengthwise, anyway. She was nearly as short as me and if our victim had stood up, it was very likely the two of us wouldn't be able to do anything about it and we'd end up dangling off him like old bits of tinsel off a discarded Christmas tree.

Time to ramp up the offensive. Both Sykes and I can do offensive no trouble at all. Especially Sykes – proud product of my own carefully thought-out and impeccably implemented training programme.

So, she bit him. Left thigh, on the inside where it's really tender. That's my girl.

He yelped then grabbed her wimple, tore her free – there was blood on her mouth – and pushed her face down into the muddy water. With his other hand he groped for his fallen weapon. I didn't think he would shoot her – it was a long-barrelled weapon and she was too close – but he could club her brains out. If she didn't drown first.

I rolled away from them, scrambled to my feet, lifted my skirts and kicked him in the ribs.

Sykes was thrashing like a madwoman. He couldn't hold her. She wriggled free, gasping and coughing, and I took advantage of his momentary inattention to kick him in the head. As hard as I could.

It must have hurt him because it certainly hurt me. A lot, because I wasn't wearing my boots. As it was, he toppled sideways and the next moment Sykes had his weapon pointing at him.

I saw his muscles tense – he was going to make a grab for it – so I ripped out my stun gun, shouted to Sykes to get clear, and gave him a good ten seconds. Because that's the standard procedure. Then a bit more because I'm not a nice person. He fell back into the mud.

Sykes lowered the gun and began to cough.

'Bloody hell, Max,' she said, straightening up.

'Yes,' I agreed, and at that moment – when all the heavy lifting had been done – Markham appeared from the trees.

'Oh, well done,' he said, surveying our prone prisoner. 'You two all right?'

I pointed to Sykes. 'She's been drinking the water.'

He grinned. 'That's just earned you an extra twenty-four hours in Sick Bay. Minimum. Come on, matey, let's be having you.'

Between us, we hauled our twitching, dribbling prisoner to his feet.

'Someone's hurt,' said Markham sharply, looking down at his blood-streaked palm.

'I bit him,' said Sykes, proudly.

'Why?'

She batted her muddy eyelashes. 'I was trained to.'

'Well . . .' said Markham. 'I . . . You . . . Yes . . . Well done. Let's get him back with the others.'

I took the weapon from Sykes and followed on behind. 'Did you get them?'

'We got four,' he said.

'No, you didn't,' said Sykes, who could argue the hind leg off a donkey. 'We got one. You only got seventy-five per cent.'

'I meant,' said Markham with dignity, no doubt deciding he didn't miss St Mary's after all, 'we –' his expansive gesture not only encompassed us but nearly everyone in the southern counties – 'got them all.'

'Hmpf,' said Sykes, which is what I say when I'm stumped for a clever reply, but it sounded considerably more forceful with her Caledonian accent.

'Behold,' cried Markham, dramatically pushing his prisoner into a grove of sycamore trees. Or possibly oaks. Or elms. Trees, anyway.

Now that I had time to look at Markham properly, I could see he was wet and muddy, his hood twisted around his shoulders, with an angry red mark on one cheekbone. 'Is everyone all right?'

'Sands reckons he's broken his hand. Keller says he's been shot but he hasn't really so don't waste your sympathy.'

'What about our friends?'

'Stunned, peppered, thumped, grappled with and heroically subdued. Just like yours.'

He pushed our prisoner to the ground and put a knee on his back. Sykes and I each stood on his calves while Markham zipped him.

I asked Markham what we'd got.

'Two sets of two,' he said. 'Just as we thought. Snipers. Professional weapons.'

202

'Are they definitely Insight? Have they said anything?'

'One has Peterson-induced concussion and isn't talking at all. The other two are conscious but not talking. But come and look at this.'

Heaving our prisoner to his feet, he led us further under the trees. The ground was a little higher here, rising gently up from the river. There was an excellent view all the way down to the glittering Thames. The king's stage was clearly visible. Except . . .

'Oh,' I said.

'Yeah.'

'You're sure this was their site.'

'Yep.' He pointed to the ground. 'You can still just about see where the sniper was lying, and his spotter was crouched over there. By that tree.'

I looked down. There had certainly been a struggle here. The ground was kicked up. Great gouges had been torn out of the earth. A snapped tree branch lay nearby. There was blood on the business end. St Mary's punching above its weight again.

I crossed to where the spotter had been and looked down at the stage.

'Again – oh.'

'Exactly.'

'Those two trees are in the way. From these positions, neither of them had a clear shot at John.'

'No.'

I moved five or six steps to the right. 'And yet, if they'd moved over here . . .' I raised an imaginary gun. 'A clear line of sight.'

'Yes. And before you ask – Keller says it's the same at their other site. Worse, in fact. The table and chair were at too oblique an angle *and* he reckons the Archbishop of Canterbury would have been in the way, as well.'

'Interesting.'

'Yeah. We're just waiting for the crowds to disperse then we'll get our prisoners back to the pod. What happened to whatshername?'

'Gone. And without a backward glance.'

'Shit.'

I looked at him. I looked at the two men, zip-tied and laid out on the ground with a dishevelled Peterson watching over them. Keller, Roberts and Sands were presumably with the other pair. I looked back at Markham.

'John wasn't the target, was he?'

'Doesn't look like it.'

I looked down at the snipers again. 'How did you find them?'

'They heard our little conversation, just as we wanted them to. These two came flying out of the trees right into our arms. The only thing that saved us was they were actually expecting the Time Police. Seeing a bunch of supposed peasants gave us the seconds we needed. Secrecy be buggered – if they could have got their weapons up in time, they'd have opened fire on us. And anyone getting in their way. And a note for the future, Max – these people are more professional than we thought. As you found out, one did get away from us so well done to you and Sykes. Peterson belted Sunny Jim here with a bit of tree which left me free to pursue your boy.'

He was right. We'd been luckier than we deserved. History had been on our side.

'So,' I said, drawing a breath. 'Do we possess some magic way to make them talk?'

'No. I mean, we can knock them around a bit more, but they're tough buggers.'

'You could try telling them Bridget's legged it and left them to their fate.'

He shook his head. 'They must know she's gone by now and I'm not sure I have anything in my repertoire that would do the trick. But we both know someone who does, don't we?'

We did.

'Any sign of other Insight pods?'

He shook his head. 'I don't think they work like that. I think there's a strict deadline to each mission and if they don't make it, that's just tough.'

I considered this. 'What happens if they're wounded?'

'They're left to die. Or are shot by their own people. Miss the deadline and you're dead. That's probably why it's called a deadline. I suspect this bunch might have been dropped off to be picked up later. Perhaps that's what Bridget was here for, which would make sense. I'm concerned she might have gone for reinforcements so I think our best course of action is to get out of here asap, return our prisoners to base, and see what Pennyroyal can pry out of them. And one of us has to be back at work on Monday.'

We gave our prisoners a couple of jolts with our stun guns, met up with the others and then carried/dragged the four of them the hundred yards or so to our pod. Peterson and Sands took care to stagger a little and sang a drinking song about an engineer and a piece of equipment he'd invented. I didn't understand a word of it.

Our new friends weren't the only ones who'd taken slightly more beer than was good for them on such a hot day and no one challenged us. In fact, there was some amusement. Sykes and I stamped along behind, giving excellent impersonations of two women just waiting to get our menfolk home for an hour-long earbashing over their behaviour. And in front of the king, as well.

Reaching the pod, I got the door open. We squeezed our prisoners inside and turned to say goodbye.

There was a silence. St Mary's isn't terribly good at goodbyes and I suspected Pros and Cons weren't going to be much better.

'Well,' said Peterson, shuffling his feet. 'Let us know how this ends, won't you?'

'We will,' I said. 'And thanks for your help. We couldn't have done this without you.'

'You mean the pair of you have bitten off more than you can chew again.'

'As if,' said Markham indignantly. 'Well, perhaps a little bit.'

I said, 'If you see Leon . . . can you tell him . . .'

'I will,' said Peterson. 'I'm not going to waste my breath telling you to take care.'

'We always do,' I said and he rolled his eyes.

'Well, goodbye.'

'See you soon,' I said and held out my hand.

He took it. 'Yeah. Well. We'll be off.' St Mary's all backed out of range.

I closed the door and without taking a last look at them on the screen because I knew they'd be waving and I didn't think I could handle it, said, 'Computer, initiate jump.'

'Jump initiated.'

The world went white.

18

'Great Scott,' cried Lady Amelia as we crashed through the back door with our wobbly-legged prisoners. 'One never knows what you two will drag through the cat flap next. Who have you brought home this time? And why are you dressed like that? I feel one of your excellent reports coming on.'

Which is Smallhope speak for *tell me what's happening right now or I'll set Pennyroyal on you.*

I left Markham to make one of his excellent reports while I made us a cup of well-deserved tea. I brought him a mug just as he was concluding with, '. . . and now we can't get anything out of them.'

Smallhope regarded the hooded figures face down on the floor. 'Really? Well, let's give them a chance to contribute substantially to our bank balance, shall we?'

She prodded one with her foot – just to get his attention, I suppose. 'Ho there, good person. Tell us what we want to know at once or I will cause your reproductive organs to be encased in twenty-five feet of razor wire dipped in sulphuric acid.' She raised her voice. 'Pennyroyal – fetch razor wire and sulphuric acid, testicles for the encasing of.'

Pennyroyal made his unhurried way towards us. 'I beg your

pardon, my lady, but being unaware of your plans for the day, I neglected to lay in adequate supplies of razor wire, sulphuric acid and the like.'

'Arseholes, Pennyroyal.'

'Yes, my lady.'

'Never mind. Continuing the playful theme, have their throats cut and plough their bodies into the soil. To ensure a good harvest. That's always fun.'

'I fear, my lady, the time for ploughing is long past.'

'Tying my hands here, Pennyroyal.'

'Apologies, my lady.'

'We could strip them naked and hunt them with hounds.'

'Alas, my lady, hunting with dogs is now illegal in this country.'

'What? When did that happen?'

'Some considerable time ago, I believe.'

'Bloody government. Make a note to do something about that bunch of arseholing killjoys as soon as we have a spare moment.'

'I shall pencil it in with all speed, my lady, but I feel it incumbent on me to point out that won't help us with our current difficulty.'

'We could chuck them in the slurry pit. No one ever finds the bodies in there.'

'Not after the unpleasantness last time, my lady.'

She sighed. 'You're not as much fun as you used to be, Pennyroyal.'

'My apologies, my lady.'

'I suppose we'd better just give them an old-fashioned kicking and hand them over to the Time Police then. Unless, of course, gentlemen, you'd like to buy your freedom? Pennyroyal will have our bank details to hand.'

There was complete silence from our prisoners. Not even a whimper of pain.

She sighed. 'Some people just won't be helped, will they? I'll leave it all up to you then, Pennyroyal.'

'Yes, my lady.'

She turned to us. 'Runnymede, eh? One of my ancestors was there, you know.'

I raised my eyebrows. 'Really? On which side?'

'Oh, I think we can all safely assume it would have been his own.'

'An ex-colleague downloaded her recording,' I said. 'Perhaps we can identify him.' Pennyroyal and Markham were hauling our prisoners to their feet. 'Ask them about the other site,' I said. 'This isn't over yet.'

Pennyroyal nodded and shunted them off to their grisly fate. Which, I should inform those of a nervous disposition, consisted of a quick injection with something illegal but effective, and switching on the voice recorder as they tumbled over themselves to tell him everything they knew. Which turned out to be not very much. I suspect Insight compartmentalised everything on a 'need to know' basis.

Lady Amelia and I made our way into the kitchen, where I sat down rather quickly because my eyes were doing the double-vision thing again. I could see two Markhams which isn't something anyone wants to happen to them. Lady Amelia plonked a margarita in front of me. From what I could see, it was just past breakfast time here, but I wasn't going to argue. If I had two Markhams to cope with, then I needed all the alcohol I could get. Anyone would.

Markham pulled up a chair opposite me. 'I've been meaning

to ask you,' he said. 'This other site Bridget mentioned – was there anything interesting about any of the other files you picked up from the conference room that might possibly give us a clue?'

'I don't think so,' I said. 'I was concentrating on the black file. Give me a minute.'

I sipped and thought. OK. I was in the toilet. Tiled floor. Cream walls. Pungent air freshener. Toilet roll to my left-hand side. I lowered the lid. I sat down. I had the files on my lap. Half of me was listening for the door opening. The black one was about four files down. I lifted the first one . . . I closed my eyes, remembering. The first one was big and blue – 17th century – I couldn't remember the number at all. The second was pink. The third was . . . red. Nineteenth century. It was cross-referenced to a lot of other files. Then there was the black file and I put the others down on the floor so I could read it properly. Of course, not one of the buggers was named. God forbid anything should be easy.

A part of my brain wondered whether this was the reason the files were only numbered. Unless you had access to the index, you'd never really be sure what you were holding. Which was a bugger. Life would be so much easier if they'd had their names scrawled across the front. King John. Magna Carta. Runnymede. William Marshal.

Hang on. Where had William Marshal come from? Why did I suddenly think of him?

Because he was probably the most important man in the kingdom, was the answer to that. Much more important than the king in the scheme of things. William Marshal was the foremost knight in the kingdom. He was everything that John wasn't. Without him to steady the ship, it was very likely that

John's feeble following would have just melted away. I sipped again – I swear the alcohol was doing me good.

John hadn't been the target; we'd proved that. So who? These Insight people were definitely snipers. Well equipped with high-powered weapons. So who had they come for? Let's narrow it down. Who else was there? Other than John, there had been the archbishop and his clutch of clerics. Unlikely targets, all of them. Then there had been the twenty-five rebel barons – it could be any one of those, I suppose, but I rather thought not. Besides, they had been standing in a clump, all together, facing the king with their backs to the snipers. Difficult to pick out any specific individual.

I had another sip. Purely for brain lubrication, you understand. Let's wind things on a little. What happened after Magna Carta?

William Marshal junior would change sides. He would join his father to support the royalists and go on to fight at Lincoln. And win. The beleaguered garrison would hold for the new king – the young Henry III – while the city supported the rebels. Everyone thought taking the castle would be a walkover and it hadn't been. The ancient and experienced castellan, Nicola de la Haye, would hold her garrison together until William Marshal turned up to lift the siege and save the day.

'Not John,' I said, more to myself than anyone else. 'William Marshal. It was William Marshal they were after. Shoot William Marshal at Runnymede and he's not around to lift the siege at Lincoln. The royalists lose the war – Prince Louis claims the throne. Could that be it?'

I was cross with myself. I should know more about this. Not many people are aware, but the Battle of Lincoln Fair is the second most important battle in English History. If the royalists had lost, then the royal line would have been finished. The rebels would have installed Prince Louis of France on the throne; young Henry III would almost certainly have suffered a tragic accident. Or a tragic illness. Or both. It would have been 1066 all over again. We'd have become part of the French Empire. Lacking a figurehead on which to focus any resistance, we'd probably never have got rid of them.

I had the feeling I'd kicked a tiny pebble and started an avalanche.

I suddenly remembered, when I was sitting my History exams, one of the questions: why was there a revolution in France and not England? I racked my brains. What had I said? I remembered citing English social mobility versus the rigid French class structure. In England, where people were no longer tied to the land, a man could make a name and fortune for himself. It wouldn't be easy but it could be done. Look at all those 18th- and 19th-century men who rose from obscurity to become rich and powerful industrialists. And, I'd argued, we'd had our Civil War in the 1640s and come down very heavily against the Divine Right of Kings.

I stared at my glass. Civil War . . . kings and Parliament. How did all this tie together? What happened next?

The young Henry III was crowned at Gloucester. With none of his father's baggage to hinder him, Henry would revise and reissue the Great Charter. It was during his reign that Simon de Montfort called the first Parliament – no, hang on, that wasn't right. De Montfort called the first Parliament *without* royal authority. For the first time, the king's permission was not sought. Parliament was called independently of the king.

And most importantly of all, it was the first Parliament ever to summon commoners. Not peasants, obviously, but two knights from each shire and two burgesses from each borough.

Why did I keep coming back to Parliament? What did my brain know that the rest of me didn't? All right, these days most people are of the opinion that our politicians couldn't find their own arse with both hands and a set of detailed instructions, but politicians aren't Parliament. The institution is a glowing beacon even if the people who comprise it are sometimes . . . less twinkly. Regardless of the human element, Parliament has been robust throughout History. It survives. It always does. There have been many threats over the centuries and it has endured them all, functioning without a break during wars, plague and pestilence, scandal, plots . . . plots . . . There had been a blue file. Blue was the 17th century. It had been on the top. I remembered how heavy it had been. An important file. For an important event in the 17th century. How did 1217 tie in with that?

No. Wait – don't call it the 17th century. Call it the 1600s. That clarified the context, didn't it? A lot happened in the 1600s. The Civil War. Charles I lost his head. The Great Plague. The Great Fire. Charles II – invited back by Parliament. His brother, James II, who didn't last ten minutes. And finally, William and Mary – again, invited by Parliament. Was that it? Was this what I was groping for? Not quite. What else happened in that century? It had been a busy time. Elizabeth at one end – Mary and William at the other. A century of Stuarts.

And then I had it. Elizabeth until 1603, yes, but then James I. And what's the one thing for which James's reign is famous? And that's Parliament-related? November 5th, 1605. The Gunpowder Plot.

Shiiiit.

I glanced up to find Smallhope and Markham watching me. 'That looked painful,' said Markham.

I pushed my glass across the table towards Smallhope. 'Can I have another, please?'

'So soon after breakfast? A girl after my own heart.'

I sipped again, suddenly realising I hadn't had breakfast today. Or lunch. I looked at the clock. Half past ten. Half an hour ago it had been around two in the afternoon. The day before that it had been . . . I couldn't remember. What time had we left London? It had been midnight when we arrived at Runnymede. My body clock was all over the place. The beneficial effects of alcohol were probably illusory. Did I care?

I frowned at the table. Something . . . there was something . . . something important and I'd been in such a hurry . . . My sleeve was wet. I stared at it. Someone had spilled something on the table – me probably – and I'd rested my arm in it and my sleeve was wet. As were my knees from where I'd knelt in the mud. I sighed, hoping it would brush out when it was dry. Although the dress was brown so not a huge problem.

'Brown dress. White wimple.'

I opened my mouth and then Pennyroyal came back into the kitchen. I had to say it before I forgot what was so important. Alcohol gave me courage.

Before he could speak, I said, 'The Battle of Lincoln Fair. Pink. Simon de Montfort. Pink. Magna Carta. Also pink. And the Gunpowder Plot. Blue. And the black file. Black files are covert ops. They're working to bring down Parliament. They're trying to stop its creation. Or if that doesn't work, then to destroy it completely.'

All right – all of that could have been better expressed but I was tired and suffering two margaritas on an empty stomach.

He joined us at the kitchen table. 'Yes. There's another attempt at naughtiness in 1848 you forgot to mention . . .'

1848? The 19th century. The red file.

Sadly, too modern for me. 'What happens in 1848?'

It was Lady Amelia who answered. 'Revolution. Everywhere. Beginning in Sicily, then France, Germany, Italy and the Austrian Empire. There were the Chartists in England and republicanism in Ireland. It might take only the smallest tweak for someone to bring down the entire edifice.'

'Someone who knows what they're doing,' said Markham. 'Where and when to apply the pressure.'

I nodded. 'Someone like an historical research organisation.'

Shit.

We contemplated this in silence for a very long time.

'Without in any way impugning your abilities,' said Smallhope to me and Markham, 'I think all this might be a little too much for one team to handle.'

We both nodded. She wasn't wrong. The implications were . . . I couldn't think of a word.

'We would need to divide our responsibilities,' she said. 'Otherwise, we risk attempting everything and achieving nothing.'

Pennyroyal nodded.

'I propose the following. You two,' she looked at me and Markham, 'jump to Lincoln and have a look around. There's a battle. Assassination would be easy.'

'William Marshal,' I said. 'It must be. He's the key player of his age. Although . . .' I sipped thoughtfully. 'The removal of Nicola de la Haye might also affect the outcome of the siege.'

In the dark days when most women went unnoticed and were barred from education or public office, Nicola de la Haye shone like a star. Inheriting the position of Constable of Lincoln Castle from her father, she so impressed King John that he made her Sheriff of Lincolnshire in 1216. It would be very fair to say that without her leadership, Lincoln Castle would have fallen. And England, too.

Lady Amelia was talking. 'Give some thought to the place from which you will operate. Inside or outside the castle. Inside is probably safer but you'll have less mobility. I'll leave that to you to think about.

'Pennyroyal and I will take 1848. A little diplomacy is called for, I think.' She looked at Pennyroyal. 'We've started a few revolutions in our time. Let's see if we're equally successful in preventing them.'

He nodded.

'On successful completion of our individual jobs, both teams will rendezvous back here and jointly jump to 1605 to see what we can do to ensure the Gunpowder Plot doesn't succeed.' She paused. 'Max, I have to ask. Do you intend to return to Insight at all?'

'I think I must,' I said, reluctantly. 'They're obviously considerably more dangerous than we thought. This is a direct attempt to change History. Why are they doing it? Who's paying them? What are they hoping to achieve? These are things we must find out.'

Markham coughed. 'At what point do we involve the Time Police? Should we play safe and let them take over? Would that be wiser than trying to do it ourselves and failing?'

'That is a very good point,' said Smallhope. 'We have always been very careful never to be associated with failure. Bad for our image. To say nothing of the possible damage to history.'

'Can I propose a compromise?' I said. 'We deal with the problems we currently have before us. On successful completion, *then* we take our knowledge of Insight's activities – past and present – together with any assets we may have acquired – to the Time Police. That's the point at which we hand the problem over to them, and collect enough bounty to enable us to retire and live happily ever after.'

There was a silence as everyone thought about this.

'That is certainly an option,' said Smallhope. She turned to me and Markham. 'It wouldn't solve all *your* problems but there would be more than enough for both of you to do whatever you want. Live wherever you want. Under the grid, of course, but perfectly doable. The only thing I would say is that if we're going to do this – and I think we all know we are – then we need to make sure the Time Police get every single one of those Insight buggers, otherwise we're going to be looking over our shoulders for the rest of our lives.'

She wasn't wrong. On the other hand, if we got this wrong then there wouldn't be much rest of our lives left in which to spend looking over our shoulders. I frowned. Margarita grammar.

'I'm starving,' said Markham. He stood up. 'Egg and bacon sarnies, anyone?'

I nodded vigorously and when I looked again, Pennyroyal had taken my glass off me. Probably a good idea.

'And what did our friends downstairs have to tell us?' enquired Smallhope to Pennyroyal. 'I'm assuming you did get them to talk?'

'Eventually, my lady, yes. And, just to be on the safe side,' he said, 'I interrogated them all, in order to verify what the first one had said. It didn't take long. I suspect they were selected for their marksmanship rather than their resistance to interrogation techniques.'

I opened my mouth to question him further.

'Food, I think,' said Smallhope, running an experienced eye over me. 'And then the rest of the afternoon off.'

Two massive Markham specials later – eggs flipped over and bacon at that perfect point between crispy and carbon, toast and marmalade plus a couple of mugs of tea – and I was raring to go. Symptoms gone. Wooziness gone. Just point me at the problem.

Markham and I went to his room to talk. His room was identical to mine except the other way around. And with a picture of Hunter and Flora on his bedside table.

'May I?'

He nodded.

I picked it up and took it to the window. 'What a lovely photo. When was it taken?'

'A while ago,' he said and I put it back. He didn't want to talk about it.

I kicked off my shoes and made myself comfortable on the window seat, arranging my dressing gown around me. Penny-royal was giving our costumes a good brush downstairs. 'What did you want to talk about?'

'Do you remember Laurence Hoyle?'

'I do,' I said. 'Vividly.' Laurence Hoyle had been one of my trainees, along with Sykes, Lingoss (who now worked in R&D), North (now with the Time Police), and lovely normal Atherton.

Hoyle had had his own agenda. Markham and I had both been with him when he died.

'Do you remember how we talked about shadowy figures behind him, how they might be part of the government? Well, they must have been to have got him into St Mary's. I think – and feel free to scoff – that the people at Insight might be some of these shadowy figures.'

'I've been thinking the same,' I said. 'And – and don't ask me how because I'm still working on that – I'm wondering if there's a link to Clive Ronan as well.'

'I know you've always had a bee in your bonnet about that but – yeah – it's possible.'

'Tentacles everywhere,' I said. 'It's a bit worrying, don't you think?'

He nodded.

'Listen,' I said, 'and I mean this, so listen carefully. You don't have to get any more involved in this. You have a young family. You have responsibilities. Your own position in law is ambiguous. Never forget why you left St Mary's. If you want to back away, then I think you should. You have an awful lot to lose.'

'The same goes for you.'

'It's not the same,' I said. 'Matthew's older. He doesn't need me.' I swallowed. 'And we've spent a lot of time apart. It's good that he's self-sufficient. If anything happened to me, he'd probably be upset but he'd carry on. I don't know about Leon but . . .'

'If anything happened to you then Leon would break,' Markham interrupted. 'You have family ties, just like me, Max. You could walk away now too. We've both got a fair bit of money put away. We could find somewhere quiet. Dr Dowson would whip us up new identities – it's not as if either of us was living under our own names, anyway – and we just quietly fade out of sight.'

'It is tempting,' I said, 'but we've started this. I'd like to see it through. And if not us then who?'

'We dump it all in the lap of the Time Police and walk away.'

I shook my head. 'They might not let us do that. They'd probably fall over themselves looking for a connection to St Mary's. And if they couldn't find it, I wouldn't put it past them to manufacture one.'

Markham sighed. 'We're in deep shit again, aren't we?'

'We're always in deep shit,' I said. 'Only this time I think we might possibly be in over our heads. Dr Bairstow told me the Time Police think this might be the opening stages of the Time Wars.'

He nodded. 'He said the same to me and I think they're right. If this organisation succeeds in its objectives – whatever they are – and manages to change History . . .'

'If History will allow them to do that,' I said. 'Although I saw no sign of History stamping on the bad guys at Runnymede, which is worrying.'

He laughed. 'That's because History has us to do it instead. Think about it, Max. Who arranged things so you and I would work with Smallhope and Pennyroyal – the very people who might be able to do something about this? Who manipulated events to get you into Insight? Who made those files available for you to peruse in the Ladies? Who arranged things so the bad guys, by some freak chance, are on our channel and we know where they are? Who put St Mary's in exactly the right spot at exactly the right time to help us out at Runnymede? That assignment was scheduled years ago and yet was never completed. We should have gone but we didn't. But, now, at the perfect moment, when we were needed – there we were. As was St Mary's, just when we needed them. No, you're right. History has really dropped the ball on this one, don't you think?'

My margarita-laden mind was struggling to cope.

'We are History's instruments,' Markham cried, dramatically.

'Tools, more like,' I said. 'We are the Tools of History.'

'No, seriously, Max. Remember Mary Stuart? Remember how difficulties just melted away before us?'

'They melted away for you,' I said. 'I was wrestling Clive Ronan in an alleyway during a monsoon and we had to evacuate Ian Guthrie in a wheelbarrow.'

'Not the point I'm trying to make.'

'You can be a tool,' I said. 'I'm off to do research on the Battle of Lincoln Fair. And don't forget one of us has to go to work on Monday and it's not you.'

He was silent a while and then said, 'Do you ever wonder what will become of us, Max? How all this is going to end?'

'I don't like to think about it,' I said, and got up to go.

19

A spell at the data table followed by a short nap and a long shower and I was as good as new. Not that that was anything to get excited about. I took Markham in a cup of tea because it was my turn and then went downstairs.

Pennyroyal had obviously been busy because our two neatly refurbished costumes hung over the back of a chair. Plus a proper wimple and veil for me.

'Have you and Markham sorted out a plan of action yet?' Smallhope asked.

'We have. We're going to land inside the castle. The city of Lincoln is about to become a bloodbath and we don't want to be caught up in that. I suspect the Insight people won't want that either so they'll be inside, too.'

'How will you neutralise them?'

'We have a number of scenarios, each based on the circumstances prevailing at the time.'

'So no idea then?'

'None whatsoever.'

'Here you are,' said Pennyroyal, emerging from the kitchen with a covered basket from which the most delicious smells were wafting.

'You made pasties?' I said in amazement. 'You do home baking?'

He shook his head. 'Delivery,' he said. 'Greggs.'

'Even better.'

Don't laugh. I always did this when I was with St Mary's. A basket would give me something to do with my hands. And the contents could be used as either a bribe or a tasty snack.

'We'll see you off,' said Smallhope, 'and then get going ourselves. Your instructions are to get the job done and rendezvous back here. We'll be along as soon as we've done what we can in 1848. A quick recap and then everyone off to 1605. Once there we'll do a recce and come up with a plan of action.'

I changed in my room. Low waistlines were fashionable but this time I wore my narrow belt up around what passes for my waist so I could hitch up my dress and run like hell if I had to. A large wooden cross around my neck and close-fitting wimple and veil denoted I was a Good Person doing Good Deeds. Someone you would think twice about accosting. Pious and devout. Respectable. God-fearing. I shook my head. I was never going to get away with any of that.

Markham was in the same tunic. Pennyroyal had found him a surcoat but he wasn't keen. 'Too much material,' he said, 'but I'll take it anyway. We can always tear it up for bandages.'

Pennyroyal's expression very clearly gave him to understand that anyone tearing up their surcoat for bandages would soon need said bandages themself and possibly major surgery as well.

Markham had also rammed a small round hat on his head and trimmed his beard. He actually looked quite smart.

He grinned and looked at me. 'All right?'

I nodded, for some reason suddenly very nervous.

'Good luck,' said Smallhope. 'Have at the bastards.'

'If I don't come back,' I said to Pennyroyal, 'can you tell Leon . . .'

'If you don't come back, we'll take it out of your wages,' he said, which was his way of being jolly and upbeat. I think.

We were heading for Lincoln on the eve of one of the bloodiest battles of the Middle Ages. We didn't know what we were going to do when we got there. We didn't know how this was going to pan out. We didn't even know if we were on the right track. Basically, we were placing ourselves in the hands of History.

What could possibly go wrong?

Lincoln Castle, 20th May, 1217. Not quite when we wanted to be. Or where – but hey, no one's perfect.

A quick update while I shut down the pod. It's almost two years since Magna Carta. John's dead because trying to cure dysentery with brandy and peaches was never going to be a good idea. But now that the English have a king who isn't John, a significant number of people have changed sides – including the young William Marshal – and now support the new, bright, shiny young Henry III.

Prince Louis was still in the picture, however, and a sizeable number of rebel barons were laying siege to the castle. The city itself was already in their hands. I assumed large numbers of townsfolk had fled. There's a tragic story of all the women and children taking to the boats to escape the battle. The boats sank and most of them drowned. You could say they'd have done better to stay put and take their chances, but the royalists would go through the city like something that moves very quickly through something else. Markham through a Spotted Dick, perhaps.

For those who mistakenly think Spotted Dick is just the sort of terrible disease he would go down with – it's actually his favourite dessert. He's almost terminally addicted to it. And the ocean of custard that goes with it. Rumour has it that Mrs Mack had been forced to employ another kitchen assistant just to satisfy his rapacious demands. I don't know about that, but I do know that at least twice a week Janet used to emerge from the kitchen and personally serve him his own individual Dick. He would beam and thank her politely. She would blush and pour his custard for him. No – that is not a metaphor. Shame on you.

Anyway, moving swiftly away from the young master and his designated Spotted Dick provider, the damage to the city was one of the reasons we'd landed inside the castle rather than out.

Nice place, Lincoln. Very prosperous. In fact, the third largest city in England. Made its name through wool and cloth. Remember Robin Hood and his famous Lincoln Green?

And strategically very important, too. They say, 'Location, location, location,' and Lincoln had location in spades. It stood at the junction of two main Roman roads – Ermine Street and the Fosse Way. The River Trent gave access to York and the north via the River Ouse, and the River Witham offered access to the eastern coast. Yep – Lincoln was a prize worth fighting over.

And Lady Nicola de la Haye, the hereditary castellan and one of the most remarkable women of the Middle Ages, was making them fight for it. Loyal to the king, contemptuous of the rebels on the other side of her castle walls, she commanded the tiny garrison and, despite an appeal from Prince Louis on the grounds of her age and gender – silly sod – she refused to

225

surrender to him. For almost three months the castle had withstood siege engines bombarding the south and east walls. To no avail – these were obviously some serious walls.

The royalists, headed by Ranulf, Earl of Chester, and William Marshal senior, were due any minute now. There would be bloody fighting. The siege would be lifted and the town plundered as its punishment.

So that's the state of play. Everyone in the right place at the right time except for Markham and Maxwell. We'd aimed for the north-west corner of the bailey on the day before the battle was due to take place – the 19th – so we'd be able to have a good look around and suss things out before events kicked off. Hence the pasties. The royalists – trapped inside the castle – had been under siege for three months now, although I don't think the siege was total. Sir Geoffrey de Serlant, Nicola's deputy, was able to get out when he needed to – but food opens doors and we intended to exploit that.

Lincoln Castle was a big place. The bailey – the area within the castle walls – was huge, which was just as well, as it had to contain all the official buildings – the courts, the administrative offices and all the men who staffed them. We'd hoped to find ourselves somewhere to blend in among the usual clutter of scruffy wooden buildings scattered about. Kitchens, smithies, workshops, poultry houses, wells, stables, armouries, storerooms – it's not all flouncing around in long skirts and pointy hats, you know. Castles were male-oriented, working, multifunctional buildings. The centre of commerce and the community. Bustling. And, with luck, too busy to notice a couple of strangers and their pod.

As I said, we'd aimed for the north-west end and missed.

We were in the north-east corner, a few yards from an old stone edifice that would one day be Cobb Hall but wasn't at the moment. I'd missed our target. Or rather, I hadn't missed but the pod had.

I think I've banged on before about the necessity for frequent pod maintenance. Without it, pods begin to drift. To prevent this happening, Leon has instigated a rigid programme of A, B and C services – all of which take priority over operational requirements.

The A service is what a pod receives after every jump. The equivalent of polishing out the scratches and emptying the ashtrays. There's always a lot of unjustified grumbling from the Technical Section, which peace-loving and very nearly innocent historians rightly ignore. The B service is the monthly check-up, and the C service – the big one – is twice yearly. That's when Leon and his teams virtually take the pod apart and rebuild it from scratch. Mischief-making historians maintain there's absolutely no difference in the pod's performance pre or post any service, just for the pleasure of winding up the techies, who retaliate with a long list of complaints and observations regarding said historians, addressed directly to the long-suffering and very nearly blameless Head of the History Department.

I remembered the brief but vigorous discussion over exactly how Sykes and Roberts had managed to break a cupholder. Both of them had strenuously denied any wrongdoing – it had come off in their hand, apparently. In our efforts to prove each other wrong, Leon and I both stamped into Number Six and demonstrated our theories as to exactly how this catastrophe could have occurred. Sadly, no sooner had the door closed behind us than we were overcome by the force of our arguments – and one or two other things – resulting in us breaking the second cupholder. We called that one a score draw.

Markham and I had treated this pod as gently as we could, keeping the power levels topped up and so forth but, sooner or later, it would start to drift. Temporally and spatially. The warning signs were beginning to manifest themselves. Very soon now I was going to have to get it a proper check-up. Somehow.

Presumably Pennyroyal and Smallhope had the same problem with their pod – or pods, because Markham always maintained they had more than one. And more than one location, too. In fact, we were convinced they had boltholes all over the place. When we saw them again, I'd have to ask them how they overcame the drifting problem.

Back to the now, however. We'd meant to land in the very early morning on the 19th and spend the day familiarising ourselves with the layout. Sadly, we were twenty-four hours and a hundred yards out. At least it was still dark. Our sudden appearance, in daylight, in the middle of a castle under siege would have been asking for serious trouble.

Anyway, here we were – wrong time wrong place, which just about summed up the two of us.

'Two hours to dawn,' said Markham. 'I strongly advise we stay put until daylight.'

'Agreed,' I said, and he curled up in the corner like a stunned dormouse and went to sleep. Just like that. I wished I could do the same. I don't sleep well. Sometimes it's so bad I can wake up if a sparrow coughs in the next street. And tonight my mind was racing, anyway.

The siege was going so badly for the rebels that Prince Louis, still in London, had been forced to send reinforcements. Which meant that over half the rebel forces were now congregated outside the walls of Lincoln Castle. Something that wily old strategist, William Marshal, was about to use to his advantage. A win today would be a massive blow against the rebels. A turning point in the war. And vice versa. Both sides had everything to play for and things were about to get very hairy indeed.

Markham and I had discussed our strategy. Land inside the castle grounds, pray everyone was far too busy to pay us any attention, wander around handing out the odd pie or pasty, and keep our eyes peeled. It seemed a good bet that a specific attempt would be made on the life of someone important here today. William Marshal senior was our first choice, followed by Nicola de la Haye. She had a very able deputy in the person of Sir Geoffrey de Serlant, but there was no doubt her death would deal the defenders a mighty blow. Markham and I might have to split up.

I folded my arms and scowled at my feet. They hadn't actually done anything wrong – I was just having a think about what was going on. Not just here, but in general. The first question, of course – what the hell were these Insight people playing at?

Because you can't change History. It's the first rule of St Mary's and what we've always been told. You can't change History. History doesn't like it.

Deep breath, everyone, because, actually – you can. I've changed History twice that I know of. Once when I'd had to engineer a meeting between Mary Stuart and the Earl of Bothwell because someone else was working very hard to ensure they were never going to get it together – and again when we'd had to move heaven and earth to get Jane Grey off the throne and Mary Tudor on it. There'd been no one person to blame for that particular problem – it was the result of what the Time Police call Bluebell Time.

A long time ago in the future – in the days when time travel for all was not only possible but legal – so many people had wanted to visit the 16th century and interact with contemporaries that many events were changed, distorted or never happened at all. The upshot was that somehow the wrong queen ascended the throne.

The Time Police likened it to a bluebell wood visited by too many people, all of whom trampled the flowers into the mud, churned up the paths, made new paths to walk on and so forth. In the end they'd all but destroyed the wood and the Time Police had had to put in a patch. They'd described it as putting down decking to give the glade a chance to recover and return to its former state.

Don't laugh – it worked. Who here remembers Queen Jane the Bloody – even though she reigned for thirty-five years and was finally defeated by the Spanish Armada? Anyone? Anyway, History had looked the other way as I'd climbed over the right wall at the right moment to catch Mary Tudor alone and per-suade her to declare herself queen. History was diverted back on to the correct path and we all went home more or less unscathed.

Even now, after all these years, I can still remember that heady feeling of invincibility. Of events falling neatly into place. Just where and when I'd needed them to. And here we were – me and Markham – interfering with History yet again.

If we got this wrong, then we wouldn't last ten minutes outside the pod. A long time ago, one of my trainees, Laurence

Hoyle, had tried to alter the outcome of Bosworth Field and he'd been trampled to death by two horsemen who had appeared from nowhere and disappeared a second later. How easy for History to kill a couple of lunatics who had no right to be here. Many and varied are the ways for an historian to die if History decides she's in the wrong place at the wrong time.

And this is why ex-historians shouldn't be allowed to sit and think in a dimly lit pod on the eve of battle. It's never a good idea to start second-guessing yourself. I switched on the kettle and made some tea, giving the young master a gentle kick.

'Early morning tea for Mr Ham. Room service for Mr Mark Ham.'

He stirred. A bit like Godzilla emerging from the primal ooze to lay waste to Tokyo. Or Lincoln, in this case. He sat up and groaned. 'I'm getting too old for this.'

I handed him his mug of tea. 'Oh, come on. We're in the middle of the second most important battle in English History. Both sides will regard us as hostile. We don't know what we're doing. We don't know what's going to happen next and we're a long way from home. Seriously – where else would we be?'

Markham grinned. 'True. Still got the basket?'

I nodded and touched the cloth covering the top. 'Still warm.'

'Good.'

'I'm hoping no one's going to stab the Good Woman bringing a small treat to the troops.'

He nodded. 'Ditto with the good woman's servant.'

'I'm not holding my breath over that one.'

We finished our tea in silence and then he said, 'Sun's coming up. Ready?'

'As I'll ever be.'

I checked my wimple and veil, shook out my skirts and pushed my stun gun up my sleeve. Markham took the basket.

'Right then,' I said, squaring my shoulders and trying to look brave. 'No reason to hang around.'

'None at all.'

'Shall we stop hanging around then?'

'OK.'

'Off we go.'

'Yep.'

'After you.'

I think he would have said age before beauty before realising that might end his life far more quickly than facing whatever was happening outside. Taking a deep breath, he opened the door and forth we sallied.

The first thing that hit me was the noise. I don't mean that there was any fighting but a lot of men were gathered together in a very small space – both inside and outside the walls – and there was noise. Men shouting, horses whinnying for their breakfast, the clang of hammers on metal, running footsteps, a clatter of pans from what I guessed was the kitchens, dogs barking, and someone somewhere was doing something to a goose and it wasn't happy.

'Good heavens,' said Markham. 'Well, at least we won't have to whisper.'

What caught my attention was the sizeable contingent of civilians. I assumed these were the townspeople who supported the king or were loyal to Nicola and had sought refuge inside the castle. Which was a big relief. There aren't usually that many women in a castle but now there was a whole gaggle of civilians to camouflage us. Things were looking better.

They'd erected makeshift tents and awnings between

buildings, against walls, anywhere there was space. They'd clearly brought as many of their possessions as they could carry, plus livestock – goats, several cows, geese, a few sheep and many, many chickens. Dogs trotted around, tongues lolling. Children were milking the goats, lugging buckets of water nearly as big as they were and generally getting under everyone's feet.

A vast stash of firewood was stashed against one wall and a nearby lean-to was stacked with kegs and sacks, full of what I hoped were supplies.

To my left stood the East Gate – soon to be the focus of the battle. Further along the wall stood the Observatory Tower and the Lucy Tower, containing Lady Nicola's living quarters, I suspected, and in a sunny spot, a little garden had been laid out. For Nicola presumably. Sweet-smelling flowers and herbs had been planted around a wooden bench. And there was an early rose, carefully planted where anyone sitting on the bench would appreciate the scent.

I could see a line of women and children drawing water at the well. There might have been two wells – one for civilians and one for the garrison. A prudent arrangement. I'd once been under siege – at St Mary's, of all places – and the whole thing was buggered when someone chucked a dead animal down the only well. That was all it took. Game over.

Anyway, I was pretty sure that among all this shouting, baaing, cackling chaos, no one was going to notice two additional strangers.

Making sure my cross was hanging prominently, I said to Markham, 'I think the kitchens are over there so we'll take care to look as if we're coming from that direction with our pies. Where shall we go first?'

'South wall,' he said, gesturing. 'To check out the damage so far. Then around to the East Gate to have a look at the state of play there. Shall I help you up the steps?'

I impaled him with a Look and it just glanced off him. He did, however, help me up the steep stone steps to the top of the wall. Deference to one's elders and betters was very important in the Middle Ages.

The stone steps running up to the ramparts were the usual breakneck affair. Unevenly spaced, worn, slippery with dust and grit, and no handrail. If Hyssop – St Mary's almost completely disregarded Health and Safety Officer – had been here then there would have been a colossal cat's cradle of black and yellow tape, warning notices, safety nets, at least two handrails and probably several forms you had to sign, in triplicate, declaring you'd attended all the relevant courses in the hazardous art of step-climbing. And were signed up for the refresher. As usual, thinking about Hyssop made me angry – too angry to worry about toppling off the steps to my death – so she was at least serving some useful purpose.

The ramparts and battlements were not packed with soldiers. There weren't enough of them. The garrison was indeed tiny. All credit to them – and the castle's wall builders – for holding out so long. Most men were just rousing themselves, emerging from their cloaks or blankets, standing up and stretching. Three or four were peeing over the battlements.

I could see archers, crossbowmen, and ordinary soldiers. Many had been wounded. The man nearest me had a dirty cloth wrapped around his head. From the position of the crusty bloodstain, he might have lost part of his ear.

Markham and I edged our way along the ramparts. Most

men politely stepped back to give me room, touching their caps or their forelocks if they weren't wearing headgear. I smiled and nodded, moving slowly along the wall, while behind me, Markham distributed pies and pasties which were very well received. We had nowhere near enough to give one to everyone and men broke the pasties apart and distributed the pieces around their mates. Most got at least a mouthful or two.

I had to watch where I was putting my feet. There was clutter everywhere. Old cloaks and blankets in which they had slept, helmets, stacks of weapons, and their own packs and personal effects lay all around. Piles of rubble and broken stone were assembled into neat heaps – impacts from the siege weapons' assault on the walls, I assumed – all carefully collected and ready to be thrown back at the invaders when the time came. Some of the ramparts had been knocked about quite badly but the walls themselves still stood firm. Lady Nicola and her garrison weren't going anywhere.

We worked our way towards the tower on the second, smaller motte – known today as the Observatory Tower. Two soldiers were just sorting themselves out for the day, rolling up their gear in a scruffy blanket.

We handed them a pasty and Markham indicated we'd like to see what was happening below. Munching appreciatively, they moved aside for us.

Very, very cautiously, we peered out over the wall.

'Shit,' said Markham and I didn't blame him.

20

I'd done my homework, reading up everything I could find on Lincoln in the Middle Ages, and I was still unprepared.

We were a long way up. A hell of a long way up. I'd heard the castle was at the top of a steep hill but this was . . . well, a very steep hill. It was actually named Steep Hill – just to give you a clue.

The view of the surrounding countryside was magnificent, though. I could see all the way to the hazy horizon. Ground mist was still rising off the lower areas and around the river. The town lay before us – a sea of uneven roofs. The East Gate was over to our left – the Lucy Tower to our right.

Down below in the town, a small trebuchet stood ominously close, pointing towards the gate. Two more, larger and more solid, stood away to our right – to target the south wall, presumably. Trying to gauge the angles, it seemed to me that anything fired from the smaller one would probably sail harmlessly over the walls. Which might have been the point. We've all heard of dead and diseased animals being hurled over the walls to spread sickness among the defenders. And even the smallest rock fired from one of those beasties would be lethal if it found a target. The pockmarked ground inside the bailey and especially around the East Gate seemed to indicate that this had been happening, and quite often, too.

Almost directly opposite the castle stood the cathedral, its spires jutting heavenwards. Another colossal building. They really didn't mess about in Lincoln, did they? Think big – build big.

The area between the castle and the cathedral was just a seething mass of men. There were no horses that I could see, meaning these were probably common soldiers. Either the rebel barons were in their tents somewhere or, more likely, had seized comfortable accommodation in the town.

As with the garrison inside, everyone out there was preparing to face the day. I could see smoke curling from occasional fires. Men sat in groups, cleaning their weapons, opening their packs, pulling out lumps of bread and such. Presumably the local butchers and bakers were either willingly providing provender or they'd fled and their shops been looted. I could smell the sharp smoke in the early morning chill. Interestingly, no one was firing at anyone else. Those below were sitting targets – quite literally in most cases – but those up here weren't taking a blind bit of notice of them. The rules of medieval warfare always baffle me. You didn't fight in the dark. You didn't fight until everyone was ready – unless you were a complete bastard, of course. Often, you didn't fight in the rain. You didn't fight on major saints' days. Looking at this lot, presumably you didn't fight until everyone had had their breakfast, either.

On the other hand, this siege had lasted three months so far. I think some of the initial excitement might have worn off.

Speaking of breakfast . . . we distributed the last of our pasties to random men around the walls. As far as I could see, no one was paying us even the slightest bit of attention. In the bailey down below, a number of serving tables had been set up and men were appearing from stone halls and wooden huts to form lines. Breakfast was being served. Around us, men were leaving the wall to trot down the steps. With complete disregard for health and safety, I might add. In fact, many of them were looking over their shoulders and talking to their mates as they descended the breakneck steps. Were they all insane?

'Should we split up?' enquired Markham. 'I'll stay up here and check out the rebel force. You go down there and search for Lady Nicola.'

This was the point at which all our advance planning had ground to a halt. We didn't know who the target would be. I didn't know whether to hope Insight were here or not.

I nodded. 'Start at the north wall. William Marshal approaches from the north. When he turns up, find his standard – he'll never be very far away from that. Although if Insight make an attempt on him before the battle, there will be bugger all we can do about it from here. I'll try to find Lady Nicola. She must make an appearance soon.' I sighed. 'I wish we knew what we're looking for.'

'You can potter about until the siege engines start up again,' he said. 'And then, wherever she is, we're both back under cover. And this is Markham, Head of Security, saying that.'

'OK.'

We were interrupted by bells. Lots and lots of bells, seemingly ringing from churches all over the city. Lincoln had rather a lot of parish churches as I remember.

'Prime,' I shouted in Markham's ear. 'Early morning prayers.'

Most men dropped to their knees, crossing themselves in

silence. A priest appeared from the Lucy Tower, descended the motte and began to pass among them. The bells fell silent. Markham and I stood very still, backs to the wall, heads bowed. There was silence on the other side of the walls as well.

'I suspect,' I said softly, 'that it'll all start kicking off after prayers.'

'Yes,' he said thoughtfully. 'As soon as they're finished, we get cracking. For God's sake, try and stay out of trouble, Max.'

'I'm hoping to be with Lady Nicola,' I said, 'and I doubt she'll personally supervise the defence of the castle. She's over sixty, which is quite an age for the 13th century. She might come out to inspect the garrison and encourage the men, but only once the royalist forces are outside the town. I don't think she'll be the primary target.'

'Agreed,' he said. 'If there's a target today, then it's going to be William Marshal. And remember – if you must use your com, stay off our usual channel. If you can't use it, then either tap your ear or take the low-tech option and scream your lungs out.'

Below us, prayers had ceased. There were a few moments' blessed stillness and then men began to move purposefully within the bailey, kicking their packs out of the way, seizing their weapons and awaiting orders.

'This is it,' said Markham.

And then it all really kicked off.

21

This wouldn't be my first battle. Agincourt, Thermopylae, Hastings – I've seen a few – but usually either from a safe distance or tucked away inside a pod. Not today. Today I was right in the middle of the action.

The sounds of horns drifted over the wall, high and urgent, eliciting a response from everyone, no matter which side they were on. I could hear men shouting orders. Followed by a thousand voices raised in some sort of battle cry. I couldn't make out the words but likely it was a demand that God strengthen their sword arms and sow confusion in the enemy ranks. To me it sounded like the medieval equivalent of, 'Oggy, Oggy, Oggy – Oi, Oi, Oi.'

Inside the bailey, everyone was galvanised. I could hear feet pounding up the steps and see men running along the walls. Everyone was running. Platters and bowls were thrown aside – breakfast forgotten. Men shouted orders, shoving their colleagues into position.

Up on the wall a man bellowed a warning, gesturing wildly into the sky. I looked up but in completely the wrong direction. I remember only the far-off sound of creaking wood, followed by a crash, a rush of wind, a moment's silence, and then an impact that made the whole wall shudder.

'Bloody hell,' said Markham, grabbing me with one arm and the wall with the other as we staggered back. I could only agree.

The rebels fired again. Hit the wall again. The whole walkway bounced under my feet.

Believe me – to be on the receiving end of a trebuchet is terrifying. First you hear the sounds of wood and rope under tremendous strain. Then the warning shout as they let go. Then the crash of the giant wooden arm as it's released. Then there's that moment of deadly hush as the missile is airborne and no one has any real idea where it will land. And then the rush of wind as the medieval equivalent of a V2 rocket hurtles overhead. And then the impact. The earth-shaking impact.

And then they fired again.

Down in the bailey, people scattered, running for cover, although I doubted a flimsy wooden hut would offer much protection. I heard something shatter somewhere. Voices were raised – alarm, fear, anger, warning. One or two children began to cry. Dogs barked and ran about, their tails between their legs – but on the whole, there was less panic than I would have imagined. They'd had three months of this.

I could hear the sound of falling stones but on the other side of the walls. I guessed some of the facing stones might have been shattered but the south wall itself was still holding.

Because I couldn't help myself, I leaned out over the wall to see what sort of damage had been done. This wall must have sustained many such impacts but only eight or ten craters showed, and those not large. More serious, I suspected, was a long crack running vertically down from the ramparts, zigzagging almost to ground level.

Steep banks ran down from the walls and were littered with

rounded stones from the trebuchets, broken pieces of masonry from the walls, and a number of impact craters in the ground. Once again, I was conscious of how high up I was. I just had time to be grateful Peterson wasn't here because he doesn't deal well with heights when Markham hauled me back again, as yet another stone ball crashed into another section of the wall, nearer to the East Gate.

'You go down,' said Markham, pushing me gently towards the steps. 'Shout if you see anything odd.'

I nodded, waited until the steps were clear of running men and then carefully made my way down to the bailey. They were clearing the decks for action. The tables were being bundled away. A man ran past me clutching a heel of bread. Sensible chap. He had no idea when he'd next get the chance to eat. Or even whether he'd be alive to enjoy it. Markham says soldiers always eat and sleep whenever they can because they never know when they might get another chance.

The garrison was lined up along the walls, pulling on helmets and buckling their breastplates. Every hit to the wall was greeted with shouts of abuse and derision and many, many rude gestures. Including a few I'd never seen before.

With the sound of rushing wind, yet another stone hurtled straight over our heads, dark against the bright sky. To me it seemed to travel exceedingly slowly, turning as it went, to drop with a thud right in the middle of the bailey, not that far from where I was standing.

Bloody hell.

Between the lack of rain and the number of feet pounding on it daily, the earth was rock-hard. Any grass had long since been scuffed into non-existence. The stone ball bounced, landed and bounced again, finally coming to rest near the place where the tables had been. About the same size as a football is all I can tell you. Two men ran forwards, scooped it up and disappeared with it. Sooner or later the invaders would be getting that one back again.

I should move, but where? No one knew where the next ball would hit – not even the attackers themselves. This whole stone-slinging thing was completely random. I had no idea where the safest place to stand would be. And staying safe wasn't the reason I was here, anyway. I should find somewhere that gave me a good view and watch for anything or anyone suspicious. And, with luck, not have a bloody great rock fall on my head.

Another stone whizzed over the wall to hit in almost exactly the same place. There were more shouts of warning. This one disintegrated on impact, sending shards of shattered stone flying in all directions. I saw a man fall, blood running down his face.

I shouldn't have done it but it's instinct. I ran towards him. He rolled over, cursing. A small piece of stone had nicked a lump out of his forehead and thick red blood was running down into his eyes. He looked as if someone had tipped a bottle of tomato ketchup over his head. I had no idea what he was saying but I think I'd be using the same sort of language if it had been me. Angrily, he tried to dash the blood out of his eyes with his sleeve.

I pulled him to his feet and yanked off my veil. For those of you reeling in horror at this unwomanly act, my wimple was still preserving my respectability. Using the veil, I cleared away the blood. In holos and books the heroine – always a resourceful wench – starts ripping up her clothing to make bandages in a crisis. Trust me – it can't be done. Well, not by me, anyway.

After three embarrassingly unsuccessful attempts, I held out the veil and made *ripping it up to make bandages* gestures, because I'm a heroine. The man took it from me somewhat dubiously so I did it again. He tore off a strip – as easily as anything – and I tied it around his forehead.

Still somewhat confused about what was happening here, he held out the bloody remains to me. I pulled it through my belt because it was useful bandage material, and with a steady bombardment of rocks and stones crashing all around us, I could see I'd be needing it again in the very near future.

He picked up his sword, nodded, adjusted his bandage for that fashionably rakish battlefield look and set off for the east wall.

As he ran off, a big man appeared outside the door to the Lucy Tower, high above the bailey. He was roaring instructions down to the running men. I wondered if this was Sir Geoffrey. I craned my neck, searching for Nicola de la Haye. She must be here somewhere, surely. The woman who defied Prince Louis wouldn't remain quietly in her room while all this was going on.

She hadn't. And she wasn't at ground level either. A small group of people had appeared at the top of the tower on the other motte. The one in the south-east corner. Even as I watched, they all began to shout and point north. I squinted up at them. There were at least two women up there. I could see their veils streaming behind them in the wind.

Markham's voice sounded in my ear. 'William Marshal's forces have been sighted. That's what all the excitement is about. Eyes peeled, Max. If Nicola's standing up there on the tower, then she's an easy shot for someone with a sniperscope. Or even a sharp-eyed bowman. And remember, they could be dressed as someone from either side.'

I interrupted him. 'Something's happening down here as well.'

The man I assumed to be Geoffrey de Serlant was running down from the Lucy Tower towards the north gate. One hand on his sword, the other waving in the air to keep his balance, he was tearing down the rough steps cut into the steep-sided motte. Yet another example of armour not being as restrictive as sometimes thought. I sighed. Still thinking like an historian.

He was shouting as he ran. I couldn't pick out what he was saying. Word of the reinforcements must have got round very quickly because everyone now was shouting and cheering him on. I could almost smell the relief. William Marshal's army had been sighted. The siege would be lifted. They waved their hats in the air, yelling and slapping each other on the back.

Two men dragged a plunging horse from the stables. Sir Geoffrey hurled himself dramatically into the saddle. The horse himself reared dramatically and then set off across the bailey at full gallop. Men dramatically threw themselves out of the way because it was very apparent neither horse nor rider had any intention of stopping. It was a splendidly theatrical gesture and both horse and rider were lucky the guards got the gate open in time. Sir Geoffrey thundered through to cheers and whoops and disappeared in the traditional cloud of dust. The gate slammed to behind him.

I drew back into the angle of a wooden hut built against a stone building. Somewhere quiet and discreet but I could still see what was going on. I watched the people run past, looking for someone – or more likely several someones – who just didn't look quite right.

'Hope the pod will be OK,' said Markham in my ear as yet

another missile dropped from the sky to hit a range of long, low wooden buildings over to my left. They exploded in a shower of splinters, manure, dust and terrified chickens.

I straightened up. I hadn't been in any sort of danger – the hit had been well to my left – but you do tend instinctively to duck when bloody great rocks are hurtling down from the heavens.

I tried to reassure him. 'That pod's taken everything I've thrown at it over the years – I wouldn't worry too much. Plenty of other things to worry about.'

Having said that, typically, after those exciting few minutes, everything went quiet. Men slowly emerged from whatever cover they'd managed to find, looked up at the sky for a moment and then carried on with their normal morning tasks.

This often happens in warfare. It's all go for half an hour and the rest of the day is spent hanging around waiting for someone to kill you. I suspected the impending arrival of William's army was causing a massive strategy session at rebel HQ and they'd ordered an immediate ceasefire to rethink their tactics.

If William hoped the rebels would march out to meet him on the flat ground outside the city, he was to be disappointed. They would refuse to surrender their advantage, stubbornly remaining in the city.

'They're in a sandwich now,' said Markham, from his eyrie up on the ramparts. 'There's the castle, held by royalists – one slice of bread. Then there's the rebel-held town – that's the filling. Then there's William's royalist army – the other slice of bread. It's going to be interesting, don't you think?'

There was no 'going to be' about it. It was interesting right now. There were shouts from the other side of the walls. And then everything went very quiet.

'Don't like the look of this,' shouted Markham, running down the steps. 'Heads up, Max.'

Barely had he spoken when something black and trailing flame like a comet came whistling over the walls to fragment on impact. Hundreds of pieces of burning shrapnel whizzed through the air in all directions, showering everyone in the vicinity. A man stared stupidly at his burning arm. Markham appeared from nowhere, threw the man to the ground, ripped off his hitherto despised surcoat and used it to bat at the flames. In a few seconds the flames were out. The man nodded vaguely – shock and pain, I suspected – and wandered away.

Markham climbed to his feet, took one look at me and shouted, 'Max, you idiot – you're on fire.'

Bloody hell – so I was. Well, that made a change. Usually it was the other way around.

Half a dozen smouldering embers had landed on my dress and caught in the folds. Even as I looked down, the glowing edges were slowly spreading outwards. No flames as yet, perhaps the modern material was fire-retardant, but any minute now . . . I remembered the man with the burning arm.

We slapped at the fabric until everything seemed more or less extinguished. I was just gloomily contemplating the damage – there went Markham's deposit – when an elderly man appeared at my side, frightening me half to death. He was gesturing towards the Observatory Tower. He was well dressed and wore a modest chain around his neck. I wondered if he was Nicola's steward but I couldn't make out what he was saying.

I spread my arms in an eloquent gesture of non-understanding and in sheer exasperation, I think, he took my arm. Not roughly, but there was no chance to argue. He'd clearly been given instructions to remove me and removed I was going to be.

'You're either under arrest or being taken to a place of greater safety,' hissed Markham, melting away out of sight. 'Leave what's happening out here to me. If you are under arrest, I'll rescue you as soon as I have a moment.'

I was hustled away. Respectfully but firmly. No one else was taking any notice. They were too busy putting out the small fires around the bailey. Some of those wooden structures were well ablaze. Dark smoke and the smell of burning wood filled the air.

Up on the walls, however, men were cheering. William Marshal's reputation preceded him. Many here obviously considered the battle as good as won. The difference in the atmosphere was amazing. Not only had reinforcements arrived but they were being led by the great William Marshal himself. Well, no, officially they were led by the Earl of Chester, but I suspected it would be William that everyone looked to.

If the steps up to the top of the wall had been bad, the ones in the Observatory Tower were even worse. I struggled to the top of the motte and stepped in through the open door. It seemed very dark after the bright sunshine outside. I took a moment to blink then gathered up my skirts and proceeded with caution. It was a long way to the top. Turn after turn after turn. I had to stop – once to get my breath and once to get a better grip on my skirt. Sixty years old or not, I bet Lady Nicola cantered up and down these ten times a day.

Eventually, hot, breathless and with aching legs, I emerged, slowly and cautiously, out on to the roof. I took a moment to let my skirts fall and arrange them decently. Despite my singed and bloody appearance, I wanted to look respectable. The steward pushed past me and went to speak to the older of the two women looking out at the fighting from the tower.

No one turned to look at me so I took the opportunity to stand quietly for a moment, getting my bearings and blinking in the sunshine. And the wind. I hadn't realised how sheltered I'd been at ground level. The wind was really gusting up here. Over my head a pennant of some kind flapped and snapped in the breeze.

OK, Max. Concentrate. The first thing was to check out those who were up here. There was the elderly man who had brought me and a younger woman – probably Lady Nicola's maid. A guard stood either side of the doorway – the absolute minimum she would accept, I suspected. Every other able-bodied man would be manning the walls. There were also two young lads, small and light and similarly dressed in blue. She was probably using them as runners. Carrying and receiving messages to other parts of the castle. She would expect to be kept abreast of developments at all times. This was not her first siege, after all.

Finally, Lady Nicola turned away from the view northwards to look at me.

I remembered she was a great lady and bowed. Her gaze lingered on the bloody veil still hanging from my belt, which I hoped was reinforcing my credentials as a Good Woman.

Sixty was a great age in medieval times and Lady Nicola looked every inch of it. Her hair was completely covered but her eyebrows were snowy white and her skin was criss-crossed with fine lines. Her most prominent feature was her great, bony, hooked nose. Like a parrot's beak. Her hands, clasped before her, were arthritic and freckle-speckled and she had a prominent dowager's hump. I think her eyes had once been brown but were now a milky grey. Faded they might be, but they were still fierce and I suspected she missed nothing.

I greeted her in Latin which I think she understood. She didn't ask for my name and I didn't give it. She spent a few seconds looking me up and down. I tried hard not to imagine her giving the order to have me hurled from the tower. Then she nodded and thereafter completely ignored me. Which suited me very well.

I looked around. Bloody hell, I was a bloody long way up, and the ramparts were barely higher than my waist. Lower in a few places. The gusting wind was whipping Lady Nicola's veil around her head. She was so small and slight I was surprised she wasn't blown off the tower completely.

We were standing on top of a tall tower, itself on top of a sturdy motte in a castle built on the top of a very steep hill. On a clear day I could probably have seen all the way to the Nether-lands. And, for the record, no one was clinging, white-fingered, to the stones in their efforts not to be blown into the middle of next week. Not even me, although that could all change at any moment. But this was exactly where I wanted to be, so take a deep breath, Maxwell, and hang on to something solid. This was probably the closest I was ever going to get to heaven.

I tried to manoeuvre myself into a position where I could see what was going on and stand close to Nicola at the same time. Her maid stood just behind her and her steward at her right side, leaving her left side exposed to whoever should be out there. I was edging my way cautiously towards her when her maid very gently pulled me back, shaking her head. I was spoiling her mistress's view. Reluctantly I took a small half step back. The old lady pointed her beaky nose at me so I took the other half as well. You didn't argue with Lady Nicola de la Haye, even if you were trying to save her life. I'd have to think of something else. The chances were that those buggers from Insight were out there somewhere, position unknown, purpose unknown – but probably not good – and she was the second major player on the stage today.

'Hey, I can see you up there,' said Markham chattily in my ear. 'Can you see me?'

I glanced around and spotted him over near the East Gate. I raised a hand and then pretended to adjust my wimple.

There are varying accounts of what happened at Lincoln, who was where and how brave they were, and sometimes it's difficult to pick your way through it all. But most reports agree that the Earl of Chester attacked the north gate in the city walls as a diversion, while William's men made for the north-west gate, which had been blocked up and was therefore unguarded, and entered the city that way.

Things were moving just outside the castle walls, as well. A man I suspected might be the royalist Falk de Breauté was leading a counter-attack. A small contingent of crossbowmen – about ten that I could see – was creeping across the rooftops to fire down on the besiegers. There weren't many of them but given the way men were crammed into the place below, Falk's men could hardly miss. Each man found himself a place, loaded his bolt, and at some signal I couldn't see, began to fire volley after volley into the massed ranks of rebels.

'Are you seeing this?' said Markham, softly in my ear. 'If there were any Insight people up on the rooftops, they'll soon push off when they see this lot up here as well.'

'Unless they're disguised as Falk's men,' I whispered. 'In which case we're sitting targets up here.'

He swore briefly and closed his com.

For such a small contingent, Falk's crossbowmen were having a massive effect. There was panic and confusion in the square below. Men fell over each other in their efforts to find cover. Between Falk's people on the roofs and Chester's at the gate, it was an excellent distraction from Marshal's forces still toiling to unblock the other gate.

Nicola clapped her hands together, uttering a 'Ha!' of satisfaction.

It was short-lived, however. Such was the rapidity of their fire that Falk and his men soon ran out of bolts. Nicola flung a command to her steward that between the gusty wind and her Norman French, I didn't catch. He replied briefly and pointed urgently down into the square.

Not content with assaulting from the roofs, Falk had led his men down to the streets below for a spot of hand-to-hand combat. Swords drawn, roaring defiance and death, they streamed across the marketplace, taking the fight to the rebels. Seemingly unstoppable, Falk's men fell on them with massive ferocity, striking right and left, leaving the rebels with no option other than to fall back towards the cathedral. Which they did, but in good order, and once there and with their backs protected, they made their stand. There was fierce fighting.

I am always shocked by the savagery with which men fight. The strength, the power of their blows. The intent to kill or maim. To fight in battle is very different from a scrap on the football pitch or in the bar. All these men were fighting for their lives. They shouted, roared, hacked, kicked, stamped, stabbed. No one gave any quarter. Lose your footing and you were dead. Hesitate for one moment and you were dead. Two-handed, they

252

hewed at each other. Even from all the way up here I could hear the clash of metal on metal, the war cries and the shrieks of the wounded and the dying. The tide of battle flowed to and fro. From up here it was very hard to tell who, if anyone, was winning.

I was dividing my time between watching out for Lady Nicola who appeared to have been born without fear and was hanging over the battlements in a way that made my blood run cold, keeping an eye on the fighting below, ensuring Markham hadn't been caught up in all the chaos, and not being blown off that bloody tower.

I've never forgotten standing up there, halfway to heaven, with the wind whipping at my skirts. I remember the brilliant forget-me-not blue sky above me, with its scudding white clouds; the beauty of the distant landscape, serene and silent. And the red slaughter below. Men locked together in their death struggles and barely able to move. The dead held up by the living.

The ferocity of Falk's attack had cleaved a great wedge through the rebel forces. The din was terrific. With their backs literally to the wall, the rebels rallied. Reinforcements erupted from the surrounding streets and suddenly the wedge became a trap. Falk and his men were surrounded. Cut off from the castle and slowly being hacked to pieces.

Lady Nicola slammed her fist into the stonework. I might have only a little Norman French, but I know bad language when I hear it. She fired off a series of rapid instructions. The two young runners disappeared through the doorway. I began to edge towards her again. Should anyone have any ideas about eliminating her, now would be the ideal moment. With Sir

Geoffrey on his way to meet William Marshal, Lady Nicola was the person very much in charge.

Below us, soldiers of the garrison were opening the East Gate. Four men struggled to remove the giant wooden cross-beam and another four – two on each side – began to heave them open.

Everyone's attention would be on the drama below. There would never be a better moment to take out Lady Nicola. I stood as close as I could get to her left-hand side. Her maid was on the other. It was only afterwards that it occurred to me that a sniper would be unable to distinguish between the women on top of the tower. And wouldn't care anyway. All three of us – mistress, maid and me – would have died.

A body of men erupted out of the castle through the open gate and fought their way to join those of Falk de Breauté. There was utter confusion. I had no idea who was who. In any Calvin Cutter holo, medieval armies were always beautifully dressed. One side would be in jaunty red and yellow and the other side in blue and white check – thus enabling audiences to know who is who at any given point. This was just a struggling melee of similarly grey- and brown-clad men.

The rescue party were successful, however, retrieving the overenthusiastic de Breauté and his little band and fighting their way back through the gates, to the accompaniment of loud cheering from the garrison, who were supporting them with arrows, bolts, rocks and great enthusiasm.

The diversion had succeeded in its purpose. With everyone's attention on the exciting events outside the castle, the city's north-west gate was finally breached. We heard the horns, the hoofbeats, the war-cries. William Marshal himself led the charge even though he was seventy years old. The story goes that so keen was he to get to the fighting that he nearly galloped off without his helmet. A man had to run after him with it.

Banners flying, the mounted knights were galloping through the streets. I could hear them before I could see them, appearing and disappearing between gaps in the houses.

And then – without warning – they were here. Suddenly. Below us. Erupting into view. The sight was terrifying. Enormous horses with equally enormous hooves struck sparks from the cobbles. Echoes bounced off the walls. The narrow streets were packed from side to side with riders and horses and nothing could stand against them.

Their riders were equally terrifying. Fully armoured, visors down. The area was too cramped for lances – they held their bloody swords aloft and got stuck in. Anyone getting in their way or losing their footing wouldn't stand a chance. They'd end their days as an unpleasant stain on the cobbles.

Still tightly packed, the entire mass of horses and riders turned, almost on a sixpence – I was very impressed at their control over their horses – to approach the castle from the north. With a roar, they erupted into the space between the castle and the cathedral. The rebels didn't stand a chance. Many flung down their swords to flee but more and more riders were piling into the square, pushing the solid mass of foot soldiers back before them, either to fall and be trampled under the horses' hooves or crushed against the walls.

Their horses fought too. A good warhorse was a knight's third arm in a fight. Ears laid back, they reared up, bringing blood-splattered, iron-shod hooves down on those trying to get out of their way, eyes bulging with battle fury, teeth bared, and snorting foam everywhere.

At this exact moment, the Earl of Chester and his men broke through the north gate as well, surging into the narrow streets and driving all before them. Swords and axes rose and fell. There was no quarter. This was the make-or-break battle of the barons' rebellion and everyone knew it. Lose this one and you'd lost the war. The cobbles ran with blood. Groaning men struggled to drag themselves clear of the fighting, leaving long, shiny red trails behind them. Horses were bloodied to their knees. A tangle of limbs and heads were trampled underfoot. A single arm, still holding a sword, was kicked from one side of the street to the other. Fierce-eyed horses trampled anyone in their path – friend or foe.

The heaviest fighting was in front of the cathedral where the bells were tolling wildly. What that was supposed to signify I never knew. The noise was deafening – adding to the shouts of the victors and the screams of the wounded. I wondered what it was like to be down there. The heat . . . the smell of blood . . .

I could see William Marshal's banner. He was in the thick of the fight outside the East Gate. I was trying to watch out for him while still keeping an eye on Lady Nicola. She couldn't know how dangerously exposed she was. I scanned the rooftops below because if I were Insight, now that Falk's men had gone, that's where I'd be. Peering through a sniperscope at the women at the top of the tower.

And then I had a thought. I stared at Lady Nicola and the two guards up here with her. Neither of them would be any protection from a modern sniper but they would easily be able to protect her from me. And I was an unknown quantity, as far as they were concerned. Suppose Nicola slumped suddenly to the ground, dead. They wouldn't recognise a bullet wound. They certainly wouldn't hear the shot. A sudden patch of red on her dress – they'd assume she'd been stabbed and that, as the only stranger there, I would be the one doing the stabbing.

On the other hand, now that William Marshal was in town, I rather thought Nicola might be of secondary importance. Killing her now wouldn't affect the outcome of the battle in any way. No – Marshal was the target and always had been, I was convinced of it.

Everyone was craning over the battlements, twisting their heads to watch the progress of the fighting below.

I tapped my ear and said very quietly, 'Where are you?'

'Outside,' said Markham, meaning outside the castle. I assumed he'd gone out with Falk's rescue party. 'I'm about to check the rooftops.'

'I don't think I'm serving any useful purpose here. On my way,' and closed the link before he could argue.

I summoned my Latin and addressed Lady Nicola. 'Lady, I have healing skills. I can tend the wounded.'

There was a moment . . . those milky eyes regarded me. I waited. One word from her and I'd be dead. Then she nodded. Just once.

I didn't hang around. I backed slowly out of the door, turned, picked up my skirts again, gave my eyes a moment to adjust to the dark and set off. Very slowly because I was almost blind. There was no wimpy handrail. Not even a rope to hold on to. The treads were very narrow. I always thought this type of stairway was supposed to favour the defenders but that definitely wasn't the case here.

I did briefly contemplate coming down on my bum but my bum's a lot bigger than my feet. All I could do was inch my way down, making sure of every step, and hope for the best. Slowly, slowly, Maxwell. You'll get there. It can't go on forever.

Markham's voice sounded in my ear. 'Where are you? You've disappeared.'

I whispered, 'I'm struggling down these bloody stairs. I don't think killing Nicola now will affect the battle in any way so I'm on my way to you. I'm certain William Marshal will be their target.'

There's nothing the universe likes better than proving me wrong.

22

The tower walls were thick, muffling the sounds of the bells, the fighting, everything. All I could hear were my own footsteps. One-one. Two-two. There was dust and grit on the stairs and every now and then my foot would slip forwards, making my heart leap with fear. One broken ankle and we'd be in dead trouble. And I had work on Monday.

The walls were becoming lighter. I could see the outlines of the individual stairs. And my own feet. I was nearly there. I couldn't wait to be off this bloody staircase no matter what awaited me out there. I rounded the last turn. There was the open door with bright sunshine beyond. I'd made it.

No, I hadn't. Two men appeared in the doorway and there was something about them . . .

If they'd fallen back and made way for me – as they should have done given my age and status – then I probably wouldn't have looked at them twice, but they didn't so I did.

And then I looked at them a third time.

Their backs were to the daylight but I knew these men. I'd seen them before and very recently, too. They were Snipers Three and Four from Runnymede. They were even wearing exactly the same clothes. Greyish-brown camo-style top and trousers tucked into boots. I knew them immediately.

I didn't even have time to wonder how they could possibly have got away from Pennyroyal. He was like the waiting room to hell. No escape, no returning to the real world, the only way forward was to an unavoidable and unpleasant future.

I had no place to hide. The sunlight streamed through the doorway, hitting me full in the face. They couldn't miss me. I didn't dare move. Not even to tap my ear. I waited for the shot that would end my life.

Seconds ticked by as we all stared at each other while my heart rate and breathing accelerated a thousandfold. I had vague thoughts of fishing up my sleeve for my stun gun but by the time I dragged it out they could have shot me thirty times over so I didn't bother.

Think, Maxwell. Think, think, think.

No useful course of action occurred to me. There must have been chaos, confusion and a hell of a racket going on outside but I wasn't aware of any of it. The world had narrowed to just me and two men and a patch of bright sunshine on a stone floor.

This was an extraordinarily long silence. They were holding guns. Discreetly and at their sides, but guns nevertheless. Why hadn't they shot me? Why wasn't I bleeding all over the flagstones? Surely they knew who I was. There was something wrong here.

Stop.

Think.

I knew them but they didn't appear to know me. They couldn't have or I'd be dead by now. Why didn't they know me? They should do. I'd met them at Runnymede. Markham and I had

260

dragged them back to Home Farm. They'd seen our faces. We hadn't tried to hide them. Why didn't they recognise me? And how did they get here?

The answer – when it came – was blindingly obvious. They didn't know me because they hadn't met me yet. Because Markham and I were doing things the wrong way round. We'd made a basic rookie error. We'd assumed everyone was working chronologically – like us – and they weren't.

Yes, yes, of course. That made sense. Of course they'd jump to the Battle of Lincoln first. It's much easier to kill someone during a battle than in a water meadow by the river. These two had probably come for Lady Nicola and Snipers One and Two were almost certainly out there looking for William Marshal.

For some reason – and I could only hope it was something we'd done – did – would do – had done – whatever – their mission here failed and that was why they'd trotted off to Runnymede to implement Plan B. That was why Bridget had been there. To make sure they got it right that time.

Another thought slammed into place. *Tertiary.* She'd ordered everyone to the *tertiary* site. Implying Runnymede had been their second attempt. And this must have been their first. Unbelievably, they didn't yet know who I was. To them, I was exactly what I appeared to be. A contemporary woman on her way to do . . . women's things.

In almost every assignment there's a pivotal moment on which everything hangs and this was it. That these people were using the same channel as St Mary's was a massive coincidence. Almost too massive a coincidence, perhaps. However, let's not look a gift horse in the mouth. I could use this.

Sometimes I do best when I don't stop to think. Acting without rational thought isn't always bad.

I held up one finger in the classic *one moment, please* gesture and tapped my ear.

Markham said, 'Not now, Max. Halfway up a roof.'

'Yes, now,' I said firmly.

The two men stiffened as they realised I'd spoken in English.

'Change of plan,' I said. 'Return to the original frequency.'

'You mean channel.' There was a pause. 'Problem?'

'Change of plan,' I said again. 'Quickly.'

I looked at the men. 'Shan't be a moment. Good job I caught you,' and adjusted my com to its original channel.

'Attention, all. Attention, all. Abort. Abort. Abort. I say again. Abort. Abort. Abort. This mission is terminated. Board authorisation.' I took a chance they already had Runnymede set up, just in case of failure here. 'Rendezvous at the secondary site. Immediate withdrawal. Go.'

I shut down my com. 'Quick,' I said to the men. 'They're all dead up there. I saw an opportunity and took it. They'll be raising the alarm any minute now. I'll tidy up here – you get out while you still can. Move.'

The trick is not to give anyone time to stop and think. No time to say, 'Hang on a minute . . .'

Casting anxious glances over my shoulder at the empty staircase, I moved towards the door. Instinctively they fell back before me.

'You know what to do?' I said.

They nodded.

'Then go. Job done here. Get yourselves to the second site, and for heaven's sake, don't let Marshal escape this time.'

One moved. One stood firm. Bugger. 'Who are you?' he said. 'Identify yourself.'

Dammit – I was going to have to zap them after all, which I really didn't want to do because it was vital they got themselves to Runnymede or we'd be in all sorts of trouble.

And then – believe it or not – the god of historians, so often absent in my life and obviously still not completely up to speed regarding my current employment status – sent me a flash of inspiration.

I drew myself up. 'My name is unimportant. You need only know that I'm from the top floor and a member of the Board. I don't know your names. Would you like that happy state of affairs to continue?'

They were gone almost before I'd finished speaking. I took a deep breath and wobbled my way back to the bottom steps to sit down for a moment.

That had been a very close call. Insight had very nearly got to Lady Nicola. Suppose they'd killed her – killed us all up there – and thrown our bodies down into the town. The uproar and confusion might well have turned the battle.

Speaking of which, a runner arrived – another young lad – hot and panting. Obligingly I stood up to let him pass. He raced up the stairway with a careless speed that made me want to hack his legs off. At the neck.

I hoped Markham understood how important it was to let these Insight people go. How to contact him?

I'm an idiot. This was Markham. He would be waiting to contact me. I switched my com back to our discrete channel.

'. . . you there?' he was saying. 'Come in, Max. Are you there? Are you there?'

'Yes,' I said. 'Let them all go. Don't get in their way.'

'Wasn't going to,' he said, with the air of one settling down to a comfortable gossip. 'What was that all about?'

'Are you safe to talk?'

'I'm on someone's roof, hiding behind a smoke louvre and staying out of the way, so yes. For the time being.'

'We've made a huge mistake.'

'Have we?'

'What are we always telling people about History?'

'Stand well back?'

'You can't change it.'

'Well, yes, we can, but no, we shouldn't.'

All my words were scrambling together as I tried to convey my thoughts in some sort of order. No one knows better than us that things don't always happen in the right sequence. I'm always saying – effect before cause.

'We've made a stupid mistake,' I said, desperate to get him to understand. I trotted down the rough steps cut into the motte and headed towards the open East Gate, sidestepping to avoid a stream of running men. 'We worked in chronological order – they didn't. We did 1215 then 1217 – they've done it the other way around. *That's* why they were yammering about a woman in a brown dress when we got to Runnymede. Because they met me here first. I took a chance. I bluffed. I've cancelled the mission and sent them off to Runnymede. Sometime between here and there they compare notes – with Bridget, probably – and realise they've been conned. We have to let them get out of here so we can arrest them at Runnymede or we're in deep shit.'

There was a long silence as he thought about this. 'Get yourself to the pod, Max. The battle's nearly won but it's going to be hell on earth afterwards. We both know what the royalist troops will do to the town.'

'The same goes for you,' I said. 'The snipers will have withdrawn by now and there's no point sitting quietly on the roof if the house is burning beneath you. Thatch goes up like a torch, you know.'

'I do know and I shall join you at the earliest opportunity, trust me. Go and put the kettle on and run a duster over the place so it's all nice when I get back.'

'On second thoughts,' I said, 'stay where you are. Thatch hardly burns at all.'

The siege was raised. Roaring men were pouring into the streets because now the castle was a secure base from which to attack. I stepped aside and took a look around. The wounded were helping each other back in through the gate. More serious cases were being laid out in the shade of the wall. Time passed and still no sign of the young master. You have to ask yourself, how long does it take to climb down off someone's roof?

I opened my com. 'Where are you?'

No response.

For heaven's sake – if it wasn't one of us, it was the other.

Carefully I switched to the Insight channel and listened. Just static. No coms were open. There was no one there.

I walked to the gate and looked out. The fighting was fanning out from the square to the streets, leaving bodies, badly wounded men, piles of detritus, abandoned weapons and riderless horses. Faintly, I could smell smoke. Traditional après-battle behaviour. Looting and burning.

I made my way around the very edge of the square, from

doorway to doorway, until I found a gap between two houses, wide enough for me and too narrow for a horseman. The world was suddenly cold. Even bright May sunshine couldn't make it into this narrow space. The alley smelled of piss and mould. Green slime grew up the sides of the houses and the bare earth was sticky, dragging at my shoes as I walked. At least I hoped it was earth, although I wasn't optimistic. I sighed and hoisted my skirts out of something unspeakable. Why was I doing this? Instead of sitting in my quiet, shady pod and enjoying a nice cup of tea, I was slithering my way down Shit Alley in pursuit of an idiot last heard of crouching behind someone's smoke louvre.

I looked for some way to access the rooftops. Aha – a lean-to with a sloping roof. I climbed on to an old stool which might have been placed there just for that purpose and scrambled ungracefully up. There was a tiny window in the house wall. No glass, just vertical wooden slats, but it was a perfect foothold. I heaved myself up and looked around at a sea of rooftops, all of different heights and angles and materials. Most had smoke holes so that was something else to watch out for. A few of the larger, more imposing buildings had louvres over theirs. To keep the rain out. And prevent careless historians falling in.

I edged very slowly and very carefully along a roof I thought would give me a good viewpoint. Yes, all right, there was a socking great castle over there and a socking great cathedral over there, but without any ground to refer to, it was hard to get any sense of direction. Plus, I couldn't proceed in a direct line because some roofs were either inaccessible or looked to be in too fragile a condition to support my weight. And my skirts didn't help.

I crouched in some sort of gutter between two houses. I don't think it was supposed to be a gutter – it was just an area where two roofs met, all clogged up with mouldy straw and old birds' nests. But it was a useful crouching place and so I crouched.

Any minute now, William Marshal would be riding through the East Gate to meet with Lady Nicola. There would be rejoicing and congratulations, and then he'd be off to Nottingham to take the good news to King Henry. I was hoping for a glimpse. Just for once, I might actually have a good view of a major historical event in contemporary time. A bit of a treat for me.

At that moment Markham appeared on the roof over to my right, climbing across a flattish surface lined with wooden planks grey with age.

I stood up and waved. He stood up and waved. We grinned at each other. Two battle-hardened professionals enjoying the moment. A job well done. In complete control of ourselves and the situation. I could taste the tea already.

And then – without warning – he disappeared from view.

O . . . K.

For a second, I was too stunned to move. I started working my way towards the place I'd last seen him – without looking where I was putting my feet, obviously – somehow lost my balance and began to slither down a steeper than usual roof. Something went crack and then I was slipping on the mouldy thatch and heading rapidly towards the edge. The thatch smelled of wet rats. Don't ask me how I know that.

I somehow jumped the very narrow gap between my roof and his, landed as softly as I could and looked around.

Oh, for God's sake. The silly sod had fallen straight through the smoke hole.

As I saw it, he fell through the smoke hole because he wasn't looking where he was going. He maintains he was turning in his usual stellar performance when the roof collapsed underneath him. Which – since he has the body mass of a moth – trust me, is unlikely.

He was making a hell of a racket. Crashing and banging and cursing. And an odd sort of metallic bonging noise. I suspect the only reason no one came to investigate was that no one could hear him over the celebrations taking place in the streets around us.

The city was being sacked. That's what happens when you're on the losing team. You're fair game. This was their punishment for supporting the rebels. I could hear the crash of doors being kicked in as soldiers swarmed into the houses looking for anything valuable. No one and nothing was spared. That's why it's always referred to as the Lincoln Fair – because of the amount of plunder seized and the good time had by the winning team.

Most of the townspeople had long since fled and as far as I could see all these houses were standing empty. But probably not for long.

I hitched up my skirt and crawled carefully across the roof

on all fours because it was quicker and easier – although a lot less dignified. I tried to ease my way around the saggy bits – very unsuccessfully as it turned out, because without even the courtesy of a warning groan, the whole roof sagged beneath me and then collapsed in a shower of rotten timbers and straw.

I grabbed at something – don't ask me what – and for a second I hung, swaying to and fro like a pendulum in a high wind. I tried to struggle for a better grip and that only made things worse. The timber slid through my hands leaving splinters and pain in its wake. I couldn't hold on any longer. I shut my eyes – because that always helps – and landed with a crash on something soft.

I think we can all guess who.

The language was horrendous.

I scrambled to my feet, adjusted my clothing, peered through the gloom and said cautiously, 'Is that you?'

There was a lot more bad language along the lines of *who did I think it would bloody well be?*

'What's that noise?'

There were more hollow metallic noises. And more bad language. 'Now look what's happened.'

'How can I? I can't see a bloody thing. Come outside.'

I groped my way to the door, pulled it open, and staggered out into the now setting sunlight.

He followed me out.

I collapsed in helpless laughter.

He had a metal pot stuck on his foot and he wasn't happy. 'Stop messing about and do something useful, will you?'

I opened my mouth to make a really clever remark about a mess of pottage but thought better of it.

'I put my swiving foot in it in the dark and now I can't swiving get it out.'

'Course you can. If it went in, it'll come out. Sit down.'

He sat down on the step and lifted his leg. I tugged. Nope – it wasn't coming off.

'Well,' I said heartlessly. 'You've really put your foot in it, haven't you?'

Which gives you a pretty fair indication of the standards of humour prevailing both in and out of St Mary's. 'Good job you didn't get it stuck on your head because then you'd be a pothead.'

I nearly had to sit down over that one. Lovers of sophisticated humour and witty repartee should move on to the next chapter now because it's not going to get any better.

'I can't walk around like this. Give it another go.'

I did. Because actually, the situation was more serious than I was letting on. If I couldn't get it off him then there was a very good chance the pod wouldn't jump. A medieval cauldron was just the sort of thing the onboard sensors would pick up. Markham actually wearing the thing wouldn't make it any more acceptable.

I broke it to him gently. 'I'll have to leave you behind to die alone.'

'I'm not staying here.'

'Or chop your foot off.'

'Not an option.'

'David Sands manages.'

'Could you be more constructive?'

I thought hard. 'No.'

'This is your fault.'

'How? How can you being stupid enough to put your foot in a pot be my fault? You're the idiot here. In fact, you're a tosspot.'

And off I went again.

A group of three or four men turned into the alley, paused in a manner I didn't much care for, and then headed towards us.

'Shit,' said Markham, attempting to get to his feet.

'Stay there,' I said. 'Leave this to me.'

I put my hands on my hips and stood squarely in their path.

'Thank heavens,' I said, raising my hands skywards. And, incidentally, checking my stun gun was still up my sleeve. And yes, I was speaking in English but spouse-slagging-off is common to all languages. They stared at me, not understanding a word, but, I hoped, definitely getting the gist. Time to make them grateful they weren't married to me.

I gestured at Markham. 'Look at what this clodhopping fop-doodle has done. I take my eye off him for one moment and see what happens. Did you ever, in all your born days, meet such a sottish, quisby cumberworld?'

'Steady on,' said Markham, shocked. I ignored him.

'I swear he's nought but a harecop. A raggabrash. A scob-berlotcher from the day I married him. Shame it's not on his head. Do any of you have an axe?'

They were laughing at us both. We might get away with this.

'Loiter-sack,' shouted Markham, who has a head start on the world when it comes to insults in any century.

'What?' I screamed. 'Wandought.'

'Fustylugs. Driggle-draggle,' he roared, getting into his stride.

'Bollock-brained moron,' I yelled, reverting to modern times.

By this point I rather hoped the men would have gone away in search of more beer and younger women. I should be so lucky. Two of them seized Markham and hauled him to his feet.

'I've got my stun gun,' I said. 'You kick them with your pot.'

Laughing and shouting jokes I fortunately didn't understand, they hauled Markham away down the alley, leaving me alone.

'Seriously,' I shouted after them. 'What about me?'

Oh, the shame of it. If we ever got out of this, I was going to have to kill Markham to stop him spreading the story. On the other hand, he had a cauldron on his foot, so it wasn't really a shining hour for either of us.

If they were taking us away to be killed, then it was a bloody long way to go. We staggered up and down a couple of alley-ways – twice in some cases. They were very drunk.

'Just go with it, Max,' sang Markham under the guise of a drinking song. 'Let's see where they take us.'

Believe it or not – they took us to a smith.

His smithy was a square space where three buildings met. The floor was of stone, supporting his anvil. Horseshoes and odd bits of metal hung from hooks and were piled against the walls. A giant pile of firewood stood ready for use. A sturdy roof on four thick posts covered everything. That was about all I had time to take in.

The smith wasn't a big man – not much taller than me – but his shoulders and arms were massive. He was bare-chested but wore a scorched and stained leather apron. He was sitting with three or four friends around a dying fire. A small boy sat nearby. The bellows boy, I guessed.

A peaceful scene. Whatever was going on elsewhere was nothing to do with them. A good smith is a valuable member of society. I wondered if he'd worked for both sides.

272

Markham was presented with much hilarity. No one even looked at me, so for once in my life I thought I'd shut up and let the men sort it out.

On the other hand, the smith was pissed as a newt. Two newts, actually. As he lurched to his feet, he managed to kick an empty flagon across the floor. One of many.

'Um . . .' said Markham.

I stood just outside, because smithies were the domain of men, and pushed up my sleeve so I could get to my stun gun if I needed to. Although there were five – no, six – of them, and I'm not bloody Wonder Woman. I decided if everything kicked off, I'd take out the small boy.

Another flagon was found and everyone had a go at that one – even Markham. I didn't blame him. Having guzzled some evil rotgut, they hoisted him up, still enpotted, in their arms. Someone laid his foot on the anvil.

'No,' he wailed. As did I. I couldn't see this ending at all well.

The smith picked up a hammer the size of Mjölnir, examined it closely and then discarded it in favour of something that looked as if it could fell a large elephant.

'No,' I said, starting forwards, because this wasn't funny any longer.

One of the men caught my arm and pulled me back, shaking his head.

'But . . .' I said.

The smith swung. The anvil rang. Markham yelled. I screamed. The men cheered the mighty blow. The pot fell to the floor in two pieces. The flagon went round again. I had a swig this time because enamel on your teeth isn't anything like as important as dentists would have you believe.

Gently, they set Markham on his feet. 'I don't feel very well,' he said feebly.

'I don't blame you,' I said, clinging to him for support.

'Is my foot still attached?'

'It is. Did it hurt very much?'

'Not at all. I didn't feel a thing. Are you sure it's still there? Perhaps that's why I'm not feeling any pain.'

'Either that or the stuff you were drinking,' I said. 'Would you like me to take you home now?'

He turned pitiful eyes on me. 'Yes, please.'

Turning to the smith, he bowed low. As did I. That had been some blow.

I drew his arm firmly through mine. 'Time to go.'

We backed out of the smithy and turned in the direction of the castle.

As we left, their laughter echoed off the walls.

'Another century we can never go back to,' said Markham, gloomily.

Just a quick footnote to that rather shameful episode – we were both nearly run over by William Marshal as he made his triumphant entry into the castle. You have to ask yourself – where's the gratitude? And – silly old fool – he hadn't learned anything from the day because he'd taken his helmet off again. To reassure his followers, perhaps, although I suspected just seventy-year-old bravado. He was a game old boy. And he wasn't finished yet. He had a few years still to go.

His long hair was yellowy white and he had a surprising amount of it, given his age. More than John, anyway. His beard was also full and long. He rode through the streets with his clenched fist raised, acknowledging the nearly hysterical cheers.

Lady Nicola stood at the now wide-open East Gate, her veil blowing gently around her. He dismounted and strode to meet her. It was rather sweet, actually. He bowed his head and kissed her hand. She touched his cheek. And then he straightened up, took her arm and the two of them walked in triumph through the gate. I could hear cheering ringing around the bailey.

We followed them in. Well, we joined the crowd who followed them in, but I did feel a little of the reflected glory was ours.

The pod was exactly where we'd left it. No giant boulder had landed on it, which was a relief.

I hadn't realised it was so late. The day seemed to have flown by and now long shadows were stretching across the bailey. All the gates were open. There was a constant stream of people in and out of the castle grounds.

It was only as we approached the pod that I realised I'd lost my basket. I genuinely had no idea where I could possibly have left it. Pennyroyal takes a very dim view of lost equipment so I made a spirited attempt to blame Markham, claiming he had it last. He responded in kind and I'd like to think it was our very public argument that got us across the bailey with no trouble at all. No one even looked at us. The rebels had mostly been rounded up and were awaiting the king's justice. I wasn't sure what would happen to them. Most had surrendered. If William Marshal was clever, he wouldn't begin the new king's reign with mass beheadings and hangings.

When I was at St Mary's, we normally finished every

assignment with a quick cup of tea – unless we'd been running for our lives, obviously – during which I'd carry out the headcount and wound inspection. There would be tall stories, exaggeration and mockery.

There was none of that today. I think both of us were fairly shattered. We'd both fallen through a roof. Markham had invented a new kind of footwear. I'd been set on fire and had to climb nearly every set of steps in the castle. Time to go home, as I think everyone will agree.

I was conscious of a certain amount of apprehension over the return trip and noticed Markham unobtrusively easing himself out of vomiting range. I checked over the coordinates one last time, crossed my fingers, and the world went white.

24

Finally, we were back at Home Farm.

I leaned over the console, pretending to shut things down while I waited for the world to stop spinning. Various read-outs blurred and faded. If Markham asked me to report, I wouldn't have a bloody clue.

His silence spoke volumes.

'It's nothing,' I said, eventually. 'I haven't eaten all day and I had a couple of mouthfuls of that rotgut stuff. Still – that's soon remedied. Come on, let's go and find our employers.'

We left the pod and Markham hit the keypad to get us access to the house. I followed him into the hall.

Home Farm greeted us with total silence. The sort of silence that says there's no one home.

Markham stood still.

'There's something wrong,' he said.

'No,' I said, a few minutes behind the world as usual. 'It's just a slight dizzy spell.'

'They're not here. They should be back by now.'

I blinked and looked around. 'Not necessarily. And they could be back at any moment. Have they left a message?'

'Not that I can see.'

Smallhope, Pennyroyal, Markham and I had ways of communicating with each other which I can't mention here, and none of them had been utilised. On the other hand, nothing was out of place. There were no signs of anything untoward having happened. Certainly no return visit from Insight.

I looked around. 'Is it possible they've been offered a better-paying job and abandoned us?'

'No,' Markham said. 'They wouldn't do that,' and he sounded so confident I knew he was worried. '1848 is probably taking longer than they thought and they're not back yet.'

That might well be the case. Pennyroyal and Smallhope certainly had the more complicated assignment. The revolutions of 1848 were sometimes known as the Springtime of Nations. Everyone was at it. Over fifty countries were affected in one way or another. In France, the monarchy was overthrown. Again. I really don't know why they bothered to unpack. Germany and Italy were each moving towards becoming unified countries at last. After a series of uprisings, Austria had to introduce a more liberal constitution and grant Hungary and Czechoslovakia more autonomy. It was a year of massive change for everyone and I was certain that Insight would be in there somewhere, seeking to tweak History to their advantage.

But I had every confidence in Smallhope and Pennyroyal. Between them, they had the entire social spectrum covered. I suspected they had talents, abilities and resources we didn't know anything about. And besides, however long it took them shouldn't make a difference. The return coordinates had been agreed. Even if they'd been in 1848 for ten years they should still be here. Unless they were dead. That really wasn't something I wanted to contemplate.

'In that case,' I said, 'and lacking instructions to the contrary – shower, shit, shave and straight back out again. We'll meet them in 1605 instead.'

'Let's get something to eat first. And for God's sake, put some cream on your nose, Max – you'll have to account for your sunburn on Monday.'

Markham crashed around in the kitchen while I went off to see to the pod.

I set everything to charge so we could career around the timeline with full power. It wasn't going to solve our drifting problem. I'd be extra careful with the coordinates, but if the pod took it into its head to dump us in China 1483 instead of London 1605 there wouldn't be much I could do about it. And I might not even be able to get us back home again afterwards. I remembered the time when Leon and I had been leaping around the timeline on the run from the Time Police – he'd been almost continually under the console fixing something or other.

I dropped to my knees, pulled out the first board, stared at it in complete incomprehension and told myself to put it back before I made things even worse.

I emptied and refilled the tanks as appropriate, topped up the Turd Tumbler, checked the lockers, swept the floor and used my sleeve to dust down the console, because if you can't be accurate, at least you can be clean and tidy. We might end up in the middle of nowhere but at least we'd be able to have a comfortable crap when we got there. Although not me – wrong time of year.

Markham had done eggs, bacon and fried potatoes. Every mouthful was bloody wonderful. As I've said before, he's not a bad cook – although, in our dim and distant youth, he'd once made a stew in which, he said, the main ingredient had been a recently discarded placenta. He'd been having us on – he has a very strange sense of humour – but that's definitely not something you want to hear. Especially when you're halfway through what, up until that moment, had been a delicious bowl of stew. Or do I mean a bowl of delicious stew? Anyway, Major Guthrie had walloped him round the head with a spoon and it must have done him some good because we'd never had placenta stew since.

I tucked in. There's something about fatty, salty, cholesterol-laden food that does you the world of good even if you haven't been investigating major historical events in a wonky pod. I was a new woman. I also made a mental note to take some cheese with me when we next jumped, in case I had a funny five minutes again.

Markham locked all the doors and windows, set the security alarms and we went off for a nap. Because it's not when you leave – it's when you arrive that's important. We could actually have gone off and enjoyed a three-week holiday in the Seychelles – well, I certainly would have – before setting out to foil yet another dastardly scheme, but I very much doubt Pennyroyal would have been happy to see that on this month's expenses claim. I could hear him now: 'You are not an MP, Dr Maxwell.'

I climbed the stairs, enjoyed a long hot shower and fell into bed. Obviously if I was a heroine, I'd have lain awake fretting, but I'm not so I didn't. Just for once I was asleep almost instantly. And I don't think heroines snore.

And I bet they don't have to go to work on Monday, either.

*

Scorched patches and burn holes aside, the brown dress still looked moderately respectable. Cooking over open fires meant many people's clothes were covered in tiny holes and grease stains so I shouldn't stand out too much in Jacobean England.

I found a full black cloak in the costume room – because it would be November, after all – and tied a plain white scarf around my head. The previously despised mob cap went on over the top and I wore my own boots again. The effect wasn't that bad.

Markham would be unable to get by with his mid-calf tunic. Doublets, hose and trousers were now in – tunics were definitely out unless you were some sort of yokel from the country. Perfectly possible in his case but it would certainly draw attention in the centre of fashionable London. He was now a vision in knee-length trousers and muttering about it. There was no hose available so he'd gone with long socks which looked odd, but, believe me, he's appeared in worse. A close-fitting jacket with a pointed waist and floppy hat completed his ensemble.

'How do I look?' he said, surveying himself in the mirror.

I patted his arm to reassure him. 'It's not rose. Just keep remembering that.'

We locked up and reset the security system.

I was doubtful. 'Should we leave a message? Tell them where we've gone?'

He shook his head. 'They know our schedule. Runnymede. Lincoln. House of Lords. They'll find us somehow.'

'If they can. This isn't like them. Perhaps we should . . .'

'If the worst really has happened, do you want to meet the people who were able to take down Pennyroyal and Smallhope?'

'Good thought,' I said, and we set off for the pod.

*

281

I did everything I could to ensure a safe and accurate landing. Sadly, I failed across the board. Not only were we in the wrong time and the wrong place but whatever was wrong with me manifested itself in an unexpected but spectacular bout of projectile vomiting, after which I fell out of my seat.

I lay on the floor. Here it came again. A great, greasy wave of disorientation. My eyes were closed but that didn't help. I could still see. One London was superimposed over another over another over another like an image in a series of mirrors disappearing off into the distance and I was swept away.

The Great Fire of 1666 exploded before my eyes in a roaring dance of orange and crimson flames. Everything was ablaze. The heat seared me. I could feel my skin crisp. At the same time, the icy waters of the Thames closed over my head. I couldn't reach the surface no matter how hard I struggled. A giant weight was pulling me down into the dark depths as I ran and ran and ran. Dear God, how I ran. My footsteps echoed off the dank brick walls that hemmed me in. There was no way out. And all the time he was behind me. Above me. In front of me. Waiting for me. In fact – he'd never gone away.

The alleyway ended in a brick wall. I turned to face him.

He was exactly as I remembered. Man-shaped. A bloodless thing. His damp skin glistened. Like a huge white slug. His hands were as big as shovels, the thick, yellow nails still caked with Kal's blood. And mine. His eyes were dark. They reflected nothing. His face was all wrong. The much too big mouth was halfway up his face. The chin was long, pointed and not symmetrical. His nose was set off to one side. I could smell bad earth and blood. My stomach clenched in fear. The Ripper was here and he had found me. Finally, he had found me.

My face burned with sudden familiar pain. Almost forgotten scars throbbed. I'd always known this day would come. That one day he would find me again. That we would face each other and my nightmares would come true.

And then he moved. Faster than sight. One minute he was lurking in the corner of my eye and the next he was right in front of me. I reached for my knife. I stabbed. I slashed. As hard and fast as I could. There was a sharp pain in my forearm, lancing all the way down through my wrist and into my thumb. My hand went numb. No matter how I struggled I just couldn't hold on to the knife any longer. It fell from my hand. I heard it hit the floor. I was defenceless.

I couldn't get my arms free. I needed to get my arms free. I struggled but he was strong. I was crushed in his grip. I struggled again, kicking out, headbutting, biting, frantic in my efforts to break free and run. Run until I could no longer put one foot in front of the other.

In the distance, I could hear Markham's voice. He was talking. His voice was all around me. I tried to tell him he should get away. He kept talking over me. He should get out. While he still could. This thing was hideously dangerous. He knew that. Why was he still here?

I heard my name. Was he calling me for help? I should respond. I stopped struggling and began to make out individual words.

'It's all right, Max. You're here with me. You're still in the pod. We're on the floor. And one of my legs has gone to sleep because you're not light and it hurts like hell. We'll be talking about that later. You're in London, 1605. You're having a bit of a moment. Just breathe. Ground yourself. Find your centre and breathe. In and out. That's fine. Just keep still and breathe. And don't worry about my leg – it'll probably be fine. It's all right, Max. You're safe. It's all good.'

A long white face swam in front of mine. I struggled in the water, enveloped in flames.

'It's me, Max. I've got you. You're safe. You're fine. I'm here. Keep still now. I don't want to have to hurt you again.'

Where was I? Where was I at this specific moment? My eyes said one thing, my brain another, my body something else. And then I was falling. I was upside down. I reached out, groping for something to hold on to, and a warm hand grabbed mine. 'I've got you, Max. Steady now. Just breathe.'

And then I was back. I was in Leon's pod. Sitting on the floor. Markham had one arm clamping me to him and the other grasped my hand. Gradually, things sorted themselves. I was the right way up. I was here. I was Max. I wasn't drowning or burning and the thing from my nightmares had gone. My head rested against Markham's shoulder. I could smell the dry-cleaning chemicals on his jacket. Feel the rough material under my cheek. My heartbeat slowed. My thoughts unjangled themselves. I was aware of myself and my surroundings again.

Slowly he let me go. I stayed on the floor because there was no going anywhere at the moment. I could barely function. I didn't even want a cup of tea. Anything hitting my stomach was going to make the return trip at the speed of light. There was a pool of vomit on the floor which Markham cleared up. He was such a hero. I know this because he told me so. Three or four times.

My knife was still on the floor. He picked it up and gave it back. 'How's your arm? Sorry about that but you were about

284

to slit me from gut to gizzard. Good move, by the way. Did the major teach you that? Close your eyes for a moment and I'll help you into your seat.'

I did as I was told and muttered, 'Sorry.'

'Not a problem,' he said cheerfully. 'Although if you'd upchucked all over me then there would have been a row. We're a long way from the nearest laundrette.'

He bustled about, giving me the space I needed. Slowly, turning my head as little as possible, I scanned the console. Where things did not get any better.

'We're early,' I said in despair. 'Far, far too early. I was aiming for the second or third of November and it's only the 26th October. That's ten days to wait. The longer we stay here, the greater our chances of either being discovered by someone or offed by the Insight people. I'm not even sure we have enough supplies for ten days.'

'Relax,' he said soothingly. 'You'll think of something. In fact, you sit quietly and make a start with the thinking and I'll have a firkle around the rations and find you something to eat. Soup, perhaps. Did you think to pack cheese?'

I nodded.

'OK, you sit tight and surround yourself with historian mystique. Or take a nap – it's not always easy for us lesser mortals to tell the difference.'

I'd printed out everything we needed at Home Farm, not wanting to run down the power by using the computer unnecessarily. Carefully I spread my maps and documents across the console and tried to reassemble all my scattered thoughts.

Right. Concentrate. 1605. The old queen, Elizabeth, was dead and the first Scottish king of England, James I (or VI depending on which nation was claiming him), was the new kid on the block.

He'd inherited a country still riven by religious dissent – and also the country that had murdered his mother, Mary Stuart. It seemed strange to think that I might have seen as much of his mother as he had. He was only thirteen months old when he was crowned king after her abdication.

James came to the English throne in 1604. To be a Catholic in England at this time was to lead a restricted life. Public positions were closed to them. They were forbidden Mass. Attendance at Protestant churches was compulsory. On his succession, however, James seemed moderately well disposed towards his Catholic subjects and there was a general feeling of optimism.

That didn't last. Parliament re-enacted Elizabeth's anti-Catholic legislation. There was great outrage at what was seen as James's betrayal and the conspiracy was born.

The leaders were Robert Catesby, a popular and charismatic young man, together with Thomas Percy, Francis Tresham and, of course, their explosives man, Guy Fawkes.

In our modern times of massive security surrounding anything even remotely official, it seems strange that Thomas Percy was able to lease a house right next door to the Palace of Westminster. Large areas of the palace were open to the public. Ordinary people actually lived there, carried on their trades there, and generally wandered about as they pleased. Anything could be bought or sold at Westminster. Nothing really changes, does it?

Guy Fawkes would live in Percy's house in his role as John Johnson, Percy's servant. To cover all his frequent comings and goings, he would put it about that Percy's wife was joining her husband and the house was to be got ready for her.

Catesby found himself a house on the south bank almost directly opposite the palace and was able, slowly, to amass at least thirty-six kegs of gunpowder.

By yet another massive stroke of luck – they really must have thought God was on their side – a coal merchant was vacating the undercroft directly under the House of Lords. Again, Percy grabbed the lease and now the way was clear for Catesby to begin to ferry the gunpowder across the Thames. Every day he rowed himself across the river, bringing just a few barrels at a time. No one noticed one small rowing boat among the many hundreds of boats trading up and down the river every day.

Estimates of the exact number of barrels vary but thirty-six seems a consistent number. Depending on their size, thirty-six barrels equals at least one ton of gunpowder and very probably a lot more.

Had the conspirators succeeded, the effects of the explosion would have been massive. The undercroft walls were nine feet thick so the force of the blast would have been channelled upwards. Like a fireworks factory. The House of Lords was directly above. Everyone would have been killed and the building completely destroyed. Vapourised, probably. No one would have stood any chance of survival.

And this was the fiendish bit – it wouldn't have been just the king who was killed, but his two sons as well, including the future Charles I. Also present for the opening of Parliament would be the archbishops and bishops of the land, plus all the judges and peers of the realm, together with their assistants, clerks, recorders and advisors. Imagine this country – any country – with its entire ruling class wiped out in the same instant. Yes, tempting, I know, but think of the power vacuum. And then think what would move in to take its place.

And not just the House of Lords. Westminster Hall and Westminster Abbey would have been destroyed. Along with all the surrounding buildings, taverns, shops, alleyways, houses, stables – everything. Together with the hundreds of ordinary people who lived in the area. Merchants, clergymen, labourers, tradesmen, shopkeepers, servants, families, ordinary members of the public who just happened to be passing at the time. Plus horses, dogs, cats, rats – everything.

There would have been a vast smoking crater left behind which almost certainly would have filled with water as the River Thames rushed in. Those who had survived the blast and the subsequent inferno would drown.

And that would have been only the beginning. With the usual tolerance shown by one religious group towards a different religious group, there would have been a massive Protestant backlash. Catholics – men, women and children – would have been dragged out of hiding and massacred on the spot. Hundreds, possibly thousands, of people would have been killed. There would have been decades and decades of bloody murder.

It might have been at this point that one or two of the more thoughtful conspirators began to have second thoughts. Especially Francis Tresham, a close relative of Lord Monteagle who, as a member of the aristocracy, would certainly be attending the opening of Parliament on 5th November – that fateful day.

What happens next is a mystery. On 4th November, a letter was delivered – anonymously – to Lord Monteagle at his house in Hoxton, warning him to stay away. The letter doesn't specify why.

Monteagle immediately took the letter to Sir Robert Cecil, the Secretary of State, who, despite being quite a bright bloke and in possession of an extremely sophisticated intelligence network, had no idea what was going on literally right under his nose.

He raced to the king, who had just returned from a hunting trip, and at nearly midnight, the day before Parliament was due to be opened, the premises were searched. Not tremendously efficiently, it would seem, because they didn't find the thirty-six barrels of gunpowder. Easily missed, I suppose. They did, however, discover an enormous amount of firewood, and fortunately this did arouse suspicion and the guards were sent back to search again.

This time they found the barrels, together with poor old Guy Fawkes, cloaked and spurred, all ready to light the slow fuse and ride like the devil.

That's how close the gunpowder conspirators came. Either to success or utter catastrophe, depending on your point of view.

The rest is History. The plot was smashed. Catesby's plans to capture the Princess Elizabeth and set her up as a puppet monarch came to nothing. And probably never would have anyway since the lady later declared she would rather have died with her father and brothers than fall in with his schemes. In fact, the lady would probably have put a musket ball through him at the first opportunity.

I was lost in thought when Markham thrust some soup at me. Wading through this lot and sorting it into chronological sequence had calmed my mind a little and I was feeling better. I took the soup, said thank you, and sat back to have a think.

Insight would undoubtedly have access to the exact same information. Someone like me would have studied the evidence and looked for a weak spot. There's always a weak spot that can be exploited. Somewhere you can point your finger and say, 'If this doesn't happen at the right time . . .'

Or, 'If he misses that rendezvous . . .'

Or, 'If this marriage doesn't take place . . .'

. . . then the whole of History will be changed. We'd just seen that with John at Runnymede and Nicola at Lincoln and now here in London. And the weak spot here was blindingly, glaringly obvious.

The letter to Monteagle. Supposedly written by Francis Tresham although there's no evidence.

If that letter is never delivered then the plot will succeed. As simple as that. Cecil and the authorities were completely ignorant of the conspirators and their plans. The letter was the key. All Insight had to do was literally shoot the messenger, destroy the letter and nothing would ever have been the same again.

And we'd arrived dangerously early. And dangerously in the wrong place. I'd aimed for further along the river and out of the immediate blast zone, but here we were right on top of things, actually within the precincts of Westminster itself. If I opened the door and it wasn't too foggy then I could probably catch a glimpse of the House of Lords from here. Should we get this wrong, then it might not be just the king and Parliament blown to smithereens.

I sighed. Nothing's easy, is it?

25

The only good thing about our current position was that we were on the right side of the river. In 1605 there was still only one way across the Thames and that was by London Bridge. There was a gate at the south end – the Stone Gate – where they displayed the parboiled heads of traitors, setting them on pikes as a gentle warning to anyone who might be contemplating anything treasonous. I really don't know why pictures of the parboiled heads of traitors sprang into my mind at that particular moment, but if this all went tits up and they closed the bridge then at least we wouldn't find ourselves stuck on the wrong side of the river and unable to return to the pod.

'Because we'd be dead,' said the part of my brain not currently occupied with the parboiled heads of traitors.

For God's sake, Maxwell – focus.

The downside was that we were far, far too close to the danger zone and if the gunpowder went up, then so would the pod, and that explosion would take out the half of London that hadn't been flattened in the original blast. And if anyone survived that, then the accompanying radiation would certainly finish them off.

'Probably best we don't let that happen,' said Markham when I casually mentioned this. 'Now, about this letter . . .'

'There must be a letter,' I said, urgently. 'It's how the conspiracy will be discovered. Cecil had no idea any of this was going on and if the letter is never delivered then History will be . . .' I struggled. Altered? Changed? Completely rewritten? None of those words conveyed the vast extent of the implications. Large numbers of people's ancestors would be wiped out. Possibly even some of mine.

The only one who probably would escape was Markham, who had sidestepped History in 1483 only to reappear some time in the future. He'd probably be OK, but everyone else . . .

Why would Insight be doing this? There was a more than equal chance they themselves wouldn't exist – at least not in their current form. We could be looking at the grandfather of all grandfather paradoxes.

Although not necessarily. There have been many theories about time travel.

Some people say you can't change the past because it's already happened and it is, therefore, unchangeable.

Some say you can change the past but those changes are already built in and therefore any action is unnecessary.

Then there's the retro-suicide paradox, the Hitler paradox, the Bootstrap paradox, and many others. We'd studied them all during training in my early days at St Mary's and I could barely remember any of it. It's all gone the same way as *the angle on the hypotenuse is* . . . something or other.

I know the Time Police rely heavily on the *Don't meddle with things man was not meant to understand* as part of their *Let's frighten everyone to death now and then we won't have to bother shooting them later* public awareness scheme. The one they take round schools to educate young people on the evils of time travel. Just say no, kids.

Anyway, years and years ago, the parallel universe idea began to gain some headway, was subsequently disproved, raised its head again, was disproved again and is currently hovering on the borders of mainstream thinking. Basically, it says that should a time traveller kill their own grandfather – in the course of time travel, obviously, not just because his grandfather was getting on his nerves – then it's not his real grandfather he kills but a grandfather from a parallel universe. The universe protects itself from paradox by ensuring the original universe remains unaltered and all changes take place in parallel universes.

I always keep my head down and my mouth shut during these sorts of discussions. I myself am no stranger to parallel universes. What can I say? We all have our secrets.

Anyway, perhaps this theory had once again become part of mainstream thinking and this could be Insight's approach. That whatever action they took – whatever event they influenced – whoever they killed – they could do that because it wasn't affecting their own universe. Did they think they could hack their way through History with impunity because an obliging universe would create a series of alternative worlds to accommodate these changes? All very well if they were right – disaster for everyone if they were wrong.

Except – and I'm aware I'm on very dodgy scientific ground here – there are nasty little things called bubble universes and they're really bad news.

Bubble universes are a bit like scabs. They form to protect the timeline. Having done that, they disappear because the job's done. Universe corrected – by the Time Police, usually – the scab flakes off, leaving the nice, pink, shiny, unharmed universe underneath. Unless you're me, of course, notorious scab-picker, and make a mess and get an infection and everyone shouts at you.

Anyway, setting all that aside, the really bad news is that if you're in said bubble universe at the time it disappears then so do you. You don't die – because that implies a cause of death – you simply cease to be. And it's not quick and painless. The bubble universe contracts, getting smaller and smaller until you're the last thing in it, scrabbling for a toehold, watching your feet, your legs, everything fade from view, sucking in one last, desperate breath, and then – poof – you're gone.

The Time Police deal with bubble universes all the time and they say there's nothing you can do to prevent their slow annihilation. The only thing to do is get out – asap.

I looked around. Markham and I could be in a bubble universe now. One which might roll up and disappear at any moment.

Or something could change the course of History and we could be caught in a massive explosion as thirty-six barrels of gunpowder prematurely blow the guts out of the city.

Or we could both be captured and executed as traitors.

Or Insight could turn up and kill us both.

Or . . .

Stop it. Stop it right now, Maxwell. You're here to do a job. Get on with it and leave the universe and the timeline to look after themselves.

'Eat your cheese,' said Markham. 'You're looking weird again.'

I sighed. Back to our current dilemma. 'The Monteagle letter was delivered, anonymously, on 4th November.'

He nodded. 'And Monteagle takes it to Cecil who takes it to the king. Who had been away hunting.'

I said slowly, 'Let's assume Insight's plan is to intercept the letter. Because without that warning, the gunpowder plot would almost certainly have succeeded.'

'What are you suggesting?'

'How do you mean?'

'Come on, Max – this is you. Don't tell me you haven't had a Brilliant Idea.'

'I might have.'

'And it is?'

I sat up straight. 'We deliver the letter ourselves. Early. As soon as possible, in fact. Before the Insight people even turn up. Perhaps our arriving so early is actually a Good Thing. We have time to manoeuvre.'

He looked uneasy but I pressed on.

'Look, once Monteagle has that letter, he'll go straight to Cecil. Once that letter is in Cecil's possession, there isn't anything anyone can do to prevent the plot collapsing. Insight will no longer have any control over events. The king is warned. The undercroft will be searched. The plot will fail. Everything happens exactly as it should, except it happens a few days early. Which, given the alternative, I think we could all live with.'

'All right,' Markham said, slowly. 'Yes. Good as far as it goes. Except – how do we get our hands on a letter that hasn't been written yet? Especially when we don't know who writes it.'

I looked at him. 'We write the letter ourselves.'

He opened his mouth – presumably to say don't be so bloody stupid – and then closed it again as he thought it through.

'That . . . might . . . work.'

'It will work,' I said stoutly. 'No one ever found out who wrote the original letter. There's no reason it couldn't have been us.'

'So what happens to the original letter? Will we end up with two?'

'No. My theory is that no one wrote a letter warning Monteagle. I think it's really unlikely anyone would commit themselves in writing in case it all blew up in their face. No pun intended. No, I think Monteagle was warned verbally. Someone whispered in his ear. He was horrified but couldn't take the risk of being implicated so he sat down and wrote the letter himself. To himself. It was his brilliant way of tipping off the authorities. But that's not important. As soon as the existence of our letter is known there's no reason for the original letter to be written. It will be superfluous. The would-be composer will probably think thank God for that – someone else got in before me. Now I don't have to stick my head over the parapet and can join everyone else in looking as unimplicated as possible.'

Markham was silent a long time thinking it through.

'Actually, Max, that's . . .'

'Bloody brilliant?'

'Yeah – actually it is.'

'Finally, my talents are recognised.'

'Except . . .'

'Except what?'

'How do we forge the letter?'

'Well, we know what it said and how it looked. The original is in the National Archive and there are plenty of images out there for us to copy. All we have to do is . . .'

I tailed off.

'Exactly. *We* can't do it. I mean, we could try, but if there's the slightest suspicion it's not kosher, then Cecil could just dump it in the bin and then if the original letter *does* turn up, he'll probably do the same with that. If we're not careful, we could make things considerably worse. We'll only get one chance at this and we have to get it right.' Markham paused. 'We both know someone who can do it – and do it well – but frankly, I don't think either you or the pod are in the best condition to make the jump back to St Mary's.'

'All right – we have choices about our next course of action,' I said, rubbing my eyes. 'Work with me on this. For the purposes of this argument, I'm assuming that for some reason Pennyroyal and Smallhope aren't coming to join us any time soon. We have to manage alone.'

He nodded.

'OK. If we *both* jump and for some reason can't get back, then there's no one here to ensure the plot is uncovered, and everything is buggered.'

He frowned. 'Agreed. But if *I* jump away, leaving you here, and the pod doesn't return, then buggeration will also occur.'

I tried to speak but he swept on. 'But if *you* jump away and I stay here then I might still have an outside chance of influencing events if you can't get back. I could attract the guards' attention – denounce the conspirators – whatever – and they *might* listen, but if you try that, there's a very good chance the guards won't believe a woman. So it makes sense for you to go and me to stay behind. I'm sure if you take it slowly, you and the pod will be fine.'

'There's no way I'm leaving you here alone,' I said. 'Forget it. You'd be completely exposed. If I can't get back, you'll be stuck here. And if the plot succeeds, you'll be blown to pieces in the explosion because you won't have had the sense to get out of the way in time.'

Markham shook his head. 'No, Max. It has to happen that way. You're the one who's going back. For hundreds and hundreds of good reasons that I haven't thought of yet and are too tedious to cite anyway.'

'It's too dangerous,' I said.

'No, it's not,' he said seriously. He came to stand beside me, folded his arms and leaned against the console. 'I think we're meant to do it, Max. I think we've been working towards this for years.'

I blinked. 'Have we?'

'We have. Don't you remember little Aline?'

I have to admit it took a while to recall little Aline. And then I had it. Christmas Day, 1066. A snowy forest just outside London. We'd turned up to witness William the Conqueror's coronation. We hadn't actually made it because, inexplicably, the pod had dumped us in exactly the wrong place for the ceremony but at exactly the right place to save an injured woodcutter.

I stared at him. 'Oh my God.'

'Exactly, Max. We saved her father. Which, in turn, saved her. Which saved all her descendants. Including Simon de Montfort. If we hadn't landed in the wrong place at the wrong time and rescued her father, then History might have been very different.'

'We landed in the wrong place to witness William's coronation,' I said slowly. 'But exactly the right place to save de Montfort's ancestors. And de Montfort was a major player – *the* major player . . .'

'In the development of Parliament. There's a common thread to all this, don't you think?'

I did. At the time – Christmas Day, 1066 – I'd just written our landing off as one of those unfortunate things that happen occasionally. Later, I'd wondered. And now it seemed I hadn't been the only one.

And his remark – that St Mary's had, unknowingly, been working towards this for years – struck a chord in me. If History *was* with us . . . On the other hand, that might just be wishful thinking on my part and we were both going to die. Horribly.

'All right,' I said, with some reluctance, because Markham's argument was sound but I really wasn't looking forward to the return trip. The last jump had been no fun at all.

'OK,' he said. 'Practical stuff. You bring back Dr Dowson to knock us up the letter but we'll need contemporary materials. I'll exercise my former talents and acquire parchment and some ink.'

'Too risky. Suppose you're caught. We can bring something back with us.'

He waved his hand. 'No, you can't. We can't have a modern watermark. The thing's in the National Archive. Think of the embarrassment.'

'Unimportant as long as we succeed.'

'No point in storing up future trouble for ourselves. Suppose an anomalous letter is what sets Insight off in the first place.'

There were hundreds of things wrong with that argument. I just couldn't think of any of them at the moment so I changed tack.

'My worry is leaving you here. You're going to be very vulnerable, you know. And what will you do if Insight turn up?'

'I'll be fine,' he said bravely.

'No, you bloody won't. You'll fall in the river again and then catch something unpleasant and hugely contagious and I'll be forced to shoot you.'

'Well, at least you won't be here and throwing up all over me every ten minutes, which is a huge improvement as far as I'm concerned. Shall we get you going?'

Markham took a pack of high-energy biscuits from the locker and went to wait by the door while I sorted out the coordinates. My conscience insisted I make one final effort to change his mind.

'No – this is wrong. You should come back with me. If the pod is wonky, then where better to fix it than St Mary's? And then we can both come back to sort out whatever's going on here.'

'It's not about the pod. It's about someone staying here and keeping an eye out for Insight. We have to stay ahead of them on this one, Max.'

'Even so . . .'

'Even so nothing. If the situation was reversed, you'd be kicking me back to St Mary's with threats and bad language. Fortunately for you,' he said, scratching himself somewhere not normally accessed in public, 'I am a gentleman.'

Still, I hovered.

'We need to get moving, Max. You go and get Dr Dowson – try not to fall foul of Treadwell – and I'll see what I can do regarding materials. Off you go. Now.'

The last I saw of him he was crossing Old Palace Yard. It was one of those cold, dank days. River mist twisted and curled its way through the narrow streets, reached Markham, recoiled, and continued hastily on its way.

I checked the console, sat on the floor, took a deep breath and said, 'Computer, initiate jump.'

'Jump initiated.'

The world went white.

26

And so, I went back to St Mary's.

I was much more prepared this time and initiating the jump from the floor saved me the embarrassment of falling out of my chair again.

I didn't do anything for a long while after I'd landed. I stayed perfectly still with my eyes closed while the world adjusted itself around me. But I didn't actually throw up so, you know – progress.

When I eventually staggered to my feet and looked at the chronometer, I'd been on the floor for nearly ten minutes. I'd been extraordinarily lucky; anything could have happened during those ten minutes. But no one was trying to kick the door in so I appeared to have got away with it. For the time being.

I took a few deep breaths, sipped some water and eventually felt well enough to get to work. I panned the cameras around the paint store. No one was around but I initiated the camo device anyway.

This wasn't the first time I'd been back to St Mary's since being chucked out but I didn't have the strength to disguise myself as a kitchen assistant again. Not that I thought Mrs Mack would ever let me back into her kitchen after my last visit.

For those considering it, the best time to invade St Mary's is mealtime. Seriously. Forget all this creeping about in the small hours stuff – because that's not suspicious at all, is it? Simply march your invading army through the doors at half past six in the evening and St Mary's is yours.

It was ten past three in the afternoon. The pod had missed again.

I took a deep breath because my hands were shaking a little bit and called up Peterson. I had no idea whether calls were monitored under Hyssop's regime so I kept it neutral.

'Dr Peterson, sir, good afternoon. Sorry to trouble you.'

And waited. He might not even have his com switched on.

There was a long pause – presumably while he tried to remember who I was – and then he said, quite normally, 'Hello there. What's the problem?'

'Sir, the research you requested has thrown up an anomaly. I wonder if you could spare me a moment. At your convenience, of course.'

'Of course,' he said. 'Are you where I think you are?'

'Yes. Thank you, sir.' And closed the com.

I put the kettle on and sipped a cautious cup of tea.

He turned up about ten minutes later, obviously having taken the time to finish what he was doing and waft graciously through the building. He was alone though, which was the main thing.

I let him in. He didn't look any different. A fixed point in a tumultuous universe.

'Hello, again.'

I was so pleased to see him. 'Tim – hi.'

He looked around the pod. 'Is this anything to do with Runnymede?'

'Yes, but . . .'

He stepped back and looked at me. 'Have you been on fire?'

'Only a very little.'

'What's going on?'

'It's a long story,' I said. 'And I'm not just saying that. It really is a very long and complicated story.'

He looked over my shoulder. 'Where's the other one?'

'Not in a particularly safe environment. I know it doesn't make any difference but I really would like to get back to him asap.'

'What do you need? Rations? Medical care? I have to say – you look terrible.' He sniffed. 'Has someone been sick in here?'

'Yes, but no time for that now. The Monteagle letter.'

He blinked. 'Francis Tresham. Gunpowder Plot. Oh God, Max. What . . . ?'

'I need a really good copy. Could you ask Dr Dowson if he could oblige, please? We need to fool everyone. Not just Lord Monteagle but possible future scientific analysis as well.'

'Why?'

'Because there's a very good chance the original letter will never make it.'

He stood for a moment, taking in the implication, then nodded. 'All right, I'll go and speak to Dr Dowson. How long have you got?'

'It doesn't matter – you know that. As long as I can get this slightly unreliable pod back about an hour after I left . . .'

'No, I meant for you. I'd like Dr Stone to look you over.'

'I don't think I should leave the pod . . .'

'Hyssop's not here. She and her team are out with Roberts and Atherton. Lost Libraries of Timbuktu.'

'Treadwell?'

'In his office.'

'Bugger.'

'No problem. He'll never know.'

'How's he doing?'

'Not too badly. He's been asking for money-making ideas and someone mentioned having another Open Day.'

I groaned. 'Oh God. Do we never learn?'

'It's all right – he wasn't that keen.'

'Thank God.'

'Until someone pointed out that you'd been shot at the last one and he suddenly became quite enthusiastic.'

'I'm not even here any longer.'

'He said that wasn't a problem. Historical re-enactments are our thing and could he volunteer to pull the trigger.'

'He was joking, surely.'

'Not sure. Hard to tell with him. Anyway, wait here.' Peterson deepened his voice, intoning impressively, 'I'll be back.'

'Sorry – what?'

'I said . . .' He deepened his voice even further. I swear I felt my chest vibrate. 'I'll be back.'

I blinked. 'Yes, I know.'

He sighed. 'Remind me again why I bother.'

He disappeared. I put down my tea because I didn't really want it.

Minutes later, he reappeared with Dieter.

Dieter sniffed the air a few times. 'Is the problem with you or the pod?'

'Drifting.'

'Badly?'

'No, but getting worse.'

'Thirty minutes.'

'OK.'

Peterson passed me a black jumpsuit and a baseball cap to hide my hair. It would seem I'd been promoted to the IT Department.

'Oh,' I said. 'Yes. Good thought.'

'Other people do have them, you know.'

They waited outside while I changed.

'It's mid-afternoon and the place is heaving at the moment,' said Peterson, as I emerged. 'I'm surprised you didn't aim for around half past six in the evening. That's what I would have done.'

Sadly, the many and brilliant responses to this remark formed a kind of logjam in my brain and instead of annihilating him on the spot with my caustic comeback I could only stare at him. I told myself I was tired, obviously.

He patted me on the shoulder. 'Never mind. It was a good effort.'

Never have I more longed for the power to strike a man dead where he stood.

'Come on,' he said, cheerfully, 'and whatever you see or hear, stay close to me. Dr Dowson's waiting for you. Just tell him what you want. Dieter will do the biz here. Then you shoot off to Sick Bay for an overhaul and Bob's your uncle.'

Well – it was never going to be that simple, was it?

We'd barely got out of the paint store when the racket started. I heard someone shout a warning in the distance. There was a rumbling noise as of something heavy being trundled around the building. Followed by a sudden, sharp cry of warning. Followed by the sound of breaking glass. Followed by screams. And overturning furniture. And shouting.

306

Instinctively, I set off in the Direction of Doom.

'No, no,' said Peterson. 'We'll go around the outside and in through the Library windows. Like normal people.'

'But . . .' I said.

'Just ignore everything.'

'What have you done?' I said in alarm.

'I haven't done anything,' he said. 'I simply asked for a small diversion to keep everyone congregated in the Hall while you and I scamper happily around the outside of the building.'

'Who did you ask?'

'Professor Rapson, of course. Can't wait to see what he's come up with. Stick with me now. And do try to look like a normal member of the human race.'

We let ourselves out of one of the back doors and trotted around the side of the building. Even from out here I could hear sounds of . . . let's go with 'agitation'.

Normally the Great Hall – home of historians – is the preferred venue for whatever has just gone horribly wrong. With R&D running a close second. Followed by the Library – usually an unwilling and bitterly complaining participant. The car park too has had its moments of drama over the years. And the lake, of course. Even Wardrobe has seen its fair share of tense moments. On reflection, it might be quicker and easier to list the areas where nothing untoward has ever occurred.

Pause for reflection.

No – sorry, I've got nothing. All of St Mary's has figured in what Pennyroyal would no doubt refer to as another Catalogue of Catastrophe.

It's going to take me a while to climb through the Library windows because we always have to keep an eye open for swans. Other organisations might have guard dogs or robot security systems. We have swans. And before you laugh – the Romans had geese and it worked for them. Anyway, to help you pass the time, let me list the component parts of this afternoon's particular incidentette and you see if you can work it out more quickly than I did.

Item 1. Broken glass all over the Hall. Everywhere. Masses and masses of broken glass. It looked as if some sort of giant glass tank had sustained some sort of giant accident.

Item 2. An upturned flatbed trolley – possibly borrowed but more likely stolen from Hawking – on which the giant glass tank was seemingly being transported.

Item 3. A vast quantity of what looked and smelled like wood shavings. Pine, if I wasn't mistaken. Rather a pleasant smell. I made a mental note to discuss scattering them around the pod instead of our traditional floor covering. To counteract the smell of cabbage, of course. And, more recently, sick.

Item 4. Slightly more puzzling – dog food. A lot of dog food. I knew it was dog food because it was pink. These days the law says that pet food must be pink or blue so people don't confuse it with human food. I don't object to the government being idiots – if they weren't idiots then they'd have a proper job like the rest of us – but I do object to them thinking we're idiots. However, pink dog food is here to stay.

Item 5. Perhaps I should have led with this. A rather large dead pig. Which appeared to have tumbled from the now shattered glass tank. Either it had sustained a lot of damage during its tumble or it hadn't been good to start with, being full of holes and with bones and things poking out. Moth-eaten was my first impression. It had obviously rolled some distance from the flatbed and had come to rest against an already laden table which was showing signs of imminent collapse.

Item 6. Scattered across the floor, a very large quantity of cheap jewellery. From Wardrobe. I thought I could see one or two pieces I'd worn to Babylon.

Have you got it yet? Need any more clues? OK then – last clue. The Big Finish.

Item 7. A large number of beetles. Not the car – the insects. Lots and lots of scuttling, crawling, scurrying, running beetles.

Got it now? Just let me get in through this window and I can describe the scene properly.

It was some time since I'd last seen the Hall and I could recognise Treadwell's influence immediately. All the tables were in straight lines, parallel to each other and at right angles to the walls. All the files were neatly stacked and not toppling over. All the whiteboards were arranged against the walls where no one could walk into them. All the scruffy notices, rosters, reminders, and Post-its had been taken down. All the fire exits were clearly marked. The floor was cleared of trip hazards and the secondary filing system. The place looked clean, tidy and efficient. It was enough to rot your soul just looking at it.

Except today. Today was the St Mary's I knew. Today there was screaming and mass climbing on to furniture. We at St Mary's – sorry, St Mary's personnel – are as brave as lions when it comes to the animal world. Dinosaurs, mammoths, horses, even swans (as long as we're standing behind someone else) – we've dealt with them all. But beetles – thousands of beetles – were another matter. And if these beetles were what I thought they were, then we were due a panic of biblical proportions.

It was at this point that Commander Treadwell made a tactical error and appeared on the gallery demanding to know what was going on.

I drew well back in the Library and stood behind Peterson.

Just for the record, the correct procedure – as employed by Dr Bairstow – should have been to close his office door and become massively busy with an important telephone call to the exclusion of all lesser matters. Treadwell still had a lot to learn.

'Oh, good afternoon, Director,' said Professor Rapson, who, with the other members of his department, was scurrying around, picking up beetles and dropping them into anything that looked fit for purpose. He gestured expansively. 'Museum bugs.'

I suppose he thought that sounded better than the more well-known name, and for all I know he was right.

'Museum bugs?' said Treadwell.

The professor beamed and moved sideways. Treadwell turned to keep him in view. Peterson nudged me into an alcove. Dewey number 236 – Eschatology, if I remember correctly. Which seemed very appropriate under the circumstances.

'It's an experiment,' said the professor. 'In conjunction with our colleagues at Thirsk. Inter-site cooperation.'

He stopped, obviously assuming this explained everything.

Treadwell now had his back to me. 'An experiment?'

'Well, more of a race, really.'

'A race?'

He really wasn't going to get anywhere just repeating everything the professor said.

'Fascinating to watch,' continued the professor, seemingly unaware he had completely mistaken his audience. 'And to listen to. If everyone could just stop screaming for a moment, you'll be able to hear them at work. They sound exactly like that breakfast cereal when you pour your milk over it.'

He tilted his head to one side in an attitude of intense concentration.

Several people turned green although you'd think anyone daft enough to engage with milk – the juice of the devil – would have a strong enough stomach to cope with a few beetles, wouldn't you?

Treadwell, who obviously hadn't learned anything during my absence from St Mary's, continued with his interrogation. 'Exactly what has occurred here, professor?'

'Well, as I said, it's an experiment with our colleagues at Thirsk to discover which strain of flesh-eating beetle . . .'

That was as far as he got for quite some considerable time. I think it would be fair to say mass consternation ensued.

'. . . is most efficient at stripping skeletons of their flesh,' he continued happily. 'We each constructed an equal-sized glass tank – for the purposes of observation – and obtained similarly sized pigs. But – and I think you'll agree this is the fascinating part – we are using different sub-species of beetle. I know this will excite you, Director, since several well-known museums – our friends at the BM, for instance – have registered an interest in the results. Our plan is to breed the winner on a commercial scale and thus obtain some much-needed income for St Mary's – as you continually exhort us to do, Director.'

His face afire with an evangelical fervour which wouldn't have deceived Dr Bairstow for a microsecond, he continued. 'I thought some of the empty rooms along the admin corridor would be ideal for our purpose.'

Mrs Partridge's expression invited him to try.

'Although we haven't met with quite the enthusiasm we expected from our co-workers . . .'

He appeared to contemplate this sad state of affairs for a moment and then gave himself a little shake. 'Anyway, the jewellery was concealed inside the pig – much as ancient people were buried with their valuables.'

He picked up a small diadem last seen adorning Rosie Lee and which now had something pink and wobbly dangling from one end. 'The object was to see which species of beetle would uncover the jewellery most quickly so that we could begin commercialisation as soon as possible. We really are quite excited about this one, Director. And to appeal to your competitive instincts, we here at St Mary's are definitely well ahead and . . . Or rather we were. Our attempts to move the tank will almost certainly set back our progress and . . .'

'And the dog food?'

The professor radiated innocence. 'In case they didn't like the pig.'

Bashford started to scratch. 'Oh my God, I think one's just run up my leg.'

Many people tried to climb up on to trestle tables not designed for this purpose. Those who had already gained the illusory safety of being off the ground showed no signs of willingness to share their refuge. Shouts of 'Bugger off and find your own table' echoed around the Hall.

'Flesh-eating beetles?' said Treadwell, apparently under the impression this wasn't an actual thing.

The professor frowned reproachfully. 'Their proper name is Dermestids, Director. Flesh-eating beetles sounds a little melodramatic, don't you think? I always feel it's important not to overdramatise this sort of situation.'

'They eat flesh?'

'Well, not live flesh, obviously. Only dead flesh. Could someone reassure Mr Bashford as to the safety of his external reproductive organs? Unless he falls off the table and kills himself, in which case, one lucky little beetle has a head start on his friends.'

Bashford screamed and scrabbled to rip off his clothes. His boots, jumpsuit, socks . . .

Several other people screamed, but not for beetle-related reasons, I suspected.

'Or,' continued the apparently oblivious professor, 'if they can't get dead flesh, they're rather partial to wool . . .'

Mrs Enderby screamed and fled into the Wardrobe Department, slamming the door behind her.

'. . . wood . . .'

Mr Strong screamed. Ditto with the front doors.

'. . . paper . . .'

Dr Dowson screamed and headed towards the Library. Exactly where I wanted him to be. I cast a suspicious look at Peterson, standing innocently in the End of the World section.

'. . . cotton . . .'

Mrs Midgley screamed and surged up the stairs. To defend her airing cupboards to the death, presumably. Although whose death wasn't entirely clear.

How Treadwell dealt with all this I never knew. Peterson and I followed Dr Dowson into his office. He shut the door behind me and beamed. 'How are you, Max?'

'Very well,' I said. 'But I desperately need your help, doctor.'

'Yes, so Dr Peterson explained.'

'And we can't wait, sir. The only way we can be truly certain the letter is delivered is to deliver it ourselves. As soon as possible.'

He sat for a moment, drumming his fingers on his desk. I waited.

'The letter itself is not a problem. A simple enough matter to copy, I think. The problem is the paper or parchment. I'm certain I don't have anything suitable here, and we're talking about a national document so it's going to have to be spot on. How easy would it be for you to acquire something suitable at the other end, so to speak?'

'I think Mr Markham has that in hand, sir. What about ink?'

'If you can acquire paper then you can probably acquire ink at the same time. If not, we can probably knock something up from soot and gum arabic. I must say, Max, you appear to be leading a very adventurous life since you left us.'

'Well, it wasn't exactly a quiet life while I was here, was it? And now St Mary's is grappling with ten thousand flesh-eating beetles.'

He shook his head. 'No, it isn't.'

I pointed back towards the Great Hall. 'But I just saw . . .'

'No, you didn't. No more than five hundred at the most.'

I don't know why he thought five hundred flesh-eating beetles would be more acceptable than ten thousand and said so. 'Aren't you a little concerned they'll eat St Mary's around your ears?'

He shook his head. 'We'll entice them back with the dead pig. That's what it's there for. The old fool upstairs has a second tank all set up and ready to go and they'll all be back on the job by nightfall. It's a genuine thing, you know – stripping flesh

314

this way doesn't damage the skeleton underneath. And if this works well, we're thinking of trying it on a dead mammoth.'

'And Thirsk?'

'No, I don't think we can try it on them, Max. I can't see the Chancellor being at all happy about that.'

'I mean – the experiment.'

'Enthusiastically on board with this one,' he said cheerfully. 'Just in case Treadwell checks with Dr Chalfont – although he won't, I'm sure, because he's no fool – and I have to say, Max, St Mary's flesh-eating beetles are considerably more efficient than Thirsk's. Bets have been placed and I myself stand to win a handsome sum.'

'They'll say we cheated,' I said, unable to avoid being dragged into these deep academic issues.

'Dr Black is adjudicating. No one argues with her. Now – to business.'

Not without some difficulty, I dragged my mind away from flesh-eating beetles and the only marginally less apocalyptic sight of Bashford taking his clothes off in public. Because now it was time for the difficult bit. Time to persuade Dr Dowson to entrust himself to a sick historian, enter an unreliable pod and jump to a hazardous destination where anything could be waiting for us – up to and including the world's scruffiest partner in crime. I was going to have to exercise all my powers of persuasion and probably borrow a few more from someone else.

'Give me a minute to grab my other spectacles, Max, and I'll be with you.'

It took me a few moments for his words to sink in. I was so busy trying to think up ways to entice him to the dark side I hadn't realised he was already there. Although I should have.

'Er . . .'

'Well, that is why you're here, isn't it? To jump me back to the 17th century?'

'Um . . .'

'Good. Meet you . . . where?'

'Paint store,' I said weakly, feeling my grasp on reality slacken even further.

He disappeared into his little storeroom without a backward glance. I looked around his empty office. Peterson had disappeared. Might as well visit Sick Bay, I suppose.

Which went slightly worse than even I expected.

I climbed out of the Library windows again, trotted round the outside of the building and was able to get in through a deserted Hawking where, for some reason, the outside door had been left open.

Dr Stone had me in the scanner before I could say a word.

Afterwards we just looked at each other.

'Tell me your symptoms again.'

The correct answer would have been: generally falling apart, nausea, vertigo, flashbacks, one world superimposed over another, feelings of overwhelming fear and panic, everything getting worse, barely able to function.

I went with, 'A slight disorientation, mostly.'

'Including hallucinations.'

'Not all the time,' I said, anxious he should know it wasn't that serious.

'The thing is, Max . . .'

My heart sank. This was the traditional St Mary's preface to bad news.

'It's your body clock. I can't decide if it's on overdrive trying to keep up or whether it's just given up and stopped working altogether. One of the two, anyway.'

'What does that mean?'

'You've made too many jumps.'

'No more than anyone else.'

'Max, you've made far more jumps than anyone else. And that's just the official ones. Don't tell me you haven't been shooting off whenever the fancy takes you because I wouldn't believe you.'

'Peterson . . .'

'Hardly jumps at all now he's DD.'

'Kal . . .'

'Ditto now she's our liaison officer. And Sands and Roberts left St Mary's for a year.'

'Bashford . . .'

'Is so weird it probably doesn't show.'

'Van Owen . . .'

'Is beginning to exhibit symptoms. The thing is, most of our jumps here are in one direction. To the past. But I'm guessing you've been jumping in both directions. To the past and the future. In which direction was your last jump?'

'Forward. To here. The present.'

'And the one before that?'

'Back. To the past.

'And before that?'

I scowled with the effort because I genuinely couldn't remember. 'To the future.'

'And before that?'

'Back.'

'And before that?'

317

'Forward.'

'And . . .'

'Yes, yes, I get the message.'

'No, you don't, Max. Let me put it in terms you can understand: like an overused pod, you're beginning to drift.'

I must have looked unconvinced because he continued. 'The point I'm trying to make is that you've been ricocheting around the timeline for far too long. Your body clock doesn't know whether it's morning or October. No wonder you only open your bowels twice a year. You can't go on like this – your body's beginning to break down, and I'm guessing those periods when you don't know whether you're up or down are increasing in frequency and duration. My main concern is that you're being confronted with two or three worlds simultaneously and the possibility that one day, Max, you might step into the wrong one and we'll have lost you forever. You're discombobulated, disoriented and God knows what else besides. And you had a dose of Bluebell Time not so long ago, which hasn't helped at all. My recommendation is that you remain in one time and one place and wait for your body clock to sort itself out.'

'I can't stop,' I said. 'I'm in the middle of something important.'

'If you were still at St Mary's, I'd take you off the active list.'

'But I'm not,' I said, gently.

Dr Stone sat back and thought. 'Let's try this, shall we?' He pushed over a piece of paper and a pen. 'Make me a list of all your jumps over the last three months.'

I scowled, thought, and wrote for a few minutes.

'Now for the three months before that.'

I wrote again and had to ask for another sheet. I honestly

hadn't realised I'd done so much. And I'm certain I missed a few as well.

'Right,' he said, taking it off me. He punched away at his screen. 'I'm bringing up a list of your jumps – your official jumps – over the last two years . . . and adding these in . . .'

He turned his screen to show me the total.

'Shit,' I said, seriously surprised. 'That can't be right.'

'It's probably an underestimation,' he said. 'We haven't even started on the unofficial stuff. I'm gobsmacked you're still on your feet.'

I didn't dare tell him that a lot of the time I wasn't.

'What about the Time Police, though?' I said craftily. 'They're all over the place. In every sense of the word. To the future – to the past – back to the future. You don't see them fainting like a bunch of wusses.'

'That's true but I believe the Time Police have already identified this as a problem.'

'And have they identified a solution?'

'I believe so. Your problem is that you're not spending long enough here in your own time. They take care to ground themselves after each assignment. Even something as simple as just a stint with the Time Map. Relating themselves to the here and now. To regain their sense of . . . well, their place in time and space. It's simple but effective, apparently. You should do something similar.'

'Not a possibility at the moment.'

'In that case, all I can advise you to do is keep the jumping to an absolute minimum. I mean it, Max. I don't know what you're up to at the moment – nor do I want to – but unless you drastically cut back – the day will come when you can't jump

319

at all and wherever and whenever you are – that's where you'll
be stuck. Think about that. In the meantime . . .' He got up and
began to rummage in a cupboard on the wall. 'This might help
a little. Bend over.'

'What?'

He reappeared with a syringe apparently modelled on one of
Lingoss's giant steam pumps.

I put my back to the wall and prepared for death or glory.

'It's a form of cyclizine although you won't find this on the
high street. Very effective at treating nausea, vertigo, disorientation, travel sickness and so on. A warning though – this is
only temporary. You will need to address this, Max. And soon.'

'Understood,' I said. 'But if you can just keep me on my feet
for a couple of days . . .'

'This will help. It won't cure. Bend over.'

Well, that was unpleasant.

I snuck down the stairs, along the deserted corridor and met Dr
Dowson in the paint store.

There was a small yellow Post-it stuck to the pod door.
Dieter's handwriting informed me it needed a major service
but should be OK for a few jumps.

I peeled it off, screwed it up and tucked it down the back
of a shelf.

'Are you ready, Dr Dowson?'

'Of course,' he said, quivering with excitement.

I've no idea what colour the world went. My eyes were tight
shut and my bum was killing me.

27

Markham wasn't at the rendezvous point. A hissed conversation over his com informed me he was in a bloody tavern about a quarter of an hour away. The Catherine Wheel. The fact that this was the place where Catesby and the others had been meeting to lay their plans was, apparently, a complete coincidence.

He was so dead.

I left Dr Dowson in the pod and went off to look for the prospective corpse.

Last time I'd seen Markham he'd been trudging pathetically down the foggy street. Now, he was the centre of attention in a hot, smelly, smoky room and he was doing conjuring tricks. I seriously contemplated killing him on the spot. He had a comfortable seat near the fire. A small crowd had gathered around and he had several tankards lined up on the table. I gritted my teeth. He was definitely marked for death.

I didn't go in. I stood just inside the doorway and telepathically instructed him to get his arse over here if he wanted to live.

Astonishingly, he got the message, waving goodbye to his new friends, who saw him go with huge regret. I prodded him back to the pod at a great rate of knots because we couldn't afford to hang around.

The pod seemed very warm after the cold air outside. Dr Dowson was happily flicking through images of the Monteagle letter on the screen.

Markham and Dr Dowson were very pleased to be reunited. I was too busy being cross. I'd been quite concerned about him and there he'd been, sitting by the fire, best seat in the house, having a great time, while I'd been suffering bum trauma. That last bit sounded better in my head so feel free to ignore it.

'Dr Dowson says we might be able to make our own ink. Parchment might be a problem, though, and . . .'

'Yes, such a pity we don't have a handy goat,' said Dr Dowson. 'I keep telling Treadwell this is what happens if you don't have your own goats, but he doesn't listen.'

'Everyone calm down,' said Markham, grabbing the seat before I could although I don't think I was much interested in sitting down anyway. 'I haven't been wasting my time, you know.'

'Of course you haven't,' I said, nastily. 'You've had a full day performing in pubs for free drinks.'

'That was my reward,' he said, throwing me a hurt look which I ignored. It doesn't work on Hunter and it doesn't work on me, either. 'Ask me how I spent today.'

'No,' I said.

'No matter. I shall tell you anyway. I took a pleasant stroll along the river. A bit chilly but at least it wasn't raining. Lots to see. Finished up at Old St Paul's. Remember that place?'

'Is there some point to these maunderings?' My bum was giving me hell.

'Yes, indeed. I maundered in the direction of Paternoster Row.'

'I remember that place. I was about to overstay my time there and you were going to shoot me.'

'I don't think you should keep harping on about that,' he said, reproachfully.

'First time I've mentioned it in years.'

'Anyway . . .' he said patiently, 'Paternoster Row is where one Christopher Barker and his son ply their trade.'

We stared at him.

He heaved a martyred sigh. 'Christopher Barker. At the sign of the Tyger's Head? The printer?'

He rummaged under his cloak, eventually producing several sheets of stiff paper, a phial of dark fluid and a handful of what looked like goose tail feathers.

'Oh,' I said. And then as the implications dawned, 'Oh.'

Dr Dowson took them from him. 'My dear fellow, well done. Well done, indeed. Max and I were formulating all sorts of plans for obtaining gum arabic and lampblack and here you are providing everything an ambitious forger could possibly require. Except . . .'

'What?' I said, alarmed. 'Except what? What did we forget?'

Markham calmly laid a small lump of red wax on the console.

'Brilliant,' I said. Because it was. I hadn't thought of sealing the letter. I grinned at Markham. 'How did you manage to steal all this?'

'I didn't,' he said, dredging up yet more hurt reproach. 'Three hours' labouring. God knows what was in those barrels they wanted moving – dead elephants probably – but at the end of the day, at my request, they paid me in kind. It just struck me that we should get this done as soon as possible.'

'Yes, indeed,' said Dr Dowson. 'Max, if you can just clear

me a little room, please . . . thank you very much . . . I need to spend a while studying the original.'

He elbowed Markham out of the seat, turned back to the screen, said, 'Hmm,' thoughtfully, and then regarded us brightly. 'Perhaps you'd both like to take a walk.'

In other words, push off and let me get on with it.

'Of course,' I said. 'Is the light good enough for you?'

Dr Dowson nodded vaguely, peering at the screen as he enlarged the first line of the letter. He'd forgotten us already.

Markham and I set out into the cold, damp air. The morning fog had cleared but the sun was going down and it was definitely the sort of afternoon best spent in front of a roaring fire with a nice glass of something, rather than having to encounter the slimy low life of Westminster. But it was an opportunity to take a good look around because none of this bore any resemblance to the Westminster of modern times.

The pod had landed in a corner of Old Palace Yard. There were ancient stone buildings behind and to our right, but their function remained unknown to us throughout the whole time we were there. We walked to the top of Parliament Stairs and looked out over the river. The biggest difference was the lack of an embankment. I was accustomed to seeing the river enclosed between neat walls. This straggling shoreline always seemed unfamiliar to me. It was low tide and mud glistened in the cold, weak sunlight, littered with debris – driftwood, discarded nets torn beyond repair, the remains of old jetties, even some quite large rocks. There was a strong smell of dirty water, with top notes of sewage. Small groups of birds pecked away, leaving tiny tracks in the mud. I could see where boats had been dragged up out of the water. And a surprising number of people – children mostly – were bent double, rooting around at the water's edge. Mudlarks.

A fairly sturdy-looking jetty provided a mooring for half a dozen rowing boats. The boat owners, temporarily unemployed, squatted at the foot of the steps doing something noisy with dice and small pebbles. Markham and I exchanged glances. I think it's fair to say neither of us had happy memories of the river and its wooden jetties.

I shivered and we turned and made our way back into Old Palace Yard.

To our right, sandwiched between two private houses, was the House of Lords. This was the former Queen's Chamber and horribly scruffy and undistinguished. Frankly, if it wasn't for the unfortunate people inside, blowing it up might have been the kindest thing to happen to it. The steeply pitched roof was poorly tiled and thick with green moss. It must be hideously damp in there. A thin wisp of smoke drifted from the very tall chimney so at least someone had a fire going. Lucky devil. I pulled my cloak around me and stuffed my clenched fists into my armpits to keep them warm.

The upper windows were tall and arched and I suspected had once been very fine but now the stained glass was nearly all gone, replaced with thick green stuff through which it was impossible to see. I suspected very little light filtered through. Unlike modern times, Parliament sat in the mornings – by early afternoon it was probably too difficult to see clearly.

The building wasn't even detached, being joined at each end to much more prosperous-looking private houses which faced away from it as if ashamed of their scruffy neighbour.

We studied our target carefully. I nodded to a small door recessed deep within the wall with two worn steps leading down to it. The actual Lords' chamber was on the first floor so that must be the entrance to the infamous undercroft.

We both stared. Such an insignificant door. Wooden, grey with age, slightly rotted around the bottom, with rusting hinges and a latch.

'We'll come back to that,' said Markham. 'Come on.'

We strolled through Old Palace Yard. Despite being a cold afternoon, the place was humming with life. Security was non-existent. I couldn't see any guards anywhere. There was nothing to stop anyone strolling in, doing something naughty and then just strolling straight back out again. Seriously, the only astonishment was that something like this hadn't happened sooner.

Men rolled empty barrels over the cobbles. The noise was deafening. You couldn't hear yourself shriek. Someone was trying to tempt a horse to pass a group of small boys who alternately jeered and threw small stones. A shopkeeper – a butcher, by his blood-crusted apron – chased them away. His hands were black with a nasty combination of dirt and dried blood. I made a mental note – no pies. Ever.

On the other side of the narrow lane was a glove-maker, and on the other side of him, a printer.

I turned to Markham who shook his head. 'Tried him,' he said. 'Closed. So I had to go looking.'

I put my arm through his. 'You did very well.'

He patted my hand. 'I did, didn't I?'

And then the lovely smell of leather wafting from a boot-maker's stall momentarily blotted out the pong of bad fish, piss, sour ale and unwashed people.

To our left, Westminster Abbey loomed, and on a darkening afternoon such as this, trust me, it really did loom.

We walked through the Yard, turned sharp right and passed under an old stone archway. The building to our left was some sort of court building, to our right, the House of Commons. Interestingly, twice the size of and in much better nick than the House of Lords.

There were a lot of men about here, rushing to and fro, laden with documents. Well, their servants were laden with documents, but you know what I mean. The point being that all of them were better dressed than us. One or two paused to stare. The archway obviously delineated some sort of social barrier which it would be unwise to pass.

We backed out slowly and strolled along St Margaret's Lane, past Fish Yard – the source of the all-pervading smell of muddy fish – and into New Palace Yard.

I couldn't help noticing how very masculine everything was. There were very few women around. Until nightfall, of course, when, given this was Westminster, all that would change.

The Palace of Westminster had been a proper royal residence although the last monarch to live here had been Fat Harry, I think. As a palace it was rather a disappointment. In fact, the whole area was. There certainly wasn't much going on. On the other hand, of course, Parliament didn't open until the 5th. Here, all was quiet emptiness. Blank windows stared down at us, daring us to enter.

'No further, I think,' said Markham. 'Let's not ask for trouble.'

We retraced our steps through the crowds. Darkness was closing in and lights were springing up everywhere. Shop-keepers were taking in their produce, shouting to each other, enquiring as to the day's business and putting up their shutters.

The air was damp. Tiny droplets of water clung to my sleeve. I was suddenly very tired. We should go back to the pod, watch Dr Dowson in action, return him whence he came and, at a suitable time, deliver Lord Monteagle his History-changing letter.

In between all that, perhaps I could grab a few hours' sleep, try and eat something and have a think about what Dr Stone had told me.

'I've made some tea,' announced Dr Dowson as we entered the pod. 'Max, you look chilled to the bone. Careful not to smudge it, now.'

The letter lay on the console, kept flat by a half-drunk mug of tea at one end and his spectacles case at the other. I could see wet ink glistening.

'You've done it already?' I said in astonishment.

'Oh yes,' he said airily. 'It wasn't difficult.'

I peered at the letter, comparing it with the original on the screen. 'Oh my God, great job, sir. It's magnificent. It's practically identical to the original.'

'It *is* identical to the original,' he said, proudly. 'That . . .' he pointed to the letter on the screen, 'is that.' He pointed to the letter on the console. 'This is the original letter. I wrote it. Don't you see? There's only ever been my letter.'

'So . . . it wasn't written by one of the conspirators?'

'No, it was me,' he said complacently.

'*Not* Francis Tresham?'

'No – me.'

'Not even Monteagle himself because some said he did it for the reward?'

'No – I wrote the letter.'

'And to save his life, of course.'

'No,' he said, patiently, explaining things to the hard of understanding. 'It was me. I wrote the letter. That's why *my* letter is identical to *that* letter. They're one and the same. I wrote the Monteagle letter.'

'Bloody hell.'

'Take a look.'

I did. And there it was. The familiar image made real right in front of me. Even to the error on the first line. Today, the original letter is in the National Archive. Correction – *this* letter is in the National Archive. Go and look for yourself.

'Well,' said Markham. 'I suppose that solves the question of its origin.'

I read slowly.

'My lord, out of the love I beare to some of youere frends, I have a care of youre preservacion, therefore I would aduyse you as you tender your life to devise some excuse to shift youer attendance at this parliament, for God and man hath concurred to punishe the wickedness of this tyme, and thinke not slightly of this advertisement, but retire yourself into your country, where you may expect the event in safety, for though there be no apparance of anni stir, yet I saye they shall receive a terrible blow this parliament and yet they shall not seie who hurts them this cowncel is not to be contemned because it may do yowe good and can do yowe no harme for the dangere is passed as soon as yowe have burnt the letter and i hope God will give yowe the grace to mak good use of it to whose holy proteccion i comend yowe.'

Under the last line the letter was addressed 'To the right honorable the Lord Monteagle'

The stiff paper crackled under my hands. 'Let it dry thoroughly,' said the master forger masquerading as a respectable member of society, 'and then roll it up and seal it. My work here is done.'

'In that case,' said Markham, 'can we offer you dinner, sir?' He gestured to our stack of ration trays.

'No,' said Dr Dowson quickly. 'I'd better be getting back. God knows what the old fool has been up to in my absence.'

'St Mary's might have been eaten by now,' I said, suddenly remembering their current insect-related crisis.

'What?' said Markham, in astonished delight. 'Never tell me they've taken to cannibalism. Although now you come to mention it – not unlikely.'

'Ten thousand flesh-eating beetles,' I said.

His face fell. 'Oh. How disappointing.'

'Disappointing?'

'Well, you know. Flesh-eating beetles . . . yeah, OK, I suppose if you like that sort of thing, but actual *cannibalism*, Max . . .'

Dr Dowson intervened firmly. 'Absolutely no cannibalism. For heaven's sake, what sort of people do you think we are?'

There was a very long silence as the pair of us mentally assembled and discarded possible answers.

'I've got nothing,' said Markham to me.

I shook my head. 'Nor me.'

'And certainly not ten thousand of them,' continued the doctor. 'Only about five hundred. All of whom are guaranteed not to eat anything untoward. Not even Bashford's testicles. And definitely no cannibalism.'

'None at all?' Markham turned to me. 'The place has really gone downhill since we left.'

I nodded. 'It has, hasn't it.'

I can't say I was looking forward to the return trip. My stomach had settled, my eyes were working properly – in that I was only seeing one world and not two or three simultaneously – and I was really quite reluctant to set it all off again. Especially after what Dr Stone had told me. I didn't really think that each jump might be my last but even so . . .

Markham picked up the writing materials and carefully stowed the letter away inside his doublet while I ran an eye over the console. Everything seemed fine – no flashing red lights anywhere.

Markham grinned. 'See you soon, Max. Dr Dowson – many thanks, sir.'

He disappeared out of the door.

I gave him a moment to get clear and then said, 'Ready, Doctor? Computer, initiate jump.'

'Jump initiated.'

I can confirm that this time the world did go white. My eyes were open.

28

I had the door open as soon as we landed.

'Good luck in your endeavours,' said Dr Dowson, hopping out of the door. 'Whatever they are. And you can use that letter with confidence, Max.'

I nodded. 'Thank you, sir. Take care.'

I waited until he'd left the paint store and then set the coordinates for 1605 again. I shouldn't be doing this. This was exactly the sort of non-essential jump Dr Stone had warned me against. I could have sent Markham, found a quiet spot and waited for his return. He knew how to operate a pod. It's just . . . there's something about that moment – the moment your pod disappears – and you're all alone. Really all alone. And if anything goes wrong, you'll never see home again. Given the choice between that and quietly imploding on the floor I'd gone for implosion. Although the return jump hadn't been too bad. The injection was working.

Markham met me at the door.

'Well,' I said, peering out at Westminster's dim outline. The fog was back. 'Here we are. Late afternoon, 26th October 1605. Cold. Damp. Anyone with any brains is snug and warm inside. Only mad dogs and historians on the streets.'

Markham pulled out the letter, now rolled into a little tube of paper and sealed with a blob of red wax. 'We should get rid of this before one of us drops it down the toilet or spills our tea on it.'

I nodded very unenthusiastically. It really wasn't nice out there. And Monteagle shouldn't get the letter until 4th November, but did it actually matter?

I tried to think it through. The king was away hunting. If we delivered the letter tonight, would Monteagle sit on it for a couple of days until the king returned? Would that matter? On the other hand, if we kept it here and something happened . . . Suppose Insight turned up tomorrow and killed us before we could deliver it. Or the pod blew up? Or we lost the wretched thing? We couldn't afford to take the chance. We had to seize the initiative and deliver the letter tonight. Because once the letter was with Monteagle then events should take their course. Once we'd delivered it, even if Insight did kill us afterwards, it would be too late.

Markham looked at me. 'Do you want to stay behind?'

'Of course not,' I said. 'There's no chance of you finding Hoxton by yourself and I'll have to fish you out of the Thames again.'

'Yeah, but I was worth it though.'

I stamped off into the bathroom.

Now that we'd made the decision, we didn't hang around. Markham had eaten in the pub and I wasn't hungry.

'It's a good hour from Westminster to Hoxton,' said Markham. 'Longer in this fog.'

'We should start as soon as possible in that case. We know

the letter was delivered around seven in the evening so we'll follow the original version of events as closely as possible. And afterwards we'll still have to get all the way back here again.'

'But then,' he said as I pulled the pod door closed behind us, and we set off, 'our duty is done, we can finally go home. I can't tell you how knackered I am.'

'Me too.'

'I tell you, Max, when this is over I am going to get right royally rat-arsed.'

'For a week,' I said.

'With luck, Smallhope and Pennyroyal will have given events in 1848 the kicking they deserve. All set for a big party-pooh, as Lady Amelia would say.'

The first thing Markham did was steal a lantern off someone's wall. I opened my mouth to remonstrate, realised we weren't going to get far without one and closed it again.

He asked if Dr Dowson had got back all right.

'Yes – everything was disappointingly quiet. No flesh-eating beetles were galloping around the building seeking what they might devour. Not even Treadwell rampaging around the place doing the same.'

He shook his head. 'Place has gone to the dogs since we left.'

'It certainly has.'

We fell silent and concentrated on finding our way, following the river for a little while and then striking out north, making our way through the maze of narrow, deserted streets. Anyone sensible was either inside in the warm or, judging by the occasional roar of noise from an open door, enjoying a convivial evening with their mates in the pub.

Eventually, I plucked up the courage. 'Can I ask you a question?'

'Sure.'

'How much of all this did you tell Hunter?'

'All of it. Well, everything I knew at the time. Not Insight, of course, but I discuss most things with her. She usually has something useful to contribute. Why?'

I said nothing.

'Max? Why do you ask?'

I answered with another question.

'Before you left St Mary's – did Dr Bairstow talk to you about . . . things?'

'A bit. Probably as little as he could. You?'

I shook my head and sought to change the subject. I don't know why I bothered. He's not an idiot.

'What about you and Leon?'

'How do you mean?'

'Did you talk about things?'

I shook my head. 'Not really.' Which I thought was a nicely ambiguous answer that in no way implied that no one – including Leon – had told me anything. 'It all happened so quickly.'

'Mm,' he said.

'I mean . . . I just . . . I wasn't as involved as some people were.'

'Mm,' he said, and was silent for so long I wondered if he was thinking about something else.

Wrong. Out of the blue, he said, 'Did you ever tell Leon about the tickets?'

For a moment I couldn't think what he was talking about and then I remembered. A while ago Leon had been arrested on suspicion of murdering his first wife, Monique. Anyway, the three

335

of us – Peterson, Markham and I – set off to prove his innocence. Which we did, but, while searching her flat for evidence, we came across tickets showing she was about to return to England. There was a pandemic raging at the time. Both his sons were in hospital. Monique was about to give blood which would possibly save them. Clive Ronan killed her before she could do so.

After his sons died, Leon had more or less fallen apart with rage and grief. He'd come to terms with it in the end but I'd never told him of Monique's intentions. Never told him that, without Ronan, there was a chance – albeit a small one – that his boys might have survived. Knowing that, he would have abandoned everything and gone after Ronan in a frenzy of revenge that neither of them would have survived. So, rightly or wrongly, I'd never told him what I'd found.

'It's not the same thing,' I said.

'No.'

We walked in silence for a while. Leaving the city was no problem. The gateman let us through without question.

In these times, Hoxton was still a village, surrounded by fields and open land. There was, however, a well-defined track which we had no difficulty following. First, however, was Smithfield.

'Fun Fact,' said Markham, lightening the mood.

I followed his lead and sighed. 'It never rains but it pours, does it?'

'This area was originally known as Smoothfield, from the Saxon word "smeth" which means . . .'

'Smooth,' I finished for him.

'Well done,' he said, happily teaching his grandmother to suck eggs. 'They used to joust here, you know.'

Resistance is futile. There is, literally, no way to shut him up. Attempting to interrupt or divert him not only prolongs the agony but encourages him to dive down all sorts of conversational back alleys. I usually just let the words wash over me and think about what to have for lunch.

'And then, of course, in the Middle Ages, it became the big livestock market. And Wat Tyler was executed here. And William Wallace. And there was the infamous Bartholomew Fair. Debauchery and vice,' he said with enthusiasm. 'We should check it out one day.'

We were walking down the middle of what would one day be a street. The ground was slippery. Dark houses showed on either side. We were avoiding doorways and alleyways and whatever they might contain. Silence was all around us.

I stopped dead. 'When did this stop being fun?'

Markham actually carried on walking a few paces before realising I wasn't with him. Holding up the lantern, he said, 'What?'

'When did this stop being fun? When did our world become so dark?'

He didn't speak for a long time. We plodded on. Finally, he drew breath, saying sadly, 'I don't know, Max. I suppose, when we were at St Mary's, we pretty much lived in a bubble. The world didn't impinge a great deal, did it? We weren't in it half the time. We had food and shelter and a moderate amount of pay and just got on with things. Now, we're out in the real grown-ups' world. Doing grown-up things. For grown-up money, but that means taking grown-up risks.'

'Yes, I know, but it's not that. A year ago, I'd have bounced all over this. I'd have been full of plans for overcoming Insight and returning victorious with an armful of plunder. Look at that

337

Flying Auction we attended. Neither of us even hesitated. I arrested a roomful of people right under the noses of the Time Police and you stole enough stuff to fund St Mary's for years. We didn't think twice, did we? And now . . . ?'

'Keep walking,' he said, consulting his compass and taking my arm. 'We can't afford to lose any time.'

I started walking again.

'The reason for you,' he said, 'is that you've lost control of your life. It's not the risk that's upsetting you – it's because things are being done to you instead of you doing them to other people. Max, if you weren't included in Dr Bairstow's briefing, that was for a reason and . . .'

'I'm never included in anything,' I said, angrily. 'He never told me about you – even after he knew.'

'That was for your own safety,' he said quietly. 'You acknow-ledged that yourself.'

'Not the point,' I said, not sure what the point was. 'I had my mind messed with – yes, for my own good. It's amazing what you can do to people if you tell them it's for their own good.'

'This is about Leon, isn't it?'

'What? No. Of course not.'

'Max, he didn't know Treadwell was Time Police. None of us did. Dr Bairstow set that up by himself. His plan was to spread the risk. Scatter his key people and leave them free to act as they saw fit. And he employed Smallhope and Pennyroyal to oversee everything. He was almost certain he'd be removed from St Mary's at one point and he was. The only thing he got wrong was how that would happen. He thought he'd just be sacked – not kidnapped and locked away out of sight with everyone being told he was dead. He intended to make contact eventually and plan our next step. And I'm pretty sure he had no idea how powerful these people were. Are. Or how far their influence reaches. Past, present, future – they're everywhere. Insight might have been tampering with History for hundreds of years. Of course I think they're Hoyle's shadowy figures, and possibly even behind Clive Ronan – though he might have been a double-edged weapon. And the more we do, the more we uncover. I suspect we're getting to the point where we need to involve the Time Police. Let them take over. In fact, our esteemed employers might be doing that at this very moment.'

'But . . .'

'And our problems will resolve themselves. If we prevail, then Dr Bairstow is reinstated and you and I will no longer be criminals. We can return to St Mary's. If that's what you want,' he said, raising the lantern to look at me. 'The thing is, Max, you'll be back in control of your life. Whatever decision you make will be yours. Matthew's growing up. And he'll be off to the Time Police soon for his sixth-form work – your respon- sibilities to him are changing. And obviously I don't want to hurt your feelings in any way, but at the moment you're crazier than a sack full of very crazy things. We finish here and then we go home. A good night's sleep or two, some decent food that doesn't come out of a tray, and you'll be in a much better condition to make decisions about the future. I'm right, aren't I?'

'You're a pain in the arse,' I said, because he was. And he was right, as well.

'Nearly there,' he said, raising the lantern. Our talk had taken us through Charterhouse, the site of a Carthusian monastery.

Not seeing why he should be the only one flinging around Fun Facts, I chipped in with a few of my own. 'Apparently,

Thomas More came here a lot. The monastery was dissolved by Fat Harry and the prior hanged, drawn and quartered, after which the site was purchased by Lord North.'

'Any relation?' enquired Markham.

'No idea. Probably.'

'Wonder how she's getting on.'

'I wouldn't worry too much about Miss North. Save your concern for the poor sods in the Time Police.'

We both laughed and I suddenly felt a little better. Still knackered but slightly more cheerful.

'Nearly there,' said Markham, again.

Hoxton was very much what estate agents would describe as an up-and-coming location. Still in the country but conveniently close to London, it was popular with members of the aristocracy, courtiers and foreign ambassadors who were snapping up property as fast as it could be built. Not least because its seclusion gave Catholics the privacy to celebrate Mass – forbidden throughout the country.

Even through the mist I could see this was an unexpectedly prosperous village. The main street was actually paved, which was more than could be said for most of London. I counted nearly twenty big houses along the main street. Mostly built of stone, with tiled roofs. Proud homeowners had set torches or lanterns to burn beside their front doors so we weren't in complete darkness.

Lord Monteagle's house was diagonally opposite as we lurked in the shadow of a large tree.

'That's the difference between rural and urban lurking,' said Markham chattily. 'This is a much healthier environment. More scenic, too.'

Lord Monteagle had a nice house. A very nice house. We knew it was his because of the crest over the door. Also stone built, gabled at each end, with three storeys. Two long wings led back from the street and framed a central door which was covered by a small porch. A burning torch had been thrust into the ground to light the way up the three semi-circular steps that lifted it above the level of the muddy cobbles.

No lights showed anywhere, but probably the servants would have put up the shutters as soon as darkness fell.

'Are they in?' whispered Markham. 'Suppose they're out.'

'They must be in,' I said with far more confidence than I felt. 'Where else would they be? The weather's awful – I'm frozen, by the way – the king's away hunting and Parliament hasn't opened yet. They'll be inside, by the fire, drinking wine and looking forward to their dinner. As I wish I was.'

I didn't mean to snap. Meddling with History always makes me nervous. My little heart was pounding away.

'No sign of anyone anywhere,' he said, peering up and down the street.

That was another thing. In the original version, the letter was delivered to Thomas Ward, one of Monteagle's servants. If no opportunity presented itself, then we were going to have to bang on the door which was a little more obtrusive than I was happy with. And which door? Front or back? It would make a difference. Front door would mark out the letter as important but we weren't dressed for that. They might take one look and set the dogs on us, in which case the letter would never be delivered. If we nipped down the alley on the right-hand side of the house and banged on the servants' door, then no, they probably wouldn't set the dogs on us, but that approach marked the letter as not that important. It might not be taken directly to Monteagle, it might be set aside for a while. Or even mislaid. Or not delivered until it was too late.

I peered up and down the street. Everything was silent. Not even a dog barked. The night smelled of smoke, horses and cooking. For how long could we safely stand here? Would the village employ a night watchman?

'I'm going to knock at the front door,' said Markham. 'We can't stand around all night. Someone will report us. Or set the dogs on us. Monteagle's not likely to answer his own door so I'll just hand the letter to whoever does.'

A sensible course of action. I should agree. Except . . .

I put my hand on his arm. 'Wait.'

'Why?'

'I don't know. Just give it a minute.'

'Max . . .'

'I don't know why. Just . . . wait . . . please.'

We stood silently. Water dripped off something. Me, probably. Long minutes passed. Neither of us moved an inch.

And then . . .

'Someone's coming,' hissed Markham. 'I can see a light.'

A man was approaching the Monteagle house. Could this be Thomas Ward? I could make out a tall-crowned hat and a good thick cloak. He was on foot – his footsteps ringing loud in the cold night air – and he was carrying a small keg under one arm.

My mind was still running on gunpowder. 'Oh my God, Insight are blowing up Lord Monteagle.'

'No,' said Markham, in the sort of voice you use with a not very bright puppy who still hasn't quite mastered not peeing

342

in the corner. 'He's been to scrounge a keg of spirits for his master. Brandy, probably.'

My legs sagged with relief. Actually, nearly all of me sagged with relief.

'Don't sag too soon,' warned Markham. 'He might not be part of the Monteagle household.'

'If luck is on our side, then he is.'

'Luck is something we shouldn't push.'

'Who are you and what have you done with the real Markham? Look – according to contemporary reports, at around seven, a footman is approached by "a man of indifferent stature". That could easily be you. You charge him to put the letter into his lord's hands presently and he does so. By then we're halfway home and looking forward to a nice cup of tea.'

He nodded. 'Give me your cloak.'

'What?'

'It's more respectable than mine. Hand it over.'

I unfastened it and passed it to him. He swirled it around his shoulders. He was right. With his hat pulled low and his scruffiness concealed by the cloak, he looked nearly presentable. Which, with Markham, is about the best you can ever hope for.

'Got the letter?'

His face changed. He began to pat himself down.

I watched with increasing panic.

'Um . . .' He patted himself down some more.

I couldn't believe it. This could not be happening. We had a God-given opportunity . . . 'You idiot,' I hissed, 'don't tell me you've lost the bloody letter.'

'Um . . .'

'You've lost it, haven't you?' I stared wildly around as if I might see it lying somewhere in the dark. 'How could you be so . . . ?' And then I realised. 'Bastard.'

He was laughing at me. 'That's better. There's the Max we all know and love. Ricocheting between ice-cold calm and flat-out panic.'

I went to punch his lights out but he'd already stepped into the street.

The servant – Thomas Ward, I hoped – was approaching the alleyway. Obviously, he'd use the servants' entrance.

Markham raised his hand. 'Ho there, good fellow.'

There's no escape. I think Lady Amelia rubs off on everyone, sooner or later.

The servant stopped, peering suspiciously. Sensibly Markham made no move to approach, giving him time to assess the stranger accosting him.

I held my breath. Would he just walk away? And if he did stay, would he take the letter? And if he took the letter, would he simply throw it away as soon as we disappeared back into the night? We had no money with which to bribe him. A huge oversight on our part. Would he shout for the watchman, sound the alarm? Would we end up, yet again, running for our lives?

Slowly Markham held out the letter. 'Lord Monteagle. His life depends upon it. Deliver it to his hand this night, I charge you.'

The servant glared suspiciously. I really didn't blame him. He was in a Catholic household. These were suspicious times. For all he knew this was one of Cecil's traps.

His next actions confirmed this. Firmly shaking his head, he took two steps back and refused to take the letter.

I couldn't believe it. We'd striven to overcome every obstacle.

We'd identified the pivotal point, run the risk of returning to St Mary's, forged the letter, braved London at night, found Monteagle's house, attempted to hand over the letter – and then the bloody servant wouldn't accept it. I don't know if it was because he was naturally cautious, or because Markham hadn't greased his palm or what, but the bugger wouldn't cooperate at all, backing away, waving his hands in refusal, and when Markham tried to force it on him, he let it fall to the ground. Fortunately, it wasn't raining and the street was damp but not puddle-ridden.

I scampered to pick it up before something terrible happened to it because there are no do-overs in History. If anything went wrong then we were buggered. That's an historical technical term.

'I come from London,' said Markham, speaking quietly to make him listen. 'I have an urgent letter for my Lord Monteagle. As he values his life, he must have it in his hand tonight.'

The servant shook his head and went to turn away.

Shit.

Markham raised his lantern. The Bristol accent had disappeared. '*Thomas Ward.*'

The servant stopped dead, visibly shocked at both the tone and that Markham knew his name.

'Do you travel with my lord to London for Parliament?'

Grudgingly the servant nodded.

Markham stepped closer, saying softly, 'Make your goodbyes before you go, Master Ward. Neither you nor your master will survive the day.'

He turned his back and pulled his cloak around himself, saying curtly to me, 'Come.'

Still clutching the letter, I fell in beside him, sick at heart and wondering what the hell to do next.

'Wait.'

We turned.

The three of us stared at each other.

'Don't move,' whispered Markham to me.

Still Thomas Ward hesitated. I held my breath. We'd come so far, overcome so much – to fail now was unthinkable. Had I overestimated the benevolence of History?

I began to formulate alternatives. Knock him on the head, and Markham could deliver both the keg and the letter and hope no one noticed who he was. I couldn't see that working at all.

Knock him on the head and leave him on the doorstep with the letter lying on his chest, bang on the door and run away. That would be one way of getting Monteagle to read it, I suppose.

Back out in the road, Thomas Ward had edged away. Markham followed him but slowly, maintaining at least two sword lengths between them.

I passed the letter to Markham who held it out, angling it so the red sealing wax was visible in the flickering light. The two figures stood motionless. I gave Markham full credit for not trying to force him into a decision. To wait, patiently, for the man to come to him.

Time ticked on. Somewhere in the distance a dog rattled his chain and barked. How long before someone realised Thomas was taking an age to fetch the brandy and came out to look for him. For God's sake, we were trying to save hundreds, possibly thousands of lives here, but he had to take the bloody letter first. So much hung on such an insignificant action. I willed him. Reach out. Take the letter. Deliver it to your master.

Finally ... finally ... Thomas Ward – remember his name because he's one of the most important people in History – it's not always about kings and battles – reached out towards Markham. Markham himself leaned forwards, the letter in his hand. The gap closed. Markham released the scroll and stepped back.

Ward looked down, examining it in the light. I was still holding my breath. If he didn't get a move on, I was going to pass out. And then, with a brief nod to Markham, he turned on his heel and disappeared down the alleyway.

Markham stood stock-still. As did I. Somewhere a wooden door banged and then there was just the silence of the night.

We left nothing to chance. Markham shot off with his lantern to make sure Thomas Ward hadn't just tossed it aside as soon as he was out of sight.

I drew back into the cover of the tree again, trying to picture the scene.

Thomas would get inside, put down the keg and ... what?

Take off his hat and cloak.

Yes, and then what?

Would he take the letter to his master immediately?

Would he leave it on a table somewhere?

No – he wouldn't do that. I was almost certain that once the letter was inside it would find its way to Lord Monteagle. Perhaps not by Thomas, who might only be an outdoor man, but a household servant certainly. It might be on its way to him now.

I pictured Lord Monteagle sitting by a leaping fire in an ornate wooden chair. There would be candles flickering in the draughts – and there would be plenty of draughts. I saw a glass of brandy winking in the firelight. He might not be able to afford glass, but in my mind's eye he held a crystal goblet.

He might be alone – he might not. I had no idea who comprised his household. He might be waiting for his dinner. He might already be at dinner. In the original reports the letter had been delivered around seven-ish, and apart from the difference in the date – 26th October instead of 4th November – we'd adhered as closely as we could to the original version.

In my mind I saw a manservant approaching with the letter. Monteagle would examine the seal which, since it was only Markham's thumbprint, wouldn't give him any clue at all. Although once Monteagle had read the contents, he would understand why the writer hadn't used his personal seal.

What would he do then?

Sit and have a think?

Finish his dinner before taking any action?

Throw it on the fire? He hadn't in the original timeline and there was no reason he would do that now, but still I fretted.

Long, long minutes passed. Markham reappeared and joined me under the tree. 'Nothing in the alleyway,' he said in a low voice. 'The letter's definitely inside the house. And that's half the battle.'

I nodded. He was right. In fact, the only question could be how long it would be before any action—

A door slammed somewhere. A man's voice was raised, shouting for a horse. Another door banged. A dog began to bark and a horse neighed. I heard the sound of hooves on cobbles. Men were shouting to each other. Lights blazed as servants ran around with torches.

I couldn't believe it. After all Thomas's shilly-shallying around, it would appear Monteagle had no sooner assimilated the contents of the letter than he was roused to action. Popular report always said Monteagle was horrified at its contents and made haste to present the letter to Cecil, but I honestly thought he'd wait until the morning at least. It was as black as the Earl of Hell's waistcoat out here.

The shouting had increased. As had the sound of clattering hooves. Several men and horses by the sound of it. With one last warning shout, a gate was flung open and suddenly the now brightly lit alleyway was full of men on horseback. Three or four of them. Two held flaming torches. They paused briefly in the street, gathered themselves into a tight group and then, with a thunder of hooves, they galloped past us and off into the night.

'Well,' said Markham, handing me back my cloak. 'Job done and done, I think.'

29

It was well past midnight when we eventually got back to the pod. We passed the time by getting lost. Twice. It's really not easy finding your way around rural England on a dark October night. On the plus side, neither of us fell into the eventually located River Thames. As Markham said, either we were getting better at this or were so tired we couldn't even be bothered to throw ourselves into the river properly.

We approached Westminster with some caution, fully expecting the area to be alive with torches and shouting soldiers ransacking the House of Lords, turning people out of their beds for questioning and generally Foiling the Gunpowder Plot of 1605.

Well – that wasn't happening. No soldiers. No shouting. No searching. And definitely no Foiling.

'What is wrong with these people?' demanded Markham as we surveyed the empty street.

'I don't know and I'm too tired to care,' I said. 'Let's get our heads down and talk about it in the morning.'

We didn't even stay up for the traditional mug of tea and assignment inquest. Markham pulled out the blankets and pillows and we curled up on the floor and went straight to sleep.

I did remember to lock the door but that was about it as far as security precautions went. Had Insight turned up that night we would probably have been theirs for the taking.

They didn't, however – poor planning on their part – and both of us awoke the next morning, stiff, cold, with still damp clothes and shoes and pretty pissed off with things in general. We settled down with our early morning tea, each contemplating the other.

'You look like shit,' said Markham.

I nodded. 'Feel like shit, too. You, on the other hand, look as rough as you always do so it's hard to feel any sympathy.'

We sipped in silence for a while.

'Well,' said Markham, eventually. 'Now what?'

I shook my head. A very good question to which I did not have a very good answer.

I wanted to go home. I could make a very good case for jumping away from rat-infested Westminster for the bright lights and soft beds of Home Farm. Things weren't that simple, though. My instincts were telling me to stay put. I hate my bloody instincts.

'Let's go with what we know,' he said. 'The letter was delivered. Not fifteen minutes later a group of horsemen disappeared dramatically into the night. Heading in the right direction for London. That we know.'

'Monteagle must have given the letter to Cecil,' I said. 'He'd surely want to get rid of it as quickly as possible so he races to London. But unaccountably, it doesn't look as if Cecil's acted on it. Why not?'

I stared down at my tea. With a threat of this magnitude, Cecil should have gone straight to the king. Who would certainly have ordered a search of the entire area. They wouldn't have known what the threat consisted of – the letter was very vague – but they'd have searched until they found it. It seemed safe to assume that some, if not all, of the thirty-six barrels of gunpowder were already on site.

And they hadn't. Searched, I mean. Had King James urged caution? Did he not take the threat seriously? He was an intelligent and conscientious man so . . .

'He's not here,' I said, suddenly.

'What? Who's not where?'

'The king's not here,' I said, gabbling like an idiot. 'Remember? He's out hunting. The original letter was delivered to him on his return from a hunting trip. He's not in London.'

'Could Cecil have sent word to him?'

'Possibly,' I said, because we were in uncharted waters now. This is what happens when you attempt to change History. You don't have a clue what's going to happen next. 'In fact, probably. The gunpowder is almost certainly in place because Parliament's opening was delayed from its original date until 5th November. The king will return on the 4th. They'll discuss the letter, a search will be ordered, and the plot will come to light. The king's absence is just a very tiny hiccup and then everything will proceed exactly as it did before.'

I wished I sounded more convinced. This was the morning of the 27th October. There were nine days to Parliament opening. How much could go wrong in nine days?

The answer was – a lot. In fact, everything could go wrong in nine days. Or, given our luck, in nine minutes.

I looked at Markham. I could see by the expression on his face that the same thought had occurred to him. Far from being able to go home to fix ourselves and the pod, we were going to have to stay – another nine days here. I felt my stomach twist. I wanted to go home. I wanted a bath and one of Markham's magic breakfasts and to sleep for a week. None of that was going to happen.

'We have to stay,' I said. 'Otherwise, it's all in vain. We took a chance last night and so far, it seems to have paid off, but we're not out of the woods yet. Suppose Insight turn up on the 3rd or 4th of November, all ready to intercept the original letter and it doesn't show. They'll guess they've been rumbled. That might precipitate events and all our efforts will have been in vain. Think how we'd feel if, having got this far, we pushed off and something went wrong at the last moment. The job's only half done. We have to see it through to the end.'

He looked uncertain. 'I'm not sure, Max. If Smallhope and Pennyroyal were here then yes, possibly. If you were firing on all cylinders then possibly. But they're not and you're not, so I think you, at least, should leave.'

I could see I was going to have to box carefully with this. Markham's really easy-going and he doesn't say no very often but when he does, he means it. And he had a point. How much more could we or the pod do before something went badly wrong? If he was saying we'd done what we could, then maybe we should let events take their course.

'The problem is,' I said, carefully, 'if we do leave and then have to return, I might not be able to get the pod back to the precise time and place. We're here now – I think we should stay. There were quite a large number of conspirators. For all we know, some of them were members of Insight. Or Insight could be sponsoring them. They could be all over this even as we speak.'

He shifted position. 'We will get them, Max.'

'You don't know that.'

'Yes, I do. Something we do seriously pisses them off. Have you forgotten the night at Home Farm? When Bridget died?'

Actually, I had. I'm no stranger to provoking my managers to fits of homicidal rage but it's just a little disconcerting knowing that something I would say or do would provoke her to such an extent that she would put together a team to take out me and my innocent colleagues. It puts a crimp in the development of harmonious workplace relationships.

'Our main problem,' he said, 'is that we never expected to be here for nine days. We don't have enough rations or water.'

'We could split the difference,' I said, knowing he'd never agree. 'I stay and you go back for supplies and reinforcements. Smallhope and Pennyroyal are bound to be back by now.'

He just looked at me. OK – spectacularly bad idea.

'I'm sorry,' I said, 'but I feel very strongly that we shouldn't take any chances over this. I'm not leaving until I know the plot has been discovered and all danger past. I accept your arguments but they aren't strong enough to weigh with me. Sorry.'

'All right,' he said, getting up and rummaging in the locker. 'Let's take stock. Food for three or four days – if we share one meal once a day, we have enough for eight days. We have water purification tablets but we'll still need to be careful with the water. I am not drinking from the Thames and neither are you. No showers. We shut down all non-essential systems. We crack the door occasionally to let in some fresh air. One of us regularly goes on patrol to watch the undercroft – the other stays inside monitoring the cameras and surrounding areas. Deal?'

'Deal,' I said.

*

It was shit. Utter shit. The weather was shit. It rained every day. Markham, busy checking out the area in his own, unobtrusive way, came back soaked to the skin. This wouldn't normally be a problem but we had no way of drying clothes. He insisted I stay inside, arguing quite sensibly that there was no point in two of us being cold, wet and uncomfortable.

He would stagger, shivering, back inside the pod, strip off and wrap himself in a blanket to try to get warm again. I insisted he have the lion's share of our tray because he deserved it. Re-dressing in wet clothes two or three times a day is no fun.

I kept the door open whenever I thought it was safe but the inside of the pod was becoming more than a little ripe. You never see this on time travel holos, do you? People sniffing their armpits, checking their clothes for mould because everything's damp, and fantasising about hot baths. Still, as Markham said, at least we blended in with everyone else, olfactorily speaking, so that was all right then.

Boredom was the biggest problem. We played word games. We played guessing games. We tried to play two-person chess. I mean chess with only two pieces – him and me. That didn't work at all and we nearly came to blows. We even spent one morning trying to stand on our heads. I can only say it seemed a good idea at the time – and we only desisted when Markham collapsed sideways, crashing into the locker door which sprang open and the kettle and mugs fell out on top of him. I rushed to save the kettle because if anything happened to that then we were definitely going home. Fortunately, it was unharmed.

'What about me?' said Markham indignantly as I cuddled the kettle.

'I'm sorry – I don't understand the question.'

So desperate were we that on the fourth or fifth day, I think, we discussed Markham taking my clothes and going outside dressed as a woman.

He objected on the grounds that delightful though it would be to be encased in something warm and dry that meant my clothes would then be wet as well. It was a good idea, he said, even if the universe was forcing him to appear in public in women's clothing for the umpteenth time, but we'd keep that for emergencies.

I worried about him. He went out into the rain four or five times a day, splashing through the streaming streets, and there was never, ever anything to report. The whole area around the House of Lords was deserted and the undercroft door remained firmly locked. I would make him a hot drink on his return, endlessly reusing the tea bags until they split. We ran out of milk and lemon juice. Then we ran out of sugar. This was suffering on an epic scale.

And it wasn't doing me any good, either. This long inactivity was tearing at my nerves. I honestly thought the violence at Lincoln had been easier to deal with than this. I'm not very good at sitting still and doing nothing.

By the 3rd November we were running short of nearly everything. Time, patience, supplies, places to spread out Markham's clothing and my cloak. This wasn't a Jane Austen novel so he hadn't caught a fatal illness just by getting wet, but I worried for him nonetheless. I tried putting the heating on but it took too much power and the solar panels were almost useless and, as he pointed out, when midnight struck on 4th November, whatever happened, we would need to get out of here fast.

*

The morning of the 4th November dawned. Well, no, it didn't, actually. The cloud cover was too low. It had stopped raining and now we were doing thick, wet smog. We'd had everything else, so why not?

We dared not take our eyes off the undercroft. I'd given Markham the last tray of compo, saying, quite honestly, that I wasn't hungry. I sat in silence, sipping some weak black tea and vowing to give up all things time travel and get a nice office job.

'Like the one you had at Insight?' said Markham.

'Exactly like that. Warm office, vending machines, sandwiches delivered at lunchtime, coffee machine – all right, forget that last one – but yeah, I didn't know when I was well off.'

'Until your boss tried to kill you.'

'Other than that,' I said, with dignity.

We walked the streets together that day, looking for any signs that Insight was or had been here. Nothing. We looked for signs of Cecil and his soldiers. Nothing. We looked for Guy Fawkes disguised as the servant John Johnson, or Catesby delivering kegs of gunpowder – anything that would give us a clue as to what was happening. We even looked for signs the king had returned. We walked and walked. There was no point in returning to the pod since it was now warmer and dryer and less smelly outside in the street than inside. We strode briskly to try to stay warm. Markham occasionally complained about his wet clothes chafing. Apparently, he had a rash. You don't see that on fashionable time travel holos, either. He offered to show me. I declined on the grounds of safeguarding my mental health.

And then, in the afternoon – excitement. Huge excitement. A squad of soldiers turned up.

'This is it,' said Markham as we crowded into a convenient

doorway to watch events unfold. 'Thank God. Bugger saving the country and the future of democracy – I want some dry underwear.'

There were six of them with a guard commander. The men wore what looked like their own clothes with a breastplate and helmet. They carried pikes. The officer – no idea what his rank was – was very young and wore a black suit with a very dashing short cloak and a tall hat. He marched his men around the corner, shouted a command and stood back as they got stuck in.

We kept well back behind the curious crowd that had gathered.

Someone apparently had a key to the undercroft because they didn't break the door down. One remained outside and the officer led his men down the steps.

'Oh my God,' I said, hardly able to breathe with excitement. 'We've successfully saved History. We're heroes.'

'Thank God,' said the hero next to me. 'I definitely need to get out of these keks. I'm rubbed raw, you know. Raw!'

We waited for the shouts of discovery. The officer would send a messenger for reinforcements and someone more senior than he to carry the can should everything go tits up.

They weren't in there very long. And there was no shouting. No messenger. No excitement. No nothing.

'No,' I said, sliding effortlessly into panic mode. 'No, no, no. What's happened?'

The officer emerged, dusting off his gloved hands. I don't know why. He obviously hadn't done anything.

Markham sighed. 'Seriously – you have to be a member of the officer class to miss thirty-six barrels of gunpowder.'

They even relocked the door. Then he lined up his men and marched them off again. The sound of their steps died away.

'Shit,' I shouted after them. 'Come back, you dozy pillocks. There's gunpowder everywhere down there. How could you miss it?'

Markham patted my arm and gently recommended I not shout at the soldiers.

'Perhaps they did find it,' I said, clutching at anything that even remotely resembled a straw. 'Perhaps they've gone away to report.'

'They didn't leave anyone on guard,' said Markham, who had remembered to count everyone in and everyone out again. 'So that's not likely.'

Excitement over, the crowd began to disperse and we returned to the pod.

I tried to calm down. I sat down and attempted to formulate a plan in which one of us could raise the alarm without incriminating ourselves. I got up and paced. Insomuch as three paces one way and three another could constitute pacing. And Markham had to keep getting out of the way which he obligingly did the first ten or twelve times and then became irritated and told me to pack it in.

I packed it in and tried to think what to do next.

'For God's sake,' he said five minutes later. 'I can hear your brain working from here. Will you please start pacing again?'

'Sorry.' I went to sit beside him on the floor. 'OK. Suppose we've got this wrong. Suppose by delivering the letter early we've changed some small detail we don't know about and the plotters are successful after all.'

Markham tried very hard to reassure me but his heart wasn't in it. It was all so obvious. We'd done something. Somehow, unknowingly, we'd done something. Our presence here had changed a tiny detail. Perhaps the soldiers hadn't found the gunpowder because Catesby and Fawkes had stored it somewhere else. In which case we were buggered. Or Monteagle had ignored the letter and the horsemen galloping from his house were just on their way to a dinner engagement and were late. Or those soldiers had just been carrying out a routine, not very important check prior to Parliament re-opening tomorrow. Suppose, although Catesby and his friends initiated the plot, Markham and I were the ones who actually made it happen.

Or – and trust me, I was well down the Purple Path of Paranoia by this point – it might even have been something we'd done at Runnymede or Lincoln. Some tiny action or inaction that had worked its way down the centuries and would culminate in the success of the Gunpowder Plot and the end of things as we'd known them, and it was all our fault.

Time dragged by. We talked and talked. The best plan we could come up with was to have Markham break into the under-croft, 'discover' the gunpowder and raise the alarm.

Even I could see a lot of things wrong with that plan. 'They'll almost certainly take you away for "questioning" and not everyone survives that. I won't let you do it.'

'In that case, allow me to introduce Plan B. I set off a small explosion – just a pinch of powder, perhaps. To attract attention. Except I don't have a slow fuse or any method of making one. I suppose I could make a tiny pile of gunpowder, chuck a lighted match at it and run like hell.'

I frowned. 'The chances of setting off the other thirty-six barrels . . .'

'Would be good, yeah.'

'Looking on the bright side,' I said, gloomily, 'we wouldn't have to worry about an exit strategy.'

'*You* won't. You won't be here.'

'I'm not leaving you.'

'I'm not taking you down with me.'

I grabbed his arm. 'No . . .'

'No, Max. Listen to me. You know who I am. I have responsibilities. They're bred into me. I can't run away from this. I'm duty-bound to defend the realm. To keep this country safe. Admittedly it isn't quite as glorious as defeating our enemies in battle – I've always thought I'd be quite good at that – but that's not really important, is it? The important thing is that the country's government survives.'

'But you wouldn't.'

'Not important.'

'It's important to me.'

'Well, thank you, but let's face it, Max, I've been living on borrowed time since 1483. I've had a great life. I'll be sorry to leave it. Desperately sorry. But it's my duty. You could say it's my job.'

I was crying.

'Hey,' he said, gently pulling my hands away from my face. 'Don't cry. Perhaps this is what you saved me for. Why you were in the river that night. You saved me so I could do this. It's ironic, isn't it? I went into the river not that far from here – I think you could call this my destiny.'

I would have called it his stupidity but I couldn't get the words out. I hung on to him as if I could physically prevent him putting either of his daft plans into action.

'As soon as it gets dark, I'll nip in there. That door won't give me any trouble. I'll take a matchbox, break open a keg – if they're actually there – lay a trail of powder and . . .'

'No,' I said. 'That plan is off the table. Don't even think about it. We'll work on Plan A. I stand outside keeping watch while you break in, grab a couple of kegs and rush into the street shouting, "Look what I've found."'

'Yes? And then what?'

'You drop the evidence, leaving it for all to see, and we both leg it to the pod before the guards turn up.'

He gestured at the screen showing the foggy street and a few hazy buildings. Well-muffled men were walking past, heads down, cloaks pulled tightly around them, heading for home. 'How many of those out there are Insight, do you think?'

'Not a problem. I cover you while you're breaking in. Anyone looking even remotely threatening gets a jolt from my stun gun.'

He smiled at me. 'You and your stun gun against . . .'

'Against the world,' I finished. 'Start feeling sorry for the world.'

'You could just go and get help,' he said. 'Home Farm. Smallhope and Pennyroyal. London. Leon. Evans. St Mary's. Treadwell and Peterson. Even the Time Police.'

'Firstly, I'm not leaving you on your own. You need me to tell you what you're doing wrong. And secondly, you know as well as I do that the chances of getting this pod back to the right time and place are almost zero. And thirdly, any attempt by you to get me and the pod out of here . . .' I pulled out my much-discussed stun gun, 'will be met with deadly force. Just as long as we're both clear on that. You need me at your shoulder telling you you're an idiot.'

He scowled. 'A compromise,' he said eventually. 'You stay in

362

the pod and monitor the street. If Insight are here then there's a good chance they'll drop me before I can even get the door open.'

I nodded.

'And that will be the moment to go for help.'

I thought about it. 'Reluctantly – agreed.'

'OK – no more messing about with guesses and speculation. I'm going over there to take a look around.'

'Take my cloak again.'

He flung it around his shoulders. I went to the console, split the screen, and set one camera to show the door to the under-croft. The rest were on the street in both directions.

'Right,' he said. 'I nip over the road and check things out. If it all goes pear-shaped then you're out of here at the speed of light. Come back with the cavalry.'

I nodded – filling the pod with unhappy historian vibes.

He paused and took my hand.

'Max,' he said gently. 'You have to accept this.'

'Accept what?'

'This is why you saved me. This is what I was saved for. This is my duty. My responsibility.'

'I'm pretty sure it isn't.'

He pulled away. 'You have to let me do it.'

I had such a bad, bad feeling about this. So much could go wrong. Insight were out there somewhere, I was sure of it. And they were deadly. But, try as I might, I couldn't think of an alternative plan. Perhaps I could delay him until I could come up with something.

'Do you miss it? That other life?'

He shrugged. 'Don't remember a lot of it. You and I are the same, Max. Our lives are what we've made them.'

'But you were a prince.'

'Still am,' he said. 'No one can take that away from me. I'll always be Richard of Shrewsbury. Son of one king, brother of another. Ancestor of many more.'

'Do you think one day they'll kill you?'

'Who?'

'Anyone. The government because of who you are. The Time Police because one day, like Clive Ronan, your influence on events is over. Hunter, because she fell over your boots again . . . even a couple of rogue bounty hunters.'

'If I pull this off, think how grateful people will be. I might even be accepted back into society.'

I must have looked distressed.

'Max, I know things aren't good at the moment but this too will pass. Everything does. In the end.'

I shivered. 'Don't talk about the end.'

Markham smiled. 'To quote someone not a million miles from here – everything's going to be absolutely fine.' He drew a deep breath. 'Right then. Off I go.'

I wiped my nose on my sleeve. It's not as endearing a habit as it sounds. 'Can you remember the way?'

'Any more cheek from you and I'll knock you unconscious, lay in the coordinates myself and send you to safety whether you like it or not.'

I tried to smile. 'You don't know how.'

'Course I do,' he said. 'Who do you think taught Evans? I love the way historians think only they can say, "Computer, initiate jump."'

The computer trilled.

'See?' He turned his head. 'Discontinue.'

364

The computer trilled again.

I addressed the console. 'We will be taking a few minutes to discuss pod disloyalty later.'

'Look,' he said, gently pulling his hand free. 'I'm not going to take any chances, I promise you. I've got a daughter, remember. I'll just nip over there and check things out. Then I'll come back, report, and depending on what I find, we'll both decide what to do next. OK?'

Reluctantly, I nodded. 'Yeah.'

He let himself out. I watched him cross the road and disappear into the shadows.

And not come back.

30

Of course he didn't come back.

Of course something had gone wrong.

Of course he'd been caught poking around. Either by Guy Fawkes, or by Insight, or by the palace guards. Let's face it – if anyone's going to be caught red-handed – actually standing over the gunpowder – it's going to be Markham. I should never have let him go by himself.

The minutes ticked by. I couldn't take my eyes from the screen. The last days had dragged past like treacle struggling uphill – now, typically, the minutes were flying by and it was very nearly eleven o'clock. If we were adhering to the previous timetable then the soldiers should turn up at midnight, but we weren't adhering to the original schedule. History had come loose and was flapping in the wind and anything could happen.

Come on, Markham.

I swear if he was in there doing his conjuring tricks again then he might as well die in the explosion because I myself would rip him from limb to limb and feed his spleen to anything that liked the look of it.

I drummed my fingers on the console. I know he'd said to

stay put but this was really not the moment to start doing as I was told.

Instinctively I engaged the camo device. It wasn't too late for Insight to turn up and I didn't want them recognising a pod. That done, I let myself quietly out and into the thick, foggy, moisture-laden night. And, for the record, it was very cold without my cloak.

I squinted around. There was no one in sight. No sound from the dark shapes of the buildings. No movement in the streets. It was on nights like this, nearly three hundred years in the future, that the Ripper would walk. I should know. I was there.

There was a hazy golden nimbus at the entrance to St Margaret's Lane which might have been a lantern high up on a wall, or perhaps a candle in a window, lighting a husband's way home from the pub. Although given the silence around me, everyone was asleep.

I stayed in the shadows as long as I could, trailing my fingers along the damp, sooty walls to find my way towards the door to the undercroft. Which was ajar.

I stood on the threshold, held my breath and listened.
Nothing.

The few steps led down from street level. This wasn't strictly a cellar, although it's often described as such. This was a lower floor, slightly below street level, with the House of Lords directly above it.

I put my hand on the wall, leaned forwards a little – as if that would help – and listened as hard as I could. Silence. Not even a rat scuttering in the corners.

I could feel grit under my fingers. It still smelled of the coal that had, until recently, been stored here.

I pushed at the door, opening it wide enough for me to slip through. At first, I thought it was my imagination – seeing light where none could possibly be – but the more I looked, the more I was convinced I could see a faint gleam in the darkness. Silently, one careful step at a time, I eased my way down the shallow stairs and into a narrow passage which doglegged left.

I was right. A closed lantern stood on the floor just around the corner. No naked torches here, obviously. Not with thirty-six barrels of gunpowder in such close proximity.

Now that I was around the corner I could see more clearly. The passage ended in a doorway, currently propped open.

I crept down for a closer look.

The far end and the corners were lost in shadows but I could see a long space ahead of me. Much bigger than I had imagined, given the meanness of the building above. Perhaps it extended under the two private houses as well.

The floor was paved, I think, but covered in mud. I suspected frequent floods and heavy rain had washed in whatever shit was lying in the street above. The walls were an odd mixture of old flaking stone patched with brick in places.

The undercroft was empty.

Shit – the undercroft was empty. No Fawkes, no barrels, nothing. The sick, bitter disappointment nearly overwhelmed me. Far from saving the day, we'd only made things worse. Somehow our interference meant they'd stored the gunpowder elsewhere and we had no idea where and it was too late to search now. Parliament would open at first light and *boom*. This is what happens when people try to interfere with History. Catastrophe.

This was why Insight weren't here. They weren't here because the gunpowder wasn't here either. *This* was why we'd had a completely free hand. We were in the wrong place. Either by accident or design, Insight had outsmarted us.

Sick fear battled with sick disappointment, robbing me of coherent thought. All this work and all this effort and it was very possible we'd actually brought about the thing we were trying to prevent. A lot of people were going to die and it would be our fault. And that wasn't taking into account the bloody aftermath. How easy to take over a country when the entire government has been wiped out in a second.

I stood up straight and took one or two deep breaths. No. Wait. Wait. Stop and think, Maxwell. The House of Lords is just above you. Unless they'd packed the chamber itself with barrels of gunpowder – and someone would have noticed that – then this was the only place it could be. It *had* to be here. Stop panicking and look properly. And watch out for Insight. If they were here.

About to take a step into the dark undercroft, I stopped. No, Insight weren't here, were they? Why not? You'd think the place would be crawling with them, standing in the shadows, watching to make sure nothing went wrong with their precious scheme. Where were they? We were in the final hours before Parliament opened. This was 4th November. Midnight approached. In the original timeline, the soldiers turned up in time, but now . . .

Something danced on the edge of my thoughts. November 4th . . . original timeline . . . What was it?

And then it came to me. The letter. The key to the whole business. I'd been right all along. In the original timeline the letter was delivered to Lord Monteagle on the evening of 4th November.

That's where Insight were. They were at Hoxton. They had to be. I'd put good money on it that at this very moment they were all standing in the shelter of that tree opposite the Monteagle house, wondering where the original messenger had got to. All set to stab him – and possibly Thomas Ward as well – and grab the letter. I could picture the scene. See the tiny flame in the dark as what could be called the second most important document in British History went up in flames. Drop the burning letter – grind the ashes into the mud – step over the bodies – and vanish into the night.

Only that hadn't happened. The letter hadn't arrived. Because Monteagle already had it. How long would they wait there before . . . ?

Before making their way back here. At speed. Their plans had been derailed but it might not be too late. They'd be on their way to make sure everything here could still proceed according to plan. They could be here at any moment.

They could be here now.

Watching where I put my feet, I took two silent steps down into the room. Which altered my perspective slightly. And there it was. A series of six deep archways ran along the left-hand wall. I took two more steps and now I could see – not clearly because the light wasn't good enough – that each alcove was neatly stacked with half a dozen small kegs, set well back and forming a neat pyramid. Three on the bottom row, two on the next and one on the top. Thirty-six in all.

I bent forwards, resting my hands on my thighs, light-headed with relief. I should stop cursing the soldiers because this might well account for their inexplicable failure to spot the gunpowder during their earlier search. Anyone just sticking their head around the door would see nothing in the main body of the undercroft. Only a series of broken pillar bases that had once held up the beamed roof. I could easily imagine a bunch of grumpy squaddies, turfed out of their warm barracks on a shit afternoon for a very perfunctory security check, giving this only the briefest glance before deciding there was nothing to see here, boys, and pushing off again. That I could see the arches at all was only thanks to another closed lantern carefully placed as far away as possible from the powder.

And then, somewhere in the depths, a shadow moved. I thought I heard a foot scrape across the dusty floor. Heart thumping, I eased back to the wall, head tilted, listening. A stealthy footstep? Or just a rat? Or Markham? Or even Guy Fawkes lighting his bloody fuse?

What should I do?

I knew better than to call Markham's name. I should wait to see what happened. There was a corresponding series of arches over to my right – empty, as far as I could see. And a rotting wooden door that led only into darkness. That was a nasty thought. Was there actually another way in and out? Had we wasted our time watching one door while Guy Fawkes brought the powder through another? That would be so typical.

Markham could be anywhere. I eased myself back the way I had come. My main concern was that someone – I don't know who, anyone – could slam the outside door shut and I'd be trapped here, so I stood stock-still and waited in the dark, listening to my heart thump and trying to think what to do next.

And then, thank God, a figure emerged from one of the arched recesses off to the right. My massive surge of relief was short-lived. This man bore a lantern and it very obviously wasn't Markham. Even more worryingly, he was carrying a drawn sword and even in the wavering light I could see the tip was stained with something dark.

Shit – this must be him. Guy Fawkes. Guido Fawkes. John Johnson. Whatever he was calling himself today. Had he already lit the slow fuse? Was he already making his escape? Should I try to detain him or let him get away? Where were the guards? Shit – would all this go wrong at the very last moment?

Shit. Shit. Shit.

I acted without thinking. Again.

I stepped into his path. He started back in fear, lantern swinging. Shadows jumped around the walls and ceiling which didn't do anyone's nerves any good. I saw him open his mouth in surprise and hissed, 'Guido Fawkes,' which must have frightened the living daylights out of him because, as far as he knew, no one here was aware of his true identity.

He staggered back two or three steps, collided with a pillar base and lost his balance. His hands were full – lantern in one, sword in the other. He dropped his sword. I heard it clatter as it hit the stone base. The mud floor was damp and his foot slipped beneath him. I saw the long skid mark in the mud and then he was on the ground.

I didn't hesitate. Stepping up, I gave him a good zap with my stun gun. Possibly a little more than he deserved but there had been blood on his sword.

His lantern was still lit – perhaps they had a design that kept them alight even if they were dropped. I didn't know and I didn't care. I grabbed it and held it high.

Guy Fawkes was much younger than I thought he would be. His skin was pale although a good zapping might be the reason for that. His hat had fallen off, revealing shoulder-length dark hair and the almost obligatory moustache and beard, somewhat grown out. I wondered if he'd actually been living here in the undercroft. That would certainly account for never seeing him go in or out. His clothes were black but so were everyone else's these days. His white collar was grubby though. He'd obviously been wearing it for a very long time. He smelled very similar to me and Markham, so yes, he probably had been living here.

Lying there in a pool of lantern light and with his eyes closed, he looked very young and vulnerable.

What clinched it for me, however, was that he was spurred and booted. Ready to light the fuse and ride like the devil, leaving the citizens of London to their fate. Heartless bastard. His religious fanaticism would have led him to murder hundreds of people and be responsible for the deaths of thousands more.

I hardened my heart and went to look for Markham.

Who was in a heap in the second archway to the right. I rolled him over. The front of his doublet was wet. As I raised the lantern, he opened his eyes. 'The swiving swiver swiving well stabbed me.'

There was no time to waste on comforting him. 'You're a bloody idiot. Where are you hurt?'

'Left shoulder.'

'You have to get up. Use me.'

He groaned and pulled himself up.

'Come on,' I said, pulling his right arm around my neck. 'It's not far. Just put one foot in front of the other.'

'Wait.'

I remembered why we were here. 'Has he lit the fuse?'

'Yes,' he said faintly. 'Far arch.'

I did not just drop him. I want that made perfectly clear. I simply released him so he could lie comfortably on the ground, grabbed the lantern and sprinted to the far end of the undercroft.

I could see something glowing. Before anyone panics utterly – that's my job, so hands off – it was a slow fuse, a simple hemp rope soaked in something I really didn't care about. I could see the glow travel imperceptibly towards the barrels. Less than an inch a minute, I discovered afterwards.

My first instinct was to run. My second was to yank it away from the barrels, but it might be firmly secured and if I brought the barrels down and the powder spilled everywhere . . .

Trying not to think about the time, or the soldiers, or Markham bleeding to death over there, I set down the lantern because my hand was shaking and pulled very gently. The fuse didn't appear to be attached to anything so I did it again. I felt movement. From the weight of it this was a very long rope. It would have to be. If Parliament opened just after dawn . . . although how much earlier would the lords have to assemble . . . at around an inch a minute . . . For God's sake, Maxwell – focus.

Very, very slowly I pulled. It moved, but reluctantly. It was no good. I was going to have to get up close and personal. I left the lantern where it was – if Fawkes had kept it well away from the gunpowder who was I to do differently? I followed the fuse with my foot, eventually locating the other end, resting on a small pile of gunpowder in the very last alcove.

Very, very carefully I dragged it away from the barrels. I could feel the sweat rolling down my back. It would be so typical if something went horribly wrong now. When I decided I'd achieved a safe distance, I stamped on the end to try to extinguish it. I failed. I don't know what it had been soaked in but it was certainly unputtable outable.

In desperation, I picked the whole thing up, coiled it like a snake, and heaved it over one shoulder. I certainly wasn't going to leave it here. It still wasn't too late for something to go horribly wrong.

I left the lantern where it was, raced back to Markham who was struggling to his feet, gave Guido another conscienceless zapping because, yes, all right, he was going to be tortured and executed, but he himself was no angel. He fell back into the mud, moaning and dribbling.

I grabbed Markham again for attempt number two. He was surprisingly heavy. As I told him. He grunted. The steps were a struggle. He was bleeding everywhere. Nothing I could do about that at the moment.

We emerged into the street. I've never been so pleased to see fog in all my life. I dropped the fuse into a nearby horse trough and tried to get my hip under Markham's to give him some extra support. His arm was slipping through my blood-covered hand and I had a horrible feeling that if he fell now, I'd never get him back on his feet again.

Just as I was thinking we would make it back to safety after all, there was the sound of running feet. Heading in our direction. Men were shouting commands. I could hear clinking metal. Lantern light flickered off grubby walls. The time was nearly midnight and the guards were coming – just as they should do. We'd done it after all. Markham got suddenly heavier.

I tightened my grip on him and said, 'You're drunk.'

He grunted. 'I wish.'

He staggered artistically, nearly dragging me to the ground with him, and raised his voice in song. Apparently he got knocked down. But he got up again. I wasn't ever going to keep him down. And on and on and on. I made secret plans to hurl him into the Thames. Someone would rescue him. They always did.

The ringing footsteps were very close now.

I slipped effortlessly into *martyred woman slagging off useless male* mode. As a head of department, wife, mother, and fifty per cent of Pros and Cons, it gets a lot of practice. I was giving Markham a right earbashing when a platoon of soldiers trotted around the corner. These were a whole step up from the unenthusiastic amateurs from earlier today. They had their hands on their swords and definitely meant business.

They'd seen us. They'd certainly heard us. I reckon half of London had heard us. It was vitally important not to look the slightest bit guilty. Not even a little bit. I was just an honest goodwife bringing the man of the house safely home after a night in the tavern with his good-for-nothing mates.

And the fuse was at the bottom of the horse trough and nothing to do with me.

They didn't even look at us. In fact, we had to flatten ourselves against a wall as they trotted past. Men on a mission. And for anyone querying the current whereabouts of Guy Fawkes – he was still in his beloved undercroft. Trust me, I'd been keeping one eye on the exit. If he had appeared, I'd have lightly tossed Markham into the nearest gutter and kicked Fawkes back down the steps. I was in no mood to mess about with anyone.

All I wanted was to go home and have a bath.

And I still had to go to work on Monday.

Longest weekend ever.

31

As usual, my problems came from an unexpected direction.

The soldiers trotted past us without a second glance. Not a problem. They vanished towards the undercroft and I and the drunken sailor staggered back to the safety of the pod.

Except – and I wasn't going to mention this bit, but Markham laughed like a drain when he found out and said if I didn't tell people then he would. Fine. Here goes.

I couldn't find the bloody thing.

I always knew this would happen one day. Every time someone said, 'Why don't we use the camo device?' I had to point out how difficult it is to find anything when you're in a hurry. Think back to the last time you couldn't find your keys in your handbag. The fumbling. The cursing. The rummaging. The panic. Even though you know they have to be in there somewhere. The final upending of the bag all over the floor. And that's just a bloody handbag and a set of keys.

Now scale that up to an invisible pod. In the dark. And the fog. While struggling to support a slowly bleeding to death ex-Head of Security. Trust me, a camouflage device is all very well but not in a major crisis when a quick getaway is imperative. Leon had taught me always to exit the door, turn around and remember whatever was to the left and the right so I could easily locate the pod in an emergency.

Guess what I'd forgotten to do?

Yes, all right, but I can't think of everything. I was too busy saving the young master. Who was never going to let me hear the end of this so it would be just as well if he died now. I'd activated the camo device in case Insight had turned up while I was out looking for him. Now, of course – sensitive readers look away now, please – I couldn't find the useless, arse-wiping, bastard, useless, swiving, pox-ridden, useless, futtucking pod.

I kept moving, honestly expecting to run into it at any moment. Well, that didn't happen.

I staggered on and on, eventually reaching a wider thorough-fare. I could see the Thames through gaps in the buildings. I'd come too far. I'd missed the pod completely.

I wheeled around, dragging a protesting Markham with me and that's when it all went wrong for me.

The world canted sideways. Suddenly it was daylight. The Thames was packed with boats full of screaming people. Boatmen were coming to blows. The city was on fire. Spanish ships sailed up the river, raking both banks with gunfire. Houses exploded. Giant fires broke out. People screamed and ran and were crushed. Or fell into the river and drowned. And then I was in a shadowy place and Peterson lay at my feet. White and bloody. A massive bubo throbbed in his groin. He called to me to save him and I couldn't reach him. I reached out and my arms met only tendrils of fog. Thicker and deadlier than mere river fog. This was a real pea-souper from Old London Town. Something dark rushed past me. I felt the air move. The fog swirled in its wake.

I panicked. I couldn't find the pod. I couldn't get myself or

Markham to safety. We would die here. From the guards. From the Spanish. From the flames. From the plague. From the thing that waited for me.

This could not be happening. Not now. Not at the very worst possible moment. An old enemy waited for me in the dark and I could barely keep my balance.

The fog moved again. I couldn't see him but he was here, I knew it. Suddenly I felt his foul breath hot in my ear.

See . . . Me . . .

I shook my head. 'No. No. Get away.'

I felt Markham lift his head. 'Max, look at me. At *me*.'

Blood was running down his arm. My own hand was slick with it. I was losing my grip on him. I was losing my grip on everything. Darkness awaited me.

'See me . . . see me . . . see me . . .'

The words whispered around me. Thick. Sibilant. Pushing their way through the fog. Filling my world. I could neither see nor hear. He was standing beside me. Reaching out for me. There was no escape.

Something slapped me hard across the face. Really hard. My head snapped back with the impact and I tasted blood. Salty and warm. And then again. My head snapped back the other way.

Something heavy dragged at me. I was doing something important. Why couldn't I remember what it was? Whose blood was this?

A voice shouted, 'Max . . .'

Who was that? Who wanted me? I couldn't see anything in the fog. Somewhere over to my left, a bell rang.

Markham's voice intoned, *'Ask not for whom the bell tolls. It tolls for thee.'*

And suddenly I was back. I knew where I was. I was standing in a foggy street in 17th-century London with a bloody and near unconscious Markham draped around me, black treason was abroad, and I couldn't find the pod. Just a normal day at work, really.

I heaved Markham into an even more uncomfortable position and said, 'We have to get out of here now,' because sometimes stating the bleeding obvious is very comforting.

We lurched a couple of steps, listing heavily to the right, and walked slap bang into something substantial. I don't know if anyone's ever walked into a plate glass door. Hurts, doesn't it? This was no different.

'Bloody hell,' muttered Markham. 'Could you just leave me in the gutter, please. More chance of survival down there.'

I told him not to be such a baby.

There was a lot of shouting coming from the undercroft. Two guards appeared and set off down the street at a run, to raise the alarm and bring reinforcements. We should definitely go.

I groped my way around the pod. 'Door.'

I was groping around the wrong wall. The door was in the left-hand wall. You see – I told you. That bloody camo thing is more trouble than it's worth.

I dragged Markham towards the door. I might have been complaining about a few things. The weather, Markham, the mess, the pod, the soldiers, and back to the weather again, because if I was complaining about something then I didn't have to think about what was behind me in the fog. Waiting. Or might even now be slipping through the door as I struggled to reach it.

I shook my head. I had to get Markham to safety. Don't think about anything else, Maxwell.

We staggered inside. He maintains I dropped him but he literally slipped through my bloody hands. I left him for the moment to get the door shut. We were safe.

I fumbled for the first-aid box and dragged out the scissors, cutting straight through his doublet, so that was me on Pennyroyal's hit list. The wound was high up on his shoulder. I didn't think anything vital had been punctured but he was losing an awful lot of blood. I applied pressure with one hand and sorted out dressings with the other.

He was slipping in and out of consciousness. I commanded him to keep looking at me and he said he'd rather not if I didn't mind. I don't know if it was wishful thinking on my part but the blood seemed to be flowing more slowly. Of course, that could be because he had none left. As I told him. I packed the wound and bandaged it tightly.

I was just finishing when the floor tilted. The world stretched away from me in a series of broken images. Shit – not again. I suspected Dr Stone's temporary solution had expired. I really did need to get this sorted out. But first I had to get Markham out of here.

Leaving him on the floor – his natural habitat as I informed him – I sat myself down and squinted at the console. Not only could I barely see but a strange ringing in my ears was slicing my head in half like cheese wire. I struggled to flick through the coordinates. I wanted Home Farm. I would put good money on Smallhope and Pennyroyal being able to get their hands on a good – if slightly dodgy – doctor within minutes.

The pod looked dreadful. There was blood everywhere. I

lay on the floor as Leon hacked away at my arm. A deep gash gushed blood in a rich red river across the floor.

I poured Kal a glass of blood-red wine and she put her feet up on the console. Both the wine and the feet were against the rules but there's always a little leeway on a last jump. We toasted each other while, on the screen, Joan of Arc burned in the marketplace at Rouen and Randall died in his own blood under my hands.

I was losing control. Pictures flickered through my mind and each one was real. I was there. My senses told me so. I could smell the blood. Hear the screams. Feel the panic. I was here. Then I was there. Then I was elsewhere. This time. That time. I tried to breathe, to find my centre, but I was completely over-whelmed. Einstein said, 'Time is a river,' and he was spot on. I was drowning in the River of Time. And with that thought, the waters closed over my head and down I went. Down to the depths and whatever lurked there. Hands clutched at me, dragging me deeper. I was falling.

No. I had a job to do. I had to get us both to safety.

There's a thing you can do. Big Dave Murdoch told me about it, years ago during my training.

'Run your finger along your jawbone, Max,' he'd said. 'Feel that slight nick?'

I'd nodded.

'Stick your thumb just underneath. Like this.'

He'd stuck his giant thumb under my jawbone. 'And just a little pressure – because you can always add more – and . . .'

I'd yelped. 'Bloody hell, that hurt.'

'It's supposed to,' he said, patiently. 'Really useful for recalcitrant old ladies.'

'What?'

'Oh, they're the worst, trust me. If I had a fiver for every time I'd been beaten up by an old lady then I'd have . . .'

I'd never found out how much he'd have because Guthrie had called me over to be hurled around the exercise mat by yet another member of his team.

I ran my thumb along my jawbone and pushed.

Bloody hell, I'd forgotten how much that hurt. Definitely not doing that again.

But it worked. I could see again. I mean I could see proper things now – things that were actually here and not things that had once been. I found the coordinates I wanted and—

There was something in the bathroom.

No, there wasn't. Don't be so—

Yes, there was. I caught a flicker in the corner of my eye. There was something in the bathroom.

The truth dawned on me. It had got in through the door while I wasn't looking. That was what it did. It would wait and we would be trapped forever because I wouldn't open the door and it would play its games of blood and pain and torment with us until the end of time.

No – not this time.

This time I knew better.

When all is lost. When everything is ending. When there's no hope. When you can't win. That's when you attack.

Pepper in one hand, sonic in the other, I kicked open the bathroom door and stepped into the darkness beyond.

32

I woke to silence. Thick, heavy silence. No sound. No movement. As if time itself had ground to a halt.

I think the accepted behaviour for heroines in these situations is to leap to their feet, brandish a hastily assembled weapon acquired from God knows where and begin to lay about them, vanquishing all their enemies before leaping from an upstairs window to continue their Quest.

I lay very still. I wasn't prepared to commit myself to any sort of action until I knew exactly where, when and what I was dealing with. And any Quest hanging around on the off-chance could just bugger off.

I could smell lavender. And, very faintly, smoke. There was a fire somewhere close by.

I lay motionless for a very long time but nothing happened. If there was something waiting, it obviously possessed infinite patience. Which was more than could be said of me. Time to open my eyes and deal with it.

I don't know what I expected but it wasn't this. The last I'd seen of the world had been around 1605 with fog and soldiers, and a pod reeking of mould and people and with something unpleasant in the bathroom.

This was a bedroom. Quite a large bedroom, with an elegant wallpaper of oriental birds and flowers. Dark, highly polished furniture gleamed in the flickering flames of a small fire. I could see a dressing table, a bureau and a tall chest of drawers. All very elegant and fashionable and only slightly let down by the commode in the corner. Slightly yellowed lace curtains hung at the windows.

I turned my heavy head. I was in an old-fashioned brass bedstead with a feather mattress, by the feel of it, but very comfortable. I wouldn't be leaving this any time soon. The bedding was old-style, too. Crisp white sheets and heavy blankets were topped with something big and fluffy and full of even more feathers.

This was a lovely, peaceful room and I'd be quite happy to stay here forever. Warm, comfortable and reassuringly alone.

Oh no, I wasn't. Markham was standing by the window, looking out at the fog. He looked fine. The last time I'd seen him he hadn't been. Fine, I mean. There had been quite a lot of blood but now, other than having one arm in a sling, he looked – for him – very normal. And clean. He was wearing modern clothes. I recognised his jacket and jeans. Was I back at Home Farm? This wasn't my room there. What was going on? Was I dead after all? That would account for a lot.

He was talking to me. I could see his mouth moving. I wasn't listening because there was a long white thing on the quilt beside me. I stared, because I'd never seen anything like it before. Long, white and completely motionless.

'You're not listening to me,' Markham said. Not for the first time.

'Stop talking,' I whispered. Not for the first time.

Worryingly, the thing was still there. I stared at it in horror. 'Can you see that? What is it?'

He sighed. 'It's your arm, Max.'

'Really?'

'Yes. If you turn your head, there's one on the other side as well. Look.'

Good God – he was right on both counts. I gawped at this phenomenon. And my arms, as well.

'Anyway,' he said, letting the curtain fall on the fog which was clawing at the window in the best house-of-horror style. 'How are you feeling?'

I suppose my first words should have been to thank him. Obviously, he'd managed to get us both to safety, but why break with tradition? 'Like shit.'

He came to sit down in the chair beside the bed and poured something into a glass. 'Here, have a sip of this.'

My head weighed a hundred tons. I could hardly lift it but the drink was very nice. Sweet and fruity. I sipped some more until he took the glass away.

'Better now?'

I croaked, 'I'm absolutely fine,' and let my head fall back on to the pillows. The lovely soft feather pillows.

There was an awkward pause. In my mind I was assembling a list of all the questions I should be asking. What happened? Why am I here? Where's here? Where's Leon? And Matthew? Did Fawkes manage to blow up the House of Lords after all? What happened in the bathroom? But I lacked the strength. And the interest. At the moment I really didn't care. Let someone else do the heavy lifting for a change.

I said, 'How are you?' at exactly the same time as Markham

said, 'Thought I'd lost you there.' We both looked at each other. Apart from the occasional spark from the fire, this room – wherever and whenever it was – was very quiet.

'Did we do it?'

He hesitated.

I struggled to lift my head. 'Tell me. What happened? Did we do it? Did the plot succeed?'

'No, no, relax. We did it.'

I let my head fall back again. 'Was your wound that bad?'

He looked down at his sling. 'This? Oh, no. Once you stopped the bleeding – thank you very much – it was fine. I got this when I tried to lift you up. How much do you actually weigh?'

I ignored this.

With the air of one steeling himself for an ordeal of some sort, he sat forwards in his chair and took my hand in his unslinged one.

'Max – I'm glad you're awake. I didn't want to go without saying goodbye.'

I panicked. 'Goodbye? Where are you going? Why are you going? What's happening? You're leaving me?'

'For God's sake, keep your voice down or we'll have Mrs Brown in here, and while she doesn't shout, she has a very nasty way about her when she's not happy about something.'

'Ah – well, that answers where and when I am.'

A vague memory. A blow. Out of nowhere. I raised a wobbly hand to my face. 'You hit me.'

'Sorry.'

'You hit me.'

'It was the only way.'

'You hit me.'

'I had to, Max. You don't know your own strength. Time was running out. There were soldiers everywhere, kicking doors in and dragging people out into the street. It was only a matter of time before someone ran into our pod. And then everyone would be crowding around and the pod wouldn't be able to jump. And I swear that Insight were there. Do you remember that bloke you once pointed out – the one with the two-tone hair? The light wasn't good but I'm sure I caught a glimpse of him. I think they'd come to check out what had gone wrong. They didn't look very happy about something and I wasn't going to hang around to find out. I couldn't take the risk of them discovering us. I was slowly bleeding to death. You were battling something that didn't exist so yes, I did hit you. But not very hard. In fact, I think you were already on your way groundwards before I gave you what was really no more than a gentle tap.'

I felt cold air on my face. It was only a draughty Victorian house but the bad memories were too recent. For a moment I was lost again. I scrabbled at Markham's free arm. 'Oh my God – he's here. We brought him back with us. He's here.'

He put his hand over mine. 'No. I know what you're talking about and we didn't bring anything back with us. Just you and me. It's all in your head, Max. Dr Stone will explain it to you.'

'Dr Stone is here?'

'He will be. Leon's fetching him now. It'll be his second – no, third – visit.'

I looked down at myself. 'Am I hurt?'

He shook his head. 'You haven't been well.'

Now that he mentioned it . . . 'I feel terrible.'

'I'm not surprised. You were in quite a state but they tell me you're on the mend.' He looked at me and then away again. 'Max . . .'

My stomach turned over. 'You said you were leaving. You can't do that. *Why* would you do that?'

'Max, it's over. I brought you here because we were both hurt and didn't have anywhere else to go. But I'm worried about Hunter and Flora. We've seriously annoyed Insight and I have to make sure they're safe.'

I didn't get it for a moment and then I did. He wasn't talking about leaving our flat in London. Or Home Farm. He was talking about leaving me.

I felt my eyes fill with tears. We'd been through so much. How could he leave? 'No. You can't go.'

'I have to. You don't know what's happened, do you?'

My stomach turned again. I could taste the sweet stuff in my mouth. 'Leon? Matthew?'

'No, no – not that bad but still not good. Home Farm's been attacked again. One end's completely gone. The roof has caved in. There's obviously been some sort of titanic struggle.'

'Smallhope and Pennyroyal?'

'Not there.'

'Not even in the bunker?'

'No.'

'Insight came back?'

'Possibly. Either Insight or some of the millions of people they've managed to piss off over the years. Could be anyone from the Time Police upwards. The farm's still working and the Faradays are all over the damage but there's no sign of our employers anywhere.'

'Any blood?'

He paused. 'A lot. Max, I think you're missing the point. If we'd returned to Home Farm as we originally planned, then we'd have been caught up in it, too. Whatever has happened to Smallhope and Pennyroyal would have happened to us as well. Electing to remain in London to see things through probably saved our lives. As it was, we didn't hang around and got out as quickly as possible.'

'We?'

'Me and Evans. We went to look for clues as to our employers' whereabouts.'

Shit.

'I managed to scrape together most of your gear. A few clothes, books, your Trojan Horse, your teddy bear. In a bag in the wardrobe.' He nodded at the overdecorated structure on the far wall. 'Anyway, I've been waiting for you to wake up so I could say goodbye.'

'But you'll be back,' I said, with more hope than conviction in my voice.

He tried to smile. 'Max . . .'

'No – it's nothing. I feel fine now. I just need a day or so.'

'No, you don't. Look at us, Max. You're out of the game for the foreseeable future. I'm wounded. Our base is wrecked. Our employers are missing, presumed badly hurt. If not actually dead. I can't risk Di and Flora. I have to go back to make sure they're safe.' He tightened his grip. 'This is the one we didn't win, love. Let it go.'

I groped for words but nothing came out.

He stood up. 'I'm off now. I'm not sure when I'll see you again. Get well and be happy.'

No. I tried to throw back the covers and get out of bed. Even sitting up made the room spin.

'You need to listen to what Dr Stone tells you.'

'You can't leave me . . .'

'I'm not abandoning you. They're all here. The Boss, Mrs Brown, Leon, Matthew, Evans, Mikey, Adrian, Professor Penrose. You'll have a whole army with you.'

I could feel the tears running down my cheeks. He didn't look too dry-eyed himself.

'But what about us? What about Pros and Cons? What about investigating Insight? Flying Auctions? Being bad-ass bounty hunters? I don't think I can do it on my own.'

He took my hand again. 'You're not doing it at all, Max. Listen to me. It's finished.'

'Fine,' I said, flinging his hand away because I was too angry to think straight. 'I don't need you. I can do it on my own. In fact, I'll be better off without you.'

I regretted the words as soon as they were out of my mouth but you can't ever unsay things.

He looked at me sadly, bent and kissed my forehead and walked out of the room.

I'd have cried properly but I didn't have the strength.

Next in was Leon. Back from fetching Dr Stone, presumably. An hour later and I might have been calmer. Less distressed at losing Markham. Less pissed off with people in general. No, I wouldn't. Who are we kidding? The only thing I can say in my own defence is that my temper wasn't Leon-specific. The next person coming through the door – whoever it was – would have had the bed thrown at them. Chance decreed it would be Leon. A tired and worried Leon.

He began with a simple query I chose to regard as criticism and things went downhill fast.

'Why didn't you tell me how sick you were?'

I raised my eyebrows. '*You're* complaining about not being told something important? Welcome to my world.'

Strangely, these words did not have a mollifying effect on my husband.

'All right – if that's how you want to play it.' He compressed his lips. 'You just had to do it, didn't you?'

'Do what?'

'All this.' He gestured around at the innocent bedroom. 'You could have just walked away. You could have let well alone. Ronan was finished. It was over. We were all set for a happy ending, but no, you had to find something else to get involved with, didn't you?'

I wasn't going to let that go. 'Not my fault Dr Bairstow got himself captured and I had to save the day. If *people* . . .' mere print cannot possibly convey the sarcastic emphasis I put on the word, 'if *people* had kept me in the loop, given me just the faintest idea of what was going on, where the threat would come from, then I might have acted differently, but I only say "might" because I'm sure you and Bairstow would have found another way to manipulate me into yet another hazardous situation and then blame me for it afterwards.'

I would have swept on but sadly I haven't yet evolved past needing to breathe occasionally when yelling at my husband.

He didn't actually wave his arms around because he's not a windmill but there was a certain amount of angry pacing by one of us.

Hint: it wasn't me.

'You were sacked and safely out of St Mary's. Why couldn't you just have waited quietly with Ian Guthrie for me to . . . ?'

He stopped. I think most husbands have some sort of fail-safe mechanism somewhere – deep in their brains, perhaps – which kicks in and shuts down their mouths before they can complete potentially life-ending sentences.

Fortunately, I don't have one of those. '. . . to rescue me,' I finished for him.

'I wasn't going to say that.'

'What were you going to say?'

'Well, I can't remember now. You shouting at me like that has driven it out of my head.'

'So your inability to remember more than three words is also my fault.'

'I wasn't going to say that either.'

'As far as I can see, you're not saying anything other than to drop a whole shedload of shit on my head simply for doing my job.'

'You don't have a job.'

'I have a very good job, actually. I'm doing quite nicely and earning considerably more than you.'

'But you don't need to do that any longer – I . . .'

He stopped again.

'I . . . what?' I said, dangerously. 'I'm here now? I'll make everything better?'

Belatedly, his fail-safe mechanism ground into first gear and he said nothing.

Strangely, this was even more infuriating. 'Nothing to say?'

'Plenty to say,' he said grimly. 'It's your inability to listen that usually defeats me.'

'You should be grateful,' I said nastily. 'When my husband complains because I'm a high-achieving, high-earning wife, my ears just pack up in self-defence. Otherwise I'd be out of this bed and clattering your head against the coal scuttle. And before you give way to another bout of husbandly indignation, I'll say it again: I don't work for St Mary's any longer.'

People say women who argue are shrill. That may be true – I don't know. I do know that when I'm angry – really, really, head-burstingly furious, I get *Exorcist* voice. Not often, because it hurts like hell afterwards, but this was one of those occasions. If you want to imagine the windows rattling and horses bolting in the streets below then that's fine with me.

There was a long silence, during which more optimistic readers might like to imagine us stepping back from the brink.

He took Markham's seat and said slowly, 'I've never told you what you can and can't do. I'm not that stupid. But you've always said that if I don't want you to do something then all I have to do is ask. I'm asking now. Please stop. This is killing you. And that's not a figure of speech. It really is killing you and I need you. Matthew needs you. Please – stop.'

Dammit – with one mighty leap he'd gone from being an arsehole to being everything that was reasonable and patient and fair.

I, on the other hand, was not. They say it takes two to quarrel. No, it bloody doesn't. It's harder work, of course, but with a little flair, imagination and a complete disregard for the damage done, one person can have a really good quarrel.

'No,' I said, flatly.

He looked puzzled. 'What?'

'I'm keeping it simple so there's no possibility of anyone

misunderstanding my intentions. No. I'm in the middle of something, and this time tomorrow I'll be gone again.'

'No,' he said flatly, obviously having learned from the master. 'You won't.'

Well, Mr Reasonable and Patient and Fair didn't last long, did he?

I sat up straighter and pretended the room wasn't whirling about like a bicycle going down the plughole. 'You want to put money on it?'

'Dr Stone says . . .'

'I don't care what Dr Stone says. I'm fed up with people controlling and manipulating me. For my own good, of course.'

'Dr Bairstow agrees with me.'

'Really? That makes sense, I suppose. He has no more use for me so I'm just discarded. Like an old glove. Sent here, there and everywhere while I'm still useful, and abandoned when I'm not. Well, it's not going to happen this time. I shouldn't have to tell you this, Leon, but I make the decisions in my life. Not you, and definitely not the old man downstairs. For whom I no longer work.'

'Max . . .'

'You can't keep me here.'

'I thought we could spend some time together,' he said, quietly. 'With Matthew. He's getting ready for his exams. Don't you want to be here with us?'

Have you ever been in one of those stupid arguments where every word you say gets you more deeply entrenched in a position you really don't want to be in? I'd love to spend some quiet time with Matthew and Leon. Enjoy the really large meals I suspect were regularly served in this house. Just sit back for a few weeks and let someone else take the strain.

I shrugged. 'Not particularly. Job to do, remember? The one everyone was briefed on but me.'

'We've all had a job to do.'

'But only some of us knew that. The rest of us just bimbled around in the dark, didn't we?'

'If you won't listen to me then perhaps you'll listen to . . .'

'I'm done with listening to Dr Bairstow.'

'I was going to say Dr Stone. He's here. That's where I've been. To St Mary's. Will you at least listen to him?'

'Why should I? He's only Dr Bairstow by proxy.'

He opened his mouth to say something and someone tapped at the door.

'And here he is now,' I said brightly. 'Another one who won't listen to a word I say.'

Silently, Leon got up to let him in. They passed each other in the doorway. I could just imagine the superior, masculine *she's being difficult again* looks they exchanged.

I folded my arms.

Dr Stone took Leon's seat. That chair was certainly getting a lot of use this morning.

'Well now, Max, you have got yourself into a bit of a pickle, haven't you? Again.'

I said nothing.

'Let me guess,' he said. 'Too angry to talk to me.'

I said nothing.

'I suspect you don't realise just how sick you are.'

I opened my mouth to say probably not. Certainly not without some big strong man to explain things to me – and then stopped because even an argument is a form of communication. A word of advice to those who frequently find themselves in holes of their own digging – silence is much more difficult for your opponent(s) to deal with. And yes, I am aware there's a lot of crap talked about passive-aggressive behaviour and the value of open and frank communication, but you can take your open and frank communication and shove it where the passive-aggressive sun never shines.

Some of this must have shown in my face.

'I can see you're not happy,' he said, 'because I'm a highly trained and competent medical professional. Would you like to take it all out on me instead of laying waste to your nearest and dearest?'

'I'd love to,' I said, 'and it's so sweet that you think sacrificing yourself will save these alleged nearest and dearest. Trust me, I will kill them all and raze this house to the ground before I believe a word anyone ever says to me again.'

He rubbed his nose. 'I'm not making a very good job of this, am I?'

I let the silence speak for itself.

'Well, I'm going to carry on anyway no matter what the personal risk. Max, you're going nowhere for quite some time. And that's not a threat – that's a medical diagnosis. At this moment, I'd be astonished if you could even get out of bed. But whatever you do when you leave here – and we can talk about that another time – you have to heal first. You have no choice. Like it or not, you're here for at least a couple of weeks. When you're more recovered – and complete recovery will take some time and there's nothing you can do to change that so don't bother arguing – when you're on the road to recovery, that will be the time to discuss . . .'

'That will be the time for me to leave,' I said, growing angrier by the moment.

He sighed. 'I can see I'm not getting through.'

'No, you're not. Perhaps you've forgotten, doctor, but I don't work for St Mary's any longer.'

'No, I haven't, but that doesn't make what I'm about to say any less relevant. You need to reset your personal clock so your body knows what's going on. You can't be at midnight one moment and ten past three in the afternoon the next. Dark – light – winter – summer – often all on the same day. Do that too often and for too long and this is the result, Max. I'm guessing this has been coming on for some time and for some reason you haven't mentioned it to anyone, but you need to talk about it now. You need proper days followed by proper nights. You need regular meals at regular intervals. A solid routine. Something your body can work with. And it will take time. You cannot run before you can walk. In fact, I would be surprised if you can walk at all at the moment. Stay in bed and get as much sleep as you can.' He stood up. 'And try to relax. Stress will not help.'

'Depends who I'm stressing at the time,' I said, looking up at him.

Dr Stone paused, went to say something, changed his mind and left the room.

Great job, Maxwell. Two out of two. Three out of two if you counted Markham. I looked forward to dealing similarly with Dr Bairstow.

And I might well have done so had he turned up before I fell asleep.

33

There is nothing more infuriating than being all geared up to have a major row with your ex-boss and for it not to happen. I'd thought it all through. I had all my arguments marshalled. I knew exactly how I was going to leave Dr Bairstow without a leg to stand on, and he didn't bloody turn up. And I couldn't go looking for him because Dr Stone had been right; I couldn't even get out of bed.

Visits to the commode were brief and assisted by Kathleen or Sarah, both of whom were clearly having the time of their lives. I suspected the fell hand of Mr Evans who, like most of the Security Section, seemed to have an unsettling effect on otherwise quite intelligent women.

Meals turned up at regular intervals. A lot of meals. There was a substantial breakfast and then the always popular elevenses. Then lunch. Then a mid-afternoon snack. Then afternoon tea. Then dinner. Then supper. And there was always a plate of homemade biscuits on the bedside table to see me through the rigours of the night.

Mrs Proudie bustled in several times a day, either to oversee the maids cleaning my room or to check I was eating everything put in front of me. To be fair, I made every effort. Everything was beautifully cooked and presented on pretty plates that matched the wallpaper. It would have been churlish to send anything back. The menu was heavily cheese-based – I suspected Mikey had been offering advice.

Matthew came up, as well, to talk to me. I must be getting the hang of this mother business because even as he showed me something he and Professor Penrose were making together, and told me about the visit to the park with Mikey and Adrian to fly their homemade kites, and demolished a whole plate of jam tarts specifically sent up to guide his mother's faltering footsteps along the road to recovery, I could see he was struggling to tell me more than he was saying.

I tried to sit up a little higher on the pillows instead of sprawling like a bed-bound jellyfish and waited for him to finish his description of that most cool of all hobbies – trainspotting.

'We saw the Black Prince and the Flying Dutchman and the Iron Duke and they were huge and the pistons were thicker than my arm and the fireman let me into the cab and I saw the boiler. It was really, really hot. And really, really smelly . . .' He talked himself out and silence fell.

'So,' I said, crossing my fingers beneath the bedclothes, 'what's the problem?'

Matthew didn't answer, just scowled at his feet. I waited as long as I could but if he didn't say something soon then the chances were I'd be asleep again. I reached out and shook his hand. 'Hey.'

Silence again but something was coming. I could tell. You just can't rush him. The more you try, the less comes out. He has to do these things in his own time.

Eventually, he said, 'My exams.'

I nodded. 'Yes?'

'Suppose I . . . I mean, suppose I make a mess of them. Everyone's been . . . I mean, Mrs Brown helped me with my writing. And Dr Bairstow with the History. And Dad with the maths and science. And Uncle Evans with revision and things. And Kathleen and the others listen to me reading when they're polishing the silver. Well . . . suppose I can't answer any of the questions. They'll think I wasn't listening. Or I'm stupid.' He tailed away.

I believe the accepted response is to say, 'No, you'll do fine. I've every confidence in you,' or words to that effect, but I've never thought that was particularly helpful. In fact, it only adds to the pressure when everyone tells you how well you'll do, as you career, terrified and out of control, straight into the Ditch of Disappointment. Other people's disappointment, that is.

'That's a good point,' I said, 'but, think carefully – how likely is that actually to happen? I mean, have you been able to cover the syllabus?'

He nodded. 'Most of it, yes. The professor says I should know enough to answer at least the minimum number of questions on each paper.'

'That's sometimes the best way,' I said. 'You won't be wasting time trying to make the best choice. How many must you answer?'

'Four,' he said. 'Usually. And there's a choice from about eight.'

'Has he talked to you about the best way to approach the papers?'

'Yes. Read it all through. Make my choices. Stick with those choices. Start with the easiest. Leave enough time to read everything through afterwards.'

'Good. How do you begin?'

'Jot down the main points. Write an intro. Answer the question. Write a conclusion.'

'That sounds very sensible. Do you think you'll have a problem with any of that?'

'No . . . I don't know . . . my handwriting . . .'

'Trust me,' I said. 'It's not that bad. Have you never seen Uncle Peterson's scribble? Uncle Markham says it's like breaking the Enigma code. Without the benefit of the Enigma machines.'

Matthew looked unconvinced. I tried again. I didn't want to seem to make light of his problems but I didn't want to add to his stress, either.

'I think a system that can cope with Uncle Peterson's mysterious glyphs isn't going to be too worried about your writing, don't you? Besides, if there was a problem, the professor would have flagged it up with the exam board, so I wouldn't worry too much about that. There weren't any difficulties when you handed in your course work, were there?'

He shook his head.

'OK. Is there anything in particular you're worried about? A particular subject, for instance, or what to do when you get into the exam centre?'

He shook his head. 'No, just . . . not doing very well. And worrying so much about not doing well that I don't do well.'

'Fear of failure can be quite useful,' I said. 'It keeps you on your toes. The real enemy is complacency. That feeling that you've done enough to get by and don't need to do any more. That's what trips people up. Trust me, everyone taking their exams is feeling what you're feeling right now. That thumping heart and dry mouth as you turn over your paper is what ramps your brain into top gear so you can do your best.'

He nodded.

'Which paper worries you the most?'

'English Language. Grammar. Punctuation. Sentences, phrases and things.'

'OK,' I said, 'well, I don't know if this helps, but I had an excellent teacher at school and she explained sentences in a funny way. There was a book out at the time – a really rude book – they tried to ban it – lots of truly toe-curling sex in it – something you don't know anything about, obviously.'

He grinned and blushed.

'Anyway, she'd confiscated it from someone. Not me, before you ask. She pulled out the book, opened it up and read a sentence at random. I always remember it and now I bet you will as well.'

I cleared my throat and intoned, '*Algernon, take me, take me, my body is on fire for you.*'

He blinked. Teenage boys are convinced their parents know nothing about sex. Heaven knows how they think they were conceived.

'And then she broke the sentence down. *Algernon* is a word. *Algernon, take me* is a phrase or clause. And *Algernon, take me, take me, my body is on fire for you* is a complete sentence. Easy.'

He stared at me.

'So,' I said, 'what's the verb in that sentence?'

His lips moved as he thought it through. 'Take. To take.'

'And the nouns?'

He frowned. 'I know *fire* is a noun. A naming word.'

Well, he would know that, wouldn't he? Given the number of fires I've started in my life, it was in his genes, probably.

'And so is *body*, I think.'

403

'Yes, it is, because body is the name of the bit between your head and your bottom. Well done. Can you do the rest of the sentence?'

'*Me* is a . . . a . . . a personal pronoun.'

'That's right. *My*?'

'*My* is the single person . . . owning . . . possessive.'

'Well done. I never know that one. *Is*?'

His eyes crossed with concentration. '*Is* . . . is . . . third person singular present. *On* is a preposition – a connecting word. *For* – is a preposition I shouldn't end a sentence with.'

I coughed meaningfully.

He grinned. 'With which I shouldn't end a sentence.'

'Well done, you.'

'And *you* is another pronoun.'

'Brilliant. When you sit down for the exam, scribble *Algernon, take me, take me, my body is on fire for you* on the top of the exam paper, keep it in front of you and you'll have no problems at all. Tell me the phrase again.'

He drew himself up, threw out his arms and declaimed, '*Algernon, take me.*'

'And the entire sentence?'

We chanted together. '*Algernon, take me, take me, my body is on fire for you*,' and then fell about laughing at exactly the moment Mrs Brown appeared in the open doorway.

Ignoring her, I said to Matthew, 'If you genuinely think you've done everything you can to prepare, then you really can't do any more, so try to relax. And as I said, don't worry about exam nerves – they turn up to help you do well. Greet them as old friends.'

He nodded.

404

Mrs Brown tapped gently. 'Don't let me interrupt.'

'Finished,' said Matthew. 'See you, Mum,' and shot out of the door.

She came in and sat down. Yet another bum in the chair. She was wearing a dark, high-necked outfit and looked every inch the Victorian grand lady.

'Given your reluctance to discuss your current situation with Dr Bairstow, he has asked me to inform you of the arrangements that are being made.'

'How kind of everyone,' I said. 'I shall listen with the utmost attention and then completely ignore everything.'

She brushed this aside. 'No, you will not. You will listen because this is important.'

'To whom?'

'To us all. Events have moved on in the few days you have been here. You know about Home Farm. Chief Farrell, together with both the Meiklejohns, is examining the scene now. Whatever the reason for the attack, at this moment Home Farm is no longer either habitable or safe.'

'Any news of Smallhope and Pennyroyal?'

'No sign of them anywhere. No clue as to their whereabouts.'

'Are there any bodies?'

'None. Well, none found.'

That meant nothing. Smallhope and Pennyroyal might not have been there when the building was attacked. Or they might have been and were killed and their bodies removed. Or, and most likely, they became mildly irritated at this intrusion into their privacy, exterminated everyone within a five-mile radius and were off concealing the bodies somewhere in the 6th century BC.

'This does mean, however, that whatever your original plans may have been, you cannot return to Home Farm.'

I shrugged. 'No problem. I'll soon find somewhere else.'

'It is felt you are not yet well enough to undertake the search for a new home. In fact, there has been some discussion that this house might not be safe any longer and it would be prudent for us all to evacuate and regroup elsewhere. As you know, Matthew is about to return to his own time to take his exams in Rushford. He will be accompanied by Chief Farrell and Professor Penrose. The rest of us – excluding you, Max, since you have stated quite vehemently and on several occasions that you wish to have nothing to do with us – will make alternative arrangements that we need not trouble you with. You, however . . .'

'I can shift for myself,' I interrupted. 'I'll take my pod and be gone by tonight.'

'No.'

'Is there a problem with the pod?'

'No, the problem is you. Yes, sooner or later we must all leave this place, but you are by no means recovered. Either with us or on your own, you must return to your own time to complete your recovery. And wherever you go, that must be your permanent residence, at least for the foreseeable future. Chief Farrell will search for suitable accommodation for you. Do you have a wish list? A list of requirements?'

'I can do this myself.'

She said patiently, 'We have covered this. You cannot. You will have to give way over this, Dr Maxwell. The alternative is to remain here, and if you choose to do so, then obviously we will remain as well. To all our detriment, I suspect.'

Oh, bloody hell. I've said before that St Mary's is harder to shift than an STD and I was right.

'All right,' I said, being sensible. 'I'd like somewhere quiet. In the country. I don't want to have to be bothered with people. Close to Matthew so he can come live with me after his exams.'

She raised her eyebrows. 'With me?'

'Sorry?'

'You said *with me*. Not with *us*? You don't include your husband in your plans?'

'Leon will surely return to St Mary's,' I said. 'Since he works for them and I do not.'

'Great allowances are being made for you because you are unwell,' she said, 'but don't push it.'

'I'll make the same response I once made to Commander Treadwell: I was born to push. In fact, no one pushes better than me.'

Mrs Brown regarded me for a moment and then got up and left the room. I tried to work out whether there was anyone in the world I hadn't annoyed over the last few days. Nope – couldn't think of anyone.

I lay back on the pillows to think. This was serious. Anyone capable of taking out Smallhope and Pennyroyal and destroying their base of operations was not someone I wanted to meet.

Dr Bairstow and Mrs Brown could look after themselves. Especially since they'd have Evans with them. And Mikey and Adrian had been looking after themselves almost their whole lives.

Which just left me. The weak link. As always. No – that wasn't true. I could manage. I had money and I had skills. All right, I didn't have my health – not just at the moment, anyway – but that wasn't permanent. I'd soon get well again. I always did.

I folded my arms, scowled at the bumps in the bedclothes that were my feet and tried to think of a Brilliant Idea which would not only miraculously save us all but render everyone involved eternally and publicly grateful to me.

And fell asleep again.

Oh, for God's sake – Dr Stone was back. I knew I'd been asleep for some time because someone had come in, drawn the curtains, banked up the fire and lit the candles. This was slightly concerning. I've always said I don't sleep well, that I wake at the slightest sound and can't get back to sleep again. That certainly didn't seem to be the case these days. The knowledge that someone could come into my room, hurl some coal on the fire and draw the curtains without waking me was disturbing.

He was standing at the foot of my bed, scribbling some notes. Trust me, it's never good news when Dr Stone starts making house calls. I probably had only minutes left to live.

He looked up and nodded. 'All right?'

'Absolutely fine.'

He came to sit on the chair – still warm from the last visitor possibly.

'Here's what's going to happen,' he said, with all the smiling calm of someone who always gets his own way. 'No more jumping. As of now.'

I looked at him with all the smiling calm of someone who rarely gets her own way but never stops trying. 'Well, I can't do that, can I? This is 1893. You said I had to return to my own time to reset my body clock. How do you propose to get me home?'

'We'll jump you back – and that's not an experience you will enjoy – but that's it, then. You're done.'

'For how long?'

'As long as it takes you to recover. And even then, any future jumps will have to be restricted. For your own sake.'

'You can't do that to me.'

'I'm doing it to everyone. We don't want this happening to anyone else. My predecessor, Dr Foster, has left some notes about this very problem. The effect of persistent time-jumping on a person's body clock. She recommended that every historian only undertake a specific number of jumps in any twelve-month period.'

'No, I mean, I'm not a member of St Mary's any longer. Whatever rules St Mary's operate by don't apply to me.'

'You are, at the moment, dependent upon St Mary's, so yes, they do. And since most of your jumps happened while you were in his employ, Dr Bairstow feels a certain responsibility. I understand you've now moved into a related area of employment. If you want to continue with that, then you have to give yourself time to get over this.'

'Will I recover completely?'

'I don't know for certain. I don't see why not but I can't guarantee it. I've had a word with Dr Bairstow and he recommends you regard this as a sort of sabbatical.'

'Isn't that some kind of devil worship?'

He frowned and said, with unusual severity, 'No. Don't try to change the subject, Max. I don't care what you're doing or who you're working for – once we get you back to your own time – you're grounded.'

Well, bloody bollocking hell. That wasn't good.

34

Two weeks of bed rest and Mrs Proudie's cooking put me back on my feet again. I could walk. I could turn my head without falling over. I knew when I was and where I was going. Sometimes I had to work on the *why* I was actually going there, but for me that's always been a dodgy area anyway. As the old saying goes, 'I went upstairs and couldn't remember why. I went back downstairs and remembered. I went back upstairs and forgot again. And now I have to pee.'

I refused all visitors except for Matthew. We stayed in my room, playing chess, and he was really good. I didn't have to pretend to lose at all. He knew he could beat me, he explained as he carefully laid out the pieces for the rematch. The challenge for him was to beat me in fewer and fewer moves each game.

I'm not sure if *enjoyed* is the right word, but I also enjoyed visits from Mikey and Adrian, because no sooner did they learn of my ban on visitors than they rose to the challenge and were in my room in minutes. Adrian through the window, fractionally ahead of Mikey disguised as Sarah and bearing scones. They'd had a bet, apparently. We spent the afternoons playing cards and I now owe them everything I'll ever earn in this world and the next.

Gradually, I recovered my equilibrium. I calmed down a little.

I remember talking with Leon long into the night as the candles flickered and the fire crackled. We stopped messing about and talked about the things that were really important – Matthew, the future, St Mary's, Insight – and eventually I allowed myself to be talked into seeing reason. I had to, really – I couldn't do anything without help. Leon said I'd been running on fumes for God knows how long and I grudgingly admitted he might be right. And the recent attack on Home Farm had left me with no choice, anyway. As Mrs Brown had suggested, we drew up a proper wish list of where and how we wanted to live and Leon disappeared with it the next day.

Other than the one visit, I saw no more of Mrs Brown and I didn't see Dr Bairstow at all.

Two weeks later and *la famille* Farrell plus Professor Penrose were set to go. I wasn't looking forward to returning to my own time but there wasn't any choice. We left TB2 for Dr Bairstow and made the return trip in Leon's pod. It was a little tidier and less blood-soaked than the last time I'd seen it but there was still a certain whiff of too many soggy passengers suffering too much travel sickness.

Heroically, Leon said nothing.

We were heading for Streetley, a small village somewhere between Whittington and Rushford. Just under twenty minutes from St Mary's and Dr Stone and ten minutes from Rushford. It's a pretty place. Not that we'd be in the village. Our little cottage was about half a mile up the road and stood alone.

I'd argued. 'Why so close to St Mary's?'

'I need to give this pod some urgent attention. It's not particularly safe to use at present.'

'But . . .'

'And Dr Stone will be nearby should you take a turn for the worse.'

'I like how the needs of the pod come first.'

'And Ian Guthrie won't be too far away in the event of an emergency.'

'But . . .'

'No one will expect you to be that close, Max. Everyone will assume you've done the sensible thing and fled to the other end of the country. Or somewhere in time. Or both. No one will think you're stupid enough to be on St Mary's doorstep.'

'Wouldn't it be easier to be at the other end of the country? At some randomly chosen location?'

'No, I need to be there with you because you can't be left alone in case you walk into traffic.'

I huffed.

'And Matthew has his exams, so at least one of us needs to be close by. Streetley is far enough away but not too far. Now stop arguing.'

'I'm not arguing – I'm just pointing out . . .'

'Please just get into the pod.'

I sighed. 'Everyone wants me back at St Mary's, don't they? This is the first stage.'

'Except Treadwell,' said Leon. 'He'll probably have ten thousand fits if he finds out you're virtually on his doorstep.'

I looked at him. 'You should have led with that.'

The jump wasn't as bad as I had imagined it would be but it still wasn't fun.

We arrived at night. Don't ask me to describe anything

412

because I was concentrating on putting one foot in front of the other. I went straight to bed and woke the next morning in a warm cocoon of blankets. Miraculously the world was still and solid. And there was only one of it.

I was in a big square room with a double bed facing the window. The curtains were drawn but they were thin, and grey daylight filtered through. I could hear birds singing. I'd asked for a place in the country and it seemed I'd got it.

The ceiling sloped at one end and the walls were supported with thick beams. The original old black fireplace was full of red and orange paper flowers which gave a bright effect. The bare boards had been stained dark to match the beams and a couple of red and orange rugs matched the flowers.

An old-fashioned dressing table stood by the window to catch the light, along with two wardrobes, one on either side of the fireplace. One big and one small. His and hers, I guessed. At the moment I didn't own enough stuff to put in a small carrier bag.

At almost that same moment I saw my old sports bag standing on the dressing table. All right – I did own enough to put in a small sports bag.

There was no art on the walls. No books on the shelves. No ornaments on the windowsill. The house had a slightly disused, musty smell. The furniture was the absolute minimum. Rented property, I decided, and empty for some time.

I'm not famed for doing things slowly and carefully but that was how I lifted my head and sat up. It took some effort. I was surprised at how weak I felt, even after all this time.

There was a little clock on the bedside table. I reached out to turn it towards me, misjudged the distance and knocked it over with a clatter.

Immediately the door opened and Matthew came in. I had the impression he'd been waiting outside. 'Are you awake?'

I would have said no but he would only have turned around and left the room because teenagers only understand sarcasm when they're the ones doing it.

I said, 'Hello. Where are we?'

'Here,' he said, with perfect logic. 'It's nice.' And disappeared. I heard him clattering down the stairs shouting, 'Dad, Dad, she's awake.'

A minute later Leon appeared, wearing his oldest sweater and a pair of jeans that had presumably been worn for thirty years, kicked around in a swamp and then used to dredge a slurry pit.

I stared at him in horror. I'd married this man. 'What are you wearing?'

'Old clothes,' he said. 'We're moving in. Mucky work.'

'Did I survive the jump? Is this Streetley?'

'It is. It's very quiet here. No one knows us. They'll think we're a perfectly normal family. Right up until the moment they clap eyes on you.'

I ignored that. 'I want to get up.'

'Bath first,' he said. 'Take your time. Give me a shout when you want to get out. If I make you some lunch, will it subsequently reappear from every orifice?'

'Why don't we try it and see?'

The bathroom was just across the landing. All the usual equipment was present, plus fluffy towels, nice and warm. I enjoyed a lengthy and not very energetic bath. That done, I donned my own jeans and one of Leon's sweatshirts because it was warmer and set off to explore.

Upstairs was my bedroom, Matthew's bedroom, an empty

414

spare room and a bathroom. From there, narrow stairs doglegged into a stone-flagged hall. A door opened into a living room, the oldest part of the house, with a real fire laid all ready to light. Two small windows looked out over the front garden. Which was just a little paved area leading to a drystone wall and a wooden gate.

The kitchen was nice – very modern. Leon was unpacking saucepans. I blinked. 'It's only part furnished,' he said, 'I've had to buy what's not provided. What do you think?'

'It's very nice,' I said politely.

'You don't like it?'

'Yes, I do. I'm sure we can make it very homely.'

'Actually, I didn't rent it for the house.'

'OK,' I said, mystified, because he and Matthew were grinning like idiots.

'Do you feel up to a walk outside?'

'OK,' I said again.

'Wrap up warm.'

I wrapped up warm and we stepped out of the back door. The day was cold and the sky grey. A tiny snowflake drifted down. And then another.

'It's snowing,' said Matthew in delight.

'Great,' said Leon, apparently thrilled by the news.

I could hear rushing water somewhere.

As well as the cottage behind me, there were a number of stone outbuildings built around three sides of a paved yard.

'This was the old gamekeeper's cottage,' said Leon. He pointed. 'There's the stable where he kept his pony. There's a couple of outbuildings where he raised his birds, apparently. That's the old privy – which still works – and here's the fortunately empty pigsty.'

I nodded.

Big blobs of snow began to fall. I wondered if my family were perhaps plotting my death. I would die of exposure and the snow would cover my lifeless body. Quick, neat and efficient. I felt quietly proud of them.

'That's the woodshed.' He gestured to another stone-built structure, full of – surprise – logs. 'And that's the old workshop. Behind that is a little orchard. We'll have our own fruit.'

I nodded, slightly disappointed. 'No garden?'

'Just a little bit,' he said. 'We have to go through this gate over here.'

The blobs of snow were growing larger and falling more thickly. Normally I like a fall of snow as much as the next woman but not today. Today I wanted to go back inside, light the fire, and try out the sofa for size and comfort. I turned to go back into the house.

'Through here,' he said, and I knew him well enough to know he was very nearly bursting with excitement.

He pushed open the five-barred gate between the woodshed and pigsty and I stepped through.

Into a magical wonderland.

I stood in light woodland. Trees stretched away from me – mostly silver birches by the looks of them, but some rowans and others I didn't recognise. Their bare branches were dark against the sky. Little paths wound through the trees and tempted me to explore. About twenty yards away to my left, a fast-flowing stream dropped from one pool to the next, splashing and gurgling around big, water-smoothed boulders. An ancient oak tree overhung the water, its roots exposed where the bank had been cut away by the rushing torrent. I thought it looked like a refugee from Middle Earth.

I looked around the silent wood. There were only two colours in this world. Green and white. Snow fell from a white sky. White trees. Clumps of thick green rhododendrons. At ground level, densely planted clusters of green leaves were topped with little nodding white flowers. Snowdrops. I'd never seen so many. The ground was thick with them. Big flakes of snow fell softly – the only things moving in this quiet world – slowly covering the leaves until only the white flowers were visible above the white snow. The world was as still as only snow can make it.

I couldn't believe it. I was standing in a snowdrop wood as snow actually dropped. I stood, entranced, as the world was slowly enveloped in a blanket of white silence.

I turned to Leon. 'Leon, this is magical.'

He smiled down at me. 'Well, I just thought the stream and the woodland were pretty. The snow turned up all by itself but since you're impressed, I shall take full credit.'

'Do magic moments like this make up for all the rest?'

He smiled down at me. 'With you, all moments are magic.'

Matthew groaned, rolled his eyes and headed back to the safety and security of his bedroom, firmly designated a parent-free zone. There was a notice on the door to that effect.

Leon and I stayed there for a long time, just watching the snow fall. I stood happily in the crook of his arm and remembered Dr Stone's advice. To focus on the now. Here. This time and place. Not to fret about where I had been this time yesterday. Or where I would be next week. Or what was happening at Insight. Or the fate of Smallhope and Pennyroyal. Or whether Markham was safe. They could all look after themselves, he'd said. I was here with Leon and we were watching the snow fall together. The future could sort itself out without any help from me.

The days passed happily. My main fear had been boredom. How would I fill all this time that had suddenly come my way? I'd worked hard at school, even harder at uni, travelled the bits of the world that interested me, been a casual worker on various archaeological digs, been recruited to St Mary's, been sacked from St Mary's, been reinstated, been sacked again, and now I was a recovery agent. Frankly, I'd hardly had time to sit down over the last God knows how many years. Now I had nothing to do but sit down. Not wanting to hurt anyone's feelings, I'd reconciled myself to a prolonged period of tedium, selling it to myself on the grounds it couldn't last forever.

That – the boredom – didn't happen at all. I simply could not stay awake.

At night I would fall asleep as soon as my head hit the pillow. I would sleep late. Leon had a few weeks off to be with me but Matthew was working hard for his exams so Leon would drive him to St Mary's for his lessons with Professor Penrose.

Returning an hour later, Leon would wake me gently with a cup of tea and we'd have a leisurely chat. I'd shower and wander downstairs where he'd be preparing lunch. I'd sit on the sofa meaning to read the paper but drop off to sleep instead. He'd wake me with lunch.

I usually managed to stay awake long enough to help him clear away, then it was feet up on the sofa to watch an afternoon holo. I never made it past the opening scenes. I usually opened my eyes just in time for the closing credits.

Matthew would arrive back from his lessons and would sit at the table doing his homework, after which Leon would chivvy him off the table to lay for dinner. We'd eat, Matthew would disappear to his room to do whatever teenagers do in their room all evening – Leon had warned me not to ask – and Leon and I would settle down to an evening's viewing and conversation.

He'd wake me in time for bed and I'd do it all again. It was as if I was making up for all those years when I'd slept only a couple of hours a night – if that. At one point it was so bad I didn't dare sit down in case I lapsed into a coma. Matthew and Leon thought it was hilarious. Leon said it was the quietest I'd been in years.

The two of them spent a lot of time in the dark little workshop next to the pigsty. God knows what they were doing in there. Leon said they had to pass the time somehow while I spent my days spark out on the sofa. I know there was a lot of banging, some smoke and the occasional shout of alarm. A bit like my cooking, really. I didn't ask what they were up to in case they told me, which would make me an accessory.

But it was nice. It was family time and I enjoyed it. Neither Leon nor I were dashing off somewhere to deal with something. There was no passing on the stairs or scribbling notes to each other. Finally, at long last, we had time. Time to talk – properly – about important things. Time not to talk – just be together. Time to think about our lives, time to plan, time to walk in the wood, time to sit on the big round stones and watch the stream rush by. Time just to be Leon and Max. I was happy. This was the life I'd never had. A home and a family, together with the temporal stability Dr Stone had said I so badly needed.

After a fortnight, and somewhat reluctantly, Leon went back

to work. The little interlude had done him good as well. He looked happier, healthier, more relaxed and less tired. He would kiss me goodbye every morning, whisper something improper, and then return mid-afternoon to carry out his threat. Usually around three thirty after a slow lunch and a couple of glasses of wine.

And Matthew was happy, too. He liked being at St Mary's. He enjoyed his lessons with Professor Penrose. Since Leon and I paid for Professor Penrose's board and keep, Treadwell had little to complain about. And he was Time Police which meant Matthew probably couldn't be in safer hands.

To my surprise, this was working out much better than I had expected.

35

My only excuse is that I was left unsupervised. Leon had driven Matthew to St Mary's, the weather was too bad for me to venture outside, and I decided, just for once, that I would shoulder my share of the culinary chores. I'd barely even made a cup of tea since we'd arrived at the cottage. Apparently, the drugs I was taking precluded me making any important decisions or operating heavy machinery but I think they meant JCBs and high-speed trains and combine harvesters – not saucepans, obviously.

Soup, I thought. It was Friday and every Friday Leon would make a delicious and nutritious soup from whatever was left in the vegetable rack. I could do the same.

I contemplated my resources.

A round knobbly thing with fronds. I googled and couldn't find anything that even closely resembled it. Probably not a hand grenade. Never mind. Next.

Some sinister dark green leaves. I googled those as well. 'Not lettuce' was the best I could do. Next.

More leaves but different. Oh, for heaven's sake. So many leaves. Why? Perhaps Leon had left them here to . . . germinate, perhaps. Like potatoes. Or gestate, like butterflies. Maybe these knobbly things were some sort of pupa and the green stuff was their food. The more I thought about it, the more sensible that seemed. However – moving on . . .

A potato. Familiar ground.

And something I thought *might* be fennel.

OK – I reached for a chopping board, chopped like a maniac, staunched the bleeding more or less successfully, added masses of stuff from packets and jars and left it all to simmer.

One hour later I whipped off the lid.

I know I always bang on about not eating green food because it's bad for you, but trust me, grey food is considerably worse. I'd never seen anything like it. Perhaps it tasted better than it looked. I cracked the crust, took a cautious sip and gagged. Literally gagged. It was *much* better looking than it tasted.

I tried to tip it down the sink and it didn't want to go. It clung to the saucepan with both hands and I struggled to get it out . . . at the end of which, the sink was blocked.

OK. Don't panic. I had half an hour before Leon was due home. Think, Maxwell. Bleach. I found it under the sink and poured half a bottle down the plughole.

Nothing happened.

What else could I do? Boiling water. Boiling water can unblock sinks. I poured in an entire kettleful of boiling water.

Nothing happened. Except now I had a sink full of grey, greasy, bleach-smelling water. Refusing to be beaten, I poked about a bit with some sort of skewer.

Nothing happened.

I toyed briefly with the idea of unscrewing the U-bend but given the quality of my performance so far, that didn't seem the wisest course of action. I could picture some grey, amorphous mass crouching in the bend just waiting to hurl itself at my face. In the end, I decided to leave it. There was an excellent chance the stuff would seep away on its own.

The saucepan couldn't be saved. No more need be said. And anyway, I couldn't waste any more time because Leon would be home any moment now.

Toast was well within my repertoire. I was Mrs Mack-trained. And I could make it special by sticking some cheese on it. Cheese on toast would be lovely on this chilly day. Leon would open the door to a smiling wife and the delicious smell of toasted cheese. I switched on the grill, grated every piece of cheese in the house and lightly toasted a couple of slices of bread.

Very carefully, I arranged the cheese on the bread – right up to the corners so there would be no burnt bits – and shoved it all under the grill. A few minutes later it dawned on me there was no appetising smell of toasted cheese. Or sound of bubbling. Or any signs of life at all. I sighed. Culinarily speaking, I was not having a good morning.

I eased out the grill to ascertain why nothing seemed to be happening. Except I pulled it out too far and it came off the runners and it and the cheese on toast fell all over the floor.

Bollocks.

There was a hell of a lot more cheese on the floor than there had been on the toast. Some sort of scientific principle coming into play, I suspected. Bloody science.

I'd used up all the cheese. I studied what was on the floor – which seemed perfectly clean – so I very carefully scraped up the best bits and sprinkled it back over the toast. Sadly, there was a hell of a lot less cheese on the bread this time round.

I shoved it all under the grill again and looked for a sweeping brush because I had grated cheese between my toes and it's not a pleasant sensation. And, by this time, the kitchen wasn't looking quite as Leon had left it that morning.

I swept up what cheese I could find and contemplated topping up the toast again but there was a fair bit of fluff and dust mixed in so, sadly, I tossed it all in the bin. It could talk to the saucepan. And then I had a Brilliant Idea. I could combine the two slices into a toasted sandwich. One sandwich with lots of cheese inside was much better than two slices with a tiny sprinkling of cheese every two inches or so. Impressed at my brilliance, I pulled out the grill – a lot more carefully this time – and once again nothing had happened. There was heat. I could hear the fan going round. And I had two slices of slightly sparse but mostly uncooked cheese on toast. Bloody bollocking hell. Had the grill packed up?

No. I'd switched on the oven by mistake. In my defence, the two symbols are very similar and I wasn't wearing my specs. The ones that make me look both intelligent and sexy – although I suspected they'd have an uphill struggle today. I was actually baking the cheese on toast.

Unfortunately, the whole thing was bloody hot, including the handle, and I dropped the tray – again – and the hot cheese on toast fell on my feet. Obviously it wasn't hot enough to be appetising in any sort of way but hot enough to burn. Bloody cheese. Bloody oven. Bloody hell.

I threw the grill down one end of the kitchen and the toast down the other and hopped to the sink to splash cold water on my poor, burned feet.

The sink was full of grey greasy bleachy water. Still.

And at that moment the front door opened. Oh God, the man

of the house was home – cold, hungry, wet, and wanting his lunch, no doubt. And he had a big bunch of yellow roses in his hand. My heart melted because the woman of the house had wrecked the kitchen and had cheese-related injuries to her feet. I honestly didn't know what to say to him.

I met him in the kitchen doorway. 'Seriously,' I said. 'Divorce me. Divorce me now.'

'Well, all right,' he said amenably, 'if you say so. But can you tell me why? For the paperwork. I feel my solicitor will want something more than just *my wife told me to.*'

Wordlessly I stepped aside so he could benefit from the full impact.

There was a long silence and then he said – quite mildly, I thought – 'Did it look like this when I left this morning?'

Miserably I shook my head.

'You've been cooking, haven't you?'

Miserably I nodded.

There was a bit more silence.

'How did it go?'

Miserably I gestured.

Leon stood in the doorway, surveyed the kitchen, surveyed me – a trifle tousled – and turned away.

'What?' I said, defensively, because we can't all be at home in the culinary world.

Still with his back to me, he shook his head.

I hobbled towards him – all right, slightly exaggerating my injuries, but I was going for sympathy here. Still without looking, he reached out and put his arms around me.

'I'm fine,' I said bravely. 'Absolutely fine.'

I could feel him shaking. Was he perhaps grieving for his lost saucepan? The one with its handle poking out of the bin? Quite honestly, I wouldn't have thought he'd had them long enough to bond in any meaningful sort of way.

Pulling himself together, he said, somewhat unsteadily, 'One morning. I leave you for one morning.'

'I burned my feet making cheese on toast,' I said, piteously, shamelessly going for sympathy and understanding.

He enquired what was happening with the sink.

'Soup,' I said.

He shook his head. 'Sometimes my heart just overflows with love for you.' Which wasn't at all the response I'd been expecting.

He picked his way across the kitchen floor, rummaged in a cupboard and found some sort of plunger the landlord had provided. I hadn't thought to look.

A couple of vigorous thrusts – he's very good at those – and the sink uttered a slimy sort of exhalation and there was the smell of a three-day-dead goat giving up its final fart.

All credit to Leon, he stood his ground, merely enquiring what had been in the soup.

'Green leaves, purple leaves, something knobbly with frondy bits, something aniseedy, something red and a potato.'

'Ah,' he said. 'That would be the problem.'

'The potato?'

He nodded gravely. 'Not the easiest vegetable in the rack.'

'Oh. Well, I'll know for the future, I suppose.'

He froze. 'You're going to do this again?'

'Well, not immediately, obviously. We've run out of vege-tables, bread and cheese. I think there are some eggs somewhere. Would you like a . . . ?'

'No,' he said quickly. 'I'll take you to lunch somewhere. Go and have a quick shower.'

'I've had one.'

'Sweetheart, you have cheese in your hair.'

When I came down, the kitchen looked more or less normal and the goat fart smell had taken advantage of the wide-open windows and pushed off.

We had lunch at the pub. Leon insisted on soup and a toasted cheese sandwich – to give me something to aspire to, he said.

The good thing that came out of all that was that we sat down and divided up the housework between us. I was banned from entering the kitchen unaccompanied. He would do the cooking and washing-up. I would do the laundry and ironing. He'd keep downstairs tidy – because that's where the kitchen was. I'd keep upstairs tidy – because that's where Matthew's room was. He reckoned he'd got the best of the deal. We'd both do the shopping and the gardening.

Euphoric at being released from kitchen duties for possibly the rest of my life, I agreed and we both enjoyed our lunch. Although I should say that while his heart might have been overflowing with love for me, he still stuck me with the bill.

Weeks turned into months. Every afternoon, weather permitting, I'd walk through the courtyard and open the gate into the little wood. There was always something new to see. Fat, sticky buds, a nest under construction, dark shapes in the rock pools, a shy flower every now and then. I walked along the banks of the stream or meandered down new paths. The weather grew warmer, the snow melted and the snowdrops faded. Long woolly catkins appeared. Trees burst into new life. Birds fluttered in the bushes and trees.

This was a very neat woodland. The canopy was light enough to allow grass to grow rather than scrubby undergrowth. Hence the snowdrops, I suppose. I discovered a little path that led to a dilapidated structure overlooking one of the larger pools. An old summerhouse of some kind.

Spring began to ooze into summer. Sunlight dappled the ground, highlighting new and vivid colours and the wood captivated me all over again because – most magical of all – the bluebells came out.

I've been all over the place and seen many beautiful sights, but this one . . .

They were everywhere. The ground was covered in a thick carpet of every shade of blue imaginable. Almost as if a part of the sky had fallen down. Don't tell Chicken Licken.

Great clumps of rhododendrons had been planted at some point. Not the usual deep pink or purple – these flowers were cream, yellow and gold, because nothing must be allowed to detract from the beauty of the bluebells. With the soft golden light shafting through the trees, the brilliant green of new growth and the gentle blues – I thought it was the most beautiful place I'd ever seen.

I was lost in it, walking around and around, drinking in the colours, the sights, the smells of spring and early summer. I couldn't stay away. I think I was terrified I'd wake up one morning and it would have disappeared and I'd never see it again.

I dragged out my easel. Leon had brought all my stuff from St Mary's, including my painting gear, even though I hadn't painted for ages. I set it all up, filled a jar of water from the stream and got stuck in.

I painted like a madwoman. I couldn't stop. I painted the bluebells in bright sunshine. And the dark rushing stream frothing white as it swirled around the moss-clad rocks, iridescent green in the sunshine. And the trees, thick with lichen and leaves. I even painted the dimly remembered snowdrops, green and white and ethereal in the snowstorm.

I flung colour around like no one's business. And not just blues, greens and golds but scarlets, crimsons, magentas and oranges as well. I couldn't seem to put a brushstroke wrong. I don't know if it was the speed at which I felt compelled to work, but my style was much looser than usual – a lot of it just shapes and colours on the canvas, but there was a tremendous energy – a frenzy, almost – that translated itself into my work. Even I was pleased with the results. Leon was delighted, wrenching them from me almost the moment they were completed and hanging them up around the house.

I was busy translating sunshine into paint one day when I suddenly realised I was happy. I looked forward to each day and what it might hold for me. I had no worries. No responsibilities. I hadn't felt this carefree for a long time. There wasn't actually anywhere else I wanted to be. I loved where I was, who I was with and what I was doing. It was the most idyllic time of my life – better even than time spent on Skaxos, now sadly out of my reach.

The next big event was Matthew's exams. I asked him if he had everything he needed.

He sighed patiently. 'They're not till next week, Mum.'

'I daresay, but I am familiar with the teenage tendency to leave everything to the very last moment.'

He shook his head. 'It's all good.'

I stopped nagging.

First thing Monday morning we were all at the gate, bright and early. Leon and Matthew would drive to St Mary's to pick up Professor Penrose, who was about to discover if the last year or so had been in vain. I wouldn't be going with them. There was still some doubt as to whether I could safely be transported from A to B and Leon had expressed concerns over his upholstery.

Leon came to kiss me goodbye. 'You'll be all right on your own?'

I sighed in exaggerated exasperation. 'Yes. Obviously life is always a struggle without you but I usually manage not to burn the house down. I think a more pertinent question is whether you can manage without me.'

He smiled. 'I pray I never have to find out.'

I smiled back and Matthew groaned and rolled his eyes.

'We'll be back at the weekend, Max. When you'll probably have forgotten who we are.'

'Almost certainly. You'd better call every night just to remind me.'

His smile faded. 'I can come back every evening, you know. It's really not that far.'

'I'll be fine. You concentrate on Matthew. And keeping Professor Penrose out of trouble.'

It was his turn to groan.

'Good luck,' I said, putting my hand on Matthew's shoulder. 'Although I don't think you'll have many problems.'

He nodded, pulled open the car door, went to climb in and then stopped.

'There you are,' I said, triumphantly. 'I knew you'd forget something.'

His eyes were very bright. 'In the woodshed.'

I felt my stomach turn over. 'What is?'

'What?'

'What's in the woodshed?'

He looked at me blankly. 'I don't know. See you Friday. Can we have sausages?'

I nodded. 'We'll have a barbecue if the weather holds. Good luck.'

36

They came in the afternoon. No warning. No nothing.

It was yet another scorching day. We'd had no rain for ages. There was no wind and the air hung hot and heavy. I spared a thought for Matthew in his airless classroom wrestling with . . . what was today? . . . Thursday. I consulted his exam schedule pinned up on the pantry door. Thursday was English Language Paper 3 in the morning and Computer Sciences 2 in the afternoon.

I stepped out into the baking backyard. The heat bounced off the buildings around me. We'd bought big pots, stuffed them full of brightly coloured flowers and placed them around the walls. Scarlets, oranges, purples, blues. The effect was rather nice. I thought again how happy I was. Not head-burstingly, deliriously happy, but a kind of quiet contentment. Whatever happened to me next, I knew I would never forget this time.

I'd fully intended a morning's painting but it was just too hot. I was working in acrylics and the paint would dry too fast to be workable. Better to leave it for another time. This wasn't a day to do anything energetic on. Or, if you were Matthew, currently working his way through the grammar section of his paper – a day on which to do anything energetic.

Whatever.

I opened the gate into the wood. Perhaps it would be cooler . . . Nope – just as hot here. Stifling, even.

I wandered over to the stream and looked down at the splashing water. The level was quite low. I was just thinking what a contrast to the damp and foggy London I'd known recently, when something rumbled in the distance. I looked behind me. A huge anvil-shaped black cloud was massing threateningly on the horizon. I'll swear it hadn't been there a moment ago. Thunder rumbled again. We were due a storm. A really big one, by the looks of things.

A sudden cool wind rustled the leaves in the trees. Yep – a nasty weather front was coming through.

I folded up my easel, picked up my canvas and headed for the summerhouse. It should keep everything dry since Leon had fixed the roof. I scooted around, grabbing all the cushions, blankets and books that we'd left scattered around the place, and stacked them inside.

The temperature was dropping almost by the minute. Thunder stopped rumbling in the distance and had an overhead crash instead. Yes, this was going to be a spectacular storm. Something to be watched from the comfort of inside with a nice mug of tea.

I folded the last rug and threw it into the summerhouse, firmly fastening the door. The wind was really beginning to get up now, tossing the smaller branches around. The sun had disappeared completely, leaving just a sharp golden fringe around one of the blackest clouds I'd ever seen.

I stared. I could paint that. A whole canvas of apocalyptic sky with just a tiny, brilliant golden frill at the very edge. I could lay in an underpainting of magenta. And orange. For warmth. And the cloud wouldn't be just grey or black. It would be shades of crimson, purple, dark blue. And there would be tiny mountains on the horizon, just to give it some scale. The horizon would be very low down – in the bottom third of the canvas with just a fringe of plain, neutral foreground. Nothing should detract from the sky . . .

Something wet plopped on my head. Concentrate, Maxwell.

I closed the gate firmly against the wind and spent a few minutes pushing the tubs and pots against the walls to protect them from being blown over. There were a lot of them and it took me some time. Finally, I put my shoulder to the half-open, rickety old workshop door. It put up a fight. Quite a lot of a fight, actually, refusing to budge, so I left it to take its chances.

Something plopped heavily on the ground beside me. And then again.

I reached up to unhook the last hanging basket, which was swaying around like Poe's pendulum, and laid it gently on the ground. That was it – nothing left that could be blown away, topple over or be spoiled by the rain. Everything was either put away or made safe. Just the windows to close now.

With that, the real rain came down. Like stair rods. Even just running across the yard to the kitchen door was enough to soak me nearly to the skin. I hadn't been in a downpour like this since the Cretaceous. This was biblical. I crashed into the kitchen, closed the windows over the sink, the windows in the front room and ran – or squelched – upstairs to Matthew's room. Then into our bedroom.

That was when I heard it.

Yes, I know there was a giant storm happening outside.

434

Almost continual thunder, the occasional crack of lightning, drumming rain – and the wind was strengthening all the time – but despite all that, I heard a sound and it wasn't right.

It wasn't right in the same way as when you're not really listening to your washing machine – we've all got better things to do than that – but then it makes a click when it shouldn't make a click and you know something's gone wrong.

This was exactly the same. I heard a sound and it wasn't a storm sound. I didn't know what it was but it wasn't right.

Rain streamed down the windows. It was like being in a car wash. I padded silently into the bathroom and very, very carefully peered through the still open window into the yard below.

Even through the sleeting rain I could see a pod shape where no pod shape should be and, at the same moment, there was a faint sound downstairs. Someone had cautiously opened the back door and it had stuck slightly – just as it always did. Someone – probably several someones – were in the house.

I couldn't afford to be trapped inside. Out of the window and . . .

I stopped. I was alone. I wasn't fully fit. St Mary's was only twenty minutes away. I needed help.

Ignoring my protests, Leon had installed a panic button. Two, actually – one upstairs and one down. One on the landing and one in the kitchen. To the uninitiated they looked like thermostats. Except they weren't connected to the boiler. They were connected to St Mary's. Somehow. The process had been explained to me but guess who hadn't been listening. I had, however, paid attention to the operating instructions.

Turn the temperature control fully to the right. Depress the central knob. Turn the control fully to the left. Depress again.

Help summoned. I paused. This was St Mary's so I did it again. And again. Just to make sure everyone was aware of the severity of the emergency.

I'm not sure what I expected to happen. No alarms sounded. No doors slammed shut. No grills dropped to cover the windows. No panic room opened up. A little disappointing actually. I made a note to have a word with Leon.

Hoping someone was awake at St Mary's and mobilising what – for want of a better word – could be described as assistance, I shot back into the bathroom. I didn't hesitate for one moment. The rain was considerably reducing visibility and there would never be a better opportunity to get out unseen and unheard. I put one foot on the side of the bath, the other on the windowsill and climbed out of the window.

The rain was making a hell of a racket, masking the sound of me slithering clumsily out of the window and down on to the outside toilet roof. I crouched, peering through the downpour. I couldn't afford to hang around up here for long. They could be coming up the stairs behind me at this very minute. I had to find a secure hiding place until the cavalry turned up. I took a deep breath and dropped.

Bending low, I ran to the lowest part of the roof, didn't allow myself to stop and think about broken ankles, and jumped down into our little orchard. The ground was so hard the rain was just sitting on the top so I landed with a splash, slipped and fell sideways. Now I was not only soaked to the skin but muddy, too. This was obviously going to be one of those days.

I sat up and looked around. Thunder rolled and crashed again. No lightning this time. I couldn't remember whether being among trees in a thunderstorm was good or not. Did trees attract or repel lightning? Was that actually my most pressing issue at the moment?

Skirting the wall around the back of the outbuildings and pigsty, I reached the corner. I had choices. I could go right into the woods to play hide and seek in the thick rhododendrons, or left, around the log shed, and try to scope out who it was and what they wanted. Although I think we all know the answer to that one.

OK, Maxwell, stop and think for a minute. You should get yourself into the woodshed because firstly, you'll be out of the rain. Second, it's a good hiding place. Unless, of course, they have heat-seeking whatnots or proximity alerts. In which case, there is no hiding place. In which case, the decision is whether to run or to attack. I slid my back down the wall and crouched by the overflowing rain butt to consider my next move.

I still favoured the woodshed over the woodland. It gave me options. It was close to the house. And to their pod. Whoever they were. I know Insight was my first guess, but I'd been with Smallhope and Pennyroyal long enough to have inherited a few of their traditional enemies as well.

And then a voice I knew, nearly as well as my own, shouted, 'Search the outbuildings. Use your personnel detectors. Fan out and drive her this way.'

Bridget Lafferty. And her team. Come to kill me. Again.

Bollocks. Move, Maxwell, while you still can.

I sprinted out of the orchard and into the wood and yes, I can still do it when I have to. I swerved around trees and hurdled logs and low bushes, heading straight to the stream. Without stopping to think – my signature move, some would say – I slid down the bank and into the water.

Bloody hell, it was freezing. Absolutely bloody freezing. And the current was much faster and stronger than expected. And there were rocks and boulders everywhere. Especially below the water. I'd skinned my leg already. On reflection, this might not have been a good move, but at least now I was as cold as the water, and if they had heat detectors . . .

I struggled out of the stream, courtesy of a couple of tree roots from the Middle Earth tree, and pulled myself up to peer cautiously over the bank. They were coming through the gate – five of them. Bridget and her bloody team. As I watched, they formed themselves into a line – like the police searches you see on TV – and began, methodically, to work their way through the trees. And two of them were coming this way.

I dropped back down again and scrambled in among the exposed roots, much as the hobbits had done to avoid the Black Rider. I made myself as small as possible, clutched my knees to my chest and tried not to shiver too loudly.

I couldn't hear them over the rain but I could feel their footsteps. At least two of them, I think. They walked up and down the bank and then stopped. Right above me. I clamped my chattering teeth together.

'Could she have crossed the stream, do you think?'

I couldn't hear the reply over the water.

They stood for a while. A very long while, it seemed. I pictured them peering at their instruments, looking up and down the bank. I could only hope I was too cold to register.

'No,' said one of them, eventually. 'Nothing here.' He raised his voice, shouting, 'Clear.'

Someone far off shouted a reply and I felt them move away.

I gave it twenty seconds. I meant to give it thirty but I've

438

always been impatient. Very, very cautiously, I hoisted myself up over the bank. My instinct was to crouch and run and dodge, but running attracts attention. Their visibility would be no better than mine, and if I just moved at a cautious pace, there was a very good chance I could get myself to the already searched log store. It was only just over there. Cold rain splattered on my face and in my eyes and sodden grass wrapped itself around my lower legs. I probably wouldn't have been able to run even if I'd wanted to.

Their pod was ahead of me and slightly to the left of the log store. I remembered their cameras weren't that good and I suspected they hadn't left anyone inside anyway. They were all out looking for me.

Hugging the hedge, I skirted the pod, using my sleeve to try to keep my eyes clear. With luck they were having the same visibility problems as me. And even if they were wearing helmets and visors, they'd be splattered with rain and, with luck, a bit of fogging up as well. I blessed the rain. I was sodden, but so would they be.

Yes – they would, wouldn't they? I stopped dead, realised that wasn't the smartest thing to do, and started up again. Get to shelter and then stop to work it all out, Maxwell. First things first.

Because this was Insight. This was Bridget and her crew. The same crew that had attacked us at Home Farm what seemed like a very long time ago, now. It was pouring with rain. And when they'd come to kill us, they'd been soaking wet, hadn't they? We'd all remarked on it.

Had I got things the wrong way round again? They'd come here before they'd gone to Home Farm. And far from everyone smirking and saying I wasn't important enough to be the target – I was. It was me they'd come for. For some reason yet to be established, and I didn't have time to think about that now.

The inside was cold, dark, cobwebby and very noisy. The rain hammered down on the corrugated iron roof. Thunder crashed again, a great long rumble this time that went on and on. I looked around. Not surprisingly, the place was full of wood. A lot of wood. Some big tree trunks, waiting to be chopped up, some old pallets – again waiting to be converted into firewood – and a massive, massive pile of logs stacked neatly against two walls. In fact, so neatly were they laid that you'd be forgiven for thinking it was one of those trendy art installations people leave lying around the countryside. Unfortunately, meticulously stacked logs offer no sort of hiding place at all. Anywhere. I stared around. This was no good. There wasn't even an upstairs where I could take refuge. With hindsight, this hadn't been a good move.

In the woodshed.

I have an offspring given to obscure and unexpected utterances. They're almost always useful but there's never any context or perspective until it's almost too late. But, according to Matthew, something was in the woodshed. Something useful? Something dangerous? Something I could use?

As the line goes, there's something nasty in the woodshed.

And today there certainly was.

Me.

I looked around again. Just inside the door was a shelf at head height. Cans of oil. For a chainsaw, I assumed. Sadly, the chainsaw itself was absent. Shame. I could have gone all Streetley Chainsaw Massacre. A couple of ancient torches that certainly wouldn't work. And a small cardboard box. I recognised that box. Leon had used it to store the bits and pieces taken out of his pod. I was supposed to go through it and pull out anything I wanted to keep, and I'd forgotten. There was bound to be something useful in there.

Silently I lifted it down. Three of Markham's socks – don't ask – a tattered paperback whose title it was too dark to read, a couple of fizzers for emergencies – and a remote control.

Of course. The remote for the pod. I could summon the pod, make a quick dash through the rain and be out of here in seconds. According to Dr Stone it wouldn't do me any good, but travel sickness, no matter how bad, is rarely terminal, whereas a bullet quite often is.

I moved to the door and peered out into the now slightly flooded yard. The drains had backed up and the water was about an inch deep. Two men were climbing back over the gate just as another emerged from the privy. Checking it, presumably, rather than availing himself of the not very salubrious facilities offered in there. They looked even more drowned than me. If that was even possible. My time was running out. I couldn't get away and I couldn't dodge them forever. Time to go. I pressed the remote and waited.

Nothing happened. What?

I shook it hard because that always makes things work better and pressed it again.

Nothing.

Shit. No sign of St Mary's, either. This is how you can tell I'm not a princess. I usually have to rescue myself.

I pressed again. In fact, I stabbed repeatedly because that's always helpful. I was still stabbing when the workshop door shattered. Literally shattered. Lumps of rotten wood flew in all directions. Everyone leaped a mile into the air – including me – and with a whine and a clatter of imperfectly meshed gears, Markham's assistant – R2-Tea2 – crashed out into the courtyard.

Wasn't expecting that. Were you?

37

In a life lightly sprinkled with unexpected events, that one was right up there. What the hell? What the actual bloody hell? And then the truth dawned. It was the wrong remote. Of course Leon wouldn't leave the pod remote lying around. This was one of the remotes for R2-Tea2.

How could I ever have thought otherwise?

Because I'm stupid, was the answer to that one. And I didn't have my glasses on. And it was dark. And I was being pursued by homicidal former colleagues and my homicidal former boss.

On the other hand, I now had an ally. Yes, there were the aforementioned homicidal colleagues out there, but Markham's assistant was a force to be reckoned with. I had no idea how to operate the remote but I stabbed the controls at random, either causing a massive malfunction in its tiny brain or possibly changing TV channels for miles around.

The thing careered around in a wide circle, sending up a bit of a bow wave and shattering pots and tubs in its path. A long banner trailed behind it, carefully formed letters running in the rain.

To Mum. Love, Matthew. This was what he and Leon had been doing in the workshop. Matthew's present to me. My own tea-maker. Aww . . .

Best of all though, it was buying me time. Insight really didn't know how to react. Yes, they jumped a mile and raised their weapons, tracking it as it crashed around the yard until it became clear they were in no danger. I don't think they knew whether to laugh at it or shoot it. Whichever they did, it was only a matter of time before they wondered where it could have come from and why and who was operating it, and started searching for me with renewed enthusiasm.

'Would you like a cup of tea, master?'

Oh God, was it back on that again? We were all going to die. I twisted the controls. I had no idea what I was doing but as long as it kept them distracted . . . St Mary's was only twenty minutes away. Not much longer, surely.

Two of them put their backs to the wall and raised their weapons. Tactically a very sound move. Sadly, tactically sound moves meant nothing to Markham's PA, who veered suddenly in their direction.

'Would you like a cup of tea, master?'

It couldn't help itself. Matthew and the professor had programmed it to offer tea to everyone whose path it crossed. Its tank would be empty, of course, and quite honestly, there was so much water about that anything this demented Dalek could sling their way wasn't going to make a lot of difference, but I appreciated the effort.

I was still twisting knobs and things on the remote, so you could probably say it was something I did – although what, I've no idea – but, suddenly, appendages flailing, it went on the attack, hurling itself at the one recently emerged from the privy.

He yelled and instinctively stepped back. His two mates

444

nearly pissed themselves laughing as he jinked and dodged trying to get away from the metal monster.

I was pleased because that was three of them occupied, and every second brought St Mary's that little bit closer.

Sadly, Bridget appeared through the gate, took one look, raised her blaster and fired. R2-Tea2 exploded in a sheet of flame. Mechanical limbs flew in all directions. Black smoke poured from the shell. It was going to take more than a bit of soldering to get him going again. Matthew would be upset. As would Professor Penrose. As was I. My son had made me that. But we had the technology. We could rebuild.

The other team member had turned up while I wasn't looking. That was all five in the courtyard now. Could I somehow take advantage of this distraction?

And then I had a thought. Oozing back into the log store again, I found the box. And the fizzers therein. Because the other thing about my opponents' first attack – the one at Home Farm – was that not only had they been soaking wet, they'd been scorched. Quite badly. Not one of them had escaped unscathed. And there had been scorch marks inside the pod, as well. And that melted patch on the floor.

I looked at the fizzers. Not so much a Brilliant Idea as fulfilling my destiny.

Not that it would be easy. Fizzers aren't accurate. They're not meant to be. They're not meant to be fired horizontally, either. They're designed to soar upwards, spitting incandescent red sparks as they go, and then hang around in the air, bathing everything in a sinister red glow and probably exacerbating the problems that caused you to fire the thing off in the first place. They're distress flares, not weapons, and the one thing

Ian Guthrie had dinned into me during my training was – never, ever, point a fizzer at a person. It takes a great deal of energy to get a fizzer so high into the air and if it hits a person by mistake, it will penetrate the human body to a considerable depth. And it can't be removed. The heat thrown out is unimaginable. It's like having a small sun embedded in your arm or leg or chest. It doesn't actually matter where, because the agony and the shock will kill you. Eventually. So as Major Guthrie had repeatedly said – you never, ever, aim a fizzer at a person.

Well, he was never going to know, was he?

The rain was still hammering down. Insight regrouped and went into the house. I heard the sound of something smashing. And then something else. The bastards were trashing the place. My home. The place where I was supposed to be safe. Small mammals will fight to defend their burrows. I was a small historian defending my burrow. My scruples vanished. I would make them regret ever crossing my path. Suddenly I no longer had any problems at all with their ultimate fate at Home Farm. Even Bridget. Because this was my home. I lived here with my family and we were happy.

Perhaps they knew I was around somewhere and were hoping to tempt me out with a bit of vandalism. They got that wrong. I wriggled further into the shadows as thunder and lightning crashed overhead. I could wait. I had the advantage of knowing how this would turn out in the end. If I played everything right. I knew they didn't kill me here. They'd go on to Home Farm and meet their fate there. Something smashed in the kitchen. A whole ton of crockery by the sound of it. I imagined them throwing our books on the floor, rummaging through our stuff, breaking Matthew's carefully constructed models.

446

Bastards. They were going to fry.

I don't know how long I crouched there. My knees told me it was hours. I suspect about five minutes. Not a problem – Insight could stay as long as they liked. With good luck and a following wind, St Mary's was on the way. At least I hoped they were. Yes, of course they were. Bound to be. Weren't they?

Something was happening. The back door opened and Bridget led the way across the courtyard back to their pod. They'd grown careless. One man covered their rear but otherwise they weren't bothering with any specific precautions. They just splashed through the mini lake towards the pod.

I would need to pick my moment carefully. I wanted as many of them inside as possible but the door still had to be open. I inched my way sideways . . . just a few inches . . . for the best angle . . .

The pod door opened. Bridget and someone else went inside. Two more stood on the threshold, watching. For some unknown reason, one lingered outside. Bloody hell, get a move on, will you? One of the pair slipped into the pod. Just two outside now.

I'd have to take a chance. They might simply have returned to the pod to pick up more equipment and would leave at any moment and I'd have missed the opportunity. And if they started a methodical search with proper equipment then they'd probably find me in minutes.

There was no thought of taking aim. Fizzers don't work that way. All I could do was point it at the open door and cross my fingers. If it missed – as it very probably would – then I'd have given away my position and I had nothing to defend myself with. I wouldn't even be able to get away. There was only the one entrance. They would simply cross the courtyard, stand in the doorway and gun me down.

On the other hand, there had been clear evidence that some sort of incendiary event had occurred within the pod. Go for it, Maxwell. Place your trust in the god of historians and go for it.

I peeled back the tab and fired. The thing went off with a bang and a hiss as they always did. The flare corkscrewed across the yard towards the pod, screaming like a banshee and trailing vast amounts of blood-red smoke.

Sadly, it sailed straight over the pod roof, but the two men outside stood for a moment, paralysed, and then, obeying their instincts, ducked into the pod. Those already inside, obeying their instincts, tried to get out to see what was happening. There was a nice little scrum at the door and I had the second fizzer ready. I fired again. This one missed the doorway and bounced off the side of the pod with some force, scattering sparks over a wide area and coming to rest about two feet from the door. An incandescent ball of spitting flame. Not actually inside the pod but just outside, which was almost as good because now they couldn't get out. Until the fizzer died down of its own accord, they were trapped.

Third time pays for all. Before they had time to regroup, I grabbed the third fizzer and moved sideways for a better angle. One man saw me but too late. We both fired at the same time. His blast scorched the door jamb to my left. I felt the heat on my arm. My fizzer spiralled its way towards the pod. My memory tells me it sailed straight and true, which just goes to show how rubbish my memory is because they don't work like that and it couldn't have, but whenever I think of that moment – the rain, the scream of the fizzer, the cold, my desperation because now

I had nothing – the fizzer always sails straight through the open door to impact hard against the far wall.

Shrieks and screams came from inside the pod. Because you can't put them out. Not even with water. They're designed to burn for as long as possible and that's what this one was doing. And they burn hot. This one whizzed around, ricocheting from one wall to another. Going by the noise, there were five people all scrambling to get out of its way and failing.

I should have seized the opportunity to run but I was rooted to the spot. It was like a scene from hell. The second fizzer was still burning and hissing in the doorway, casting a sinister red glow through the sheeting rain. Men were shouting; I could hear Bridget's voice shouting to get it out, get it out, get it out. But you can't pick up a fizzer, not if you still want to have hands afterwards. The inside of the pod flickered red and orange. Like the entrance to a volcano. A high-pitched scream rose over the general clamour. I suspected someone was trying to kick it out of the door and had possibly set fire to their boots.

I'd stayed too long. I should go. Even as the thought nudged my brain, Bridget appeared at the pod doorway. I was pleased to see she had a long scorch mark etched across her breast-plate. She saw me kneeling just inside the woodshed because I was too stupid to have legged it when I had the opportunity. Calmly, ignoring both spitting fizzers and shouting colleagues, she raised her big blaster. And it was a big one. Her visor was up, and mostly what I remember is the expression on her face. We looked at each other. She took her time, lining up the shot. I knelt, paralysed, like a rabbit in headlights.

For God's sake – move, Maxwell.

The spell broke. I dived sideways. If she wanted me, she

was going to have to come and get me. If I could just entice her into the log shed . . .

Alas, she had no intention of being enticed. Not even a little bit. Ignoring everything but me, she fired.

And missed. She missed me. How could she miss me at that range?

Because she wasn't aiming at me, that's why. She'd fired at the vast stack of logs behind me. With some sort of detonation, and a rumble far louder than the thunder still crashing overhead, the entire pile collapsed.

I half turned but it was too late. Hard heavy things crashed into my legs, knocking me over. I flung up my arms to save myself and the whole giant log pile just rolled straight over the top of me. The world went dark.

It was the pain that woke me up.

And the crushing weight.

But mostly the pain.

I couldn't move.

And I couldn't breathe. Not because of the weight – although that wasn't helping – but because of the position I was in.

I don't know about anyone else but whenever I've thought about people being buried – not often, admittedly – I've always imagined them lying neatly under the rockfall – or woodfall, in my case – on their back, with their limbs picturesquely splayed around them. I was obviously doing it wrong. I was face down. My left leg was hitched up somehow and bent at the wrong angle. I had a terrible cramp and my hip was on fire with pain. My right leg was bent at the knee and ditto with the pain. Worst of all, the weight of all the wood above me was

450

crushing my face into my right arm and I couldn't breathe. At all. Not even a little bit. Couldn't lift my head. Couldn't move my arm. Couldn't breathe.

Just to keep the record tidy, I had no idea where my left arm was. Somewhere in here with me was about the best I could do.

I could feel my blood pounding in my ears. I tried to suck in some air and got nothing. I was suffocating. The weight on my back and ribs was slowly crushing the life out of me.

On the grounds I couldn't make things any worse, I tried to roll over. Give myself, literally, a bit of wiggle room. That didn't work; I was completely pinned down. I couldn't push myself up because I was lying on my own arm. I couldn't get my knees underneath me.

In desperation, instead of trying to lift my head, I tried turning it. That worked. Only a fraction of an inch but it meant a tiny corner of my mouth was clear. I tried not to suck frantically but to draw slow, smooth breaths. Again. And again. It wasn't enough. My body needed much more oxygen than it was currently getting.

A dim corner of my mind wondered whether Bridget would move in for the kill. I had a sudden, sickening vision of her unshouldering her blaster and igniting the giant pile of logs under which I was trapped. What would that be like? To lie trapped under a blazing inferno, the heat blistering my skin. Feeling my hair blaze, my lungs scorching. I didn't want to burn.

A second's reflection said no. If they killed me here, then they wouldn't have to go on to Home Farm to finish the job. Ergo – I didn't die here.

Wouldn't stop her trying, though.

I could hear wailing. Were those sirens? Or was it me? When did I suddenly have enough oxygen to make that much noise?

Idly, because my brain didn't have a lot on at the moment, and not a lot of oxygen to do it with, either, I speculated on what would happen if I did actually die here. Quite an interesting problem, don't you think? I was dying but I couldn't die. Didn't die. Wasn't going to die. Whatever. I was quite looking forward to seeing how History would resolve this one.

Unless, of course, I was a paradox. Yes, that made sense. I could easily see me being a paradox. Sadly, I didn't think I was going to be around long enough to appreciate the irony.

Paradox Lost, so to speak . . .

Hey ho . . .

Getting bored now, universe. Either save me or let me go . . .

OK – go it is, then . . .

38

The logs were gone.

That had to be good.

I was awake.

That might be good. Too early to say.

The pain was still there. My face hurt. From the tightness around my eye, I guessed there was some swelling. Logs have no give in them at all, you know. Nasty, knobbly things. My hip was throbby but strangely blunted. As if, somehow, a very large number of painkillers were wafting their way round my system, dispensing woozy pain-free goodness as they went. That was good.

I was surrounded by soft warmth. Like a pink, fluffy cloud.

Shitting Harry. Was I dead and they'd sent me to heaven and I was going to have to spend the rest of eternity sitting on a cloud listening to harp music and being nice to people? There would be no swearing, no shenanigans and definitely no chocolate. People would smile at me and everything would be sweet and serene and I was going to have to do something to get myself expelled by lunchtime. Seriously – have you seen the sort of people who think they qualify for heaven? The thought of spending eternity with that lot . . . This was definitely *not* good.

No, hang on. I knew that smell. Disinfectant and burnt paper. Again – shit. I've never been less pleased to wake up at St Mary's. Yes, ungrateful, I know, but they could have just given me a plaster and two aspirins and left me where I was. Still, I didn't have to open my eyes. I wasn't in any particular peril – I could lie here forever.

'Open your eyes, Max,' said Dr Stone. 'The machines are telling me you woke up five minutes ago.'

'They're malfunctioning,' I said.

'They're not the only ones. Open your eyes.'

I opened my eyes.

Yep. St Mary's. Bed by the door. Dr Stone. Scratchpad. Bleeping machines. All we needed was the perpetual obsession as to the state of my bowels and we'd have the complete set.

Attack is the best form of defence.

'Well,' I said. 'I carried out your instructions to the letter. I lived in my own time. I led a quiet life with no stress. Against my better judgement I ate green food. I was a model patient. How did that work out for me?'

'You're fine,' he said, failing to exude the milk of human kindness. 'No one who complains as much as you do could be seriously injured. If you manage not to piss off anyone in the meantime, you will be discharged either tomorrow evening or the next morning. I should tell you now – bets are being placed.'

'Put me down for the earliest possible discharge. Unless someone else has got that already.'

He consulted his scratchpad. 'No. Not one single bet on you being discharged early for good behaviour.'

'Where's Leon?'

'Settling Matthew with Professor Penrose and on his way.'

454

'He doesn't have to disrupt Matthew's schedule.'

'He's not. He says he'll pop in to make sure you haven't burned anything to the ground and then get back to Matthew.'

'Hmpf,' I said, and yes, that is a word. It's the traditional response to getting your own way when you've expected a struggle and are slightly disappointed. Hmpf.

'Does Treadwell know I'm here?'

'Yes, but he's choosing not to acknowledge your existence, let alone your presence. Officially, you don't exist.'

'Hyssop?'

'Haven't seen her.'

'Any chance of a cup of tea?'

'Any chance of good behaviour?'

'Any chance of not being provoked into behaving otherwise?' He sighed.

I closed my eyes.

And opened them to find Treadwell staring at me. Oh God ...

He got straight to it. 'Don't speak. I have no choice but to offer you shelter, but at the slightest sign of trouble, you're out of here. Dr Stone tells me you could be gone as early as tomorrow. Strive to achieve that target.'

He turned on his heel and walked away. He'd obviously brushed up on his having-the-last-word technique.

At the door he appeared to hesitate. 'To put your mind at rest – your cottage has been made safe. There was no sign of your assailants when St Mary's arrived.'

'They won't be back.'

'I told you not to speak. Please focus all your efforts on recovering sufficiently to be discharged tomorrow.'

'Any chance of a cup of tea?'

He looked down at me. 'Could you be more irritating?'

I grinned. 'Challenge accepted.'

And closed my eyes. He should have quit while he still had the last word.

The next day began pleasantly enough. I limped to the window seat and was looking out at a sunny day and wondering where all traces of the recent storm had gone when a voice said, 'Knock knock.'

'Come in.'

He sighed. 'No, Max. You never do this properly. Let's try it again, shall we? Knock knock.'

I sighed, too. 'I'm sick. I shouldn't have to put up with this.'

'I'm not going away. Knock knock.'

'Who's there?'

'David.'

I sighed again. 'David who?'

'David Sands. I've brought you a present.'

'How did you know I was here?'

'Mystery patient. Female. Badly knocked about. No one's talking. Who else would it be? Good God – what happened to your hair?'

'A bastard named Martin Gaunt.'

'What happened to your face?'

'Logs.'

'Yeah – that would do it. Other than that, how are you?'

'Good. How's things with you?'

'Less good,' he said, dragging up a chair and making himself comfy. 'Sykes and Roberts are an item. Bashford and Angus are distraught, which has resulted in both of them dragging themselves around the building, one sighing deeply and the other crapping on everything in sight. I leave it to you to decide which is which. Hint: it's not what you would think.

'Van Owen and Polly Perkins have taken up fencing. That's fencing with swords, not fencing as in the restraint of beasts, before you get the wrong idea.

'Turk bit young Glass. Word on the street says they had to force his jaws apart with a stick. Turk – not Glass. Mr Stone's knee is playing up and everyone is suffering. Otherwise . . .'

'Did you recapture all the flesh-eating beetles?'

'Professor Rapson says yes but after a few months in your job, I no longer believe a word anyone says to me. Sykes is doing her best to make Hyssop's life a living hell and succeeding. They're going to come to blows any day now. I've had a word with her – Sykes – and she's smiled and nodded and promised to behave.'

'Sinister,' I commented.

'Absolutely. I believe the grave has already been dug. We're all laying bets as to who will fill it.'

'Is Rosie still your PA?'

'No, Mrs Partridge knocked that on the head. I've got Mrs Shaw. Peterson's got Rosie and he hates me. Mrs Shaw's lovely though.'

'Did you tell that to Rosie?'

'Yeah.'

'Let me guess. Now she hates you too.'

'Unclear. She hasn't spoken to me for ten days.'

'Poor you.'

'Yeah. Anyway – can't stop. I'm not supposed to be here

but there are all sorts of rumours flying around and I'm nosey. Brought you something to pass the time.'

He handed me a copy of his latest book. *Species.*

'Oh, brilliant. Thank you. What's it about?'

'Well, in the past there were three species of people. Well, actually there were four, but for the sake of the narrative I haven't included the pygmies. There was us, the Neanderthals, and the Denisovans, all of whom interbred. We know this because we all carry Neander and Denisovan DNA in varying quantities. Anyway, in my book there was a long-ago war between the three races as they battled for survival and supremacy of the then world, and this is what's been the cause of wars down the ages. Nothing to do with greed, lust, violence, religion and all the traditional excuses for killing each other, but answering a subconscious urge to ensure the eradication of the other species. Fighting for the upper hand. Especially when resources become scarce. As they did when the Ice Age returned. And as they are now. In fact,' he said, thoughtfully, 'that could be why you and Hyssop don't get on. Your DNA is telling each of you to purge the other.

'Anyway, my main character discovers that's why we're the bastards that we are. We're at the mercy of our genes. Instinctive dislike of everyone who is different. The book is all about whether – now that we know the cause of our instinctive distrust and hatred of each other – mankind can rise above its own genetic programming to enjoy peace at long last. Or, will it obey that same programming and not rest until everyone who's not the same as them is obliterated from the face of the earth? One last apocalyptic battle . . . from which no one will return.'

At this point I really should say David Sands is one of the nicest people you could ever hope to meet. Heaven knows where he gets his ideas from. Too much exposure to Rosie Lee, perhaps.

'Exciting,' I said, looking at the cover. 'Do we survive?'

'Read the book and find out. Anyway, gotta go.' He paused. 'Good to see you again, Max.'

'And you.'

He disappeared, leaving me with his critically acclaimed story of the human race at its worst.

He wasn't my only visitor that morning. I was still in the window seat, enjoying the sunshine and chapter one, when I had a premonition some idiot had just entered the room. I was right. I looked up and Hyssop was standing not six feet away.

I sighed and then continued with my book in the hope she'd take the hint.

She didn't, so I said, 'What do you want?'

'I've come to see this mysterious patient everyone's talking about.'

I turned a page. 'Let me know when you've found her.'

She pounced. 'How do you know it's a her?'

'Because you're not standing in the men's ward. Although I wish you would.'

All right, yes, a touch ungrateful considering she saved my life at the Red House but if she hadn't made such a complete dog's breakfast of the Babylon assignment then neither of us would be standing here today. We could have been out having a nice drink with Clerk and Prentiss.

'Why are you here?'

459

I sighed and looked up from my book. 'I was about to ask you the same question.'

'You were sacked.'

'And yet . . . here I am.'

'Again – why? What's going on?'

I looked up. 'Treadwell keeping you out of the loop again?'

She flushed. I'd hit a nerve. I wondered how she'd been faring since the Babylon disaster. She must be aware she and her people had been frozen out. She could have solved everyone's problems by requesting a transfer but she was stubborn.

The silence lengthened. I put down my book and we looked at each other. I don't think either of us could think of anything to say. We'd parted under the very worst of terms. On the other hand, she could have let Halcombe kill me at the Red House. Revenge would have been sweet. She must have been tempted. But she hadn't given in. She'd shot Halcombe and saved my life.

And now, here she was. She must have heard there was a patient in Sick Bay, enquired who, been dissatisfied with the answers and come to check for herself.

We looked at each other some more. This was ridiculous. One of us should speak. Be the bigger woman. I prepared to be the bigger woman. I just hoped I could carry it off.

'Thank you.'

'For what?'

'You saved my life at the Red House. Did Gaunt have a go at you afterwards?'

'He tried. I just walked off and left him to deal with the aftermath. Of the two of us – you and me – it would be hard to say who he hates most.'

I grinned. 'Well, now you're just showing off. It'll be me. No question about it.'

She gave me a kind of half-smile. 'Don't kid yourself. Apparently, there are all sorts of enquiries if someone discharges a firearm in a government establishment. He'll be tied up in paperwork for the next six months. So, of the two of us, I think I can confidently take pole position.'

'I gather no one took the opportunity to be rid of him.'

'He managed to foist all the blame for Halcombe and Sullivan's behaviour on to Dr Washburn. According to Gaunt, Washburn's obviously incorrect medical assessment had placed lives in jeopardy. Washburn got the boot. Gaunt's still in place.'

'Bugger. What did Treadwell say about what happened?'

She closed her eyes. 'From memory – "You're an idiot, Hyssop. Don't do it again. Do you know how long I've had to spend sorting this out? Next time shoot Gaunt as well. Or even instead."'

'A surprisingly enlightened response.'

'Oh, he's not so bad.'

'He sacked me.'

'As I said – not so bad.'

Another awkward silence.

Eventually, she said, 'I've left Glass at your cottage.'

About to start reading again, I laid my book down, saying suspiciously, 'Why?'

'To safeguard your stuff. There's been some damage. Not to the fabric of the building, but some of your personal effects have been tossed.'

I opened my mouth to protest.

'His instructions are to sweep up, bin anything that's totalled and wait for Chief Farrell.' She looked at her watch. 'Who should be there now.'

Since I'd thought Glass's instructions would have been to have a sneak around while he could, I was a bit ashamed of myself. 'Well, that's very considerate. We don't have much but what we do have is special. Thank you. And Glass, too.'

She nodded and silence fell again.

It was good of her to have done that. And of all her people, Glass was the most acceptable. He would safeguard our stuff until Leon arrived. And then what? What was to stop Insight trying again? Could I ever go back there? What would I do when I left here? My options were narrowing. No Home Farm. And now, probably, no cottage.

I sighed. I was still too tired and fuzzy to think too deeply about my future. Something would happen which would help me make up my mind.

And it was about to.

I made an effort. 'I'll be gone soon – just as soon as I can stand up without falling over. This afternoon, probably.'

'Don't hang around here,' she said, quietly. 'For many good reasons. Not the least being you get on my nerves.'

I'm sure I had a really witty response to that but I never got to utter it and I can't remember what it was now.

A movement outside caught my attention. I turned to see Treadwell letting himself out of a side door. He stood for a moment, surveying everything around him, and then began to walk across the grass. No reason why he shouldn't – it was a nice day. I suspected he was in the middle of his weekly departmental inspection. He'd obviously finished in Hawking and was heading for the stables, and taking the scenic route across the South Lawn.

Hyssop followed my gaze. His back was to us. I watched his shadow move across the grass. He turned to survey the building, head tilted back, seemingly in no hurry and enjoying the peaceful day. The sun shone brightly, the grounds looked beautiful, nothing was on fire. St Mary's basked in rural tranquillity.

There was a noise rather like a car backfiring somewhere a long way off. Treadwell stood stock-still for a moment and then crumpled to the ground and lay still. I could see the crimson stain from here.

I sat up in a hurry and looked at Hyssop. She looked at me. And then she said, 'Stay where you are. Don't leave this room,' and ran out of the door. I could hear her shouting into her com. 'Red alert. Red alert. Lockdown. Now. No one in. No one out. Red alert. Hyssop out. Where the hell is Dr Stone? Get me a medical team now. Director down. Gunshot wound. South Lawn.'

Her voice was cut off as a door closed behind her.

There was movement outside. Atherton appeared from around the corner of the building. Closely followed by Sykes and Roberts. The ex-Head of the History Department wondered what those two could possibly have been up to.

Then Mrs Mack, closely followed by Kim and Janet from the kitchen.

Then Dieter and Lindstrom, who came out from Hawking.

Then Hyssop from the same door as Treadwell, running across the grass towards Treadwell with Dr Stone and Nurse Fortunata close behind.

They all bent over him, obscuring the body from my sight. I saw Hyssop step away and speak into her com. A moment later,

Cox, Lucca and Keller appeared. She barked a series of instructions and they scattered. To check the perimeters, I suppose. I don't know why. Complete waste of time. She knew as well as I that the shot had come from inside St Mary's.

All the remaining members of her team would be securing the building and running the CCTV tapes. I was prepared to bet they wouldn't find anything useful.

I saw Peterson running across the grass. He halted a few paces away, watching Dr Stone work. Faces crowded at all the windows that I could see. I wondered if everyone else was as gobsmacked as me.

Peterson and Hyssop conversed for a moment and then she returned to the building. The enquiries would begin. The shot had come from inside St Mary's. Almost anyone could have done it. The only person who couldn't – the only person with an absolute, cast-iron alibi – was me. She'd been standing next to me at the time. But if she wanted to – if she really wanted to – she could lie. It would be her word against mine. No one would believe me. No one who mattered, anyway. I needed to get out of here. Because I must be the number one suspect. A disgraced former employee back on the premises for a reason yet to be discovered and being concealed by certain members of St Mary's staff. If Gaunt ever found out I was here then the shit really would hit the fan.

I stood up, wobbled a little and headed for the locker next to my bed. At exactly that moment, the door opened to reveal a fully armed Gallacio.

'Sorry, Max. You're not going anywhere. Orders.'

I sighed. Hyssop wasn't as dim as I thought she was. Well, she couldn't be, really.

I climbed back into bed.

'I have to leave the door open,' he said.

'What's happening? Is Treadwell dead?'

He didn't respond and I didn't push it. He would have been instructed not to answer any questions. Especially from me.

I lay back on the pillows and watched him prop himself against the wall where he could see me, the nurses' station and the door to the lift. Sick Bay was utterly silent. I wondered if they'd bring Treadwell in for treatment or whether they'd call for an ambulance. Depended how serious it was, I suppose. He might even be dead.

And what would happen now? Was Gallacio here to keep me in or someone else out? If Treadwell was dead, then Peterson was in charge of St Mary's. He could override Hyssop's orders. But would he? And for how long would he be allowed to act as Director? Would London send a replacement for Treadwell? And if so – who?

I began to have a very bad feeling about this.

And where was Leon? Was he at the cottage or here at St Mary's? Did he have an alibi? Would he be under surveillance too? After all, he was married to Suspect Number One. Innocent or not, I needed to get out of here. As soon as possible. And then my second, more sensible, thoughts said that fleeing the scene of a crime might not be a Brilliant Idea. Better to stay put and bluff it out, perhaps. And Hyssop, unless she was a complete bitch, could – would – *should* be my alibi. If she wasn't, then I'd revert to Plan A – climbing out of the window in the middle of the night and setting fire to the place to cover my tracks.

There were so many factors. Someone in this building had shot Treadwell. He was Time Police. They weren't going to take kindly to that. He'd been appointed by the government – they weren't going to be happy, either. Would the police be involved? Or would the whole thing be handled quietly and behind closed doors?

I suppose a lot depended on whether Treadwell lived or died. Even if he survived, though, short-term, he was out of the game.

I sat up suddenly. Should someone warn Markham? No – someone would already have told Guthrie what had happened. He'd have lost no time informing Markham. Because if Hunter and little Flora hadn't been living safely with Mrs De Winter in Rushford all this time, then he was a bigger idiot than even I thought he was.

My head was spinning again. I lay back down and closed my eyes. I had no idea what would happen next.

The answer was, from my point of view – not a lot. There was a lot of activity outside the ward. I heard voices and footsteps and then Gallacio closed the door and I was on my own. I practised climbing out of bed in case I had to do it in a hurry. I went to the window and tried to devise a method of escape that wouldn't involve me fatally splattering myself on the flagstones below. Markham wouldn't be throwing me out of this window.

I wandered into the bathroom and inspected cabinets and cupboards in case anyone had inadvertently left something with which I could overcome the forces of darkness, and they bloody hadn't, which was just typical.

It was Janet from the kitchen who brought me a meal. I assumed Fortunata was busy. Or possibly under arrest. I asked Janet what was happening and she just shook her head. I wondered if she'd also been instructed not to speak to me.

I examined the food very carefully in case someone had concealed a message or a key or a remote or a weapon or a rope ladder and no one had so I just had to eat it.

That done, I put the tray to one side, lay back and waited for something to happen.

39

The hours passed slowly and I began to feel more and more frustrated. I wanted to know what was going on. I had no doubt that should I leave my room to enquire, I would very speedily find myself back on this side of the door, courtesy of Mr Gallacio. Or whoever had replaced him.

Sleep – my constant companion over recent months – had abandoned me completely. In the end I gave up. I sat up in bed, switched on the light, thumped a few pillows and had a bit of a think.

I hadn't seen Leon. Whether that was good or bad I didn't know. I didn't even know if he had returned to the cottage. Don't think about that now. Whoever was in charge of this investigation – someone in London, probably, since I was sure Hyssop wouldn't have the seniority – would no doubt consider me the number one suspect with Leon running a close second. The absent Markham would be on the list somewhere, as well. Closely followed by Dr Bairstow, recently broken out of a government establishment and in the wind with his notorious accomplice, Mrs Brown. That's the thing about Civil Servants. Once they topple off the Rails of Respectability, they really go wrong. 'Bad to the Bone Brown', they'd be calling her.

Unfortunately, the only one definitely in custody at the moment was me. But even if I could escape, where could I go? I had only a limited number of options. The cottage was the first place they'd look. I could return to Home Farm – in whatever condition it was at the moment. There was a chance Smallhope and Pennyroyal might have returned by now. There was also a chance they might be dead.

Or – and I've no idea where this came from – I could return to Insight. Was such a thing actually possible? I lay back and tried to get the timelines straight in my head, but my thoughts were still fuzzy from the medication.

In the end I stuck my head out of the door and asked Gallacio – for it was still he, gentle reader – for some paper and a pen.

He regarded me warily. 'What for?'

'To write with, of course.'

He looked at me.

'No,' I said, 'you've got me. I'm going to fashion a digging device and tunnel my way to freedom using a sheet of A4 and a 2B pencil.'

You shouldn't be sarcastic to Security. I would pay for that later on, but he did bring me the paper as requested.

I made two columns. One for me and one for Bridget. Because the first and most important question to ask myself was – I knew where Bridget was in my timeline, but where was I in hers? If I returned to Insight – would she be dead or alive?

Order of events for me	Order of events for Bridget
Attacked at Home Farm	Bridget dies
Jump to Insight and meet Bridget	When did she meet me? Here?

Jump to Runnymede	Insight team jump to Lincoln. Failed attempt to take out Nicola and possibly William. They fail. Bridget there?
Jump to Lincoln	Insight jump to Runnymede. William again? Bridget definitely there. Another failure.
Jump to 17th-century London	Insight probably there at some point. Could they identify us? It was dark. Confusion and chaos. Perhaps not. Another failure.
Jump to 19th-century London	?
Living in cottage	Insight attack me there. They get wet and scorched. Failure. Was it here that Bridget first saw my face clearly and realised who I was? I don't think she saw me at Runnymede. They jump to Home Farm for a second attempt. Failure again. Ironically, if they hadn't tried to kill us at HF, we'd have had nothing to go on and very little of the above would have happened.
Return to Insight?	What is Bridget's status? Alive or dead? If I return to Insight, will Bridget kill me or kiss me? Bugger, I've got a headache now.

If I jumped to Insight again – would Bridget Schrödinger be alive or dead? Actually, there was a very simple low-tech solution to that little problem. I could simply telephone Insight and ask to speak to Bridget Lafferty.

Yeah – that easy. Obviously, I'd have to get myself to the

future somehow, but that shouldn't be a problem. Overcome everyone at St Mary's, reacquire Leon's pod – which had almost certainly had its codes changed to keep me out – make the jump, and pray I survived. Once I'd done all that, then actually, telephoning Bridget at Insight would be the easy bit.

If she answered, then she was still alive, and if she was still alive, then I almost certainly hadn't somehow given myself away yet and she hadn't tried to kill me. Therefore, theoretically, it was still safe to return. There must be loads more to investigate at Insight. Names, places, dates – all sorts. Something I could present to Smallhope and Pennyroyal as a little package all tied up with a neat bow on their return. I refused to believe they were dead. They were simply off doing something to someone and hadn't yet returned.

My clinching argument would be that I had to do it. If you start something like this, then you have to be prepared to finish it, because you definitely don't want people like Insight after you and your loved ones. I had a very nasty feeling we hadn't seen even a fraction of what they were capable of.

I tore my list into very tiny pieces and flushed it down the loo. Which took about twenty tries and I had to club some of it with the bog brush until it took the hint.

It's actually very hard not to feel despondent when you're lying alone in a room all day and night and God knows what is happening on the other side of the door. Where was Leon? Was he repairing his pod prior to generously donating it to me for nefarious purposes? Or had recent soup trauma been the final straw and he'd fled? I knew he hadn't, not really, but imagination is not always the gift people say it is. I tried to concentrate on David Sands' book – which was really good. Everyone should buy a copy.

And then, suddenly, without warning, it *was* all happening. And worse, it was happening to me.

The door opened and in ran Nurse Fortunata. She was holding a pair of electric clippers. And a razor.

I sat up. 'What the hell?'

'Don't argue. Don't talk. Hyssop says there's a bloke called Gaunt on his way. Looking for you. We need to get you out of here. If anyone asks, you're being transferred to a civilian hospital. Into the bathroom.'

'There's no point me hiding in there.'

'I'm not hiding you. I'm disguising you.'

'How?'

She held up the clippers. 'You have very distinctive hair.'

'No,' I said. Dear God, would the assaults on my hair never cease?

'Yes. Kneel over the bath if you want to live.'

You don't argue with nurses. I knelt over the bath. She didn't hang around. The clippers whirred. I might have whimpered. And then she got busy with the razor. The last sad remains of my hair fell into the bath. She turned on the taps and the last sad remains of my hair swirled down the plughole.

I and my new shiny head were whirled back into bed. 'Quick.'

She fixed one of those surgical cap things on my head and before I knew what was happening, she'd slapped a wound dressing over the half of my face not already swollen and bruised, plonked a flexi-glove over my left hand and arm and stepped back to admire the results of her hard work.

472

'I've done a good job there,' she said. 'You genuinely do look as if you're not going to last until tomorrow. What's your name?'

'What?'

'Think of a name. Quick.'

'Nicola Hay,' I said, still bemused.

'You're an assistant librarian. You work for Dr Dowson. You were in a minor car crash and are suffering a head trauma.'

'OK,' I said, settling back on the pillows. 'Where and when did this happen?'

'You don't know. You can't remember anything. You're not sure who you are. You don't know what's going on.'

'Oh, yeah. I can do that.'

'You've been doing it for years,' she said nastily and turned to go.

I tried to stay calm. Martin Gaunt was on his way. It occurred to me suddenly that if I didn't survive this, I had important knowledge to pass on.

I caught her wrist and whispered, 'Dr Bairstow is still alive.'

She stared at me, her mouth an 'O' of surprise. I nodded. 'Gaunt had him at the Red House. Markham and I got him out. Tell Gallacio – he can pass it on to Peterson.'

She stared at me for a moment, nodded, and then whirled herself out the door.

I lay back and practised. Nicola Hay. Library. Car crash. Can't remember anything. Who are you? Who am I? What's for lunch?

And then I waited.

Not for as long as I'd hoped. I heard voices. Some sort of argument. And then the door opened a few inches and Dr Stone said, 'I warn you; the trauma is severe. You'll probably get no sense out of her. She might even be asleep.'

Well, I can take a hint. I straightened my cap and closed my eyes. Because I was asleep.

I heard them come in, Dr Stone talking in a hushed whisper. Gaunt didn't even bother to lower his voice. If I'd had any hair left then it would have crept back inside my head at the sound of him. Martin Gaunt was one of the few people of whom I was afraid. Even Clive Ronan hadn't bothered me as much as Gaunt did.

His voice brought back unpleasant memories. I certainly didn't have to open my eyes to remember how he looked. Very tall. Very thin. A shiny pink head. In fact, all of his skin was pink and shiny. His underhung jaw made him look like a well-scrubbed shark. He wore small, round glasses which reflected the light and rendered his eyes unreadable. I've never seen anyone look so completely what they were: a control freak. A compulsive, merciless, inhuman control freak.

Worst of all – an inhuman control freak who had lost an important prisoner and would be eager to make good that mistake. And extract a fitting revenge as well. I peered through my eyelashes. Two anonymous uniformed minions trailed in his wake.

Fortunata had drawn the curtains so the room was semi-dark. The surgical cap mostly covered my bald head and the enormous wound dressing covered the undamaged half of my face. He'd never recognise me.

Wrong. In three long strides, Gaunt was across the ward. He ripped off the wound dressing. Half my face came away with it.

'Arrest this woman.'

Dr Stone wasn't going down without a fight. 'What? Why? As soon as she's stabilised, we intend to transfer her to a civilian hospital with specialist facilities.'

I tried not to sigh. Where's an ash-blonde nurse with wrinkled tights when you need one?

Gaunt wasn't having any of it. 'I'd say you have been the victim of a hoax, doctor, but I have no doubt you know this woman as well as I. This is Dr Maxwell, wanted by the authorities for . . .' He stopped and then continued, 'Wanted by the authorities.'

There didn't seem to be much point in keeping my eyes closed any longer. I grinned up at him. 'Gaunt, you old goat. How are you? Still shedding prisoners like a moulting muskrat? We really made you look stupid that day, didn't we?'

I think I had some idea of enraging him to such an extent that he did something stupid that I could exploit. Or he could shoot me where I lay, of course. Possibly my scheme would have benefitted from just a little more thought.

Sadly, he had himself well in hand. This was a great day for him. The chance to settle an old score. One that must have rankled. Martin Gaunt didn't do failure. Not until Markham and I danced across his path, anyway. I'd escaped him at the last moment. And now, here I was at last. Helpless and in his power.

He didn't bother acknowledging my presence. His dehumanisation process had begun. I tried not to remember how Dr Bairstow had looked the day Markham and I got him out of Gaunt's clutches. Gaunt turned to Dr Stone. 'Get her up. An ambulance is on its way.'

He turned on his heel and strode away. Such was his arrogance he didn't even wait to see his instructions carried out. He

475

walked off knowing that if people valued their jobs – or even their liberty – they'd do exactly as he said.

Shit.

I looked at Dr Stone who looked at me. 'Nurse, find us a wheelchair, would you, please.'

'She can walk,' said Gaunt, turning in the doorway.

Dr Stone was brilliant. 'No, she can't. One of two things will happen if you try to force her. Either she will fall – and the subsequent confusion will offer her the opportunity to escape you yet again – or she will injure herself to such an extent that any statement she might make will be inadmissible. This is Maxwell of St Mary's and you know she will seize any opportunity to twist a situation to her advantage.'

Maxwell of St Mary's. Got to say I rather liked the sound of that. Better still, I'd got in before Markham decided Markham of St Mary's sounded even better. Best of all, Peterson didn't stand a chance. Although he could be Peterson of St Pomposa's if he wanted.

Dr Stone got his way and I got the wheelchair – although my right wrist was handcuffed to the wretched thing. Gaunt really wasn't taking any chances this time.

And one of his minions gagged me.

It could have been worse, I suppose. They could have drugged me. I almost wished they had. I don't know what sort of gag they used but it was metal and tasted foul and I couldn't close my mouth, couldn't waggle my jaw, couldn't swallow. It was horrible. A modern scold's bridle. I could feel saliva pooling at the back of my throat, forcing me to breathe slowly and calmly to avoid choking.

It was almost a procession. Dr Stone led the way, followed

476

by me – not that I had a lot of choice – in my minion-propelled wheelchair, followed by the second minion, followed by Nurse Fortunata.

I'd been hoping they'd whizz me out through Hawking, which would offer Leon the opportunity to do something creative in the wife-rescuing area, but – possibly because Gaunt wasn't taking any chances this time – we turned left out of the lift. He'd obviously left instructions to take me down the Long Corridor and through the Great Hall. Where everyone could watch my Wheel of Shame.

His first mistake.

The windows in the Long Corridor let in sunlight, which throws lovely patches of light and shade on the floor. From warm to cool. From light to dark. Through one of the windows, I caught a glimpse of an ambulance turning in through the gates. And not a public ambulance – a private one. Unmarked. I felt my stomach shift. These were my last moments of freedom. I was on my way back to the Red House.

We emerged into a silent Great Hall. Everyone was there. The place was packed. I was surprised Gaunt had allowed it but I suppose this was part of his revenge – my humiliation was to be witnessed by as many people as possible.

Just a tip, folks – and Clive Ronan himself would back me up on this – revenge is for amateurs. Anything personal is a waste of time. Just go for the kill – quick and clean – and walk away. I had an idea Ronan wouldn't rate Gaunt very highly.

He was waiting for me. Gaunt, I mean. Deliberately or otherwise, he stood on the half-landing. Where Dr Bairstow always stood. I was wheeled to the foot of the stairs. So I could look up at him, I suppose, as he looked down at me.

His two minions stood either side of me. Well, that wasn't ominous at all, was it?

Peterson appeared. 'What's happening here? This is a member of my unit. Take that thing off at once. Dr Stone . . .' He gestured at me.

Gaunt looked down at me and made his second mistake. He should have had me out of the door while he could. See my earlier comments about revenge.

Drawing himself up, he prepared to enjoy his moment. 'Dr Maxwell is no longer a member of this unit. Nor has she been for some time. She is under arrest for assisting in an illegal act pertaining to the unlawful escape of a prisoner from a government establishment. As such, she is in my custody.'

Peterson turned to him in simulated astonishment. 'But how could that be? The prisoner to whom you refer is dead. How could he have been held at your establishment? Is it possible, perhaps, that the prisoner of whom you speak was being held illegally and is not actually dead after all?'

Dr Stone was behind me. 'Gently, Max. I'll have you out in a moment.'

He unfastened and carefully removed the gag. It was only when it came out that I realised how much my jaw hurt, and I'd only been wearing it a few minutes. Great trails of saliva dangled everywhere. Fortunata wiped my mouth and offered me a sip of water, for which I was grateful.

Peterson hadn't finished.

Addressing the Hall, he raised his voice. 'May I have your attention, please. For anyone not already aware, Dr Bairstow is alive and well.' He turned to Gaunt. 'Since Commander Treadwell is incapacitated, as Deputy Director, I am acting Director of this unit. You have overstepped the bounds of your authority here, Gaunt. Take your people and go.'

Gaunt wasn't going quietly. In fact, he wasn't going at all. Peterson was bluffing and he knew it.

'This prisoner is mine. I have a legally obtained warrant. It is you who has no authority in this matter. *Acting Director*.'

He held up a document. I had absolutely no doubt it was a perfectly genuine, perfectly legal warrant for my arrest. Peterson could protest all he wanted – and he was – but nothing could save me from Martin Gaunt.

Casting Peterson a triumphant glance, Gaunt gestured to his minions, who immediately began to wheel me towards the front doors. I was still handcuffed to the chair and I didn't give much for my chances of a smooth and unexciting ride back to the Red House. I had only seconds left. Once I left St Mary's, I'd be lost.

It was at this exciting moment that someone politely plied the knocker. Mr Strong opened the front doors to admit a couple of green-clad paramedics – one man and one woman. Each carried a large equipment bag over their shoulder. They stopped short at the scene in front of them, located their target – me, obviously in dire need of medical attention – and approached.

Gaunt was in full flow. Striding down the stairs, he moved into maximum authoritarian mode.

'This woman is under arrest. She is a dangerous criminal and should be treated accordingly. You will not speak to her. You will not, under any circumstances, release her from her cuffs. The journey back to the Red House is short. There will be no time for the medical relapse she will undoubtedly try to convince you she is experiencing. If she demands a comfort break, let her soil herself. If, for any reason, she does not arrive at the Red House, then I guarantee not only will you never work again but neither will your families, your friends or anyone you have ever met. Have I made myself clear?'

By now he'd crossed the Hall and was standing in their faces. Wordlessly, they nodded.

'These two men will accompany you inside the ambulance and a security team will follow on in another vehicle. Radio contact is to be maintained at all times.' He gestured at Hyssop who was, apparently, supposed to supply this security team. 'Get on with it.'

There was a pause.

And then a longer one.

And then a bit more.

All eyes were on Hyssop. Who held her nerve.

Turning her back on him and raising her voice, she addressed me, but her words were for Gaunt.

'Dr Lucy Maxwell, I arrest you for the murder of Commander John Treadwell. You do not have to say anything but it may harm your defence if you do not mention, when questioned, something which you later rely on in court. Anything you do say may be given in evidence.'

Oh my God – Treadwell was dead? I didn't believe it. That didn't seem like something he would do.

I don't mind saying – my newly released jaw was on the floor. Hyssop was the one person in the world who knew I couldn't have done it. She'd only been about three feet away from me when the shot was fired. Was this her revenge? To see me charged with a crime I hadn't committed, to compensate for the crime I had?

No – that wasn't right. She could have arrested me for my

480

actions at the Red House at any time and she hadn't. What was she playing at?

And then the penny dropped. By arresting me for murder – a much more serious charge than Gaunt's – Hyssop was actually protecting me, and Martin Gaunt was just so much piss and vinegar.

She turned back to Gaunt. 'I regret to inform you, Mr Gaunt, that Dr Maxwell is now in my custody. As such, she will be returned to Sick Bay until she is in a fit condition – a legally fit condition – to make a statement. After which, at my discretion, you will be allowed one interview with her. In the presence of a neutral third party.'

I thought Gaunt was going to burst. From his point of view, defeat had been snatched from the jaws of victory. I was certain I could see a little vein throbbing in his temple. His normally pink complexion was bordering on purple. I waited hopefully for him to experience some sort of major neural or cardiac event.

And what about Hyssop? She was familiar with Gaunt and his methods. And she'd saved me. Legally! I was now in her custody. True, I was hers to do with as she pleased but more importantly, I was no longer Gaunt's to do with as *he* pleased. And she was a captain in the king's army. I had no idea whether, in matters of security, she outranked Gaunt or not, but she was on her home ground which must count for something. Bloody brilliant.

Just to put the boot in, Peterson stepped forwards. 'Thank you, Captain. Carry on, if you please.'

If Peterson had put the boot in, Hyssop rubbed Gaunt's nose in it. 'Thank you, Director.' She gestured to Lucca and Harper standing nearby. 'Return the patient to Sick Bay.' She looked at the ambulance crew. 'I'm sorry for your wasted time. Your services will not be required.'

I was still searching for Leon, who was nowhere to be seen among the sea of St Mary's faces. Everyone else was here. The kitchen staff were clustered just outside the dining room. For some reason, every single one of them had a tea towel draped over their hands.

Mrs Enderby and her team were lined up outside Wardrobe. She was holding the biggest pair of pinking shears I'd ever seen in my life. As were others in her team, except for young Glenda, who was clutching a length of material and wearing a determined expression. Was she going to hem Gaunt to death?

Dr Dowson and Professor Rapson were both waiting quietly by the Library door which, trust me, was far more alarming than anything else I'd seen so far. Was it only coincidence that every internal doorway was blocked? And that a member of the Security Section was standing casually by every exit? Not doing anything in particular. Just standing around.

But still no sign of Leon. Not that I seemed to need him at the moment. I could go back to Sick Bay and start growing my hair again.

I had relaxed too soon. Cox and Gallacio, both standing near the vestibule, stiffened. They didn't have time to do much more. The vestibule doors burst open. Not a figure of speech – they really did burst open. And not gently. I winced. The one on the right bounced off the wall, sending a great chunk of plaster flying through the air. The whole building shuddered with the impact because they were hefty doors. And very old. They'd been doing their job for a long time. When doors like that burst open, they don't muck about.

My heart sank. Oh shit – just when you think things really can't get any worse – they do. Only one organisation makes that sort of entrance.

The sodding Time Police were here.

40

Well – wasn't this interesting? Yet another body of people who would cheerfully see me dead at their feet. Was it possible they'd come to arrest me too? In which case this had to be some sort of record.

They were dressed for action. Armed and armoured. Helmeted as well. And bristling with weapons. Perfectly in step, the Time Police marched through the Hall. St Mary's fell back before them and – I'm sorry, I have to ask: does anyone else hear 'The Imperial March' in their heads every time the buggers do this? It can't be just me, surely.

Anyway, back to our improbable drama. Their visors were down so they were obviously expecting full-on carnage but at least they weren't spraying the Hall with gunfire. Not at this exact moment, anyway, although that could all change in a heartbeat.

A typical Time Police team consists of four officers – three to do the shooting while one waits outside to gun down anyone attempting to make a break for it. These buggers strode in as if they owned the place, weapons raised, just looking for trouble. This was not turning out to be my best day ever.

Back to Martin Gaunt, making every effort to regain control

of the situation, demanding to know who they were and what they wanted. Good luck with that. The Time Police were never going to play his silly games. I'm not usually an advocate of their *Let's just shoot everyone and go home early* policy but today I could well be seduced to their way of thinking. Especially if they started with Gaunt. Whose minions were almost certainly armed, as well. This, I decided, was an occasion for sitting quietly in my wheelchair, letting the big boys wipe each other out and then wheeling my getaway vehicle over their twitching bodies.

St Mary's collectively looked around for somewhere comfortable to sit and prepared to enjoy this unexpected entertainment.

The tallest of the officers levelled his weapon at me. His voice was muffled somewhat by his helmet because he hadn't switched on his mike but there was no mistaking the by now quite familiar routine.

'Lucy Maxwell, by the authority vested in me as a member of the Time Police, I arrest you for various offences including the illegal movement of people around the Timeline in order to pervert the course of justice, concealing said people in Time in order to pervert the course of justice, removing stolen artefacts from their proper Time, attending illegal assemblies for the purpose of removing artefacts from their proper Time, consorting with criminals, impersonating a Time Police officer, and any other offences which come to light during the course of our investigations, all contrary to the Chronology Projection Conjecture of 1992 . . .'

'Seriously?' I said, quite delighted. I was being arrested for crimes against the very legislation designed to make History safe for historians. Thank you, Professor Hawking, the patron saint of time travellers everywhere.

And possibly I was a little punch-drunk as well. Show me one single person who's ever been arrested three times in thirty minutes. And all by different people for different crimes in different times. Am I a legend or what? *Three times, people.*

I twisted in my chair to look up at Hyssop. 'It would appear your efforts to incarcerate me have been unsuccessful, Captain. But not unappreciated.'

She nodded. I nodded. It wasn't her fault. She'd done her best. But it would be a really good idea to get me out of here now before any unnecessary shooting happened.

I looked up at Peterson. 'You should let me go, Director. You shouldn't take any unnecessary risks.' I gestured at the Time Police with my uncuffed hand. 'Not with this bunch of Horses' Arses.'

He only faltered for a fraction of a second. You wouldn't have seen it if you didn't know him well. He nodded to the team leader. 'Your warrant?'

The officer nodded to another who produced a document. Gaunt held out his hand but the officer, bless him, handed it to Peterson, who solemnly and slowly perused it. At the end, he nodded and handed it back. 'That all seems quite correct.' He turned to Hyssop. 'Regrettably, Captain, the Time Police have overriding authority. We cannot legally impede their investigations.'

The third officer seized my chair. Which was a shame because I would have liked to see how this ended. I just caught a glimpse of an empurpled Gaunt surging towards me when, with a noise like thunder, the doors crashed back on their hinges again.

I really wasn't sure how much more of this the building could take.

Two blood-covered figures staggered into the Hall, one supporting the other.

Shit. No . . .

Pennyroyal's chest was covered in blood. His face was so white it seemed almost transparent. I've no idea whether he was conscious or not. Smallhope, struggling to hold him up, wasn't much better.

There was a long second of stunned silence and then Cox and Keller moved forwards to take his weight and lay him down on the floor. Dr Stone shouted for his team and moved to help. Even the emergency medics stepped up, unslinging their bags and pulling out their kit.

(Go on – hands up, all those who thought the two paramedics were Smallhope and Pennyroyal.)

It would appear that most of the blood belonged to Pennyroyal. I felt my stomach turn over. They'd exposed the wound and it was a mess.

Someone brought up a trolley, they lifted him aboard and disappeared in the direction of Sick Bay. Dr Stone lingered a moment, saying to Smallhope, 'It's serious but probably not fatal. Leave him with us.'

And then he was gone.

Someone offered her a chair next to me and another kind soul passed her a cup of tea.

She seemed to become aware of me. 'Good Lord. Another one who's been in the wars.'

I said carefully, 'It's Lady Amelia Smallhope, isn't it?'

She didn't even blink. 'That's right. And you're Dr Maxwell, aren't you? I remember your little boy. Don't suppose he's so little now. Hope you don't mind us crashing in like this. You were closest and as you can see, our need was urgent.'

I said quietly, 'He'll be fine. Dr Stone is very good.'

'That's why I brought him here.' She lowered her voice. 'And looking for you, of course.'

Gaunt tried again. 'I don't know who you people are . . .'

'Good,' said Smallhope, briskly. 'Keep it that way and I won't have to kill you.'

St Mary's heads were going like spectators at a particularly exciting tennis match. I swear at least half of them were clutching a mug of tea.

Switching my attention back to Gaunt – because I was still convinced he was the most dangerous man in the room – he and Hyssop were arguing. About me, I'm proud to say. It was hard to see what the Time Police were doing other than just standing around. Which they do very well.

Under cover of all the noise, I said quietly, 'Where have you been?'

She leaned towards me. '1848.'

'What happened?'

'Absolutely nothing, thanks to us. Mission successful. Ambushed by Insight on our return to base. Quite the punch-up but we got most of them. They got away before I could stop them. Pennyroyal had taken a few hits by then. How did 1605 go?'

'Mission successful.'

'Talk later,' she said, straightening up and speaking in her normal tones. Which meant they could hear her halfway across the county. 'St Mary's seems to be delightfully full of company this afternoon. Are we perhaps gate-crashing some kind of social event? Is there any chance of a drink?'

'No, you're not, and yes, of course.'

'That would be lovely. I see that dreadful oik Gaunt is here.'

I nodded. 'He's arrested me for breaking Dr Bairstow out of gaol. Over there is Captain Hyssop, who has arrested me for the murder of John Treadwell. And over there are the Time Police, who have arrested me for lots and lots of things.'

'Treadwell is dead?'

'Apparently.'

She looked around and lowered her voice again. 'If you wish, I can get you out of this in a heartbeat and then come back later for Pennyroyal, but I have to confess I would like to see how it all ends.'

'So would I,' I said, sitting back and making myself comfortable.

The best bit was watching Gaunt lose control of the situation. He was accustomed to being the big boy on the block and suddenly the block was full of boys much bigger than he was. Contrasting his congested face with his self-control at the Red House, I suspected he was one of those people who are fine when everything goes well and not fine when it doesn't. Losing control of events around him was leading to him losing control of himself.

The Time Police officer was in his face. 'Hand over my prisoner. I have the authority. Hinder me in the execution of my duties and I'll arrest you too.'

Gaunt's vein bulged even further. 'Hyssop, arrest all these people.'

'Actually, I don't think she can,' said Peterson, mildly. 'There's a treaty, you know.'

Little patches of saliva had gathered at the corners of Gaunt's mouth. 'I have written authority.'

Peterson smiled. 'And I have doubts about you, Mr Gaunt. When Dr Stone finishes with his current emergency, I shall ask him for an assessment of your mental state with a view to submitting a report questioning your suitability for the position you hold.'

Gaunt drew himself up. That vein was going to blow any minute now. 'You cannot command me. You have no authority.'

Peterson grinned evilly. 'What a coincidence. That was going to be *my* argument.'

The Time Police officer, impatient at all this civilian time-wasting, was attempting to take custody of his prisoner. Which would be me.

At exactly the same moment, Hyssop, never one to step back from an argument, was insisting that she had arrested me before the Time Police turned up and that she had priority.

Unable to resist the temptation to impose himself on everyone, Gaunt joined the fray, insisting he had arrested me first and therefore took precedence over everyone.

The bits of St Mary's visible from where I was sitting were all busy laying bets on who would eventually obtain legal custody of that legendary criminal mastermind, Maxwell. I could see myself becoming the temporal equivalent of the Dread Pirate Roberts. Eat your heart out, Markham.

Atherton brought me a very nice cup of tea for which I thanked him politely.

The noise and excitement were reaching fever pitch. Martin Gaunt was on the point of losing all control but was interrupted by the doors slamming back against the wall. For the last time that afternoon, actually, because one broke a hinge. Mr Strong added his indignant voice to the din.

To sum up: Gaunt, far from controlling the situation and bending everyone to his will, had lost custody of a notorious criminal – that would be me, for anyone who's lost the plot. An unexpected casualty was being treated up in Sick Bay. The Time Police had dropped by – except they hadn't, as astute readers will by now have realised. And now our lovely listed building had a broken door, over which, such is the authority of SPOHB, there would be repercussions. This had to be some sort of record, even for us.

And for Gaunt, things were about to get even worse.

Three figures entered the Hall. Two men, one woman. Dr Bairstow and Mrs Brown came first, followed by Leon cradling a blaster. I grinned. So that's where he'd been.

Unbidden, St Mary's shut up and stood to attention.

In silence, Dr Bairstow climbed the stairs to stand in his accustomed place on the half-landing.

The three Time Police officers pushed back their visors to reveal Guthrie, Markham and Evans. Go on – you guessed, didn't you?

The silence was absolute.

Gaunt made a massive effort. Light gleamed off his spectacles as he glared at Dr Bairstow. 'You are under arrest.'

He looked at Mrs Brown. 'And you.'

He looked at Smallhope. 'And you.'

He looked at me. 'Especially you.'

'What about me?' shouted Sykes, indignantly 'I want to be arrested, too. In fact, I demand to be arrested.'

'And me,' called Lingoss.

Van Owen waved. 'And me.'

'And me,' shouted Kal.

Shouts echoed from all around the Hall.

'And me.'

'Me first.'

I could see Gaunt flounder. Someone who could only deal with the world in terms of power and control was all at sea with ridicule. He drew himself up.

'*You are all of you under arrest.*'

Ironic cheers filled the Hall. I saw his two minions exchange dubious glances.

Gaunt turned to Dr Bairstow, hissing through clenched teeth. 'You were replaced. You have no authority here.'

'But I do,' said Mrs Brown, clearly. 'I have not been replaced. As a simple telephone call will confirm. I know you, Gaunt, and you know me. Mine is the authority here. Stand down.'

He hesitated. I suspected Mrs Brown's current status was unclear but after what had happened at the Red House, could he afford another bad mistake? And so soon after the first.

In some situations, hesitation is fatal.

'Stand down, Gaunt.'

Her voice could have shifted armies. She was the Dowager Lady Blackbourne, highly placed member of a discreet government department, mother of Celia North, and her ancestors had been trampling peasants like Martin Gaunt for centuries.

Gaunt held her gaze for one moment, hissed, 'You will regret this' in true supervillain style, and stormed towards the doors. Reaching them, he snapped his fingers for his minions – neither of whom had lifted a finger to assist him – and suddenly found himself surrounded by Hyssop and the Security Section.

Peterson climbed the stairs to the half-landing where he and Dr Bairstow regarded each other. The room fell very quiet.

492

Dr Bairstow extended his hand. 'Director, you are relieved.'

Peterson smiled. 'Director, I stand relieved.'

They shook hands to enthusiastic applause.

I was close enough to hear Dr Bairstow say, 'Thank you for your care of St Mary's.'

Peterson smiled. 'Welcome home, sir.'

As the applause died away, Dr Bairstow turned to survey the scene around him. A blood-soaked Lady Amelia getting herself on the outside of her second margarita. Various ex-members of St Mary's masquerading as Time Police officers. Another ex-member handcuffed to a wheelchair. And bald. I swear he smirked.

And Martin Gaunt. Who suddenly licked his lips. You could see him remembering that Dr Bairstow had not fared well under his regime. You could see Dr Bairstow remember it as well.

The silence lengthened. I wondered what would happen if Dr Bairstow actually ordered Markham to take Gaunt around the back of Hawking and shoot him. I think Gaunt might have been wondering the same thing.

No one moved. No one spoke. We might have been a room full of statues.

Mrs Brown stirred slightly and cleared her throat. Which broke the spell. Dr Bairstow turned his head and nodded to her.

Standing in his accustomed position on the half-landing, he surveyed his people.

'My name is Edward Bairstow and I am the Director of St Mary's.'

He turned to Hyssop and gestured at Gaunt and his minions. 'Captain Hyssop, if you would be so kind, please. *Get these people out of my unit.*'

493

41

Well, after that little lot, I think we can all agree that no one's day had gone quite according to plan, especially Pennyroyal's. According to Dr Stone he'd survived surgery and was already – although somewhat groggily – demanding to be discharged.

I'd been wheeled back to Sick Bay – protesting every inch of the way, obviously – so I'd missed Gaunt and his minions being evicted from St Mary's. I was actually quite cross about that. I'd accused Fortunata of never letting me have any fun. She'd countered with a demand to know if I'd opened my bowels recently and I'd asked if there was an 'r' in the month.

Whether Gaunt would be back – no one knew.

Whether Dr Bairstow would be permitted to remain as Director of St Mary's – no one knew. Whether Mrs Brown would be successful in getting her colleagues off our backs – no one knew.

Whether Markham would eventually return permanently to St Mary's – no one knew.

Whether Smallhope would be interested in my plans for Insight – I had no idea.

Whether Treadwell was actually dead – no one on the medical team would tell me.

Leon made a special visit to let me know what was going on. It was possible that my previous comments on being kept out of various loops had not fallen on stony ground after all. With Gaunt bearing down on St Mary's, Hyssop had told Cox, who had tipped off Guthrie, who, in turn, had contacted Markham, who spoke to Leon, who had jumped to find Dr Bairstow and inform him that the time had come for him to make his return.

'Where on earth did they get the Time Police gear?'

'It's not. Markham picked up suitably similar attire from the army and navy surplus store in Russell Street. Gaunt wasn't going to know any different. Evans and Guthrie broke into our armoury for weapons and armour while you were heroically distracting everyone in the Hall. Well done, you.'

'Yeah,' I said. 'Well done, me. You do know I'm massively under arrest, don't you?'

'Eighteen or twenty people have mentioned it, yes. I shall be interested to see what you eventually go down for.' He stood up. 'I'm off to sort out our room.' He hesitated. 'We can discuss going back to the cottage when you've recovered a little. You'll be discharged tomorrow and Matthew has finished his exams. He's kept his exam papers and is bursting to tell you all about them. Please do not inform him you're under multiple arrests.'

'I don't think he'd be that shocked.'

'That's what worries me. It's a burden, you know, being the only respectable member of this family.'

'Oh, come on – like you've never been arrested for murder. Or led the rebellion against the Time Police. Or framed my dad for something unspeakable. Or snogged Markham. Or . . .'

'Yes, yes, all right,' he said, heading for the door. 'I shall see you later. Try to stay out of trouble until then.'

The door closed behind him.

Smallhope lay in the bed opposite me. There wasn't a lot wrong with her – a little battered around the edges but nothing a half dozen margaritas wouldn't put right.

Sykes and Lingoss had brought her up a jugful. I'd been allowed one glass. No prizes for guessing who had the rest. I sipped and watched her. She looked reasonably mellow and no one was actually kicking the door in to shoot us dead so there might never be a better moment. And Pennyroyal was next door – healing in his own efficient manner, I assumed – and Markham was downstairs in the bar so, loosely speaking, the band was back together again. In the same building, anyway.

I was wondering exactly how to introduce the subject without giving her a relapse when she did it for me.

'1848.'

I jumped. Did she do mind-reading as well?

'Yes?' I said, cautiously.

'They were everywhere, you know.'

'Who?'

'Insight. Especially all over northern Europe. Setting up problems for the future was my guess. I even thought I saw that boss of yours once or twice. You know – the one who took you on at Home Farm and lost.'

This was surely the perfect moment.

'Well . . .' I said.

She drained her glass, set it down and looked up. 'Well, what?'

I grinned at her. 'I've had an idea.'

She closed her eyes. 'I don't think I want to know.'

'Bet you do.'

'Does it involve risk and reward?'

'A very great deal of both, yes.'

'How much reward?'

'A lot. If we live long enough to spend it.'

'How much risk?'

'Oh, masses. Tons and tons. It's almost certain none of us will survive.'

'And the downside?'

'It's all downside.'

'You're not really selling this, you know.'

I grinned again. 'Actually, I think I am.'

'Who else knows about this idea?'

'Right now – just me. In ten minutes – you. If I can hoik Markham out of the bar and make him understand simple words – him. Pennyroyal, I'll leave to you.'

'Wise,' she said. She emptied the contents of the jug into her glass. 'Go on, then. Hit me with the details.'

I wobbled over to her bed, found a chair and talked nonstop for about ten minutes.

Lady Amelia didn't say a word the whole time. She didn't even take a sip from her glass. At the end she just stared at me. 'Are you out of your mind?'

'There really isn't an answer which would be acceptable to both of us, so perhaps we should just move on.'

'We don't have a base from which to operate.'

'Dr Bairstow owes us. We can operate out of St Mary's.'

'That's . . . I mean . . . It's the worst idea I've ever heard. Not the St Mary's bit – the other thing. It's outrageous.'

I nodded. 'Yes.'

She sipped. 'Insane.'

'Is that another word for audacious?'

'Reckless beyond description.'

'I think you mean bold.'

'Irresponsible.'

'Dazzling.'

She snorted. 'Unimaginable folly.'

I grinned at her. There was a very long silence, during which I imagined the wheels going round, cogs engaging, bounties calculated . . .

She sighed heavily. 'You're going to make me say it, aren't you?'

I smiled sympathetically. 'You'll feel so much better once you do.'

She sighed again. 'Very well.' She drained her glass again and squared her shoulders. 'Congratulations, Dr Maxwell. It's a Brilliant Idea.'

THE END

ACKNOWLEDGEMENTS

Thanks, as always, to Phil Dawson – my go-to guy for pain, suffering and all the illegal stuff.

Thanks to Janet Thompson, winner of this year's CLIC Sargent 'Get in Character' auction, who makes a starring appearance not unconnected with Markham's Spotted Dick. I offered her the chance to be a bad-ass assassin and she turned it down for love of Markham. Psychiatric treatment has been declined.

Thanks to my brother – not the eminent author, the other one. The one we keep for emergencies because he's the most respectable member of the family, who advised me on the technicalities of head-shaving. I don't just throw these books together, you know. There was a half-hour consultation – for which he tried to charge me – on clippers versus razors, how long it would take, razor rash, etc., all of which, inevitably, led to unkind jokes about the time he walked into a lamppost and ended up in A&E. Yes, of course he was drunk.

Thanks to all those at Headline who work so hard on my behalf.

My editor, Frankie Edwards.

Jo and Shadé for Marketing.

Emily who handles the Publicity.

And, of course, everyone involved with Sales, Rights, Art, Production, etc.

And my copy editor, Sharona.

And Hannah for the Audio side.

Yes, it really does take all these people to render my books suitable for public consumption.

For those who complain about the wild improbability of my plots – and I know who you are – I'd like to state now that the events of Chapter 35 are a true and accurate account of something that actually happened to me. Even including the cheesy toes. It wasn't a good morning, culinarily speaking. Understandably, I've gone right off kale.

For the avoidance of any legal consequences, my publishers have instructed me to point out that, as far as I know, the British Museum has not drifted to the dark side. Not even a little bit. I think they – my publishers, not the BM – have concerns about being sacrificed to whatever lurks in the British Museum's Dark and Secret Cellars. Which, of course, do not exist.

To discover more about

JODI TAYLOR

visit

www.joditaylor.online

You can also find her on

Facebook

www.facebook.com/JodiTaylorBooks

Twitter

@joditaylorbooks

Instagram

@joditaylorbooks